THE GOOD POISON
CLUB

SIMON LYONS

Edited by Mairi Mayfield.
Cover by Julia Durman.

ISBN: 978-1987452372
ISBN-10: 1987452372

COMING SOON...

THE LAST WEEKEND IN WONDERLAND

BY

SIMON LYONS

FRIENDSHIP, FESTIVALS & MURDER!!?

When Jimmy is diagnosed with a rare form of early dementia his best friend Sid decides the best therapy is to go to Glastonbury to try and rekindle memories of their first festival in 1971. Things soon get out of hand as they embark on their adventure, Sid's noble intentions were strictly Rock 'n' Roll but sex, drugs and murder conspire to make it a weekend he won't forget even if his friend does!!?

DEDICATION

To the underpaid, overworked NHS nurses.

CONTENTS

	Prologue	Pg 1
1	The Pact	Pg 3
2	The Ice Queen	Pg 8
3	The Magnificent Seven	Pg 12
4	Metal Guru	Pg 17
5	Burn The Suburbs	Pg 21
6	The Professor	Pg 24
7	Bucket Lists	Pg 27
8	The Question of God	Pg 34
9	Crossing The Dots	Pg 38
10	Death By Lingerie	Pg 43
11	Plotters and Planners	Pg 49
12	The Bag	Pg 53
13	A Tale of Two Embassies	Pg 57
14	The Deposit	Pg 63
15	The Smell of Napalm	Pg 68
16	The Lock In	Pg 72
17	One Shot	Pg 81
18	Fire Fighting	Pg 87
19	The Good Poison Club on Tour	Pg 94
20	Dress Down Monday	Pg 98
21	The Confession	Pg 106
22	The Dinner Party	Pg 117
23	The Sleepover	Pg 122
24	The Tag	Pg 129
25	Kenny Dalglish	Pg 136

26	Old Dundee	Pg 143
27	Mo	Pg 146
28	The After Show	Pg 149
29	The Day Off	Pg 153
30	The Night Off	Pg 160
31	The Day After The Night Before	Pg 166
32	Inappropriate Behaviour	Pg 171
33	The Siege	Pg 176
34	The Red Lion	Pg 181
35	Rock Chicks	Pg 186
36	The Naked Truth	Pg 191
37	Sunday Brunch	Pg 198
38	The Inner Circle	Pg 203
39	The Russians Are Coming	Pg 211
40	The Ice Age	Pg 217
41	Friends And Foes	Pg 223
42	The Assassination	Pg 231
43	The Last Will And Testament	Pg 235
44	The Returners	Pg 247

PROLOGUE

(Afghanistan 1980)

"WHERE IS GOD?" A fair and, I would have thought, quite astute question for a thirteen-year-old boy. I say boy but Mohamed has seen and experienced more pain and hardship than most people will in an entire lifetime. I suppose to his peers he is very much a man, particularly to his uncle.

Mohamed's reaction to his uncle's harsh slap was initially a boyish bewildered look of injustice, he even sulked for a few seconds. But then he defiantly took the binoculars off his uncle and pressed them to his eyes to stare at the valley below. His cheek burned red from the vicious slap but there was no trace of tears.

"What can you see?" I asked in English, trying to defuse the situation.

Uncle Omar glared at me, his nephew answered. "I see where shell hit, bit too far. I see Russians in garrison, maybe seven...no, nine. They not running, they not see shell. They-"

Uncle Omar cut him short as he snatched back the binoculars. After a couple of minutes he put them down and looked directly at me, I've never seen eyes so dark and angry.

He leaned over Mohamed and pulled me over to him, turning me onto my back as he placed a knife against my Adam's apple. Calmly he told his nephew that he was to fire the second and last shell and if he didn't kill at least one Russian he would slit my throat.

Time stood still as I strained to see Mohamed load the shell into the rusty old howitzer. I knew Uncle Omar had never trusted me, I couldn't in all honesty blame him for I had little trust myself in the old relic of a gun. In my heart of hearts I knew it would fail miserably, but that wasn't the point. It was a double whammy, 'Old Dundee', as I'd christened this useless hunk of old metal, had kept me alive thus far and it was highly unlikely that I'd be responsible for anyone's demise. I felt completely helpless as I glimpsed Mohamed pick up the remaining shell and disappear to the rear of 'Old Dundee'.

The rest of Omar's tribe were silent, all I could hear was a slight metallic scraping as the shell was loaded. The pressure of Omar's blade was choking me, I gasped for air, dry unforgiving air that even at dawn was burning hot.

Where is God? It was a good question.

I'd settle for a slap, but prayer seemed my last chance. 'Old Dundee' had bought me the six weeks it had taken to push the sad old beast to this god forsaken hilltop. But she could in no way be relied upon to save me now.

I knew Mohamed would do his best for both his family and my good self. In the nine months his village had kept me captive, I'd taught him English and he'd done his best to lessen the beatings. My life was in the hands of a 'man' barely in his teens and a thirty-nine-year-old artillery piece.

It would take Mohamed, with the help of a couple of villagers, around five minutes to fire the last shell. A futile effort to take revenge for his grandfather's death, by killing a Russian soldier. Or, if the mission fails, kill a spy, for that is what Uncle Omar believes I am.

So I had just a few moments to reflect on my twenty-eight years on this planet. To think of mum and dad back home in my beloved Scottish highlands, friends, family, lovers, and of course, my beautiful Alice.

1

THE PACT

(West London 2017)

'TOXIC TINA' LAY motionless on her bed. *I'm dead*, she convinced herself, *my eyes won't open, I hear only silence, I can't physically move any part of my body, no taste, no smell. I'm dead.*

She attempted to recall how she may have died, surely Freddie wasn't a psychopath? If she'd been on one of her internet dates, well, the more chance of being murdered, her father always warned her to be careful. But she'd been on her annual New Year's Eve date with Freddie, yes, he was a strange one, but a killer? No.

She felt a throbbing pain in her head, it was encouraging. *Pain is a sense, I might still be alive.*

Tina became aware of a continuous groaning sound beside her and then felt a hand on her breast. *I'm alive.* She tried to shout but her mouth still couldn't function. *Yuk, I stink.* She could definitely smell herself.

Eventually she managed to prise open an eye. Her five senses appeared to be in some sort of working order and her memory was quickly kicking in. The beer, the wine, the shots, the weed, the MMDA. *That was quite a night*, she thought, before realising that after fourteen years, fourteen dates, Freddie and her had finally done it.

She'd met him at uni, they were mates and they were both without dates the first New Year's Eve after they met. So, they started a tradition that no matter what their situation they would go out on the lash, once a year, until one of them got hitched. In fact, they made a drunken pact when they were twenty-five that if they were both still single when they were thirty-five they'd marry each other. There was one year left before their pact would be put to the test. Last night they'd jokingly written a list of guests before things got messy, as they always did. But this year, things seemed to have gotten way out of hand.

She looked at his carpenter's hand on her boob. "Shit," she managed to croak out, "I feel like shit, I thought I was dead."

Freddie continued to snore very loudly.

"Shit Freddie, we did it, we had sex."

Freddie stirred, let out a loud, short snort and opened an eye. "I think we did Tina."

"Was it any good?"

"I think so," he replied, perplexed.

"So clearly not unforgettable?" Tina offered.

"Clearly," he sighed, "maybe we should do it again to jog our memories."

"This time next year then," Tina laughed.

"Well, according to our pact, that will be the consummation of our marriage," Freddie added with a serious tone that disturbed Tina.

"What are your prospects?" she enquired, resting her head on his hairy chest.

"Bleak," he answered, thinking about the talk of redundancy, "and yours Tina?"

"Total shit Freddie, I work for NHS for god's sake."

"So basically it would be a wonderful joining together of our overdrafts," he laughed.

"Coffee and a fry up?" Tina suggested, trying to change the subject.

"Now that's the best thing you've ever said to me."

Tina gingerly climbed out of bed and panicked when she realised she was naked. She grabbed a bathrobe that lay crumpled on the laminate floor and sought respite from her embarrassment in the bathroom, the only source of privacy in her studio flat.

A glimpse at her face in the cabinet mirror made her grimace. Her makeup looked like a face-paint artist with Parkinson's had applied it. A pang of shame hit her at harbouring that thought, but such gallows humour helped her and her colleagues survive the working day. She wondered what Freddie had made of her body, which she considered to be bordering on the obese. At best he might concede her to be 'all woman'.

THE FRY UP and strong black coffee went down very well.

"I seem to remember you telling me about a strange but positive development at your hospital Tina."

She was impressed that he could recall any of their conversation from the night before. "Ah yes, the Sanctuary, or what some of the patients have called, 'Toxic Tina's' Good Poison Club."

"Interesting…" Freddie remarked.

"Strange," Tina corrected.

"Why strange?"

Tina took a couple of Nurofen, washed down with orange juice straight from a carton. "Strange because a few months ago I was invited to a meeting with the chief executive. The management plus all the senior sisters were there and were told the Trust had overspent their budget *by millions* and there would be some tough cutbacks rolled across all departments."

"What could you possibly cut, apart from sick people?" Freddie asked, with surprising sincerity.

He lit up his last cigarette and listened to Tina describe what happened a couple of weeks after the cost cutting meeting.

* * *

Hi Tina,
Please could you join me in the canteen for Lunch 13.00 tomorrow. I have some exciting news.
Kind regards,
Sebastian

SHE READ THE email several times, particularly the address. She'd never had personal communication from the chief executive before. She felt sorry for Sebastian Phelps really. He'd arrived a year earlier, full of enthusiasm and fresh ideas but as always the grinding bureaucratic machine that is the NHS had worn him down. He'd physically aged in his time here, hair greying rapidly and bags forming under his **once bright eyes.**

She'd hardly enough time to get through the day's list of patients without yet another pointless meeting with management. But this was the chief exec. *It must be serious,* she thought, as she looked around the chemo suite.

There were a few tatty info posters on the wall that could go but not much else. The staff were stretched to breaking point, they desperately needed to recruit two experienced nurses, at least.

She entered the canteen thinking seriously about looking for another job, maybe even trying something outside the stress-filled world of front line nursing.

"TINA, THANK YOU so much for finding time to meet us," Sebastian Phelps welcomed her to a discrete table in the corner. "Let me introduce you to Rupert."

"Delighted to meet you Tina, I've heard only good things about you."

Tina smiled as she shook his hand. He was the poshest person she'd ever met. Sebastian, Rupert, these were names from a faraway planet she'd never set foot on.

"I know you're terribly busy Tina so I'll cut straight to the chase. I'm from the Ministry of Health and here to kickstart a new initiative we call the Sanctuary which, if successful here as St Peter's, we will look to roll out across every Trust in the country," Rupert stated, as if reading from a script.

What bollocks is this? Tina pondered. She'd grown cynical about the empty words the government came up with in relation to the health service, or indeed anything. As soon as she heard the words 'initiative' and 'roll out' she realised another consultation paper had been written and nothing would actually happen, not in her lifetime.

"Let me give you the details Tina," the civil servant continued.

Tina looked at Phelps, he seemed to be far away, no doubt in a world of balancing budgets. She briefly wondered what happened to the noble vocation of actually caring for the poorly.

"We are going to install a state of the art facility for your patients Tina, which we will call the Sanctuary. This will be a space they can enjoy, hopefully bringing them a positive experience to enhance their physical and mental wellbeing. This facility will be equipped with a small gymnasium, an entertainment zone and a kitchen stroke dining area, staffed by a chef and dietician."

"A gymnasium?" Tina muttered disbelievingly.

"Yes Tina, let me show you the plans." Rupert played with his iPad, an architect's plan sprung up on the screen, he pointed to a cluster of symbols in one corner. "A couple of exercise bikes here, treadmill machines there. A rowing machine-"

"Where's the Jacuzzi?" Tina interrupted.

Sebastian smiled, the man from the Ministry wasn't sure if she was serious. "Anything's possible, I'll have to check the budget of course, but most importantly we will want you to organise the Sanctuary's Good Vibes Group. It will be the epicentre of the facility Tina."

"What's the Good Vibes Group?" she asked, thinking about how many patients would be waiting for treatment that afternoon.

"One hour a week we would like you to chair a group therapy session with some of your patients. Encourage them to share their worries, get them to de-stress, if you like."

Tina stared at Rupert, then at her boss, her big boss. "Two points," she offered, "will this actually happen and how the feck can the hospital afford all this? It's already way over budgeted this year."

"I told you Tina was straight talking," Sebastian jested.

"Well, let me be straight with *you* Tina. The powers that be have given me a ring-fenced budget to make sure this project's a success. Sebastian has shown me the decommissioned Banbury ward next to your chemo suite and the builders will be commencing work tomorrow. We hope to complete the job in two working weeks."

The chief executive nodded at Tina in a gesture of confirmation.

Tina wondered if she was dreaming. Two working weeks and not two lifetimes, this was impressive. "But I'm a chemo nurse, not a therapist, what do you mean I'm going to organise the Good Vibes Group?"

"We'll give you all the support you need Tina, our thoughts are that your patients are more likely to share with someone who they know understands their particular problems and concerns. So to put your mind at rest I've confirmed to Sebastian the budget includes the immediate employment of two experienced nurses to help ease the pressure we know you are under."

* * *

"WOW, THAT'S PLAIN bizarre," Freddie said, after Tina finished the story.

"Totally fecking mental Freddie, and Rupert was good to his word, everything was up and running in just over two weeks, including the gym!"

"And did you get the extra staff?"

Tina paused before answering, an expression of pain on her face that had nothing to do with her violent hangover. "Yes but, there's always a fecking 'yes but' with the NHS, they gave me two great nurses but cut the funding on two of my patient's drug trials."

"Hmm…and is your Good Vibes Group up and running?" Freddie enquired.

"Very much so, my patients call it 'Toxic Tina's' Good Poison Club. I've only actually got a few attendees but it seems to be going ok."

Freddie took a slurp of his coffee before asking, "Any interesting characters?"

"Patient confidentiality and all that, but yes, they are very much a diverse bunch." She thought about her previous meeting with the group. "Strictly between you and me Freddie, I think one of them's a hit man!"

2

THE ICE QUEEN
(London 2016)

DECAPITATION. WHAT A fantastically descriptive word, Toby pondered. *Such a functional yet almost beautiful way of describing such a brutal, ugly act.*

Decapitation, he repeated to himself silently. This was a word a recovering stammerer could get his tongue round. Five delicious syllables. Bring on the Christmas charades, this would really stump his too clever by far siblings.

"Decapitation?"

The Ice Queen interrupted his thoughts, turning a wonderful word into a cold query, and dragging Toby back to reality.

"Is that the exact word chef used?" She addressed the seven colleagues sitting at the table.

Toby completely understood his team leader's question but felt a pang of regret that she'd in no way appreciate the technicalities of this great word. After all, the English language was a national sport to him. He'd got a first class honours degree studying it at Oxford, whilst she only achieved a second in Business Studies at a minor provincial uni. Words wouldn't excite her, but then again, what would?

Alongside his passion for words he had his rugby, which also meant auxiliary bonuses such as beer and curry. He loved music, from Beethoven to Radiohead, and he had a growing interest in foreign film, recently discovering some surprisingly brilliant Iranian cinema. But he wondered what on god's earth moved the Ice Queen?

He stared at her cold, pale face. Not a trace of makeup to lighten the harshness that was probably the product of her Norwegian diplomat father.

He was definitely responsible for her impossibly blonde, bordering on white, hair, as always, tied in a harsh functional bun.

He knew her mother was Danish but couldn't detect any physical evidence. The few Danes he'd personally met were full of fun and colour. As always she was wearing a black trouser suit with a white blouse buttoned to the neck. He'd never seen her sporting a necklace, just the same old bland white V. In the two years he'd known her he'd never seen her animated or excited about anything. She'd certainly never attended the Friday after work sessions at the Red Lion, where the rest of her team would gather and mostly indulge in their favourite pastime, discussing her.

"Defo a lesbian," Craig would offer.

"No way, and I should know," Christine interjected.

"I reckon she's asexual," Toby offered his expert analysis.

All nine of the regular attendees often expressed their surprise that none of them had ever seen her out of the work environment. They thought she lived in the Fulham area and the odds were someone would have run into her in a West End bar or restaurant, maybe in Waitrose or on the underground, but not one chance encounter to speak of.

"Does she live in the basement at HQ?"

"Maybe she's the bride of Dracula."

"Lives in a crypt..."

The quips kept coming.

"So our chef said he wanted to decapitate his clients." The Ice Queen looked directly at Sir Martin Briggs who sat at the head of the table. It was the first time in eighteen months the big white chief had chaired a meeting.

This has to be serious shit, Toby thought. Everyone and everything in their world had been stirred up by Brexit, and Trump's now imminent presidency.

"You would have all noticed the communication from our American friends. Two words underlined," Briggs addressed his troops.

"Decapitation and Afghanistan," Toby confirmed in his cut glass ascent, enjoying the moment. *Nine fantastic syllables in just two words*, he thought.

"Yes, thank you Toby, decapitation and Afghanistan. The Yanks have flagged up these two words in relation to the food poisoning incident. They're not going to let this go, they are hopping mad. They're all shitting themselves at the thought of Trump becoming Commander in Chief. They want blood, and unless we sort this problem the so called special relationship will be history."

They hadn't seen their CEO so agitated since the Iran nuclear negotiations. He motioned to the Ice Queen to carry on.

"So this is what we know thus far," she continued, perusing the classified file in front of her, the others followed the transcript on their iPads. "On November 6th a conference took place in a fifth floor room at the Queen Elizabeth Conference centre, under the title 'Global Connections'. To anyone working there it was just another geek fest. In reality it was a highly secretive meeting to discuss defence against the ongoing threat to western interests from cyber attack."

"So a geek fest then," Sir Martin laughed.

Toby and the rest chortled.

The Ice Queen glared at the team before continuing. "There were experts from across the pond, France, Germany and Holland. The conference was chaired by Nigel Bernard, from the Ministry of Defence, whom we all know. To cut to the chase, the meeting started at nine and ended at four thirty. During the course of that evening seventeen out of the twenty-one attendees were taken ill, four were hospitalised. The four that were not affected hadn't taken advantage of the lunch supplied by an outside catering company the conference centre regularly use. Because of the sensitive nature of the meeting, and the fact that everyone was over it after a few days, we decided to make a few discreet enquiries.

"We looked into the catering company, Manor From Seven. The name derives from a play on words, the biblical manor from heaven plus the fact the company are housed at unit number seven on a grim industrial estate in East London. They supply trendy and healthy food to mainly hipster businesses. Initial thoughts were that it was just an unlucky coincidence, an unfortunate case of food poisoning. The conference centre management confirmed they'd used Manor from Seven at least three times a week for three years and there'd never been an issue. They had recently been invited to the catering company's Christmas do in Soho and enjoyed a very positive relationship with them."

"But the yanks thought otherwise?" Sir Martin interrupted.

"Yes sir, they sent this communication claiming they have the transcript of a text message from a member of the catering company to a colleague claiming the chef had said he wanted to decapitate a client."

"Two questions," Toby interjected.

The Ice Queen looked slightly annoyed but invited him to carry on by turning her hand.

"Is the interception and action by the Americans legal and was the chef looking to decapitate a particular client?"

Sir Martin stepped in just as the Ice Queen was about to answer. "Legal is not something the new order are bothered about, their chief geek ended up on a drip and missed the birth of his first child. They are spitting feathers. Carry on Claire."

Claire turned a page and continued. "They want us to find out who the client in question is, they also claim the chef is originally from Afghanistan, hence the underlining along with decapitation."

"They may be adding one plus one and getting three but they also have chatter they're not sharing with us," the CEO added. "So, number one, use discretion, number two, answers on my desk within the week please. Good morning everyone."

Sir Martin stood and strode out the room, the team rose as one and mumbled their goodbyes.

3

THE MAGNIFICENT SEVEN

'TOXIC TINA' SAT perusing her shiny new empire. It was, she'd agree, spectacular, from the huge state of the art TV to the luxurious laminate flooring. The chairs were swish, modern, chrome legs, sleek red backrests and most importantly ample padding for her ample backside.

There were twenty such chairs but today only seven occupants. She was hoping for more but nature and a tube strike dictated the numbers. Two of her patients were too sick to attend and a couple would be stuck at home due to the transport problems.

The Sanctuary and its Good Vibes Group reminded Tina of her local pub. The brewery had recently spent a fortune on revamping the fixtures and fittings but they couldn't revamp the clientele, they remained unwashed and unpredictable. Not that her 'clients' were unwashed, just unwell and unpredictable.

This would be her fifth session and whilst her confidence and enthusiasm were growing, she couldn't say the same for the motley crew that sat around her in an ad hoc horseshoe shape. One or two seemed to monopolise the discussions, whilst others contributed little or nothing at all. She'd found that being herself and forgetting the meat of what she'd learnt on her crash course in group therapy was, however, drawing them out a bit more.

"Good afternoon everyone, another week and you're all still with us, that's a good start!" Tina was certain this introduction was not recommended but now she'd torn up the rulebook she was on a roll. "What would you like to whinge about today?" she asked the Good Poison Club.

She suggested this change of name after the officially named Good Vibes Club was ridiculed in the first session. Patronising codswallop, naff, crap, insulting, were among the negative adjectives used to describe the epicentre of the Ministry of Health's expensive new initiative. Later when Tina was describing the rudiments of chemotherapy, she'd called it a form of poison, a good poison. Brenda piped up, "The Good Poison Club, we are the Good Poison Club."

"Toxic Tina's Good Poison Club," the Professor added.

Tina wasn't keen on the Professor but she adored Brenda. Maybe it was the Irish connection, though certainly not Brenda's commitment to religion. Tina had lost faith in her early teens when her mother passed away. She watched her wither away, pinning her faith on her priest rather than her consultant. Tina was left full of anger rather than faith. An anger directed at God and her father, who were both absent during her time of greatest need. Her father had disappeared back to Ireland when she was six, he made a brief drunken appearance at the funeral, but Tina didn't see him again for eleven years.

Her mother would be around Brenda's age now, she imagined they'd be friends, cut from the same cloth. Brenda was uncomplaining and philosophical about her illness. Faith worked for her, plus she had the constant support of her husband John who was always there at the end of both her chemo sessions and these group meetings to take her home. Tina liked to imagine their home as a warm three-bedroom terrace with 1970s wallpaper, a cross in each room. They had two sons, both tradesmen, and three grandchildren, Brenda loved to show Tina the latest photos of them on a weekly basis. Tina genuinely hoped Brenda's story would have a happy ending.

Dennis, on the other hand, she couldn't warm to. The others gave him the nickname the Professor because he was a retired lecturer. He'd originally taught politics at a polytechnic, that later became part of a minor university. He was forced to take early retirement but was secretive about the reasons why. He was bitter and cynical about the academic system he'd spent his entire career in. Tina found him bitter and cynical about everything and assumed he was always that way. His few contributions to the group had thus far been totally negative.

"So how's your week been?" Tina asked the group.

She was taken aback when Brenda got the ball rolling. "Difficult," she croaked.

This can't be good, Tina thought. She could see the other six were curious but uncomfortable.

"Difficult Brenda, in what way?" Tina queried.

"My trial, it's been postponed," Brenda replied.

"Trial?" Veronica interjected in her raspy tones that reminded Tina of Joanna Lumley.

"My drug trial has been cancelled due to funding problems."

The others responded to this news with a mixture of sighs and expletives.

"That's shit news Bren, man that's shit news," Brian said in his deep West Indian accent.

"Hang on, how can the health authority spend a shit load of dosh on this swanky facility but can't afford Brenda's trial?"

Micky didn't often contribute so when he did the room took notice. As usual he was dressed all in black. Tina secretly called him 'the hitman'.

The others all turned their collective gaze to Tina, this was not the start she was expecting.

"I'm sorry Brenda, this is the first I've heard of this, I'll look into it. Are you sure it's been turned down?"

Brenda produced a letter from her handbag, which Tina took and read the highlights.

"I promise I'll look into this Brenda." She handed the letter back trying to keep her frustration in check.

Things then got political which, whilst Tina had stated that no subject was taboo, she wasn't entirely comfortable with the direction of this current conversation. The Professor ranted how the government had spent the money that could have funded Brenda's trial on military interventions in the Middle East. Hassan came back at him claiming that he didn't know what he was talking about, it was the fault of all the people that didn't turn up for appointments. He also claimed the Professor had never lived in the real world. "The trouble with you academics is that your parents are teachers, you go to nursery, primary school, secondary school, university, which you never leave, you've been in the bloody classroom all your life! Try living in the real world!" Voices were raised, culminating in Brian and Tina appealing for calm.

The Professor wanted the last word and addressed Hassan directly. "I'm not going to be lectured by a fucking Uber fucking minicab driver."

No one was sure if the Professor was having a dig directly at Hassan or Uber, given his views on globalisation.

Tina tried to change the subject to one less confrontational, but she couldn't change her audience. They discussed the issue of the financial implications around their illnesses, but given the varied conditions there was little input and once again only the usual suspects contributed.

Davina waffled on about her pending trip to New York.

The Professor kept his contempt for her in check, he would like to give her a slap and probably would if she mentioned her 'bucket list' one more time.

"What about insurance?" Tina chipped in.

"Fuck the insurance," Davina responded, "I might be dead in a year, I want to go to the Big Apple whilst I've still got the strength to shop."

"Well, if anything happens to you in the USA, without insurance you'd be up shit creek without a paddle," Brian exclaimed.

"So what?" Davina retorted.

"They check your paperwork before your pulse," Micky added.

"I couldn't give a flying fuck," Davina swore. "If I snuffed it in the Big Apple I would die with a smile on my face knowing the massive inconvenience it would cause my nephews who stand to inherit my three properties, the ungrateful little shits."

"Three? We know about your house in Pimlico and the apartment in Marbella, where's the third?" Brenda queried.

"Brighton," Davina confirmed, without a hint of embarrassment. "My last but one husband gave it too me as a one off divorce settlement. I love Brighton, I call it 'Camden by the sea', it's wonderful, full of the most amazing characters."

"Wannabe hippies," Dennis, the Professor, chipped in with his usual cynicism.

Micky made one of his rare interventions. "I think you'll find they are bonafide hippies. I was there the other weekend, I saw at least three demonstrations, Anti-Fracking, Surfers Against Sewage and Stop the War, proper hippies."

"Typical," the Professor snorted.

"What's typical?" Micky retorted calmly.

"What would you know about hippies, you live in some god forsaken suburb for fucks sake, you live in fucking Chavsville!"

"Calm down Dennis," Tina said, trying to placate the conversation.

She noticed Micky giving Dennis a 'thousand yard stare', she wondered if he knew the lecturer's medical history. But even allowing for his brain related illness he was an annoying bugger and probably always had been. Micky continued to stare at him. *If looks could kill*, she thought, he was a hitman after all.

She formed this theory because he was always dressed head to foot in black, literally, his swept back hair was impossibly black for a man of his fifty-nine years. Being a metal head when off duty black was her favourite colour, her only colour, but she was pretty sure he wasn't into metal. Probably a rat pack man like her father, not that he was in any way like her father. She was slightly perturbed that she found him rather attractive. Probably attracted to his mysterious aloofness rather than his looks, though she reckoned he was a handsome devil in his day. Still not at all shabby in fact. Right now though, he just looked dangerous, Tina thought he might physically attack Dennis.

Hassan chipped in, "Where is Chavsville?"

"I think the question is, what is Chavsville?" Brian added.

Everyone turned to Dennis, the Professor. "The fucking suburbs, Chavsville, where you all live."

"What exactly is a chav? I've heard the term often but I've no idea what it means," Brenda added.

"Us," Micky snapped, without averting his stare at Dennis. "We're the 'chavs' according to him, everyone who doesn't live in his fucking bubble is a chav."

"Exactly what I said before, he doesn't live in the real world," Hassan repeated. "What's wrong with living in the suburbs, isn't that where we all want to live? I've worked eighteen hours a day cabbing so my kids can grow up in a decent place, you're an idiot," he continued.

"I think you'll find Dennis, most of us aspire to live in the suburbs," Tina said diplomatically. "Shall we change the subject?"

The room fell silent, an awkward silence. Tina sensed this and tried to think of a subject that would calm everyone down. She looked at Mo, who'd not uttered a word in the five sessions. "Mo, perhaps you'd like to share something with us?"

She knew he spoke excellent English because he'd discussed various aspects of his treatment with her. Maybe he was just shy. He had a warm smile, very courteous, but didn't seem interested in joining the conversation. She wasn't the only one in the room who wondered why he bothered to attend the meetings. Rupert, from the Ministry of Health, had attended the first meeting, he'd remarked to Tina afterwards that it was a shame Mo hadn't felt comfortable enough to contribute, he was keen that diversity was at the core of this project. She didn't really have a clue what he was on about and was surprised when he mentioned the 'God' question.

"You obviously realise God will be dragged into the conversation sooner or later Tina. I'll be very interested in any theological discussion, please let me know when it was rears its ugly head."

Tina thought this strange but said she'd be in touch 'as soon as one of our respective Gods' makes an appearance.

Mo cleared his throat in preparation for his first offering to the Good Poison Club. Tina felt a pang of excitement, the other six members turned as one in mutual anticipation. He cleared his throat again but at that moment the Professor stood and started to shout, "Burn the suburbs! Burn the fucking lot of them! Burn the suburbs!"

4

METAL GURU

TINA LIKENED INTERNET dating to the lottery, you had to buy a ticket to stand a chance of winning. She'd given up conventional methods of meeting the opposite sex. In her workplace everyone was under too much pressure and the doctors she knew were far too arrogant. Though, she did have a brief liaison with a registrar, but that got a bit messy when his wife found out. Clubbing wasn't her scene, mainly due to being too knackered to be out so late. Going to gigs and films at the weekend was her passion so typing those pursuits into the online questionnaire saved a lot of time and idle chitchat.

She'd been on eleven dates, only four had led to repeat dates. She was keen to find someone to share her love of metal and chick flicks but the men were normally more interested in getting her into bed. Two close girlfriends had met their future husbands online so she was still confident it was the way forward.

Tina always met her dates in busy places, tonight's was at the legendary World's End in Camden. She text Jed, her date, telling him she would be wearing a black sleeveless turtleneck top under a jet black leather jacket, with a Metallica badge on the left hand lapel. She also described the three-year-old tattoo on her upper arm. Tina always made sure she was at least fifteen minutes late for a date. One, because she didn't want to wait in a bar or restaurant on her own, and two, she liked to create some tension, put whoever she was meeting on the back foot.

She'd arrived in Camden uncomfortably early so headed to the nearest coffee shop to waste half an hour. As she studied the frothy heart on top of her cappuccino she thought of Freddie. She'd recalled more about their night of passion than she'd let on and wondered if he thought the same.

She smiled to herself as she thought about their pact. She felt a pang of guilt that she was meeting a stranger. *This is a surprising sensation,* she thought. *What's Freddie up to? Is he seeing anybody? Would he be jealous? Could they actually be a couple…had they wasted all those years?*

"Toxic Tina."

Her thoughts were interrupted by a familiar voice. Looking up she saw a tall, slim, middle-aged man dressed all in black.

"Micky!" She acknowledged the 'hitman'. "What're you doing in Camden? Wouldn't have thought this was your scene, with respect."

"Meeting my daughter, we're going to look round the market then maybe some lunch." Micky perched on the seat opposite, declining Tina's offer of coffee. "And what you up to Tina?"

"A date," she answered feeling a little awkward, "an internet date actually."

"Sounds interesting."

"I hope so."

"I'm not an expert to be honest, I'm old school. More for the traditional approach, fate, chance, that sort of thing," Micky admitted.

"And you're married," Tina added.

"Yep, second time around, been almost fifteen years, so what would I know." Micky's smile looked more mischievous than usual. "How do you know your date isn't a psycho killer?"

"You sound like my dad, he thinks I'm bonkers."

"He might be right Tina."

"I was quite specific in requesting my date doesn't have a criminal record!" Tina laughed.

"That rules me out then," Micky replied.

"I knew it, I knew you were a naughty boy Micky."

"A very naughty boy Tina, but I'm not going to get up to much now am I," he said, despondent.

"I don't know Micky, you're very well at the moment."

Micky took a swig of water from the bottle he always carried. Tina took a sip of her coffee. *So he is a hit man,* she thought to herself.

"That was weird Tina, the other day at your meeting, the Professor and his rant about the suburbs."

"Burn the suburbs," Tina quoted and shrugged to indicate she was clueless too. "That was quite a speech wasn't it, I was particularly insulted by the bit about Prosecco, which I rather like."

"Yeah, funny, I think he's mad rather than bad though, hopefully."

* * *

THE WORLD'S END is not just the name of a pub, it's a great description of its clientele, Tina thought. The devil's local she'd describe it to those who'd never braved its cavernous bars, filled with zombie like creatures dressed, of course, in black. Not Micky the 'hitman' smart casual black, but full metal black with only beloved band names adding contrast: Black Sabbath, Metallica, Motörhead, Slayer, Autobridge, Iron Maiden, Snuff. Tina reckoned it highly unlikely any of these bands would be on Micky's playlist. There was a higher than normal tattoo count, one would assume it was compulsory. Tina too would expose her skull and crossbows on her upper arm as soon as she removed her jacket.

Because the World's End is huge she gave a fairly accurate description of where she'd plot up. The must haves in her online specifications were: Must love Metal, must be hairy, must be inked and must be employed (preferably in the public services). Secretly she confided to friends and colleagues she would like a fireman, but she didn't specify that online. She was about to be served by a purple haired barmaid when a fully inked arm emerged beside her, the hand at the end of it was clutching a twenty pound note. "I'll get this Tina, what's your poison? I'm Jed."

Tina first thought her date was standing a little too close but realised it was due to the sheer volume of punters clamouring to get served. In a millisecond she became aware he ticked all the right boxes. His shoulder length brown hair and wild beard were a great start, as well as his Judas Priest t-shirt, she loved Judas Priest. Although that was another point she forgot to mention in her CV. To top it off he had an inked sleeve, with a fire breathing dragon as its centrepiece.

He ordered her a bottle of Sol and pint of bitter for himself. *A proper bloke*, she thought. The music was deafening, this wasn't the place for casual chitchat so he led her by the hand upstairs where they shouted at each other for the next two hours.

He had her at the answer to her first question though.

"What do you do Jed?" she hollered.

"I'm a firefighter!" he hollered back.

She phoned her best friend Helen the next morning to confirm she was A) still alive and B) had met her perfect date. "It was as if the dating app had read the secret corridors of my mind. He's even a Leo for fecks sake."

Her father phoned to make sure was A) still alive, there was no B. Tina was not about to admit she'd met her perfect match to him. She checked the time, 11.30 am, she guessed he was sober.

Despite the history she liked the fact he worried about her, if only he'd been around to show concern when she needed it. She was old enough and ugly enough now to look after herself.

"You going to see Mr Right again then Tina?" he enquired.

"Going to a gig next weekend as it happens Dad."

"Is he catholic?"

"No fecking idea dad!" He always managed to annoy her.

After the call she reflected on the night before. Jed was perfect, even his name was cool, and he lived in Kentish Town. *Kentish Town! Not the fecking suburbs! Even the mad Professor would be impressed.*

5

BURN THE SUBURBS

"SO AFTER FIVE sessions, five hours, not one mention of God?" The Ice Queen questioned Toby as if it was his fault.

"No Claire, the God question has surprisingly not reared its ugly head," Toby replied, somewhat apologetically.

"And not a murmur from our friend?"

"Not a word Claire, but he did respond to a very strange rant from Dennis, whom Tina and the rest of the group call the Professor." Toby pushed his iPad across the white gloss table to his boss, she pressed play.

"Burn the suburbs! Burn the fucking lot of them! Burn the suburbs!"

The recording was taken from a camera directly behind Tina's chair, the Ice Queen noticed the Professor was on the right hand end chair, their man was directly opposite at the left hand of the horseshoe. She couldn't see Tina's reaction, but could see a clear side profile of their person of interest. She paused the recording and turned the volume up, glancing at Toby who was trying to suppress a look of excited anticipation, anticipation of how his boss would react to the recording.

She noticed his cheeks were redder than usual, he seemed to be staring at her finger lodged on the play button. She teased him by turning the iPad around slowly. She liked to tease him, she knew how to wind him up. She wasn't sure why she enjoyed it so much, maybe his cut glass accent, maybe because he was Oxbridge, mainly though because she knew he begrudged the fact she was his superior.

She looked him in the eye and pressed play, seconds later the Professor had her full attention again. "Burn the semis, the gated developments, the cul-de-sacs that, like their inhabitants, go nowhere in particular! And yes, burn the suburban people! You know the ones, they worship their shiny white gloss fitted kitchens and their flat screen TVs. They go to dinner parties and talk about 'LED' lighting like it's a new religion! They go on cruises, suburbs on the seas and to 'all inclusive' suburbs in the sun. Suburban women, don't get me started! With their nail bars and Prosecco. Limoncello, when did that happen and why? No wonder the men escape to their golf clubs, which by the way will be first on my list for incinerating! And their hateful offspring, the boy racers killing each other in their turbo charged motors. Flowers tied to lampposts, suburban shrines! The suburban teenage girls with their tattooed eyebrows. Burn the lot of them! Burn the suburbs!"

Toby watched his boss' gaze wander a fraction to the left as Hassan reacted angrily, shouting and swearing at his fellow patient only to be interrupted by a frail figure on the end chair breaking into an enthusiast round of applause. The others turned their attention away from the ranting Professor to the source of the loud clapping. "Quite a speech," Toby offered.

"Yes, but not relevant," she said coldly, sliding the iPad back to him.

Toby felt disappointed but not surprised by her non-reaction. He'd had have liked something more enthusiastic but at the end of the day she was probably correct. "What about our man's reaction?" Toby chanced.

"Well, I suppose it was at least some kind of communication," the Ice Queen agreed. "I'm just hoping we haven't wasted our entire budget on a ten-second hand clap," she said as an afterthought.

"Should I add the incident to his file?" Toby asked. He sat back whilst she deliberated, tapping the table with her fingers.

"Ok," she started, "I can see some of our friends looking at this conversation and taking it completely out of context. You can see the American's flagging up decapitation, Afghanistan and now 'burning the suburbs' and then what?"

"I agree Claire, the yanks would probably mess up all our efforts and drag him out of his hospital bed, bearing in mind I've watched the recording umpteen times and in my opinion the applause is probably sarcastic."

"Probably," she concurred.

Toby briefly felt a flicker of warmth.

"So, let's leave the speech and the clapping an off the record conversation between ourselves," the Ice Queen confirmed.

"What happens in the suburbs stays in the suburbs," Toby quipped and then felt the chill of the icy stare his boss shot back.

Claire didn't dislike Toby as much as he assumed she did. She secretly admired his intellect, but was also intimidated by it. She knew they didn't share the same connections, the ones his Oxbridge background brought him, but she was trilingual and *fuck it*, she was made team leader because she was the best. *Simple,* she said to herself in English, Norwegian and Danish.

"So Toby, we need to forward a concise, accurate report to Sir Martin outlining everything of interest since the initial meeting."

Toby couldn't recall the last time she'd addressed him by name, this was encouraging but he wasn't sure why. He opened the notes app on his iPad and waited for his boss to cover the salient points.

"First, our Imam. Craig and his team have reported hospitals, patients, dates and times. Underlined in red are the three visits he's made to our friend. There is also a historical log of some of the bad company he's kept in the past. YouTube is a wonderful thing."

Toby nodded in agreement whilst furiously typing notes.

"The Americans still won't show us the evidence but insist that ISIS are trying to recruit terminally ill patients for suicide missions. They flagged up our Imam and asked us to keep an eye on him. The attached report has no conclusions thus far but our thoroughness is there for all to see."

Toby nodded, thoroughness was another wonderful word.

"And that brings us to our chef," the Ice Queen gestured to Toby to take over.

"Yes, our chef, okay. First, yes he is from Afghanistan and we think he came here around 1990."

"You think?" she interrupted.

"Well it seems he had a sponsor who liaised with the Home Office and, bizarrely, the BBC."

"The BBC?" she repeated, with a quizzical frown.

"Yes, the sponsor, who I'm trying to track down, was working for the BBC on a documentary related to the Russian invasion of Afghanistan, I'm sure I will have the I's dotted shortly. The decapitation text - the colleague he sent it to is a female kitchen assistant from Moldova, where she returned to shortly after the cyberspace conference. Christine has emailed her a job offer from a bogus catering company, which she seems to have accepted. She's due back in London next week, so that should be a very interesting meeting."

"Very," she replied, then waited for Toby to carry on.

"The good news, well I presume it's good news, is that our chef seems to be responding to the chemo well and is due to end this round of treatment in six weeks time. What happens then, I'm not sure yet."

"In that case Toby I suggest it's vital the Good Vibes Centre yields some results. If your nurse doesn't ask the right questions at the next meeting then I recommend you replace her with someone who will."

"Leave it to me Claire," Toby replied, whilst pondering how he'd get those poor folks on board.

6

THE PROFESSOR

DENNIS WAS BUSYING himself in his Islington garden. It was the first day he'd felt well enough to venture into his pride and joy, plus it was the first decent day weather-wise for ages. He'd invested in some new gardening tools after receiving a dividend from a savings plan he'd long forgotten about. He'd also booked a boating week on the Norfolk Broads. The thought of spending twenty-four hours a day with his wife Sandra filled him with dread but he'd have to get used to it as she was retiring from her job shortly. *Why couldn't they have separate holidays like they had separate beds?*

They'd been married for thirty-five years. They probably loved each other for the first five. Tolerated each other for the next twenty, mostly for the sake of their two sons. Mutual hatred was the best description for the last ten years. Since he was disciplined at work for an indiscretion, Sandra appeared to want to punish him for the rest of his natural life. They'd considered divorce but both didn't want to move from their beloved town house, which was now worth a small fortune.

He'd inherited it from his doctor father, a fact he kept under wraps as it conflicted with his socialist politics. He also buried his expensive education, another embarrassing scar on his beliefs.

Over breakfast that day Sandra had lectured him — whilst she appreciated the chemo slowed him down, she thought he could at least tidy up the garden and do a spot of hoovering. So now he stood by a bright pink rose bush, that he'd lovingly pruned, and started to clear the weeds around its base. The handle of the brand new rake felt smooth in his hands, its steel prongs clawed efficiently at the earth. He stuck it hard into the soft mud and used it as a crutch to hold onto and rest. He looked at his watch and sighed as he realised Sandra would be home shortly. She was bound to mention the hovering, or lack of it.

Once finished he went inside and lay back on the sofa in the living room to read his copy of The Guardian. A thought entered his head, *If she was run over by a bus on the way home from work, would he be disappointed?* Of course everyone would expect him to be devastated, grief stricken, but he honestly believed he wouldn't be particularly bothered.

She'd worked as a legal secretary for the same law firm in Holborn for the past thirty years and he could never recall her telling him she'd be late home, for any reason. She only really socialised with her sister, who passed away last year. Sandra and her sister used to go to the opera together now and again, but would mostly sit in each other's kitchens moaning about everything. Since her sister died he'd had to put up with her endless negativity. He once had a bit of a spark, a sense of fun and enthusiasm, particularly for his teaching, but she had dragged him down to her miserable level.

The incident that finished his career didn't help of course but she had always been bitter and twisted. They'd only married because of two minutes of unprotected pleasure thirty-six years earlier. He was too young and bowed to family pressure at the time. How life might have turned out if he hadn't had gone to that party off the Caledonian Road. He sort of loved his sons but doubted they loved him, they'd inherited their mum's DNA. Robert, conceived in the 'Cali', moved to New Zealand six years ago and they'd not seen him since. James, who arrived two years later, had always been a problem and seemed to spend his life sofa surfing around his strange collection of arty friends. Dennis thought James probably had some form of Aspergers, he seemed incapable of showing emotion. Possibly that was his and Sandra's fault.

The back door opened and Dennis realised his wife hadn't been hit by the number 171 on Kingsway. She came towards him at a worrying pace, her bright red mac spelling danger.

"Evening dear," Dennis muttered without any warmth or affection.

"So what happened to the hoovering then?" was her greeting.

He stared at her knowing she would actually be expecting an apologetic reply, with some serious grovelling thrown in. He continued to stare for a second, thinking about the hovering, about his life limiting illness, and then looked around the freshly raked flower beds, *Not a bad afternoon's work all things considered*, he thought to himself.

She was waiting for his answer, her head tilted slightly. He looked down at his brand new rake, fresh from the gardening section at B&Q, its spiteful steel prongs far superior to the old one he'd taken to the dump the day before. *They could do some serious damage to human flesh*, he pondered.

He considered her hairstyle, she'd had her ginger locks cut into a 'bob' recently. He really quite liked it but hadn't bothered to tell her. He begrudgingly would admit she was still an attractive woman. He tightened his grip on the rake, *If she says another fucking word I'm going to bury this rake in her skull.* He imagined the stunned look on her face as the blood trickled down her rosy cheeks, just before her shapely legs gave way. It would be worth doing the time just to savour the moment. *Fuck it, I'm probably going to die before my time anyway, one more word and I'll smash it straight in her eye sockets!* His mind was racing. *No, the skull would be better, I want to see the look of surprise and horror in those hateful eyes.*

"I can see you've turned a bit of earth over Dennis but I've been at work all day. For fucks sake, it would only take ten minutes to run the hoover round."

She moved a little closer to him, he could smell Tic Tac's on her breath. "You really are fucking useless Dennis!"

7

BUCKET LISTS

DESPITE DONALD TRUMP moving into the White House, the world kept turning. 'Toxic Tina' and her team continued to go the extra mile, or ten, for their patients. She had been given two additional nurses as part of the Sanctuary initiative, but that just meant the powers that be increased patient capacity.

Tina wasn't happy with those powers that be, she'd tried to get to the bottom of why the Trust had refused to fund Brenda's trial but had been given nothing but an assortment of lame excuses. She'd requested an urgent meeting with Sebastian Phelps, the chief executive. Initially she was told he was on holiday for two weeks, which irked her, but she'd been consistently fobbed off since his return. She emailed him outlining her disappointment with the Trust's behaviour, but what she really wanted to ask him, face to face, was how they could afford the Sanctuary, as brilliant as it was, but not her patient's drug trial?

On the positive side her love life was looking on the up for once, having enjoyed two more fantastic dates with Jed. Their online profiles had obviously dovetailed nicely but Tina was still surprised by how many similar interests they shared.

She could only arrange to meet Jed on weekends as she was always so knackered after work. She recalled Freddie's favourite phrase 'less is more' and wondered how Freddie was doing, chuckling as she remembered their pact.

Tina wasn't looking forward to the next couple of days, the Professor was due in for treatment and he was bound to mess with her stress levels. It would be the first time she'd seen him since his rant. She reminded herself under no circumstances to mention the suburbs.

* * *

TINA WAS NEVER a fan of the 02 Arena, she preferred more intimate venues, but Jed had messaged her earlier in the week with a YouTube clip of the Wheatus hit from the noughties, *Teenage Dirtbag*, with the words, *'I've got two tickets for next Saturday!!?'*

She immediately started to sing the chorus, "I've got two tickets for Iron Maiden baby…"

She met him at the front entrance of Wagamama. Both were wearing identical Iron Maiden t-shirts, which was slightly embarrassing.

"We look like a metal version of Torvill and Dean," Jed quipped.

Not only does this guy love absolutely everything I do, he makes me laugh as well, Tina thought.

They were halfway through their meal when they were interrupted. "Hi Tina."

"Freddie!" Tina rarely ever caught up with her friend except on New Year's Eve, she was a little taken aback.

Freddie hugged her hello then turned to her date. "Hi, I'm Freddie," he smiled and extended his hand to Jed who shook it firmly. The introductions continued, Tina met Freddie's date, Allison, who looked in her early twenties and was a bonafide goth, complete with multiple piercings and tats. The last time she'd seen Freddie they'd been naked. She felt a little awkward and wondered if Freddie did too.

Jed invited them to join, as Tina had described Freddie as an old friend from uni. They indulged in small talk for the rest of the meal and Freddie asked Tina how the Good Poison Club was going.

Jed had the feeling Freddie knew Tina too well to be 'just an old friend' and Freddie was slightly alarmed at how silky smooth Jed was, too good looking by half, he reminded him of Jim Morrison.

As they said their goodbyes Freddie said, "See you in seven months time Tina."

Jed was perplexed by his parting comment but he noticed Tina smile, wink and nod a goodbye.

THEY HUGELY ENJOYED the concert and after Tina hugely enjoyed her first visit to Jed's small but luxurious apartment in Kentish Town. "I didn't know fire-fighters were paid so well," she stated, looking around the living room.

"Moonlighting," he answered. "I run a security company which basically employs other 'moonlighting' firemen."

"I wish I had time to 'moonlight'," Tina sighed.

"You need a stronger union like ours, you're too soft, you won't go on strike."

"That's because we are almost 100% female. Our priority is our patients, we're not selfish like men," Tina exclaimed.

"I concur." Jed put his hands up in surrender and Tina leaned over the black leather sofa they had collapsed on and kissed him.

* * *

TOBY THANKED THE Moldovan kitchen assistant for her time and apologised for the ruse he'd used to bring her back to the UK. He watched her walk out the cafe and into the Soho hustle and bustle. She crossed the road and stopped to make a call on her mobile. Toby guessed it was to her anxious family back home. She looked animated, probably telling them about the paperwork he'd just handed her giving her indefinite leave to stay and to be legally employed. He'd told her to keep the £1000 cash he'd handed her to herself.

Toby looked down at his beloved iPad and tapped its blue cover with a sense of satisfaction. He took a final sip of his latte but his now permanent smile meant he dribbled some onto his shirt. He wasn't bothered about the inevitable stain, he was completely focused on typing up the results of his meeting, anticipating the Ice Queen's response when she read his report. He would stick to the facts, there was no need for any embellishment. He planned to transcribe the Moldovan's story almost word for word and then watch his boss' reaction to what will no doubt be the most disgusting thing she'd ever heard.

He ordered another latte and messaged Christine and the sub team, who were trying to track down the chef's mysterious sponsor. He looked at the email containing a PDF of various relevant documents, a lot of information, a name even, but as yet, no joy on her location.

Toby plugged in his earphones and spent the next twenty-three minutes listening to a recording of the interview. He smiled to himself as he repeated the word tang in his mind. *Tang, their chef's client wanted more tang.*

Back at HQ Toby was writing up his report as he brought up live CCTV images from the Sanctuary. He noticed Dennis and Micky sitting next to each other eating sandwiches. They completely ignored the chef who sat beside them. There were no mics in the film room and no camera directly on their mouths, he just hoped Tina would ask the right questions at Thursday's Good Poison Club.

* * *

NOBODY LIKES MONDAYS, Tina hated them but knew her patients hated them more. This particular Monday didn't start well, there was a message from one of her colleagues claiming she had the norovirus and wouldn't be in. *Hangover*, was Tina's cynical thought, she couldn't recall the last time she threw a sickie.

This was going to be a long day.

Tina was three hours into her shift. Dennis and Micky had chemo sessions at the same time, she'd just hooked them up to their IV lines and decided to sit them together in front of the big screen in the Sanctuary. She put on the DVD of Jack Nicholson's film *The Bucket List*.

"Don't mention the suburbs," she whispered in Micky's ear.

Dennis read a book, ignoring the film at first, but began to take notice halfway through. Even after the film finished, they both ignored each other as they ate their packed lunches.

"I enjoyed that," Micky said, as he washed down his food with a gulp of water.

"Not bad," Dennis replied dismissively.

Micky wasn't looking forward to the next five hours stuck next to the Professor. He studied his emails on his phone for a couple of moments before chancing his arm, "What's on your bucket list then?" Dennis ignored the question but Micky played an ace, "apart from burning the suburbs of course."

That got the Professor's attention, he turned and faced Micky. "Well, apart from burning your fucking suburbs, there's one or two things I'd love to do."

"Travel?" Micky offered.

"Rio would be nice but, as that Brenda pointed out, insurance would be a problem."

Micky was slightly miffed that Dennis referred to their fellow patient as 'that Brenda' but at least he was engaging.

"What's yours then?" Dennis asked.

"I've been to Rio so that's crossed off," Micky replied, knowing the Professor would be surprised as he probably assumed a suburban chav wouldn't have travelled further than Marbella. "I'd like to mend some bridges with family, particularly my daughter."

"That's admirable," Dennis replied with a surprising modicum of sincerity

"The wounds from my divorce have never fully healed to be honest, my daughter was only nine at the time."

"It takes two to tango," Dennis chipped in.

"Nope, I was totally to blame, womanising, gambling, you name it, I was guilty as charged. But, I've had some meetings with my daughter recently, which have gone fairly well. So what about you, anything positive you'd like to do?"

They were interrupted by Mo having a coughing fit, they hadn't noticed he was there. He was surfing the TV channels and swigging a bottle of water.

"Depends what you mean by positive I suppose. I had a very positive idea last week..."

Micky sat up trying to look nonplussed as Dennis described the rake incident in the garden. Micky realised the Professor enjoyed shocking people and his brain tumour was probably responsible for his ridiculous rants.

"…so, despite my illness, despite my efforts in the garden, the fucking bitch got in my face and humiliated me. I had this thought going through my aching head, a vision and not a good one, I considered impaling the rake in her fucking skull."

Dennis stared at Micky, looking for signs of shock, none were forthcoming.

"And?" Micky asked nonchalantly.

"And what?"

"Did you do it, did you kill your missus?"

The Professor paused wondering if he'd heard correctly.

"I wouldn't blame you if you'd done it, I'd understand, they can drive you mad women, I know."

"Of course not, of course I didn't. I fucking apologised, grovelled like a fucking slave and went in and did the fucking hoovering!" Dennis was raising his voice and sweating, he noticed Mo looking across at them.

"And now you regret it?" Micky continued.

"Regret what?"

"Regret not killing her, regret hoovering."

Dennis wiped his forehead with his hanky and looked up at the screen, Mo had settled on Judge Rinder, which was ironic.

After a long pause he composed himself, "I don't think I'm long for this world to be honest, I want to make the most of every day." He mentioned his thoughts about the bus, his wife being hit by a bus. "It would be helpful because she drags me down. I'd like her to go, just leave me alone. She's got a lover you know, had one for years!"

He saw surprise at last on Micky's face, he also now had Mo's full attention.

"A colleague of hers, she's been late home every Tuesday and Thursday for nine years, she knows I know but we don't discuss it."

"Fuck," Micky said.

"I lost my job as a lecturer because of a misunderstanding, I can't go into details, the lover is payback."

Micky was shaking his head, Mo was still staring.

It's a good job he doesn't speak English, Dennis thought.

"You don't want to spend your last days in prison mate," Micky stated.

"I wouldn't go to prison, the irony is if I did kill her, either by sticking the new rake in her skull or any other method, nobody would notice she's not around. She's retiring next week and she has no friends, nobody would even miss her, sad isn't it."

"What about loverboy?" Mo blurted. "Loverboy will defo miss her."

Dennis looked in amazement at Mo and started to stutter, "I dddint think you sssspoke English."

"Of course he does," Mickey laughed, "he gave you a round of applause for your 'burn the suburbs' speech."

The Professor couldn't recall the applause and was confused. "I'm only making conversation my friend, I don't actually want to kill my wife, I've been talking bollocks."

"It doesn't bother me, I just thought it pretty obvious that loverboy might get suspicious if she doesn't show up."

Mo didn't just understand English he spoke with almost a cockney accent.

"Mo's right of course, what about the lover? You'd have to contact him and say you know all about them and that it was over," Micky added.

Mo continued, "Yeah, you should phone him and tell him if he tries to contact her you'll kill him, tell him you're terminally ill and don't give a fuck and he should forget about her otherwise you'll put a garden rake in his head."

"Shut up the both of you, I was only jesting, I'm not going to kill anybody!" With that he rang the bell. Tina arrived a couple of minutes later, she immediately sensed an atmosphere.

"Get me away from these morons," Dennis snapped at Tina.

She helped him back to the ward, he was sulking and muttering to himself the whole way and turned to Tina, "He speaks English."

"Who?"

"Mo, he speaks perfect English."

"Of course he does. Why are you surprised?"

"Because he's said nothing at your sessions, not a word."

"He applauded your rant. Surely you noticed that?"

"Seems I'm the only one who didn't notice," Dennis said, as Tina went off to deal with another patient.

Micky and Mo watched the screen without really concentrating on what was playing. Mo broke the ice, "You can't blame the poor fucker can you."

"What for?"

"Wanting to get rid of his wife, she sounds atrocious."

"Women can be difficult," Micky smiled.

"The rake idea would be a bit messy, I'd poison her," Mo stated as if discussing the weather.

Micky looked at Mo, his smile was unmoving. "You've killed haven't you Mo, you've killed before?"

"Yeah, but not anyone who didn't deserve it. I don't think I've ever killed a woman, not knowingly."

"Sounds like you've got quite a CV."

"I suppose so, but it's all a long time ago, and besides it takes one to know one."

"Know one what?" Micky asked.

"A killer," Mo replied coldly, looking Micky in the eye.

"What makes you think so Mo?"

"You have a confidence, a calmness, and you dress like a killer."

"Oh dear, if it's that obvious I'll start wearing pink."

"I remember you explaining to the group why you're such a good gambler, a complete lack of emotion. You're neither elated when you win or disappointed when you lose, a perfect state of consciousness for a professional killer."

"You really are quite a dark horse Mo, who'd have thought we'd have so much in common."

"No we are very different my friend, you kill for money which is immoral, I have only killed for Allah."

"So you're a terrorist?" Micky asked, taken aback.

"Oh no my friend, I was a soldier."

"In what war?"

"It's a long story my friend."

"I've got all afternoon Mo, I'm going nowhere in a hurry."

8

THE QUESTION OF GOD

TOBY DIDN'T SLEEP well, the info flooding in from all and sundry was messing with his mind. He prided himself on his professionalism but his meeting with the Moldovan girl was bringing out the worst in him. He should be processing the information dispassionately but he found himself fantasising about the Ice Queen's reaction to the kitchen assistant's story.

He knew first hand that extreme violence didn't ruffle her feathers, they'd studied more beheadings together than he could remember, and worse. Human torches and all manner of torture, not a flinch from his boss. But now *this*, messy sex that even had him squirming in disgust, this would be fun.

Now was not the time to be distracted though. It was ironic that Micky knew more about the chef than Toby. At least the sub team appeared closer to finding the sponsor, he hoped.

He got to HQ early so he could spend an hour in the basement gym, he'd definitely put on a pound or two lately. Even one or two of the Friday pub crowd had remarked his six pack was now a seven pack. He ran on the treadmill for half an hour before climbing into a rowing machine, Sky news on the screen in front of him. Despite the sweat trickling into his eyes he could make out the subtitles as the anchor described an incident involving an escaped panther at a zoo somewhere in Russia.

His pager vibrated against his wrist. Seconds later he saw 'BREAKING NEWS' dominating the screen and the words 'Lorry ploughs into pedestrians outside a South London Mosque'.

"Shit!" he shouted, climbing off the rowing machine and rushing to his office, still in his sweat drenched gym kit.

Achtar, the top 'nerd', was furiously assaulting his keyboard as the plethora of screens, one by one, showed different CCTV live streams from the area of the incident. The hub was pretty much deserted. His boss was due in any minute, she wouldn't be late, she was never late. He phoned his colleague Mittal who was heading up the team shadowing the Imam, who coincidentally was based at a South London Mosque, but the call went straight to voicemail.

He got through to Craig on first ring. "Where the fuck are you Craig?"

"Aberdeen mate."

"What you doing up there?"

"Meeting your chef's sponsor, why?"

Toby hesitated, trying to compute the info, despite all the live streams available he was only looking at the one showing Sky News. 'MANY CAUSALITIES, EYE WITNESSES REPORT'.

"Ok, speak to me later." He hung up.

He realised there was no Ice Queen, she was five minutes late. Just then his phone rang and her name popped up. "Hi Claire, you've obviously heard."

"Yep, I'm on my way to the American embassy Toby, hold the fort for me, I'll be in touch."

"The American Embassy?" Toby repeated in surprise.

"I'm meeting Sir Martin there, he called me, the yanks have gone berserk."

"Shit, why? This sounds like a nut job Claire."

"I know Toby, it's weird. I'll be in touch."

Toby wanted to shower and get changed, this could be a long day.

* * *

'TOXIC TINA' COULDN'T make up her mind whether hosting the Good Poison Club was actually a good thing. It did give her a chance to take a breather from the relentless stream of patients on the ward. She was disappointed that Brenda was too unwell to make it today but she noted the other six previous attendees were all there, which was encouraging.

A youngish man who attended the first meeting turned up. He'd come to tell Tina he was in full remission and brought a box of chocolates for the staff. Tina invited him to the meeting in the hope he'd lighten the mood.

Davina got the ball rolling by asking her if she'd had any joy with Brenda's trial, her absence was obviously noted. Tina explained that she'd been in touch with the powers that be and was waiting for the results. Hassan asked if there's anything they could do to help put pressure on, which Tina thought was a wonderful, although probably naive, gesture.

Brian intervened, "She's a good woman Brenda, God bless her."

"Where is he then?" the Professor asked.

"Where's who?" Tina queried and then wished she hadn't as Dennis carried on.

"God. Where is God when you want him? He can't even guarantee a drug trial."

"I take it you don't believe in God?" Davina pressed.

The Professor rolled his eyes and went into a sulk. The topic was picked up amongst the group, each of them offering differing views, except Mo, who sat in his usual seat, arms folded, offering nothing.

Eddie, the young man in remission, confessed he was never a believer but when he got his latest positive results he broke down and thanked God. He felt a bit foolish.

They all turned to Mo as he stood and started to wheel his drip stand towards the door.

"Mo, are you ok? Where are you going?" Tina pleaded, now wishing she was back on the ward.

Mo turned and faced the group.

"Have we offended you?" Davina called out but he turned and slowly made his way out of the Sanctuary.

Everyone was keen to quickly change the subject. Although no one would say as much, religion, and Mo's religion in particular, was the elephant in the room.

Hassan felt awkward, he'd only been to a mosque for family weddings and funerals. He was Turkish first, British second and Muslim a distant third. He felt compelled to say something, as if Mo was a kindred spirit.

"I think Mo is from Afghanistan, they take their religion pretty seriously over there…"

There was a collective mattering of agreement, the Professor felt a rant coming on but managed to suppress it.

At that moment Tina was thankfully rescued by an unexpected visitor, Sebastian Phelps entered the room flashing a well-rehearsed smile.

"Please forgive me Tina, if I could just interrupt for a moment."

Tina hoped he could interrupt for the remaining forty minutes.

"Hi everyone I'm Sebastian Phelps, the chief executive, I just wanted to inform you all that I've had communication from the Ministry of Health, they are very keen to roll out the concept of this wonderful initiative across several more Trusts and to that end the Minister of Health will be paying us a visit in a month's time."

Tina thought she might pass out. Dennis had a few choice words rattling round his head. Micky and Brian's thoughts immediately went to Brenda's situation.

* * *

MICKY LATER FOUND Mo sitting in a side room. He told him about Sebastian Phelps' appearance and the red hot news that the Minister of Health was going to make a visit. Mo didn't seem interested.

"He's not going to kill his bitch wife is he?" Mo whispered.

"The Professor?" Micky guessed.

"You know why?" Mo added.

"Because he's a spineless wanker?" Micky guessed.

"Because he has no god my friend, he has no god."

"Neither do I."

"You don't need one," Mo began to laugh.

"Do you know what 'Toxic Tina' calls you Micky, the 'hitman'. She's a good nurse and a good judge of character. You're a professional and also a nihilist, you don't need a god to kill."

"And you do Mo?"

"I don't need a God, I have a God, and yes I've killed for him, albeit a long time ago."

Micky looked at the drip stand. "And where's your god now Mo?"

Mo rattled the stand. "This is God's will, we can't all live forever."

"Maybe it's a punishment, you know, for all the killing you claim to have done."

"No my friend, maybe your cancer is a punishment, mine is a blessing. I killed for God you killed to pay the fucking mortgage."

"And my divorce to be fair," Micky confirmed, before adding, "anyway my first thought when I heard the big white chief was coming was Brenda, we should tell him about the drug trial."

Mo thought about Brenda, but bigger ideas were floating round his head. "We can do anything we want my friend, we might as well go out in style, who is the Minister of Health anyway?"

"Haven't a clue Mo, some fucker."

"We need to think about this. Play our cards right and they will have to fund Brenda's drug trial."

9

CROSSING THE DOTS

CLAIRE TRIED, IN her cool measured way, to support Sir Martin, who had to endure ongoing humiliation as the bad news kept coming.

"Have you any idea why I've called you here?" Wayne Myerson, the CIA's European chief, said as he thumped the desk.

Sir Martin jumped a little.

It wasn't his fault his American counterpart and colleagues were having a collective nervous breakdown since Trump moved into the West Wing.

Myerson thumped the desk with every bit of new information he received on his laptop.

"Anything Claire?" Sir Martin pleaded.

Her phone pinged just in time. She read Toby's text out loud. "According to a passport found, the name of the driver is James Mayer."

"Like fuck it is." Myerson thumped the desk again

"The passport was stolen two days ago," Claire stated calmly, "on a ferry from Ostend to Dover. Mr Mayer reported it stolen at the ferry terminal. He's in custody now but we are convinced he's not involved." She continued to read the text. "Lorry stolen in Ostend lorry park. Hungarian driver is missing."

"A hijacking by the sound of it," Sir Martin interjected.

The American gave him a look of contempt, it was becoming a competition to see who could get the most impressive information first.

Myerson thumped the desk again. "Two dead. No sign of the driver. I'm telling you this, if it turns out this guy's a Brit and you have his name on file, the fucking special relationship is over." He noticed Claire staring at him. "You have a problem miss?" he challenged her, just as her phoned pinged again.

She ignored his question and read out the text, "The driver has been arrested, Caucasian male."

Sir Martin wanted to hug her. The American thumped the desk again, they weren't sure why.

"He was on your ferry to Dover, what the fuck is going on?"

Sir Martin stood up and gestured to Claire to do the same. "We are returning to my office. I know you are under pressure, we all are, but I'm not going to sit here and be insulted by you, we have work to do."

Myerson was now crimson with rage and frustration, he looked at his laptop secretly hoping for more ammunition to throw at the Brits. He knew they were on the same side but he found them so fucking arrogant. Yes, they were professional, but they were so ridged and tied up in bureaucratic political correctness. Yes, they'd done brilliantly since 7/7, but their government had made cuts and it was inevitable the dam would burst. Too many incidents lately. Three thousand suspects being watched, it was too much.

He'd emailed the Home Secretary suggesting they at least tag all of them, only to receive a curt reply telling him the UK is not a police state and 'in this country we don't tag people until they have been convicted of a crime'. He replied diplomatically but made a plea that the authorities revoke the suspects driving licences so they couldn't hire vehicles. He hadn't had a response.

He felt the coldness of Claire's stare. *I'd like to slap that girl*, he thought, *who does she think she is?*

Claire and Sir Martin were just exiting the office when Myerson thumped his desk for the final time. "One minute!" he shouted and held up his hand, halting them in the door way. He was studying his laptop screen and then beckoned them back and turned his laptop round.

They returned to the desk and studied the information. There was a photo of one of the two fatalities, they recognised him immediately. Sir Martin looked at Claire, he was sweating. Like him she couldn't really comprehend what they'd just seen.

Myerson looked as if he could explode with rage any moment. "Yes, our Imam for fucks sake, I suggest you go and clean up your shit!"

Sir Martin was considered too old school by some but he would always defend his team. "Shit that you started," he replied coldly to the American, as he ushered Claire to the door.

"No Sir Martin, they fucking started it!" Myerson insisted on having the last word.

* * *

TINA TRIED NOT to reflect on the session but in some ways felt the God business was inevitable. She was relieved it had reared its ugly head now and not, heaven forbid, when the Minister of Health visited. Her first thoughts were of dread but then she remembered Brenda's trial and how she could maybe have a subtle word with the top man. *Feck it, why subtle, I'll tell him straight.*

Her immediate concern however was that she'd promised to meet her father for a drink. Apart from being knackered, she didn't fancy him droning on like an alcoholic version of the Professor.

She made sure she was half an hour late as she didn't want to be on her own in her old man's local. She found him on his usual stool, holding court with the 'early doors' crowd.

"Ah, hi Tina, I thought you'd forgotten me." He greeted her with a sloppy kiss on the cheek and bought her a pint before ushering her away from his drinking crowd towards a quiet table under a dart board.

"How long you been here?" Tina asked, meaning 'how many pints you had?'

"My second pint," he answered defensively.

Tina felt a bit foolish, she liked a drink herself, but god knows she deserved it.

They indulged in small talk for a while, he was particularly disappointed his local was soon to be demolished to make way for the new Crossrail train project. Tina thought he'd be less concerned if it was his home being demolished.

"Any love interest?" her dad asked.

This was a question he always asked and a question that always annoyed his daughter.

"Well yes actually, in-fact, I got married last Tuesday," she jested.

"Shit, I would have bought you a wedding present if I'd known."

"Oh yeah, what would you have bought me Dad?"

"Towels obviously," he laughed, "got some nice lilac ones in the pound shop."

Tina shook her head, laughing. "Actually I'm going out with a really nice guy," she revealed.

"Has this one got a proper job?"

Tina didn't expect anything other than sarcasm and negativity from her old man so she enjoyed replying, "Well, if being a fire-fighter is a proper job, then yes."

"A fireman no less, are you sure Tina? After all I could be an airline pilot online."

Tina didn't bother to reply. She thought about Micky the 'hitman' trying to build bridges with his daughter. *Why were men such fucking unreliable wankers, did they ever stop to think about the damage they leave behind whilst perusing their selfish childish lifestyles?* She was thirty-five and went into every relationship expecting nothing but disappointment. She thought about Jed, they had so much in common, he made her laugh, he was physically attractive, but how and when would it end?

Tina turned the conversation to practical matters regarding her father's financial chaos, which she knew was due to a combination of alcohol and gambling. As she offered advice she remembered what one of her colleagues had told her over an after work drink, 'Tina you are the world champion at sorting out everyone else's problems, you need to look out for yourself.'

She spent over half her life hating her father, now she pitied him. There was never a time she could recall loving him. She stared at his ruddy drinking face, his unkempt hair, his charity shop clothes. He was no fool, which made his lifestyle seem even more foolish. She stared into his green eyes, his only redeeming feature, they at least were full of life.

For a brief moment she considered asking him if he ever thought about her late mother. She took a swig of her beer. "Watch my bag, I'm going to the loo." She let the moment pass.

He father waited for her to disappear and reached into her bag for her phone. He easily guessed her passcode, her birth year, and opened up Instagram. It didn't take him long to find several photos of his daughter with her new 'beau'. *He's a hairy git,* he pondered, *look at that fucking pony tail, a fireman, my arse.*

He put the phone back and waited for his daughter to return. "So your man's a fireman Tina, where's he stationed?"

Tina accepted that all fathers concerned themselves with their daughters suitors, even bad fathers. "Camden."

"Have you got a photo of him?"

"I might have, why are you bothered?"

"Come on let's see Tina, let's see this handsome firefighter."

Tina reached for her phone and brought up a photo of a Nigerian doctor from her hospital xmas party. *That will get a reaction,* she laughed to herself.

He looked at the photo and then at his daughter. "Seems like a nice lad, nicely dressed, sensible haircut."

This wasn't the reaction she expected, her father was an old school racist. *What the feck is he commenting on his hairstyle for?*

"Sorry dad, he's a Protestant as well," she teased.

"Not a problem Tina, this is multi ethnic London, not the old country. He's definitely a fireman, you can tell, nicely turned out, neat short hair, all fireman have sensible haircuts. When can I meet the fella?" He was enjoying this.

"Early days yet dad, still doing his internship."

"Well, do let me know when he gets a full-time contract, I'd love to meet him."

* * *

IT HAD BEEN a long day, a shitstorm in fact, Toby was resigned to a night in the office. He prodded at his iPad, stopping to look briefly at his report on his meeting with the Moldovan girl. *That fucking racist Hungarian wanker has completely fucked up my day*, he thought, pondering once again what the Ice Queen's reaction would be.

He could, and should, email the report to her now but that would make redundant a bigger opportunity to humiliate his boss. No, it could wait a day or two.

He mulled over the day's events. He was reasonably confident the Imam was not a particular target and the Hungarian was just intent in killing Muslims, any Muslims. Even the yanks must agree with that.

Whilst the media went into a frenzy and the screens flicked overhead he suddenly had an idea he hoped the Ice Queen hadn't thought of.

He phoned his colleague, it went straight to voicemail. "Mittal it's Toby. Call me back any time, no matter how late. I'm presuming the Imam will be buried imminently. I need you at or around the funeral, I need photos. Call me back."

He sent his boss a brief email bringing her up to speed but didn't mention the funeral. Shit. He realised he hadn't caught up with the morning's goings on at the Good Vibes Club.

He decided he'd watch it over breakfast but forwarded the recording with the other info, adding a p.s. that he'd pop by the hospital and check up on the chef first thing in the morning.

10

DEATH BY LINGERIE

TINA REACHED FOR her iPhone and felt a flush of euphoria when she realised it was only five thirty, she had another hour before her alarm would signal another day on the treadmill. Her work wasn't always a treadmill but the last couple of years had seen the government's austerity measures take their toll. Too many patients, not enough staff. She used to enjoy after work drinks with colleagues where the conversation was irreverent and humorous. Now, they were too tired to socialise and traipsed off home like zombies at the end of their shift. *Yet somehow they've found extra dosh for the shiny Sanctuary?*

Yes, they found two extra chemo nurses but then they increased the workload. Tina had decided that she would hand in her notice after the Minister of Health made his visit. *Feck*, she thought, *Sebastian Phelps will have everything smooth and shiny that day, he will probably halve the patients and double the staff.*

She tried to go back to sleep but her mind was racing. *Shit, yes, that's it! I'll hand in my notice to the Minister of Health!* She was now wide-awake and smiling. She imagined Phelps introducing the MP to a long obedient line of nurses, each one smiling like a fecking air stewardess. 'And this is our top girl, ward sister Tina Gallagher, Tina's been running our Good Vibes Club."

'Delighted to meet you Tina, what a fantastic facility you have here. It's an absolute shining light and I plan to roll this innovation out country wide.'

Tina was certain he'd have a handshake like a wet fish, she'd seen the minister on TV, a typical wet old Etonian.

'I think what we actually need are drugs, there are drugs out there that could dramatically enhance my patient's lives. What we don't need is more fecking kick ass flat screen TV's. You've no idea how your uninformed decisions impact real people. I'm so disgusted I'm handing in my notice, directly to you.'

Tina laughed aloud thinking about the whole incident going out on the evening news. Her dad would spit his beer out. Brenda would cheer from her sofa, hugging her lovely husband John. Jed would…what would Jed think?

She wondered what they'd do on Saturday night. She recalled her drink with her father and picked up her iPhone again to google 'Rules on firemen's hair length'. The answers all seemed to be from American sites.

Why am I bothered? she thought. They had female fire-fighters. She presumed Jed would have his hair in a ponytail like them.

There was no way she was going back to sleep now, she got up and made a coffee.

* * *

DENNIS COULDN'T FACE breakfast. He felt sick and wasn't looking forward to his hospital appointment. He and his wife had slept in separate bedrooms since his misdemeanour, but there was no wardrobe storage in her bedroom so she always got dressed in his room. He pretended to still be asleep as she crept in and started to rummage through her clothes. She seemed to be taking longer than usual and was intentionally noisy.

"Are you awake Dennis?" she tried.

"I am now," he answered annoyed.

She was naked at the end of the bed holding a dress in each hand.

"What does one wear on one's last day?" she asked, but he wasn't sure if she was addressing him or talking aloud to herself.

She had a great body for her age, Dennis pondered. A little overweight perhaps but in proportion. She'd always had good boobs but tended to wear frumpy clothes that didn't do her figure justice. He'd noticed she'd recently spent a shit load of money on new clothes. He thought about all those Tuesday's and Thursday's and about the rake imbedded in her skull.

"What does one wear to ones leaving do?" she repeated.

"You're having a leaving do?" he asked, surprised.

"Apparently Raymond has arranged something," she answered matter of factly.

Dennis felt the anger surge through his chest at the mention of her lover's name. He'd met him two or three times at company dos. He was a few years younger, divorced, no kids, talked endlessly about his beloved Porsche and Range Rover.

She put a carrier bag on the bed and pulled out some new underwear.

The Professor watched his wife put on the sexiest bra and knickers he'd ever seen her wear. She admired herself in the full length mirror on the inside of the wardrobe door.

The fucking bitch is trying to humiliate me, he thought.

She then bent down in front of him and slowly pulled on a stay up stocking on each leg. His head was full of murder but as she turned round to face him, his thoughts were muddied by an erection. She pulled on one of the dresses without taking her eyes off his gaze.

"What do you think?" she asked, giving a twirl.

He stared at her in the tight fitting red dress, low cut and short. His mind was racing, his erection now aching and obviously noticeable. *I'm going to kill her tonight, but I'm going to fuck her first.*

She interrupted his dark thoughts, "Be a good boy Dennis, pop down and make me a cup of tea and some toast whilst I titivate."

He would have subserved to her wishes but didn't want to move due to his erection, he didn't want her to enjoy his humiliation more than she already had. He remembered Mo's statement that their illness gave them the freedom to do whatever they wanted, fuck the consequences. "I want to fuck you Sandra." He surprised himself at how easy the words came out. It was nine years since they'd had carnal relations, his workplace indiscretion, and latterly his illness, had put a halt to any mutual sexual relations. In his heart of hearts he couldn't blame her for taking a lover. What he really resented was the humiliation she revelled in causing.

She was taken aback by his request, her initial reaction was to laugh, which merely encouraged him to play his last card, having nothing to lose.

"You look fantastic Sandra, I'd really like to fuck you."

She stared at him lying on the bed, the duvet discarded. He was wearing his Greenpeace t-shirt and navy boxer shorts, barely concealing his excitement.

"Well, that's a sight I haven't enjoyed for a good few years, it must be the stockings." She lifted her dress slightly.

"You look very fuckable Sandra," he said, feeling brave.

She continued to stare at him, his penis looked huge but she put this down to the effect his cancer had had on his body. She looked at his tangled hair, his bad teeth. She thought of Raymond, her lover, she knew her husband knew all about them. She didn't know what Raymond had arranged for her leaving do but she was excited by his text requesting she wear sexy underwear.

"I need to get going Dennis, it's going to be a long day, and night," she added, teasing him, "so could you go and sort that tea and toast?"

"What do you want on your toast Sandra?" he asked meekly, climbing off the bed.

She hadn't humiliated him enough though. "Why on earth would I want to fuck you? Look at you. I'm sorry Dennis but you can have a good wank after I've left, you know I'm going to be well and truly fucked later."

He didn't reply, just calmly made his way downstairs to the kitchen. He put the kettle on and popped a couple of slices of bread into the toaster. He opened the cutlery drawer and surveyed the compartment housing an assortment of knives. He pulled out the biggest and then spotted the porcelain rolling pin on the worktop. He held the knife in his right hand and the rolling pin in his left. He practiced some stabbing motions with the knife and swotting movements with the rolling pin. He ignored the toast as it pinged up and made his way to the stairs. *She's not going to be fucking loverboy Raymond tonight*, he thought as he climbed the stairs.

* * *

TOBY WAS ALREADY standing by the nurses station when Tina arrived for her shift. He'd looked at the recording of the Good Poison Club footage and now had an even greater sense of urgency. Tina recognised him immediately as he offered his hand.

"Hi Tina, remember me? Rupert," he lied. "I've just popped by to see how you're getting on with the Good Vibes Centre."

Tina remembered him, he was the poshest person she'd ever met. "I'm drowning to be honest, drowning in work," she said bluntly.

Toby smiled, maybe a simple Terry would have been better than a Rupert. Rupert aka Toby, I'd never be a rapper, he pondered. "Oh dear, what about the extra staff Tina?"

"What about the extra patients?" she replied curtly.

"Oh dear," he repeated. "I'll have a word with Sebastian," he offered. He could see she wasn't impressed.

"I hear your boss the Minister of Health is making a visit, I may bring it up with him." Tina wasn't joking but Toby/Rupert's reply surprised her.

"Good idea Tina, I'd give it to him straight."

"Really?"

"Why not, he could do with a taste of the real world." He leaned forward and whispered in Tina's ear. "Between you and me Tina, the man is a complete tool."

Tina was starting to like Rupert.

"So how's the Good Vibes Group going?" he asked.

"Challenging, they're understandably a pretty prickly lot. We've had some interesting conversations, from bucket lists to God."

"God," Toby repeated. "I thought the subject would come up, must be tricky given your group probably pray to different gods, or none." He'd studied the recording on the way in and guessed the Ice Queen had watched it too. He was relieved the God question was put out there, it meant they could leave Tina alone for now.

"You're right, there was a very mixed reaction," Tina confirmed.

"Was anyone offended?" he asked mischievously.

"What happens in Vegas stays in Vegas," Tina replied.

"What I'd really like to do Tina is have a friendly chat with one of the group, if that's possible?"

"Well the only one here is Mo, he's the only one of the group that's ward based."

"How poorly is he? Could I go and introduce myself?"

This time Tina whispered. "I don't see a problem but strictly between you and me he left our meeting early yesterday, I think he wasn't at all comfortable with the where the conversation was heading."

Toby gave a knowing nod and followed Tina to Mo's room. She explained that he had his own room to limit the risk of infection whilst he was having very aggressive treatment. The door was ajar, she knocked gently, there was no reply so she slowly opened the door. The bed was empty. "He's probably nipped to the loo, he'll be back in a mo. Ha, Mo will be back in a mo," she laughed.

Toby wasn't laughing, he looked at the locker. No mobile, no wallet, he felt uneasy. "I'll wait in the corridor Tina, I don't want to keep you, I'll introduce myself when he returns."

He waited till Tina was out of sight and entered the room to study the locker. "Shit," he said aloud as he saw there were a pair of slippers but no shoes.

He phoned HQ and spoke to his team techy, asking him to track the chef's phone, this wasn't the first time he'd sneaked into his room. Within a couple of minutes a blue dot appeared on his phone map. He phoned the Ice Queen next. "Claire, our chef has gone walk about, he's on Euston Road, I'm tracking him. I think he's on a bus, I think I know where he's heading, I'll call you later."

"Ok Toby, let's keep this between us, we don't want the yanks getting hold of him under any circumstances."

Toby made his way to the chemo suite and found an already flushed Tina. "I think your patient has gone for a walk I'm going to make a move. I'll be in touch before the minister's visit, keep up the good work."

Toby was pleased to be just Toby again, he rarely felt guilty lying in the course of duty but he definitely felt uneasy about duping Tina. He checked his phone, the blue dot had disappeared. He's on the tube.

He called Ranj, "Any news on our Imam's funeral Ranj?"

"Yep, I'm on my way there now, deepest South London."

"I think our chef is too," Toby confirmed.

"Ok Toby I'll keep you informed."

Toby then took a call from the Ice Queen, Christine had found the sponsor. They agreed they'd need to catch up as soon as he had located the chef. She told him they'd be working over the weekend.

He sat in his car trying to process the situation when suddenly the tracker on his phone pinged. "What the fuck!" he shouted, as he noticed the location. He called the techy, who, within seconds, pinpointed the chef's exact location. "What the hell is he doing in a cafe in Soho? The Imam is being buried shortly in South London."

"Sorry Toby, I don't think your chef is on his way there."

Toby entered the postcode into his sat-nav, the cafe was forty-five minutes away. He started the engine.

11

PLOTTERS AND PLANNERS

MICKY AND DENNIS were already sat at a discreet table when Mo entered the cafe. He ordered an espresso and joined the others. They indulged in small talk about their health for a few moments before Micky got to their reason for meeting.

"So, do you think any of the others would be up for it?" Micky enquired.

Dennis just shrugged, Mo thought about the question for the moment. "Hassan might be. Not sure about Brian, he's too chilled. Davina, no way."

Micky slurped his coffee, he thought the Professor looked distracted. "We need to get something straight, this is not about personal politics, this is to help Brenda," Micky stated.

"And Tina," Mo added.

"And us," the Professor added.

The other two turned to face him.

"There's new drugs and trials coming out all the time, drugs that we might need in the very near future."

"You're right, so we need a plan," Mo concurred

"Well, firstly we've got nothing to lose," Micky confirmed, "and secondly we are never going to get another opportunity, it's not every day we get a chance to confront a cabinet minister."

"We need to isolate him from his entourage and demand funding for Brenda's trial."

We could get him in the Good Vibes Club and lock the door," Mo suggested.

"Then what?" Dennis queried.

"We give him a choice, agree to the funding and we unlock the door, no fuss, or we wait for the press to get hold of what will be a very damaging story."

"Seems a reasonable idea."

"I will slit the old Etonian cunt's throat," Dennis interrupted.

Micky and Mo looked on, shocked.

"Fuck it, I'll do it, I'm happy to do it, I've got nothing left, it would be a pleasure."

"Have you ever been in a fight Dennis?" Micky asked.

"Never," the Professor answered without hesitation.

"Ever been hit?" Mo chipped in.

"Never."

"I take it you're having a bad day mate," Micky found the Professor's behaviour erratic to say the least.

"I was a soldier in my country, I have killed many times. You, my friend, are not a killer," Mo said.

"Well that's where you're fucking wrong," the Professor stated, picking up a large hold-all and placing it on the table. He stood up and left a tenner on the table. "The coffees are on me, make your plan and just let me know what you want me to do, whatever it takes. I'll be at next week's Good Poison Club."

With that he walked out, leaving the bag on the table and the hitman and chef open mouthed.

* * *

TOBY WAS FIFTEEN minutes away from the cafe when the blue dot on the map was on the move again. He parked up but the signal was lost by Leicester Square station. *He's gone underground again*, he correctly assumed.

Toby diverted back to HQ. He asked the techy to collate all the footage he could from any CCTV near the Soho cafe. The Ice Queen was waiting for him and he brought her up to speed on the morning's events. She had news herself.

"Christine has found the sponsor," she stated matter of factly.

"Where is he, who is he?" Toby was curious.

"It's not a he, it's a she. Christine found her in the middle of nowhere, in the Shetlands, she isn't in a good place, an alcoholic."

"What's her story?"

His boss passed over an A4 Jiffy bag, Toby opened it and pulled out a VHS video.

"Have you seen it Claire?"

"Would you believe I'm waiting for someone to locate a VCR player."

Toby laughed.

"So we have now seen our chef likes actions rather than words," she continued, referring to his applause followed by his protest after the God question in the last session.

Toby nodded, he was wondering the best time to play his Moldovan kitchen assistant card. Suddenly he noticed the blue dot on his iPhone map, he studied it in silence for a couple of minutes before the Ice Queen interrupted his concentration.

"Has he gone to the funeral?"

"No, Claire," he replied without looking up from the screen, "he's returned to the hospital."

"Really, well, that's a surprise."

Toby received a text from Ranj with some photos from the funeral. He showed them to his boss. The techy put his head round the door and said he would send some CCTV through they might find interesting.

They studied three images on the screen that dominated the office. The Ice Queen looked blank. It took Toby a few seconds to recognise three familiar figures walking separately along Brewer Street.

"There's our chef," he pointed to a frail figure wearing a baseball cap. "That one and that one there are fellow patients and members of the Good Vibes Group," he stated, pointing to separate images.

"What do you make of this footage Toby?"

Toby shrugged.

"I'm at a loss as well," she confessed.

"Certainly nothing to do with our late Imam," he confirmed.

"Could be something as simple as a birthday," she said.

"So Toby tell me about the kitchen assistant, what's the story with the decapitation?"

Toby still got excited by the five syllables even when uttered in such a bland home counties accent. He wanted to get to the nitty gritty as soon as possible. He'd been thinking about her reaction for days but he needed to cover some important points first.

"There was no decapitation," he noted a slight look of surprise on her pale face, "something was lost in translation, the text said he wanted to cut his client's head off, he didn't use the word decapitation."

"Different words, same meaning, surely," she interjected.

"No Claire, the yanks thought that, they came up with decapitation, but threatening to cut off a client's head could be similar to when a parent threatens their child, 'If you don't tidy your room your father is going to kill you when he gets home'. Now change the word 'kill' with 'murder' and you see my point."

The Ice Queen nodded but she wasn't totally convinced. Toby felt he was impressing his boss but he couldn't tell. He looked at her cold blue eyes, *she'd make a great poker player*, he thought. *What did she do in her private life, did she have a hobby? How come no-one in the team had seen her out and about…*

"So what did the Moldovan girl have to say?" Claire said, interrupting his thoughts.

"It's a rather messy story Claire, to be honest."

"Were they lovers?" she asked, taking him aback.

"No, not exactly Claire, they were more co-conspirators."

"You've got me hooked Toby."

I've got her hooked, he thought, *now to reel her in.*

"Trip Advisor," Toby exclaimed, "she told me one of his clients had put a very negative review online, he wanted revenge and this is where things get disgustingly messy-"

There was a knock on the door and a colleague brought in a VCR player. "I had to go all the way to Kingston on Thames for this old relic," he confirmed. He was joined by Achtar, the techy had found a TV compatible with the VCR. They fiddled about with the leads and after a clumsy few moments the TV sprang into life. Toby realised his moment of humiliating his boss had been delayed yet again.

12

THE BAG

MICKY AND MO stared at the bag for several seconds, and then at each other, before returning their focus on the hold-all.

"I'm going outside for a fag," Micky said, suddenly cutting the tension.

He left Mo with the mystery and made his way out onto the bustling pavement taking in a deep breath as he leant against a doorway adjacent to the cafe. *What had the Professor done?* he pondered. *Surely he didn't have it in him…but my god the geezer had been severely provoked.*

He peered through the window, he could see Mo still staring at the bag. Micky lit up a cigarette hoping that by the time he'd smoked it the chef would have solved the mystery. He figured Mo had seen body parts before. *Was it a head? A heart? A finger? What the hell had Dennis done?*

He'd killed three times but never seen the end result. All three had been a single shot to the head, one through an open car window, one in a lift and the last, almost ten years ago, as his victim alighted from a bus. Each time he made a hasty get away and laid low until pay day. He'd earned a hundred and twenty-thousand pounds in total. He didn't know his victims but he was certain they'd done wrong to people you don't do wrong to.

He was offered many more hits over the years but he cherished his freedom. He knew the wrong people, he grew up with them but he never got too close, which made him an ideal hitman. Contacts and a complete lack of any emotion were a lethal combination. Whilst he was confident in his abilities, he knew it all depended on the rules of chance in the end. At the time he'd felt not a trace of regret, or any kind of buzz. But sometimes, now, he looked back and missed that sense of danger.

His services were no longer required, or maybe his fee couldn't be justified. You could hire a Kosavan immigrant to carry out a hit for a grand.

So he just dressed like a hitman now and would have to be satisfied with the nickname Tina had given him.

He liked Tina, but then again he liked a lot of women and had left a litany of broken hearts. He wasn't particularly bothered about most of the damage he'd caused along the way. His only concern now was about building bridges with his daughter.

He finished the cigarette, once again promising himself it would be his last, and deposited the stub in the metal box fixed to the cafe shop front. He followed a family through the front door and noticed the cafe was now full. He sat down and saw Mo was clutching the hold-all zip as if he'd just closed it.

"Well?" Micky gestured to the bag with a slight nod.

"The Professor's lunch," Mo laughed.

"What?"

"Cheese and pickle sandwich, a Penguin biscuit and a Ribena."

"Fuck off."

Mo laughed loudly then whispered, "Only joking, I haven't looked. It's too busy in here, we need to go somewhere quieter. I know a place a short walk away."

"Let's go then, the suspense is killing me Mo."

Mo led Micky to a slatted seat in Golden Square, they admired the sculpture of a high heeled shoe. "I've been to Soho hundreds of times but have never been in this square mate."

"I supplied food to that office over there," Mo confirmed, pointing at an anonymous building.

"What do they do in there?"

"Seminars, I think, a load of hipsters talking shit." Mo shrugged. They both looked down at the bag placed between them.

"What do you reckon's in there?"

"Not sandwiches," the chef answered.

"I don't reckon he's got it in him Mo."

"He's got a brain tumour, he may be capable of anything."

"Fuck it," Micky exclaimed, "let's open the fucker." He looked around the square. It was reasonably quite but a couple were walking towards the adjacent seat with their takeaway coffees. Micky gave them a thousand yard stare and they quickly changed course, nervously shuffling to a seat across the square. Micky grabbed the zip and yanked it open, he prised apart the hold-all, exposing a Waitrose carrier bag. Mo gingerly put his hands in and carefully lifted it out, placing it on his lap.

"Whatever it is, it's heavy," he stated as he put his hand inside and pulled out a package the size and shape of an American football. He peeled off the brown paper and gaffer tape and exposed another Waitrose carrier bag.

"The Professor likes Waitrose, typical champagne socialist," Micky joked, breaking the tension as Mo looked inside the bag.

"Fucking hell!" Mo exclaimed, offering Micky a view of its contents.

"Jesus H. Christ," Micky whispered.

Mo pulled out a small yellow post it note and showed it to Micky. *Phone me on 07770001430, Dennis.*

Micky reached for his mobile, nervously looking around him. "Shit my battery's dead, fucking useless piece of shit."

"Use mine." Mo handed the Waitrose bag to Micky and put his hand inside his jacket pocket. He looked panic stricken as he stood up and searched two further pockets on the outside of his bomber jacket. He patted his jean pockets, then repeated the exercise. "Shit!" he shouted, looking around the seat. "I must have left it in the café!"

Micky tried to calm him down. He placed the items back in the bag and suggested they pop back to the cafe and see if someone had found it.

Mo and Micky had no luck with the phone back at the cafe. Mo reckoned it had been stolen from his jacket pocket, which was hung on the back of his chair. His full attention had been on the bag, which he now clasped tightly in his right hand.

He didn't feel too good now, a cold sweat was starting to envelop him so he decided to get a cab back to the hospital, the phone could wait.

By the time the cab got to the hospital Mo was feeling dreadful.

"Go and tell Tina you're back, she'll sort you out," Micky suggested.

"What about this?" Mo patted the bag that was placed between them on the back seat.

"I'll take care of it, I'll sort you out a phone as well mate." Micky placed a reassuring hand on Mo's arm.

The chef smiled, lent forward and whispered in his ear, "Thanks mate, now listen carefully, I know I've told you I've only killed for God but don't fuck about with the contents of the bag. Phone the Professor and come and see me tomorrow."

Micky smiled back, winked and placed the bag on his lap. He watched as his friend exited the cab.

Mo found Tina in the nurse's station, harassed as usual.

"Mo, you look terrible, where've you been?" She led him to his side room and helped him get undressed before settling him into his bed. He cooked up a story about how he felt obliged to go to the Imam's funeral. She paged the consultant as she felt Mo needed checking over.

"Get some rest Mo, only two more blasts of the good poison and you can go home, by the weekend hopefully."

* * *

MICKY THOUGHT ABOUT the Professor's rant on the suburbs as the cab turned into his cul-de-sac. He gave the cabbie a generous tip, he was glad to be home.

He placed the hold-all on his teak dining table, put his phone on charge, poured himself a large scotch and sat down, staring at the bag. He unzipped it and removed the Professor's note, staring at the phone number. The phone needed half an hour to gain enough life for the call.

His other half would be home from work in a couple of hours. He sipped his scotch thinking about where to hide the bag. *The loft*, he thought, Tracey wouldn't ever bother to go up there, didn't have the correct footwear.

He got up and went into the kitchen where he removed various screwdrivers and spanners from his tool drawer. He returned to the dining table, placed them on a table mat next to the bag and decided to give the phone twenty minutes.

13

A TALE OF TWO EMBASSIES

TOBY PRESSED THE play button on the VCR and sat beside the Ice Queen. On screen a man was pictured, talking directly to the camera.

"My name is Scott Murdoch, I'm a photo journalist from Peterhead, Scotland. I came to Afghanistan in January 1980 with a small team in order to assist in a documentary about Russian conscripts. We were hoping the documentary would appeal to either the BBC or a major American network, as the Olympics were to be held in Moscow in the summer and the American government looked certain to withdraw their Olympic team because of the Russian invasion of Afghanistan.

"We'd heard rumours of a platoon made up entirely of convicts being released early, on condition they did three years military service. There was talk of this platoon being let loose in rebel villages, terrorising civilians, mass rape and multiple massacres. We were eager to track them down and hear their story. On arrival in Kabul we managed to find a few conscripts but most of the military personnel in the capital were special forces and not very forthcoming.

"We did meet a diplomat from the UN who claimed the Soviet government were conscripting thousands of young men every day, some were arriving in Afghanistan with barely a months training. We all had the best of intentions but very quickly learnt that to get anywhere in this country you had to be as corrupt as they are.

"For a few dollars here and few more dollars there you could buy information instantly that would otherwise take months to obtain. Within days of arrival we had a location for the convict platoon, or, should I say, I had a location. I mention this because it had become apparent that someone in our team had an agenda, a political agenda that was about to change the nature of our mission."

Toby pressed the pause button on the VCR. "Sorry Claire, looks like our chef is above ground again." He pointed to the tracker on his phone.

"Where is he now?" she asked.

"Barnes." He shrugged.

"That's my neck of the woods."

Wow, Toby thought, *that's a useful piece of info, the Ice Queen lives in Barnes.* Wait till Friday night drinks in the Red Lion, he'd be the centre of attention with this revelation. Never mind that the chef's whereabouts were back on track, he now could place his boss on the map.

"I'll just contact the lads so we can have eyes on ASAP."

"Good idea, not sure where this documentary is heading but we'd better stick with it," she stated.

By the time Toby's team arrived in Barnes the signal was moving rapidly along the A3 towards Kingston on Thames.

Heading to the funeral? he wondered.

He called Mittall, "What's happening Mitt?"

"Funeral's long over, loads of photos but no sign of chef, sorry mate."

"Ok, keep me posted."

Toby looked at Claire and shrugged, his boss nodded and he pressed play.

"I DISCOVERED THE rouge platoon was last seen on the road from Termez to Kabul, where they'd gone off piste in search of a notorious 'Mujahideen' commander. I suggested that the team get on the road the next morning but Felix, our team leader, objected. He claimed it was too dangerous and that he was more interested in interviewing everyday Russian civilians. We were surprised and disappointed at his lack of enthusiasm. The others felt this could be a real coup for us and gave no thought to the danger. We agreed to disagree and decided to spend a further forty-eight hours in the capital seeking out suitable subjects to interview.

"I had a bad feeling about Felix from the first time I met him, something didn't ring true. His negativity to our ideas since arriving in Afghanistan was strange to say the least, the more enthusiasm we showed, the more irritated he became.

"Two days later we gathered for a meeting in a cafe that had become our ad hoc headquarters. I was still dead keen on tracking down the convict platoon but my colleague, Dougie, came up with an interesting discovery. He'd found a couple of deserters hiding in a hotel basement, we'd heard there were thousands of deserters, most of which paid tribesmen to get them across the border into Uzbekistan, if they had some serious cash they could get a boat across the Caspian Sea.

"He explained these deserters were of particular interest because they were Jewish. They were part of a platoon made up entirely of Jews who'd applied to emigrate to Israel but instead the authorities press ganged them into the Soviet army and gave them the job of clearing landmines. Out of twenty-seven conscripts in their unit, seven so far had deserted.

"These two were hell bent on getting to Israel rather than facing the gulag in Siberia. If they died trying, to them it would be worth it. We all instantly agreed this

would be a great selling point for our proposed documentary. The oppressed being sent to oppress the oppressed. Felix's reaction was initially extraordinary, going into a rant about Jews, Zionists and even the Rothschild's worldwide domination conspiracy theories, the lot. The rest of us were gobsmacked.

"I couldn't contain myself. 'You don't want convicts or Jews, what do you want?' I shouted in frustration. The rest of the team made it obvious they shared my annoyance and Felix realised he was isolating himself.

"After a brief pause he suddenly relented and suggested we arrange to meet the Jewish deserters ASAP and then try and get an exact location on the convict platoon. He explained it was too dangerous to go on a wild goose chase looking for them and I conceded he was probably correct.

"We split into two teams, I was with two others trying to get, or should I say buy, information on the exact movements of the convicts. The other team had arranged to interview the two Jewish deserters later that day on the understanding we helped them get to the Uzbeki border. We managed to bribe an Afghani army officer who told us that a Mujahideen village had been attacked the day before by the rouge unit and gave us pretty accurate coordinates. We planned to leave first thing the next day but that night everything started to fall apart.

"There was a pounding on my door, it was Dougie, he was in a right state. He told me he'd arrived at the hotel where the Jewish deserters were holed up, only to see them being led out at gun point by Russian military police. I asked him if Felix knew the address of the hotel, his answer more than confirmed my suspicions.

"He fucking knew alright, I never trusted the fucker from the start Scott, I followed him after our meeting this morning and guess where he went. To the fucking Russian embassy,' he said.

"'Shit,' I replied. 'He knows the location of the convict platoon! Shit!'"

TOBY'S PHONE LIT up, the Ice Queen ignored it, she was totally absorbed in the acts of betrayal happening on the screen. Toby read the message before standing up. "Sorry Claire, this won't wait," he muttered in a daze, and fled the room.

Claire hardly averted her attention from the screen. She guessed that there was interesting news concerning the chef's phone. She wasn't sure where the documentary was heading but she felt she should stick with it whilst Toby dealt with the present matters.

Toby sat down next to Achtar who had a map of London on his screen with lots of different coloured lines on it, he explained these were routes and times emitted by the chef's phone. Starting with the hospital, then the cafe in Soho, then the blank time underground. He pointed out the signal reconnecting at Barnes, then at some red markers indicating eyes on by Craig and his team.

Achtar bought up a running commentary.

"One man wearing a blue hoodie on the high street, hang on, he's stopped at a bus stop, now getting on the 135, will follow."

There was a tense two minute pause before Craig's voice was heard again. "Suspect has alighted the bus. He's walking towards Earl's Court Station."

"Shit," Toby said, "he's going underground again."

"Maybe we should grab him now," Achtar offered.

Suddenly Craig was shouting, "Suspect getting in a taxi, following! Turning into A3218, now left into Queen's Gate!"

Achtar put the map onto the giant screen on the office wall.

"Continuing along Queen's Gate."

"Where the fuck is he going?" Toby asked.

"Hang on he's turning left into Prince Consort Road."

"I think I know where he's heading," Achtar interjected. "If he turns into Exhibition Road the Afghan embassy is just up past the Iranian embassy."

No sooner had Achtar mentioned his theory, Craig continued, "Turning into Exhibition Road!"

Toby's gut feeling was to tell Craig to stop the taxi and arrest the chef before he could seek sanctuary in the Embassy. He pondered what they could arrest him for, his investigations hadn't proven the chef had been responsible for the food poisoning and he hadn't, as far as he knew, decapitated anyone. The only useful information he'd found out recently was chef's disgusting culinary skills, which he still hadn't enjoyed describing to the Ice Queen, and discovering his boss lived in the Barnes area.

"Get ready to intercept Craig!" Toby shouted his orders into a microphone on Achtar's desk. "Under no circumstances let him into the Afghan embassy," he asserted.

There was a brief pause before Craig continued again. "Just coming up to the Iranian embassy, we are right on the taxi's tail, prepare to intercept the suspect lads."

"Got some live CCTV for you Toby," Achtar interrupted as different sections of Exhibition Road came on the giant screen. The taxi was clearly visible, studiously obeying the twenty miles an hour speed restriction. Craig's dark blue BMW was right behind.

"The Embassy is there on the right," Toby pointed out.

"Prepare to pull over and intercept," Craig warned his team.

The next thirty-seconds went by without a word from anyone as they watched the taxi continue up the road towards Hyde Park. Just as Toby realised the Afghan embassy was not the intended destination, Achtar relayed information that emerged on his screen. "The chef's not in the cab Toby, he's back in hospital bed on a drip!"

"What the fuck!" Toby exclaimed. His confusion was then compounded as the taxi pulled up just before a set of traffic lights where Exhibition Road meets Kensington Gore. Craig's team stopped as the hooded suspect paid and then exited the taxi.

"Are you absolutely sure we're tracking our chef's phone?" Toby barked at Achtar.

"Hundred per cent," he replied instantly.

"Maybe this geezer's stolen it," Craig chipped in.

They could see their team's BMW parked up some thirty meters from where the suspect now stood motionless on the pavement.

"Maybe, or maybe the chef gave it to him to throw us off the scent," Achtar surmised.

"Makes no sense Achtar, why would he suspect anything unless he really is up to something?" *The yanks might be right in their fears,* he thought to himself. He was about to order Craig to nick him when a silver Merc pulled up by the suspect, who quickly climbed into the passenger seat. Before Toby could react, the car sped off with purpose.

"We're in pursuit," Craig confirmed as the two cars went straight into Hyde Park out of range of the CCTV.

"Following the silver Merc into Hyde Park, the Merc is doing at least fifty!" Craig shouted.

"Get a photo of the number plate then stop them, nick them, I've had enough of this nonsense!" Toby demanded.

"Ok, we're closing, Mike's taking photos, will send through now. We are crossing the Serpentine, now doing sixty!"

Thirty-seconds later the registration filled their screen. Toby and Achtar looked at each other in shock.

"Merc stuck in a queue of traffic, I'm almost up it's arse, about to intercept suspects. Oh shit-"

"Yes, oh shit, diplomatic plates, United States Department of State. Just follow them Craig."

"Going round Marble Arch," Craig confirmed.

"You know where they are heading Toby?" Achtar whispered.

"Yep, the bastards stole our chef's phone, probably just to humiliate us."

"Toby, we're in Upper Brook Street, you know where they're going?"

"Yep."

"Turning into Grosvenor Square, they're stopping at the Embassy vehicle ramp."

Craig and his team pulled up across the square, looking at the stars and stripes fluttering in the London breeze. The driver of the Merc showed the Embassy guards his accreditation and gave a little wave back to his pursuers.

Toby sat with his head in his hands as Craig confirmed the suspect and the chef's phone were now safely inside the American embassy. He thought about Felix, the so called human rights documentary maker, betraying his friends in a Russian embassy in Kabul thirty-six years previously. He needed a drink.

14

THE DEPOSIT

MICKY CHECKED HIS phone, it was on fifty percent charge, he looked at the Professor's note and dialled the number. It rang three times before he answered, "Hi, Dennis speaking."

"It's Micky. I'm not sure it's a good idea discussing you know what on the phone."

"I'm passed caring, if big brother wants to know what's in that bag, who gives a fuck. Is Mo with you?"

"No, he's back in hospital but he was with me when we opened the bag. I'm going to see him before the Good Poison Club on Thursday. I suggest you join us, we need to discuss the Minister of Health's visit, as well as your bag."

"Ok, I'll see you there. Don't lose it."

"No chance of that Professor."

He heard the front door open. *Shit Tracey's home early.* As she entered the kitchen he opened the bag and started to place the screw drivers and spanners inside.

"What you up to Micky? Surely not DIY?" she asked.

"Just de-cluttering my man drawer, going to put all my shit in the loft. You're back early."

"I'm owed so much time off I thought I'd start nicking the odd hour. I dread to think the shit you've got in that loft, one day I'm going to go up there and have a root about."

"Watch your heels on that loft ladder dear." Micky winked, picked up the hold-all and made his way upstairs to the landing. He put the bag down and with the aid of a purpose made pole lowered the loft ladder. The hold-all was now noticeably heavier than before because of the added tools but he clambered up into the loft hatch with it in hand. He managed to push the bag up into the darkness and then fumbled for the light switch. The light illuminated the chaotic mess all around him.

Everything in his home, his life even, was orderly. His loft was the only place he allowed himself to be undisciplined.

He climbed across various laundry bags and black sacks of unimportant paraphernalia and sat against the water tank. Even if Tracey decided to pay this hellhole a visit she'd never come this far.

He peeped in a box of his old vinyl and pulled out a copy of Rolling Stones 'Sticky Fingers'. He played with the zip for a while reminiscing on his concert going days before putting it back and clearing a space on the board next to him. Placing the tools from the holdall onto the board, he left enough space for the Waitrose bag the Professor had left. He removed it and turned it upside down above the designated space. Ten bundles of fifty pound notes fell onto the MDF board. He sat and counted the cash, ten thousand pounds exactly.

He clambered across the loft and found an old biscuit tin containing some black and white photos of family members. There was one of his father and grandfather standing beside a fruit stall in Petticoat Lane, probably just before the war. He laughed to himself wondering how many years they had collectively spent in prison.

He placed the cash in the tin with the photos on top, closed the lid and put it in the middle of a bunch of boxes containing more crap.

* * *

CLAIRE HAD CONTINUED watching the documentary, unfazed by Toby's panicky disappearance. She'd listened to Scott describe how he'd taken it upon himself to go and find the convict platoon before Felix, whom he was now convinced was in cahoots with the Russians. Scott had paid a couple of Afghani police to drive him to the last known location of the platoon, the Mujahideen village they'd recently attacked.

She wasn't sure where all this was heading but Claire knew she should stick with it. Her viewing was once again, however, interrupted by a flushed Toby as he burst into the office. "Sorry Claire, the yanks have stolen our chef's phone. It's in the American embassy, lord knows why."

"So?" she answered, reverting to her Ice Queen persona.

Toby didn't quite know how to react to her lack of concern.

"You go and do some digging Toby, I'm going to stick with this," she said, nodding towards the screen.

Scott was explaining how one of his Afghan minders had bought a Russian video recorder, which for the time was state of the art.

"Ok Claire," Toby said, "I'll probably see you tomorrow morning."

His boss nodded dismissively.

He made for the door before adding, "One last thing Claire, do you think I should inform Sir Martin?"

Claire immediately paused the video, Toby realised she'd taken his question seriously. "Good question Toby, I'm not sure that Sir Martin will take kindly to this news. I think Myerson is trying to humiliate us, do your digging and send him a report in the morning. I think you and I need a lock in tomorrow to go through everything, including the documentary, which I intend to finish today."

He'd never shared a lock in with the Ice Queen. A lock in was a meeting with office door locked and phones off. They could only be disturbed by an absolute emergency. Toby thought about the Moldovan kitchen assistant, at last he'd be able to enjoy watching his boss' reaction.

* * *

MICKY TOSSED THE new pay as you go phone onto Mo's bed.

"Cheers Mate, and thanks for reporting the theft, appreciated."

"No problem Mo. I guess we're partners in crime now."

"Where's the bag?"

Micky explained what he'd done with the bag and suggested they meet the Professor in the quadrangle, a small garden in the middle of the hospital. He felt paranoid in the ward, maybe it was all the equipment.

Dennis was already sitting on the solitary bench, Micky and Mo sat either side of him. They looked like a scene from 'Last of the Summer Wine'.

"What do you think then lads, are you happy with the contents? There's a lot more where that came from. I guess you know what you have to do."

"Well yes, not a bad deposit, but Mo and I have two questions."

"Just two, fire away."

"Firstly, we're assuming you want rid of the missus, what about loverboy? Second is the question of the final settlement."

"Well, what will a further five thousand pounds each buy me?"

Micky and Mo looked at each other before Micky replied, "My usual fee is forty grand and that's for disposing of gangsters. You're asking us to kill a civilian, and female at that. You're also asking us to share twenty grand. I'm sorry Professor, you're not even close mate."

"Forget it, I'll sort it out myself," Dennis replied sharply.

"I can't talk for Mo but given the circumstances I'll be happy with fifteen. So thirty grand and we will sort the missus, but not both."

Micky and Dennis turned to Mo, who paused for a few seconds before nodding.

"Another ten each, it's a deal. But I want to know exactly how you plan to kill her."

"You what?" Mo chipped in.

"How precisely do you plan to carry out the act?"

"Mo and I will need to discuss tactics, you just pay us when the deed is done."

"Sorry guys but I need to know exact details, I don't want her killed just like that, I want her to suffer, I expect some gruesome torture for my money."

"Fuck off Professor I'm a pro, you really are taking the piss mate."

"Fuck you," Mo exclaimed and sluggishly stood up. "Forget it, I'm off," he added, as Micky stood up as well.

"Yes, Mo's right, let's forget the whole thing."

"Fuck you two, I'll do it myself, I'll have my deposit back please."

Mo laughed, Micky shook his head.

"Sorry mate, deposits in this business are non-returnable. We know your intentions, that deposit keeps that information in house."

Dennis stood up his left cheek twitching with anger and stress, he felt dizzy. "I want my money back!" he shouted.

"Not going to happen," Micky replied.

"This conversation is over," Mo added.

They started to walk away.

"You give me my ten grand back or I'll, I'll…"

Mo turned, walked back and stood right in Dennis' face. "What the fuck you going to do? You can't even kill your own wife who humiliates you every day. Loverboy is probably fucking her right now. You ain't getting a penny back."

Dennis wiped some of Mo's spittle from his eye and retreated slightly. "Ok, another twenty-thousand for just killing her, just get rid of her any way you want. Obviously I will need proof of her demise."

"No problem, leave it to us," Mo said. "That all right with you Micky?"

"Fifteen grand each, that's a deal. We will sort it ASAP, we've got to start concentrating on planning the reception committee for the Minister of Health."

* * *

TINA WAS DELIGHTED to see Brenda sitting amid the regular crew. They all looked in fairly good form except for Mo, who sat in his usual seat with his mobile chemo drip stand, and the Professor, who always looked like shit but this week even more so, Tina thought.

She'd received a text from Jed telling her he'd booked tickets for Donington Park, the 'Monsters of Rock' festival. She was very excited about it and feeling positive about life in general, despite her workload.

She tried to keep the conversation light, talking about the possibility of a group trip to the theatre to see a musical. She was interrupted by Hassan, the Uber driver. "When exactly is the Minister of Health coming and shouldn't we tell him a few home truths?"

Good point Hassan, I intend to give him a piece of my mind," Veronica concurred.

"He's coming three weeks today," Tina confirmed.

"Well I'm going to get him right in the ribs," Brian joined in.

"Believe me everyone, I'm with you on this," Tina agreed. "I'd like to give the man a slap, I think the least we should do is embarrass him in front of the press."

"We need to humiliate him," the Professor stated, "we've nothing to lose."

"Tina does, she could lose her job," Brenda chipped in. "I know you all mean well but I don't want any trouble on my account, I think we should be respectful and dignified."

The group looked at Brenda in collective admiration.

"What do you think Mo?" Tina addressed the chef.

He thought about the question for a few seconds, then cleared his throat and took a sip of water. "Well, Brenda's dignified approach is possibly the right way, but it's not my way."

"So what's your way Mo?" Tina asked.

"I'd like to torture him till he agrees to fund not just Brenda's trial but everybody who needs life enhancing treatment."

"And how would you torture him?" the Professor queried.

"I'd slice off his fingers one by one until he agreed to our demands."

"And if he resisted?" Dennis pushed Mo.

"I'd then cut off his toes one by one."

"Ouch," Tina screeched whilst laughing, assuming he was joking.

"And if he still didn't give in, I'd cut his head off just to send out a warning to his replacement that you don't want to fuck with the dying. Excuse the swearing ladies."

"Wow," Micky chipped in.

"I think we might be better off with Brenda's approach," Veronica exclaimed.

"Have you seen the arrogant ex public schoolboy?" Dennis retorted looking Mo in the eye. "I'd pay good money to see that parasite sorted out."

"In all seriousness I think we should come up with a sensible, cohesive plan to get our point across," Tina confirmed, once again trying to keep control of the debate.

15

THE SMELL OF NAPALM

"WITH THE HELP *of the Afghani police officers I'd hired, and approximately two hundred dollars' worth of 'baksheesh' for information from various sources, it took just three days to locate the convict platoon. They were imbedded in a Mujahideen village they'd allegedly attacked the week previously. We parked up around a mile away and walked towards the village holding up a white handkerchief.*

"Minders carried an assortment of weapons, we carried backpacks full of cigarettes and booze. A peace offering. The plan was to be a hundred per cent straight with them. Conduct a filmed interview with them in return for the goodies and then get the hell out and back to Kabul to confront Felix. Our first task was to warn them that we feared for their safety, given what happened to the Jewish deserters. We were convinced the Russian authorities feared they'd desert en-masse and that they were out of control.

"We were within a stone's throw from the village, the sun was high in the sky, we were in plain view of the rouge soldiers. Out of nowhere two Russian fighter bombers flew at tree top height over the village. We all instinctively dove into a drainage ditch beside the road. I buried my head in the dry dirt and heard at least eight loud explosions. The heat was beyond words, I waited a couple of minutes before raising my head.

"The village was completely hidden by a wall of napalm, the smell was choking. I looked behind me, my colleagues Jimmy and Andy were a few feet away huddled together, covered in debris, but seemed ok. Jimmy yelled that he thought it was friendly fire. I didn't answer because I had my doubts.

"We waited for what seemed an age for the flames to subside enough for us to enter the village. Except it turned out there wasn't a village to enter. Apparently the rouge platoon had slaughtered most of the inhabitants and now their own air force had completely obliterated all human life, bricks and mortar. It was literally scorched earth. The stench will never leave me, the afterburner of the napalm, the burnt flesh, Jimmy was physically sick.

"We ambled around looking for any survivors, there were none. Any remaining villagers and members of the convict platoon had been burnt alive. In twenty-four hours we'd lost our Russian Jews and convicts and I was convinced Felix had something to do with this mess. Andy called me over to the remains of what looked like a large dwelling. All that was left was a concrete floor with a large hole in the centre where there'd been a trap door that was blown open. We peered into the darkness as Jimmy searched his backpack for a torch. As he passed it to me we were joined by our minders who'd scoured the village in vain for a signs of life. I leaned into the abyss and waved the torch about. I could make out a few boxes surrounding a large green tarpaulin cover in the centre.

"I guessed the secret cellar was at least ten feet deep. Andy and Jimmy took one of my hands each and lowered me gently into the hole, I jumped the last few feet but discovered the cover was concealing something heavy and uneven. I slipped backwards on landing and smashed my head on a hard projection. I lost consciousness and was out for some time, when I came round I felt dried blood matted in my hair. My head was throbbing, I was in almost total darkness and the sun had set. I felt around for the torch and my backpack, hoping the video camera was still in one piece. I started to shout Jimmy and Andy's names in panic. I couldn't see anything there was no reply. I shouted for a good five minutes but no one responded."

THIS SEEMED A good place for Claire to take a break. She realised these unedited tapes would mean staying late, there were at least nine hours of footage to study.

She poured herself a latte from the coffee machine and walked around the office a couple of times. She wasn't looking forward to the lock in with Toby but it was absolutely necessary. She knew that, she'd suggested it, but there was something about him she found annoying, a few things in fact. He was just too posh, too public schoolboy. He was good at his job, she appreciated that, but she sensed he felt he should be superior to her. She was the boss and that was that and right now personality clashes were a not a high priority.

She needed to get to the bottom of the food poisoning issue and to find conclusive evidence the chef was behind it. She was under pressure from Sir Martin, who was under pressure from Myerson and the CIA. A lot of time, money and man power had been thrown at this enquiry, on top of the worldwide spate of vehicle terror attacks, which all democratic governments were frantically trying to quash.

Claire reckoned there was a good hour left on the first tape, which meant if she watched the other two back to back she'd be in the office till at least midnight. It was a sacrifice worth making to help get to the bottom of the story. She slipped her shoes off, wondering if she'd ever done that before in work, and then removed her jacket. She was ready for the long haul, she pressed play.

"I MUST HAVE fallen asleep for hours because when I woke the basement was full of light from the morning sun. My mouth was desert dry, I found my water canteen and took a huge gulp. I tried to shout out to the others again but my throat wouldn't amplify the words. I pulled the tarpaulin off the hard object that dominated the space I'd fallen into, underneath was a rusty old howitzer artillery canon. There was some writing on the side, it looked Russian, and a date, 1937. I looked around and saw a box of shells, there were four in there, to my delight I saw they were produced in a munitions factory in Dundee. I thought of Alice. I'd met her at college in Dundee, both of us confirmed pacifists, so it was ironic a box of bombs had directed my thoughts back home.

"I cleared my throat and managed to shout with gusto to the others but there was still no response. I was concerned and realised that now we were in extreme danger. I decided to try and jump up to the opening, I climbed onto the howitzer and made a couple of attempts but failed by just inches. So I placed the box of shells on the giant gun barrel at its widest point and precariously stood on it, rocking from side to side. I managed to reach the hatch and yank myself up, just as the box of shells crashed to the floor.

"Once up and out I made my way to the edge of the village, there was no sign of the others or the Jeep. I sat on a charred wall, the remains of somebody's home, and looked through my rucksack to see what provisions I had left. There wasn't a lot and my canteen was almost empty. The video camera was dented and needed new batteries but at least I had the chance to get some footage after what had turned out to be thus far a disastrous mission.

"The stench of napalm filled the air. Apart from the members of the rouge platoon, who'd probably massacred most of the villagers beforehand, I wondered how many others had perished in the bombing raid. I thought of Felix and started to make my way to the road to Kabul in the hope of hitching a ride, or die trying. I assumed if the Russians or the mujahideen didn't kill me, the burning sun probably would. I'd only walked around half a mile and I was feeling dehydrated. I had terrible nausea and felt dizzy, I started to hallucinate. I kept thinking I could see my comrades sitting in a tree a little way ahead. I managed to get to the tree in the hope of some shade, there was no vegetation to give any, just, just..."

Claire was transfixed at the man on screen, the camera zoomed in as tears streamed down his pale Scottish cheeks.

"...Just, just...three bodies hanging from bare branches. I recognised Jimmy first, then Andy, one of our Afghani minders also. I rested my back against the tree and sobbed like a baby, basically waiting for the perpetrators to return and end my nightmare. I could see a vehicle in the distance moving towards me. I said the Lord's Prayer and closed my eyes, thinking of my Alice. I heard the vehicle screech to a halt just a few feet from me but I kept my eyes firmly shut. Not sure why, maybe I didn't fancy looking my killer in the eye.

"'Mr Scott, Mr Scott!' I heard the frantic shouting, I opened my eyes and saw Achmed, our driver, holding the passenger door open and imploring me to get in. I'd intended to give my colleagues a decent burial but I scrambled to the Jeep and climbed in thanking Achmed, and God, as he sped away."

THE FIRST TAPE ended abruptly. Claire opened a drawer and took out the Jiffy bag containing the other two tapes. She didn't care how long it took she had to hear Scott's story to its conclusion. She pressed eject and replaced tape one with tape two.

She smiled to herself at the novelty of this now obsolete technology. There wasn't even a remote for god's sake. She pressed play and sat back.

"What the fuck," she swore aloud, as she stared at the screen. She knew nothing about football but quickly ascertained someone had recorded a Celtic vs. Rangers game. She frantically pushed the fast forward button and periodically pressed play, but all there was to see were green and white shirts battling with blue.

She switched to tape three. The first few seconds were encouraging, there was amateur footage of what looked like Afghan villagers, but just as she sighed with relief, a mid-1990s 'Top of the Pops' took over. She recognised a very young looking Oasis, Liam Gallagher with his hands behind his back. She pressed forward several times, more music, more football.

"Shit!"

She pressed stop, put on her jacket and headed home.

16

THE LOCK IN

MO RELAYED THE good news that he was being discharged at the weekend and arranged a rendezvous with Micky to collect his half of the deposit.

"So when and how do you think we should earn our balance?" Mo queried as they sat in the hospital garden.

"As soon as possible mate. I'm quite happy to put a bullet in her head tomorrow," Micky replied flatly.

"Have you got a gun?" Mo asked.

"What happens in Vegas…but seriously I'm happy to sort it ASAP, don't worry, the money will be split 50/50."

"Oh I know it will," Mo confirmed confidently.

"So how would you do it mate?"

"Poison," Mo smiled.

"What kind of poison?" Micky asked, surprised.

"Family recipe, if I told you I'd have to kill you," Mo replied seriously. "My grandfather was the village alchemist till the Russians killed him. He taught me all he knew. A bullet in the head is not just too easily traceable, it's also too quick."

"Surely quick is good and as for being traceable, excuse me I'm a pro," Micky interjected.

"With respect, this woman has humiliated her husband in the most despicable way imaginable. A bullet in her head gives her the luxury of dying instantly without having the time to think about her actions. My poison would produce a slow inscrutably painful death. Probably take about four hours for the vital organs to literally dissolve, plenty of time for her to think about her behaviour."

"Fucking hell Mo, I do like you."

After meeting Mo, Micky headed to an old warehouse he rented in South London, he stood at the door and surveyed the junk filling the metal container . He shone a torch around the box, it was packed with old filing cabinets and assorted white goods.

He squeezed passed a spin dryer, made his way to the back of the container and found an old wicker laundry basket. He removed the lid and pulled out an old manky duvet and some pillow cases, he placed his index finger in a small notch in the base and managed to tilt it upwards. There was a small space underneath where he felt around blindly and grasped the object of his search, a small handgun. He hadn't held it for nine years. He checked there were no bullets in the chamber and placed it in his inside pocket.

He made his way to Mayfair to put the Professor's down payment in his safety deposit box and remove six bullets.

* * *

TOBY RECEIVED THE message halfway through his early morning circuit at the gym. He was running flat out on the treadmill and glanced down at his phone strapped to his arm. He couldn't make out the details but saw it was from Claire. *Probably confirming the time of the lock in,* he thought. He wiped the sweat from his forehead with his sweatband and slowed down enough to study the message. *'Change of plan. Too many disruptions at the office. Lets meet off site, the cafe in Soho where our chef had his phone stolen. See you there. Claire'.*

Toby brought the machine to a gradual halt. He couldn't recall interrupting his strict daily fitness regime before.

He read the message again. *Is it a date?* he fantasised, perhaps they would adjourn to a pub or a cocktail bar afterwards. A smile spread across his face. The Moldovan kitchen assistant's story he'd been looking forward to telling his boss would now happen in a venue where others, albeit strangers, could witness her embarrassment. This was marvellous. And then there were Friday night drinks in the Red Lion, wait until he tells his colleagues about his date!

What do I wear? he considered, before heading to the showers thinking about his grooming products.

Toby was pleased the most discreet table in the cafe was available. He was five minutes early so he ordered a latte and studied the morning emails. Christine was holding fort in their office, he was looking forward to impressing her and the rest of the team down the pub later.

The waitress brought his latte over, the glass filled to the brim. He tentatively took a sip, concerned it might be too hot, not wanting to spill any on his white shirt.

He was disappointed his boss hadn't suggested the venue before he left for the gym, he'd have chosen something more snazzy, one of his Ben Sherman's perhaps. He briefly wondered if his boss might dress down, a foolish thought that vanished as soon as the Ice Queen entered the cafe in her usual attire. She managed a "Hi" and sat down, looking around casually.

"So I've come up with an agenda," she said as she removed her jacket. "I suggest I inform Christine we're turning our phones off now, any code reds and she will have someone come and get us."

"Okey dokey," Toby confirmed.

Claire glared at him sharply, how she hated that expression, a simple "ok" would be fine.

"I'm expecting a delivery shortly, other than that let's hope we're not disturbed, except by the waitress of course, I'm starving." She opened the menu. "You having anything Toby?"

He perused the menu and nodded.

The waitress came over, Claire gestured to Toby to place his order. He fancied a fry up but took into account he'd lost half his gym session that morning. Besides, his boss barely ever ate at work and when she did, it looked like rabbit food, nuts, raisins, berries. "I'll go for scrambled eggs with smoked salmon on brown toast please."

"That sounds nice," his boss stated.

This was turning into an interesting meeting.

"Same for you madam?" the waitress asked in an east European accent.

"No, I'm going to go for freshly squeezed orange juice, and..." she dithered for some seconds before confirming, "I'll have the full English please."

Toby thought he might be hearing things.

"Excuse me?" Claire called back the waitress, "I have a delivery coming at eleven sharp, it will be for Claire Peterson, please make sure the delivery guy comes to my table, I have tip for him."

The waitress nodded but thought it an odd request, as did Toby.

"So let's start with the Afghanistan documentary, where was Scott when you were called away?"

Toby referred to the notes on his iPad. "The Jewish conscripts had just been arrested, Scott seemed convinced his boss was up to no good."

Claire brought him up to speed with the dramatic events, before disappointing him with the news that the second and third tapes had been recorded over.

"Oh dear, just as things were getting interesting. What now?" Toby asked.

"Christine is in contact with the sponsor, apparently these were the only tapes of the unedited version, there should be a recording of the finished documentary in the BBC archives."

"It was shown on the BBC?" Toby seemed impressed.

"Only on the Open University slot on BBC Two in the mid-nineties," she confirmed.

"So either we find the recording or hope the sponsor can enlighten us to the connection with our chef," Toby confirmed.

"Yep, unless of course the narrator Scott can be tracked down," Claire added.

Before they could continue their discussion, their breakfasts arrived.

"Wow Claire, that is definitely a full English," Toby said.

"It certainly is, I haven't had black pudding in years," Claire replied, looking Toby in the eye she added, "that's not strictly true."

Toby had no idea what she meant but felt slightly hot and bothered. She continued to stare at him and his healthy looking plate of food. *He really does look after himself,* she thought, *if only he wasn't so posh, he'd be ok.* She cut into her sausage, speared it with her fork, also capturing a couple of mushrooms, and took a bite.

Toby looked down at his iPad busily reading his notes, trying to remain cool. "What's next on the agenda?" he quaffed.

"Enjoy your breakfast Toby, we've got all day."

They tucked in, Toby thought this a perfect opportunity to indulge in small talk. "Got plans for the weekend Claire?" He watched her scoff down some egg and bacon before she answered.

"Chilling."

"Good idea, it's been another manic week," he replied, waiting for her to ask him what he was up to. There was only silence as she, to his surprise, demolished her fry up, concluding with a large gulp of her orange juice.

"So, how's the Good Vibes Centre, or whatever you call it?" she asked.

"The Sanctuary, the Good Vibes Group, though the participants have aptly renamed it 'Toxic Tina's' Good Poison Club."

Clare gave a quizzical look. Toby explained, "As in Tina, the Chemotherapy ward sister who chairs the sessions, and chemo being a kind of poison."

"I see."

"It's a bit of a slow burner to be honest Claire, we've had a couple of reactions as you know, i.e. his applause for Dennis' burn the suburbs rant, and then when he stormed out when the question of God at last reared its head. Now, of course, of more interest is the off-site meeting in this very cafe with two of his fellow patients."

Claire nodded. Toby felt the Moldovan waitress's information was more of a priority and was desperate to furnish his boss with the disgusting story. He tried to change the agenda but not for the first time was foiled as the waitress came over to clear the plates. "Your delivery has arrived miss." She nodded at the figure standing at the entrance in black motorbike leathers and helmet.

Claire gestured to him to come over. Toby was frustrated but intrigued.

"Claire Peterson," the courier acknowledged.

"Ricky," she replied.

"That's me," he confirmed in an American accent.

"Have a seat Ricky. Coffee?"

Ricky removed his helmet, adjusted his well groomed quiff and pulled up a chair. "I'll have an espresso, my second name in Rossi." He winked at Claire before offering his hand to Toby.

Toby thought there was something familiar about the American as they greeted each other. "You look familiar, have we met before?" he asked.

"You've seen Ricky in action," his boss said mysteriously.

The courier unzipped his jacket and slipped it onto the back of the chair. He was wearing a blue hoodie, he placed the hood over his head. "Ring any bells buddy," he quipped.

Toby knew who it was instantly but couldn't find any words. The waitress put the visitor's espresso in front of him, he winked at her in response.

"Ricky was here the other day, you didn't have time for coffee then did you," she chided him.

"You stole our chef's phone in here?" Toby caught on.

"That's right Toby," Claire confirmed, "you followed Ricky from Barnes to Grosvenor Square."

Ricky slid his hood off and shrugged. "Just obeying orders I'm afraid."

"And?" Claire queried.

"And what?" Ricky replied.

"My delivery?" She held out a pale hand.

"Oh, sorry, here you go." He retrieved a small package from his jacket pocket and placed it in her hand.

"Thank you." She opened the package and revealed an iPhone.

"The chef's," Toby assumed.

"Is it locked?" she asked.

"Yes."

"But you know the number?" She glared at the American with her piecing blue eyes.

"I do." He was playing hard ball.

"We could open the phone in seconds, you know that."

"What reward will I get for saving you the trouble?" He winked at her. *Shit*, Toby thought, *bad mistake.*

"Give me the fucking number or there will be consequences," she whispered. Toby had heard that chilling tone before.

"1, 9, 9, 3," Ricky offered.

She keyed it in and the phone sprung into life. Claire stared at the screen wallpaper and smiled.

"Do you know who that is? Because we haven't got a clue," Ricky confessed.

Claire passed the phone to Toby who recognised the face on the screen immediately.

"We do Ricky," she stated matter of factly and gave him an exaggerated wink.

"Well?" he mumbled.

"Well what?"

"Well who is it?"

Claire moved as close as she could to the American. "So you went to all that trouble to steal our chef's phone and apart from sussing out his PIN number, you have discovered fuck all. Drink your coffee and fuck off back to Myerson and tell him his Scandinavian sister says hi and bye."

Ricky showed the palms of his hands in a gesture of surrender, put on his jacket, picked up his helmet and nodded to Toby. "Good luck buddy," he said, as he left with his tail between his legs.

Toby was lost for words, wait till he got down the Red Lion, they wouldn't believe it. He played with the phone nervously, trying to keep cool.

"So, you were saying Toby, the Good Vibes Club, whatever it's called, is worth persisting?"

The Ice Queen carried on as if nothing had happened.

Toby wondered what Myerson would say. The man was head of CIA in Europe for god's sake. "Sorry Claire, what just happened?"

"Which bit?"

"I can guess why they took the phone? They obviously got, or didn't get, the intel they wanted, but why return it to us? And well Myerson, he has a frightening reputation. Sir Martin has got our whole team jumping hoops because of that mad yank."

"Myerson took the phone for no other reason than to embarrass us, we have a special relationship him and me, we are both second generation Scandinavian. We have an understanding."

Toby wasn't sure what she meant but he could grudgingly see why she was his superior. She'd had a full English and seen off the CIA, all before midday.

"Yes I'd keep the hospital operation going until the proposed visit by the Minister of Health. Our chef is being discharged this weekend, his relationship with his fellow patients is of interest if only to prove the Americans wrong."

"And what about the 'decapitation' business, how was your meeting with the kitchen assistant?"

At last, he thought, *at last*. But now she had invited him to tell her the disgusting story he felt a pang of regret. The performance he just witnessed had left him reluctantly in awe of her. "Well, as I pointed out, something got lost in translation. According to the young lady our chef simply had some beef with clients who made negative comments on a well-known online restaurant review site."

"Nothing to do with jihad then?" the Ice Queen interrupted.

"No not at all. Apparently clients in a Soho advertising agency had complained that the salad dressing our chef had supplied lacked tang."

"Tang?" She raised her eyebrows quizzically.

"Yep, tang. The term caused some consternation in the kitchen, they received an email from the agency CEO explaining that the pan-seared sea bass was spot on but the chef's dressing lacked 'tang'. What sent our chef over the edge was that he repeated the comments to the review site. According to our girl he went berserk, shouting, swearing and smashing mugs and plates. That night he sent the text, declaring he wanted to 'cut their fucking heads off' and when he'd finished with them he'd make a visit to the conference centre."

"You mean the conference centre where the cyber-crime nerds were taken ill?" Claire interrupted.

"Exactly, and I've done some digging and come up with this review, which was published a few weeks before the tang business."

Toby passed his iPad to his boss, she read the words on screen aloud. "Today's lunch was not up to the usual high standard expected from Manor From Seven. The beef was far too rare and the tarte tatin for dessert was sour to say the least. Anon, Westminster Conference Centre." Claire turned back to Toby. "So our chef decided to exact revenge on the conference centre and it was simply a coincidence that he chose the day the world's elite cyber-crime experts were in the building?"

"Looks that way Claire."

"And what about the advertising agency, any sign that he poisoned them as well?"

"No Claire, he was more creative with his revenge on them." Toby felt she was impressed with this information and now came the moment he'd been waiting for, he paused, expecting her to next ask him the details of his revenge.

"So our chef was basically pissed off with a couple of dissatisfied clients and you've known this since before the Mosque attack. Why the fuck didn't you bring this information to me at the time and why are we still bothering wasting tax payers money on this crazy hospital charade?"

Toby was taken aback with the Ice Queen's outburst, he tried to compose himself. "The Americans would throw the Imam's meeting with our chef at us, besides I've been trying to tell you since I met the Moldovan."

"Fuck the Americans Toby, and you could have simply emailed all this info at the time."

Toby looked at his boss, the respect he had for her a few minutes ago had turned to contempt. She might be good at her job but she was a bitch.

"I didn't think it appropriate because of the difficult circumstances surrounding our chef's actions with regard to the advertising agency."

"Difficult circumstances? What could be so fucking difficult that you couldn't just send me a report?"

Toby played with his iPad and found the recording of the interview with the Moldavian kitchen assistant. He whizzed it forward, he knew exactly where to press play.

"So Anna, we've clarified that chef, as you call him, didn't actually intend to cut his client's heads off, what exactly did he do?"

"When the Mad Men agency man complain we not know what is 'tang', so we Google. We bit confused but realise it mean strong flavour, so Chef go crazy. The next night we were in kitchen alone preparing another order for the agency, about twenty dinners, I think it was tiger prawn salad. Chef was swearing, 'I give them fucking tang, I'll give them fucking tang'. He mix up his usual house dressing, balsamic vinegar, lemon juice, mustard, seasoning and then, then…"

"Then what? Then what Anna?"

Toby had been waiting for this moment, he looked around the now packed cafe and then directly at his boss.

"And then he tell me he add tang, I say what tang and he undo his zip and get out his cock. I in shock but he offer me twenty pounds to help him make extra tang."

"Wow, Anna, I think I get the picture."

"I feel bad but I behind with rent, I help him add tang to dressing."

Toby waited for a reaction of disgust from the Ice Queen but her expression didn't change one bit.

"Okay, spare me any more details Anna, did you get any feedback from the agency?"

"Yes, they said it was much better, much more flavour."

"Wow. Did this behaviour continue Anna?"

"Yes, I helped him on a few more occasions."

Toby stopped the recording and waited for his boss' response.

"Very entertaining Toby, I thought revenge was a dish served cold, not lukewarm." He thought he saw a slight cheeky smile, this was not the response he expected.

"And what about the cyber security nerds? As disgusting as our chef's actions were the worst his extra tang could do is leave a nasty taste in your mouth. I don't think his semen would be responsible for putting several of his clients in hospital."

Toby was burning hot, the only person he'd humiliated was himself. "The kitchen assistant left before the conference incident," he confirmed.

"I can't say I blame her Toby, she was paid the minimum wage to toss salads, not toss off the chef."

Toby cleared his dry throat before answering, "That was the problem Claire, our chef expected a bit more than just being tossed off."

Claire glared at him with contempt for a moment, he wondered if he had relayed too much information. The waitress came over and asked if they wanted anything else, Claire requested the bill.

"I have a terrible feeling we are wasting a lot of precious time and money on someone who is just a frustrated Gordon Ramsey and a bit of a perv. I wish you would have brought this to me earlier Toby."

"I didn't want to embarrass you Claire."

"For fucks sake Toby we are all grown ups. I must confess though I will think twice before ever complaining about my food in future."

Toby definitely saw a smile on her thin lips. "What about the food poisoning Claire, what have you heard?"

"Salmonella according to the lab, I guess it was just dodgy chicken."

"So what now boss?"

Claire liked being called boss, she placed her credit card on the saucer the waitress brought the bill on. "Ok Toby, let's get hold of the sponsor and finish Scott's story. We give the Good Vibes Group a couple more weeks, and you can make sure our chef gets his phone back." She slid it over to him.

They took out their own phones and turned them on, both watched in silence as their devices sprang to life. Both had multiple messages but were relieved there were no code reds.

They made their way out into the Soho air, Claire hailed a taxi. "Toby two more things, get that kitchen assistant back in I want to hear her story myself. Lastly, you going to the Red Lion?"

Toby felt a pang of excitement, his boss was going to join him for the Friday constitutional. "Yes, why?" he asked.

"Well no fucking tittle tattle, our conversation is one hundred percent classified, including the 'tang'. See you Monday."

Toby watched the Ice Queen climb into the taxi. He needed a drink.

17

ONE SHOT

PATRICK FELT A little guilty. He was standing outside the fire station, if Tina saw him she'd go potty. She wouldn't care he was trying to be a good father and look out for his girl. She'd quite rightly ask where the feck he was all those years she really needed him.

He'd recently been made redundant and too much time, plus guilt, was not a healthy combination. His drinking had got heavier, as had his smoking. He'd got into a row in his local when he drunkenly crashed into someone and knocked a tray of drinks over. A fight ensued, in which he'd come off worse. He sustained a black eye and badly hurt pride. He was too embarrassed to go out until his bruises had subsided, he looked and felt older.

He stood in the drizzle clutching a Tesco carrier bag containing a box of six craft beers. *Tina will fecking kill me,* he thought, as he walked to the front door. He stopped in his tracks as the giant red folding doors to his right burst open and he heard two fire engines rev up their engines, before the shrill of their sirens filled the air. They screamed into the evening rush hour traffic and disappeared up the high street.

He paused for a moment before entering the space recently vacated by the fire engines and shouted, "Hi! Anyone about?"

A women appeared on a mezzanine platform above him. "Can I help you sir?" she shouted down at him.

"I hope so mam, I've got a present for one of your firemen in here." Patrick held the bag up.

"Hold on, I'll come down!"

Patrick looked behind him at the open doors, he could end this ridiculous idea now and just leave. Instead he sucked on an extra strong mint, hoping the couple of liveners he'd had to give him courage would be camouflaged.

"How can I help you sir?" the female firefighter asked politely, whilst she kept her distance.

"I've…I've got a gift in here for one of your colleagues. He helped me get my cat down from a tree when he was off duty, which was really kind of him. He's name was Jez, or Jed, or something, had long hair and a beard, probably puts his hair in a bun at work."

"A bit like me," she answered without a smile. "What is it sir? We have strict rules on gifts."

Patrick took a box of Quality Street chocolates out of the bag.

"Ah, old school, lovely, he will appreciate them, hopefully pass them round." She walked over briskly and relieved him of the box.

"Thank you sir, I'll make sure he gets them when he reports for his next shift. Would you like to leave a name and number so he can thank you personally?" She produced a pen and small pad, Patrick felt a bit panicky.

"No, no, it's ok just pass thanks from the man with the cat, thanks for your time mam."

"My pleasure, have a good evening sir."

He left the fire station feeling like a complete idiot, he saw a pub just up the street, he now needed to get rid of the taste of extra strong mints.

What a fecking idiot, he thought as he supped his pint of Guinness. *What the feck would this Jed lad think when he gets a gift for something that didn't happen? Shit, he will smell a rat and look at CCTV footage, they must have cameras.*

On the other hand he now knew the love of his daughter's life was a bonafide firefighter, he was relieved his paranoia was unfounded. He downed the pint quickly, feeling guilty and very foolish. He hoped Jed would just enjoy the chocs and forget all about it.

* * *

TINA SAT ON Jed's new leather sofa. "Wow Jed, this is the most comfortable sofa I've ever sat on, it must have been expensive."

"Well you know what they say, cheap is dear!" Jed hollered from the kitchen as he cooked up a storm.

"Who the feck are *they*?" she replied.

"You know, *them*, them that know."

"Feck off Jed!" she jested, looking around his luxurious pad. Everything looked expensive but tasteful, she expected his cooking would be equally classy.

"Bollocks!" he bellowed from the kitchen. "I'm out of coriander!"

"Oh dear, disaster," Tina chided sarcastically.

Jed came hurrying through the living room throwing his leather jacket on, "I'm just popping over the road to get some fresh supplies, talk amongst yourself."

Tina watched him scurry out, she climbed off the sofa and looked out the window down at the high street below. She saw Jed emerge onto the pavement and cross the road to the convenience store opposite.

Very convenient, she thought.

He stopped and high-fived a very dodgy looking hooded teenager outside the store. She watched him enjoy an animated conversation with the young man before entering the store in search of the obviously essential coriander.

Tina crept into the bedroom and headed straight for the two huge black tinted sliding wardrobe doors. She slid the right hand one open and rifled through the clothes. She then flung open the other door and did the same. No sign of any firefighter's uniform. Maybe her dad was right. Besides how did he afford such a swanky apartment? She quickly searched the single wardrobe in the spare room, same result, before returning to the sofa.

Jed returned a few minutes later, gleefully shaking a bag of coriander.

"Smells delicious." She smiled.

"A touch of this and I guarantee the best fish stew you've ever tasted."

He was true to his word the meal was a triumph. He really was perfect, but there always a 'but'. *Where were his uniforms?*

* * *

MICKY SLEPT LIKE a baby, his dreams were bland and innocuous despite his intention to kill a women he'd never met that very day. His other half was sound asleep as he got up and left the room. He surveyed his face in the mirror as he shaved. *Not bad all things considered*, he thought, though he was concerned to see one or two grey hairs. *Far too young to be a granddad.*

He got dressed, all in black of course, and after a coffee and toast slid out the door quietly and climbed into his black BMW. He looked at his phone notes app where he'd put Raymond's address. His sat-nav told him it would be a forty minute drive. How the Professor must hate the fact that not only was his wife playing away but she was playing away in the suburbs.

Normally he'd spend a good week sussing out different escape routes, CCTV, etc., but now he wasn't that bothered. He wanted to get the job done and get paid ASAP. The Professor had given an extra incentive for them to dispose of the body. He had a plan in place and wanted matters concluded before Mo was discharged from hospital on Monday. He knew the Afghan wouldn't be happy, but hopefully he'd be placated by the fact he'd be paid his share without getting his hands dirty.

The drive took exactly forty minutes. He parked up in the new development, the Professor wouldn't approve at all. Manicured lawns, double garages, fridges full of Prosseco. He saw the bus stop where Sandra would arrive and leave from, Dennis had explained that neither of them drove because they'd always lived in town.

He parked in a nondescript spot, opened the boot and reached under the spare tire for the gun. He set off towards the lover's house.

Suddenly his phoned buzzed. It was Mo on the pay as you go phone Micky had got him.

"Hi Mo, what's happening?"

"The police have found my phone, they want to drop it off to me."

"Really?"

"They called the hospital to ask when I was being discharged, they say I have to make an appointment to collect it from Paddington Green."

"Fucking hell Mo, that's the anti-terrorist HQ."

"Well maybe it was stolen by a terrorist. What you up to my friend?"

Micky turned into Raymond's Street, he paused as the house came into view. "I'm going to take care of business Mo."

"Oh no you're not mate."

"Sorry pal, I'm on site now, I'm hoping to conclude matters within the hour. See you Monday, the drinks will be on me." He ended the call abruptly and continued on his mission.

He knew Mo was furious but there was nothing he could do, Mo wasn't going to go AWOL again.

Micky was outside Raymond's four bedroom semi, the brand new Range Rover on the driveway was pure white and spotless. He looked up at the front bedroom window, the Professor had told him she'd boasted about spending the weekend with her lover. The front door opened and the two of them emerged hand in hand, Raymond was wearing a grey tracksuit, she was in a pretty revealing dress. Raymond pressed the car key fob with his free hand.

Micky slowed his pace, he saw them get in the vehicle, the lover got out again and made his way back to the front door, he'd obviously forgotten something. Micky glanced back and then up and down the road, no one was about, he decided it was time to change track and free-style.

He put his hand in his inside pocket and pulled out the gun, straightening his arm so the weapon was held tight against his thigh. He turned and walked towards the Range Rover, he'd open the back passenger door, climb in and put a bullet in the back of Sandra's head. Raymond wouldn't see anything through the blackened windows, if he heard the shot he'd assume it was a car backfiring. Who expects gunfire on a suburban Saturday morning? He'd then put a bullet in the back of his head, recline the seats, push the bodies onto the back seat and drive the vehicle to his lock up, returning later by cab to retrieve his own car. Good plan, he would expect a big bonus from the Professor.

"Shit," he muttered as a text interrupted his approach. He dug his phone out of his trouser pocket and glanced at the message. *Dad, I've gone into labour three weeks early, Shirley xx.*

* * *

DENNIS PACED AROUND his study not sure what to do with himself. He'd been told in no uncertain terms not to contact them, they would let him know when the deed was done. Sandra wasn't due back till Monday morning, how would he survive the rest of the weekend waiting for his wife not to show up?

He spent a lot of time imagining the look on her face as she realised she was about to die. He would have preferred Mo's method but hey ho, as long as the deed was done. He hoped the last minute extra incentive package may have concentrated Micky's mind. He imagined them naked in Raymond's bed with their brains splattered all over the pillows.

When would the police arrive? They would inevitably put two and two together but he'd be surprised if he ever saw a prison cell. By the time the trial took place his tumour would probably have killed him anyway.

He picked up the TV remote and channel surfed until he came across a high brow opera on Sky arts. He toyed with his glass of Malbec, still thinking about the sordid details of his wife's demise. The front door opened, he sprang up in surprise and rushed out into the hallway. Sandra was halfway up the stairs, her head was clearly still intact.

"Sandra! You…said you'd be back Monday?"

She turned to face him, her makeup was a wet mess. "Fuck off Dennis, leave me alone!" she bellowed, and continued up to the bedroom, slamming the door behind her.

He followed her quietly and put his ear to the door, she was sobbing uncontrollably. He went back downstairs totally confused and saw his wife's bag and coat discarded on the floor. He went to hang them up on a hook but felt her phone vibrate in the pocket. He slipped his hand inside and looked at the text that had just arrived. *I'm sorry Sandra, I should have told you earlier. It's complicated, I hope you can in time forgive me.*

He put her phone back and returned to his wine, he felt a mixture of confusion, euphoria and a little disappointment that she was still alive. *Loverboy is going back to the ex*, he immediately assumed. Whilst he was still happy to proceed with the plan he could now at least enjoy her humiliation.

Sod it, he thought and phoned Micky, despite his instructions not to.

* * *

MICKY IGNORED THE phone vibrating silently in his pocket as he stared down at his two hour old granddaughter, cradled in his arms. He was transfixed, he felt emotions he doubted he possessed, elation, love, a desire to protect this precious little bundle of joy. His daughter and ex-wife (number one) stared at him and then each other as they saw a tear splash on his cheek.

The baby gave out a small cry and he reluctantly handed her back to her mother for feeding. He stared at them in wonderment and a thought came into his head.

He looked at his phone and saw the Professor had called but he ignored it as he continued staring at the miracle of new life.

He knew he could never kill again.

18

FIRE FIGHTING

TOBY SPENT HIS entire Saturday nursing a hangover. The early doors session had developed into a messy bar crawl with Craig and Christine. He'd probably told them more than he should but he wasn't sure.

The Ice Queen has driven me to drink, he pondered, as he surfed the channels, finally settling on the day's rugby highlights.

His phone rang, it was her, Claire. It was past ten, *what the fuck did she want?*

"Claire," he said, trying to sound nonplussed.

"Sorry to disturb you Toby but just wanted to warn you we are heading up to the Shetlands first thing Tuesday, train and helicopter, we will probably be there overnight. Just in case you've any plans."

Overnight, train, plans, he tried to not sound excited by the surprise road trip. "No problem Claire, funny enough I was about to email you about Craig's conversation with our chef regarding his phone."

"Wow, working on a Saturday night Toby I'm impressed, I thought you'd be out on the razz."

"I gave up the highlife when I joined your team Claire."

He told her about the chef, thinking the police had found his phone in the hands of someone on their watch list. He hoped he'd want to retrieve it on Monday as soon as he was discharged from hospital.

She asked him if anyone interesting had contacted the phone in question.

Toby surprised her with the revelation that there seemed to be a lot of communication with the chef's fellow members of the Good Poison Club.

TOBY DIDN'T LIKE Paddington Green, it was too busy and the air was full of stress and angst. There was also no Thames to look out on, like his office back at HQ. He didn't much like Mondays either.

He'd met with various head honchos before being given a small office, where he now sat studying the chef's phone. He thought about the coming trip with the Ice Queen to the Shetlands, he'd been impressed by the way she completely saw off Myerson's courier, he was actually looking forward to working with her on this trip.

Craig called Toby and brought him up to speed with the chef's movements. The chef left the hospital at 8.30am and was picked up in the car park by a fellow patient from the Good Vibes Group in a black BMW. They sat for half an hour in conversation before he was dropped off at the tube station. Mo emerged from Edgware Road station thirty minutes later and was currently in a cafe nearby, so he should be at Paddington Green shortly, as arranged.

Toby pondered on the chef's friendship with his co-sufferer. He doubted their conversation was medical but wasn't about to dig any further. He looked through the chef's photo gallery again, a strange collection of food and porno pics, then considered the photo on the screen saver. He'd rehearsed a few ideas but decided to freestyle, remembering his boss' words, 'As far as we know our chef hasn't committed any crime yet'.

A few moments later a police officer led Mo into the office, Toby gestured for him to sit opposite.

"Coffee?" he asked.

"No thanks."

Toby nodded at the officer to leave the office.

"You've got my phone," Mo stated.

"Yes I do." Toby held the phone up.

"Do I have to sign something? I'm in bit of a hurry, I was discharged from hospital this morning."

"I understand. No you don't have to sign anything, just a couple of questions."

Mo was surprised by Toby's cut glass accent. "You're not police are you, you're MI5," he guessed.

"Something like that," Toby answered honestly.

"And the guy who stole my phone was on your radar?"

"Something like that."

"Well I haven't got a clue who it was so can I just take my phone and get on? I don't think I would have any answers to your questions. I think my phone was stolen from my jacket pocket in the Berwick Street cafe."

Toby slid the phone across the table, "There you go, have a nice day."

Mo was taken aback. He picked up the phone, he guessed that it had been well and truly taken apart, he thought about the porno and smiled.

"So I'm free to go?" he asked hesitantly.

"I was hoping you could help with one or two questions, but it is your phone so…" He shrugged. "Before you leave though, maybe you could tell me how Scott is?" Toby looked Mo in the eye, he saw his discomfort.

"Excuse me, Scott?" Mo tried sounding mystified.

Toby pointed to the photo on the screen saver.

"You knew him," Mo mumbled.

"Sort of," Toby replied, pleased he'd got the chef's attention but unsure where to go next.

"I think I'll just go." Mo stood up looking confused and agitated.

"Well, keep well sir." Toby tried to sound nonplussed as he watched him make for the door.

Mo stopped suddenly and turned to face Toby. "How did you know him?" he asked.

Toby noticed the chef referred to Scott in the past tense. He was determined to stick close to the truth. "I knew of him, I'd like to know more about him."

Mo stood by the door considering the situation. "The documentary, have you seen his documentary?"

"Just the beginning, why?"

"It will tell you everything, I've got to go. Thanks for this," Mo held the phone up and was gone.

Toby sat collecting his thoughts. "Did that go well?" he said aloud. *Did it go badly?* he thought.

* * *

MICKY FELT AWKWARD walking back to his car with Frankie, meeting the father of his granddaughter in the labour ward had reminded him of just how tenuous his relationship with his daughter was.

They passed a burnt out car, Micky shook his head.

"Rough estate Micky, it's a start for us but we don't plan to be here long."

Micky didn't comment, he just nodded. His first impressions of Frankie were not positive. He had no right to judge, he knew that, but maybe its takes a wrongun to know a wrongun. He certainly didn't like the tattoo on his neck.

They got to Micky's black BMW. He opened the boot and took out a bumper bag of nappies and threw it to Frankie. "This should keep you going boy," he quipped. He looked around at the ugly concrete flats thinking about the little bundle of sheer joy he'd just held in his arms.

"Thanks Micky, appreciated mate," Frankie gave a cocky wink and turned to head back.

He took a couple of steps when Micky shouted, "Hey Frankie, come back here I've got something else for my granddaughter!"

Frankie turned on his heels and slinked up to Micky, who was rummaging through his boot. He turned to face his daughter's partner. "Listen Frankie, I'm the last fucking father on earth to lecture anyone about responsibility but I'm not overly optimistic you're going surprise me and be there for my Shirley and that little bundle of joy. I can't tell you to do the right thing but I promise you this, if you do the wrong thing I'm going to be very disappointed." He removed the covering over the spare tyre.

Frankie looked aghast as he saw the gun wedged in the inner wheel. "Fucking hell Micky," he mumbled.

"In the meantime I want to give Shirley this, she won't take it from me I know, so tell her you won it on a bet." He handed him a large envelope containing the Professor's deposit.

"I expect every pound to be spent on my granddaughter, don't disappoint me mate."

* * *

TINA SHOOK HER head as she read the message from her father. He'd suffered a nasty cut on his thumb and was in the A&E department, he suggested they meet in the canteen when he'd been stitched up. She made her way to the room Mo had vacated hoping it had been cleaned ready for the next patient.

"Hiya Tina, I found this in the bedside cupboard." The cleaner handed her an envelope which simply had 'Tina' written in biro on it. She could feel a paper clip inside.

"It's okay Olu I'll empty the bin." She could see the cleaner was almost done. "Thank you," she said as Olu left.

Tina sat on the bed and opened the envelope, there was a small piece of paper that read 'Thanks for everything Tina. See you when the minister visits. Mo'. Clipped to the paper were two fifty pound notes. Tina blushed, her first thought was the honesty of the cleaner, then panic, she didn't think it right to hang onto it. She picked up the bin and made her way to the nurses station.

"I've got a large contribution to the Christmas party fund," she announced to her colleagues and handed it over to the ward secretary.

She took the bin to the rubbish shoot and removed the inner sack, which disappeared into the dark tunnel. She noticed a small carrier bag stuck to the inside of the bin, which she prised off and peaked inside. There were at least eight SIM cards in there. *How strange*, she thought, wondering if she should keep them, hesitating for a moment before throwing them down the chute.

She made her way to the canteen and spotted her father at a table, grinning and giving her a thumbs up, the injured thumb sporting a thick swathe of bandage and tape.

"What you done then you idiot?" she mocked.

"Work related accident, had a disagreement with a chop saw."

"And I presume you can't carry a tray and you expect me to treat you to lunch?" Tina chided him.

"Can't even get my wallet out of my pocket," he quipped.

Tina returned with two healthy looking pasta dishes and a pot of tea. "Do you want me to feed you?" she teased her father.

They indulged in inane small talk before her father touched a nerve. "How's your fireman then?"

"He's good, so you accept he's actually a fireman then?"

"Of course, I was just messing with you, he's obviously a fireman, who would make such a thing up. If you're going to lie about your job you'd claim to be an airline pilot or a hotshot layer. No, loverboy is defo a fireman, you've got yourself a proper man at last."

Tina recalled that it was her father who planted the seed of doubt in her mind in the first place. She thought of Freddie and their pact, she wasn't sure why.

"I'm not so sure dad," she muttered.

"You what love?" He was taken aback.

"I admit you planted a seed of doubt in my mind when we last met in your local, I'm surprised you've changed your tune."

"And I'm surprised you've changed yours," he came back at her.

She was about to answer when she saw Micky at the food counter. He gave her a thumbs up, she returned with a smile.

"Who's the man in black?" her father asked.

"That's one of my patients, I reckon he's a hitman."

"Yep, I can see that," he agreed.

They were still discussing Jed when Micky came over and went to put his tray on the adjacent table. Tina gestured for him to join them. "Hi Micky, what you doing here?"

"Blood test Tina. Here, have a look at this." He placed his phone in front of her, there was a photo of him holding his granddaughter.

"Wow, that's fantastic Micky, you must be thrilled."

"I'm walking on air Tina."

"Dad, this Micky. Micky, this is dad."

They shook hands. "Congratulations Micky."

"Cheers pal."

"You two have got something in common," Tina declared.

"Really, what may that be?" her father enquired.

"You are both irresponsible absent fathers trying to make amends."

Both men looked sheepishly at Tina, and then at each other. After an uncomfortable silence Micky addressed her father. "Well all I can say mate is you should be very proud of your daughter, she's a bloody saint. Anyway I hope I'm not interrupting your private meeting."

"No Micky we were just discussing Tina's latest boyfriend and yes she is a saint putting up with me."

"Well, I hope your boyfriend appreciates you Tina," Micky smiled.

"Well, the problem is he is too perfect, there's always a fly in the ointment where my love life's concerned," Tina confirmed.

"So what's the fly?" Micky asked curiously.

"Tina doesn't believe her fella is a fireman," Patrick interjected.

"Why would he lie about that?"

"Exactly my friend, I told Tina a fella wouldn't make something like that up."

"It was dad who questioned his profession in the first place just because he has long hair. Anyway I'm going to leave the two of you to it, I've got work to do. Nice to see you Micky, hope to see you at the next meeting."

"Not sure I can make it but I will defo be there to embarrass the big white chief."

"We need to discuss a plan of action so come the week before and make sure Mo comes too."

Micky nodded, she gave her father a playful slap on his cheek and left them alone.

"So what's your name dad?"

"Patrick."

"She's a great girl Patrick, I'm the last person on earth that should give advice but whatever history you two have, you should put in the effort mate."

"I'm trying, god knows I'm trying. It may take several lifetimes to pay that girl back for the misery I caused her."

"Wow, I know where you're coming from. So what's this boyfriend like?"

"Not met him, she speaks very highly of him but she does pick em does Tina."

"Why you reckon she has doubts about him being a fireman?"

"Probably my fault for planting a seed but I know he's on the level."

"I know what I'd do if I was you Patrick mate."

"Go on"

"I'd go to the fire station and check him out. Where's he stationed?"

Patrick smiled, he liked this fella. "Kentish Town, that would be a bit sneaky wouldn't it."

"I'll check him out if you like, I wouldn't want anyone messing our Tina about."

"I'll bear it in mind Micky."

"I'll give you my number Patrick, if you need my help just give me a buzz."

19

THE GOOD POISON CLUB ON TOUR

MO WAS ALREADY on their usual bench near the giant shoe sculpture.

"This is yours mate," Micky handed him a carrier bag containing his share of the deposit.

"What horse did you put your share on?" Mo asked him.

"I invested it in the future mate." Micky smiled, he told him about his granddaughter and his lunch with Tina before Mo changed the subject.

"So you didn't kill her?"

"No, I was going to, he'd gone back into the house to get something they'd forgotten. I walked unseen to where he'd left the driver's door open, my intention was to put one bullet in her head and then one in his when he returned. I was standing there, finger on trigger, about to finish her, she never saw me. She'd picked up his mobile, which he'd left in his seat, she was looking through the messages smiling when she came across one that wiped the smile of her face. I hesitated when Raymond came back out the front door with a bottle of fizz. I crouched down out of sight as she got out the car screaming at him, 'You cheating bastard, you fucking cheating bastard!' She threw his phone at him and basically attacked him, I got the hell out of there."

"Fuck, that's crazy. What will the Professor make of it?" Mo pondered.

"We'll find out in a minute, here he comes," Micky pointed at the frail bearded figure striding across the square. They noticed the smile on his gaunt face.

Dennis sat and explained the surprising and most enjoyable turn in events. Micky told him his side of the story of what happened outside Raymond's house.

"So what now?" Mo interrupted.

* * *

TOBY WAS PLEASED to be back at HQ, he was looking forward to the Ice Queen confirming the details of their overnighter. As he walked through reception his phone rang, "Hi Craig, where are you?"

"I'm with Mittall enjoying lunch in Golden Square Soho. We're on a bench opposite your chemo club on tour."

"Sorry?" Toby was confused.

"Our chef is with a couple of fellow patients, deep in conversation."

"Which patients?"

"Hang on, Mittall's taking a photo, on its way to you."

"Ok, bon appetit, let me know if anything happens, can't you get ears nearby?"

"Mittall is going for a stroll, will keep you posted."

Toby waited a few seconds for the photo to arrive. *Strange bedfellows*, he thought.

* * *

"I MUST ADMIT I'm in a dilemma as what to suggest, on one hand I'm thoroughly enjoying watching her suffer, on the other things are much easier now Raymond is out the equation. Trust me lads nobody would notice if she disappeared," Dennis calmly explained his predicament.

Micky was quick to respond. "Well, number one, most importantly, you're not getting your deposit back."

Mo nodded in agreement.

"Number two, I'm a granddad now, I've got new priorities, so I'm not going to be killing anybody for mercenary reasons. I'm retired."

Mo looked at Micky quizzically. "So it's down to me," Mo confirmed.

"I'm afraid so mate."

"So I take it I get the full balance?" Mo guessed.

"Sorry mate, I know too much, the deal stays fifty-fifty and I know nothing. Don't forget I was a squeeze of the trigger away from putting a bullet in her head."

Mo considered the situation for a few seconds before replying. "I want seventy-five percent or I'm retired as well."

"That gives me just seven and half grand," Micky moaned.

"Plus the deposit. Not bad for doing nothing."

"Hang on a minute," the Professor interrupted, "this is my money, my idea, my wife. This isn't an auction."

"Hang on a minute, we've shaken hands on a deal, this is between Micky and me now," Mo interjected.

"Excuse me but I might decide to forget the whole thing. We have a new set of circumstances now," Dennis snapped.

"Too late Professor," Micky looked him in the eye, "too late. The deal is done, what you decide about the wife is up to you, but you owe us thirty grand."

Dennis was about to answer but they were interrupted by a passer-by. Mittal stopped by their bench looking at his phone map. "Excuse me gentlemen I'm looking for Glassblower Street, my phone is playing up, I'm a bit confused."

"Just up there mate and throw a right," Micky pointed the way.

"Thank you," Mittal replied and made to walk away when Craig came up to him hand extended.

"Doctor Patel, what you doing in deepest Soho?"

They shook hands. "Hi Trevor, I'm on my way to meet a colleague, how are you?"

"I'm good thanks to you and your team, doctor," Craig stated convincingly. "I'm in full remission."

Micky, Mo and Dennis all looked at one-another before Micky spoke up. "You're an oncologist sir?"

Mittall claimed to be the king of freestyling but this situation seemed ridiculous. "Indeed I am."

"We're all patients at Saint Peters under Mr Shepherd."

"Top chap, know him well, you are all in good hands." He felt dreadful making this stuff up. "And what brings you three musketeers to Soho this sunny afternoon?"

The 'three musketeers' all looked at each other before Dennis piped up, "We're expecting a visit from the Minister of Health, we're planning to kidnap and torture him until he guarantees funding for drug trials."

"What a fantastic idea, may I suggest waterboarding," Mittall laughed.

"Actually we all agreed that we'd enjoy a day out together having all met on the chemo suite," Micky chipped in.

"Ah! Tell me, is sister Gallagher still running things? Great girl that one, absolutely on the ball."

"Tina, yes," Mo confirmed. "She's a friend to all of us."

"Well good luck to you all and to you Trevor."

They watched Mittall head towards Glassblower Street as per Micky's instructions. They didn't notice Craig slip behind the bench dropping a small recording device on the grass.

"Nice fella," Micky stated.

"So what's it to be?" Mo asked Dennis.

"How you planning to do it?"

"Poison."

"Poison, what kind of poison?" the Professor asked.

"My own recipe, a guaranteed slow extremely painful death and completely untraceable."

"But I still want my fifteen grand as agreed," Micky asserted.

"Fuck off, no way. I get seventy-five percent or I'm off," the chef said, standing up.

Micky decided to play hardball. "Fifty-fifty mate."

Mo didn't answer, he just turned and walked off past the shoe sculpture and out of sight.

20

DRESS DOWN MONDAY

"OH SHIT," TOBY cursed. He was standing by Achtar, listening to the conversation the device had recorded.

Toby listened to the twenty-second clip five times. "Shit, I'd better go and see the Ice Queen she's going to love this."

"She not in her office," Achtar said, surprising him as he made for the corridor. "She's in the secure interview room."

"Who with?" Toby asked.

"You're not going to believe it Toby."

"What...who?"

"Wayne Myerson."

"Myerson, Wayne Myerson? What the fuck?" Toby's cheeks were crimson with stress. "Have we got ears on this?" he asked Achtar.

"Sorry mate, she deactivated sound and vision. This is a top legal one-to-one and there's something else..."

"What?"

"She dressed up for the occasion."

"She what?"

"I know he's the big chief of the CIA but we couldn't believe our eyes when she turned up."

Toby wanted to know more, *dressed up?* He quickly reverted back to being professional. "She wanted me back in the office?"

"She still does, there's an old friend of yours in there mate, another yank."

Toby found Ricky sitting in his chair, he was nodding his head to the music exploding in his earphones. "What you listening to Ricky?" he asked.

"Foo Fighters, you like em?"

"Too mainstream for me, I like my music a bit left field, out of the box."

"What the hell's going on Toby?"

"You tell me, you're the one sitting in my chair."

"Fucked if I know Toby, my boss has been a pain in the ass ever since our man got killed by that Hungarian fuck head."

"Your man?" Toby repeated.

"The Imam, he was our man, I presumed you knew that."

"Wait a minute Ricky, you're telling me the Imam was working for the CIA?"

"Oops, I may have to kill you now I've let a cat out of the bag." The American laughed.

"Shit I need to let Claire know!"

Toby ran out of the office and down the corridor to the secure interview room, he banged on the door. "Claire I need to talk to you, it's urgent!"

His boss opened the door slightly. "I'm busy Toby, I'll be with you shortly," she whispered through the crack.

"I know Myerson is with you, the Imam was on his payroll."

"I know Toby he's just told me, I'll fill you in shortly."

Toby was perplexed, he caught a glimpse of her as she opened the door slightly wider. He noticed immediately she had makeup on, not a lot, but makeup nonetheless. In the brief exchange he noticed she had at least two of her top buttons undone. Lastly, and to Toby, most incredibly, she was wearing a skirt. He tried to look like he hadn't noticed.

"Sorry Claire, there's a development regarding the chef and his fellow patients I need to discuss with you."

"Ok Toby," she replied cooly, "as soon as I'm finished with Myerson."

* * *

CLAIRE RETURNED TO sit opposite Myerson. "Seems it's now common knowledge that the Imam was your man."

"Well, as I said Claire, we're on the same side. Yes, the pressure got to me, I fucked up, I shouldn't have made that call. I'm hoping we can draw a line in the sand and work together."

Claire sat back chewing her pen, she knew she had the head of CIA Europe in her pocket. She knew her silence was irking him.

"I've given you the heads up on the Imam, I've told you I will big you up to your boss, what else can I do Claire? I'm sorry."

Claire looked him in the eye, the dirty old bastard must be at least twenty years older than her. She knew right from the beginning he hated her and Sir Martin but she was completely taken aback when he called her.

There was no recording of the conversation, it was her word against his, but he knew mud could stick and he was strictly on probation with his wife Monica. What really irked him was how much she was enjoying his humiliation, and he was right.

"When you leave this room Mr Myerson I don't want to hear from you again so if you have anything else to say, best say it now."

He looked at her pale blue eyes, she looked slightly less fierce than on their first meeting, he wasn't sure why. She'd got to him, he knew that. The stuck up, ice cold, English bitch had got under his skin. The Trump administration had driven him to drink heavily. He was severely under the influence when he'd phoned her. If she divulged the contents of that conversation he would deny it but the fall out would be irreparable. No, he'd have to give in to her every will and whim. He said those things to her and, despite the drink, he'd meant them and now he'd have to pay the price.

She gestured to him, inviting him to make a final plea.

Fuck it, he thought, *I messed up but who the hell does she think she is*. "I'm sorry Claire, but I must admit I meant every word."

"Including the ones about you intending to put a smile on my miserable face."

"Especially those ones, though I have to say your face doesn't look as harsh this time."

"Well, thanks, I'll take that as a compliment Wayne and as disgusting as your suggestion was, I've heard worse this week. Word of advice, never complain about your food till you've finished the meal."

* * *

TOBY AND RICKY spent their time guessing what their bosses were discussing. The American confirmed that Myerson absolutely detested the Ice Queen and Toby suggested his boss detested all men full stop.

They both looked very sheepish as she returned to the office, looking completely unflustered. She simply gave a dismissive nod to Ricky towards the door, he got up and left to join his boss without another word.

Toby should have been thinking about the Minister of Health and the Imam, in that order, but his mind was too busy computing his boss' attire. Her usual white blouse had taken on a new persona with three buttons undone exposing a gold crucifix. Her breasts were definitely more defined, he could see a trace of a black bra through the material. Her breasts had been the subject of feverish discussion in the Red Lion. The pill, pregnancy, and nip and tuck had all been muttered, the latter two deemed highly unlikely. He then realised he was staring at her legs for the first time. It seemed that the skirt matched her discarded black jacket perfectly, probably came as a suit, as an alternative to her usual trousers.

Why wear the skirt for the first time today? he pondered.

"Yes Toby, they are legs," she said sarcastically, catching his stare.

Toby's public schoolboy cheeks were burning crimson. He thought he might faint when, instead of taking her seat opposite him, she came round to his side of the conference table and sat on its edge, taunting him as a bit of thigh was exposed. The Ice Queen's smooth legs dangled inches from him, his mind was mash.

"It's a strange thing Toby, Myerson is probably the most powerful man this side of the Atlantic. He has hundreds of thousands of armed men at his disposal, a phone call to his president could result in a nuclear strike. I know for a fact he is responsible for a military coup in at least one small Balkan state and yet, I've got him here." She unfurled a clenched fist. "I've got the head of CIA Europe in the palm of my hand and all because of one thing." She hoisted her skirt a little higher exposing a stay up stocking top.

Toby reached for a glass of water.

"Myerson didn't get to his lofty position through luck. He is a Harvard graduate, a genius in some respects but at the end of the day he's just a bloke, just a fucking pathetic bloke."

She nonchalantly slid off the desk and returned to her seat.

"You had something to tell me Toby," she said coldly as if the previous rant had never happened. He stuttered as she did up her buttons and put her jacket on.

"There's been a development, a bit of a strange one." He related the events at Golden Square. "I think our chef is planning to poison the Minister of Health."

Claire put her hair back in its normal functional bun, considering the new information. "Are we sure the conversation definitely related to the minister, Toby?"

Toby shrugged before replying. "It certainly looks that way, who else would he be looking to poison?"

"What about the money, what's all that about?"

Toby had wondered that himself but the Myerson business had completely thrown him. He suddenly remembered the impending trip to meet the sponsor. What would the Ice Queen be wearing for that?

* * *

BRENDA HAD NO reason to get up, she felt guilty that her husband had gone off to work, battling through the rush hour traffic, whilst she sipped tea and read the paper sitting up against her pillows.

There again *he* felt guilty that his wife had a life limiting illness and was forced to take early retirement. He had a nasty chesty cough but didn't dare complain, he'd grin and bear it, it would go as it came but the future of his wife of thirty-three years was uncertain.

Brenda had no grandchildren duties today and intended to read the Daily Mail back to front, do the cross word and then go the local charity shop where she'd had an eye on a designer handbag, though she thought it was probably a snide.

The news was never good and the headline today about the NHS was all doom and gloom, she wondered why she read this crap.

She heard the letter box give out a metallic clang. *The post is early today*, she thought, *junk mail most likely*. The crossword was more of a challenge than usual, not for the first time she cheated with the help of Google.

She looked at her watch, it was ten thirty, *this is ridiculous*, she thought. She crawled out of bed, showered, dressed and sat in front of the mirror. There was no physical sign of her illness but she was constantly reminded of it by her regular sweats. She thought of Tina, her consultant, the Good Poison Club, then that handbag.

She made her way downstairs and noticed a fat brown envelope on the door mat, surprised it had got through the letter box. She took it into the kitchen and placed it on the breakfast bar whilst she made a coffee. Kettle, cup, instant coffee, spoon, the usual routine.

Her phone rang, it was her youngest son checking up on her. After a couple of minutes chit chat they said their goodbyes and as she made her way to the living room she remembered the package. Probably raffle ticket books from the church, she guessed. She picked it up nonetheless and noticed 'Brender' was crudely scrawled with a black marker on the envelope. *Some idiot can't even spell my name.*

She turned the TV on just in time for a bit of Jeremy Kyle. She took a slurp of coffee and laughed to herself as she watched a sister-in-law claim she was expecting her brother-in-law's twins. She placed the package on her lap and tore off the brown envelope without taking her eyes from the screen. Her actions temporarily halted whilst a security man held back the women's sister, who was shouting death threats at her pregnant sister. The programme cut to a commercial break.

Inside the brown envelope was a Sainsbury's carrier bag with brown tape around it. *This is like playing pass the parcel with the grandkids.*

She peeled away the tape and managed to open the bag.

"Holy mother of Jesus!" she shouted aloud.

She didn't know what to do first, phone John, her sons, the police… She spent several minutes studying the contents. She ignored the coffee and went over to John's shelf and poured herself a large Brandy, which she knocked back in one before returning to the sofa and counting out five thousand pounds in twenty pound notes.

She then saw a yellow post it note in the bottom of the bag, '*For your trial, hope it helps*'.

* * *

TOBY WAS DISAPPOINTED, his boss joined him in the first class carriage at Kings Cross in her usual attire, confirming that the previous day's performance was definitely for Myerson's benefit.

She placed her overnight bag next to his, this was encouraging. He made a point of looking at his watch, letting her know she was cutting it fine, he doubted she noticed.

His phone buzzed, it was Craig.

"You on the train Toby?"

"Yes I'm with Claire, just about to leave."

"St Pancras?"

"Yes, why?"

"I'm outside the station, we've had eyes on the chef since Golden Square yesterday and this morning he took a cab to a property belonging to a fellow patient, put something through her letter box and then has carried on to Kings Cross."

"A coincidence maybe, which patient by the way?"

"Maybe, Mittall followed him into the ticket hall. The patient was a Brenda Callaghan. Hang on Mittall's back, he wants to speak to you."

A breathless Mittall came on the phone. "Toby," he sounded panicked, "he's bought a return to Edinburgh, I just saw him sprinting to the platform!"

Toby stood up and looked out the window, the immediate departure of the train was announced.

"Everything ok Toby?" Clare asked casually.

"No, fucking no it's not!" he exclaimed, before realising he was drawing attention to himself.

The train started to pull out the station. "I think the chef is on this train."

Claire tried to remain cool but this was more than unexpected.

"This is no coincidence, he's on the train for a reason. We need to think through the options," she reasoned.

"I think I might have provoked him Claire, when I returned his phone I asked him how Scott was."

"Clever I think Toby, how did he react?"

"He was stunned but spoke of him in the past tense, I definitely touched a nerve."

"Are you thinking what I'm thinking Toby?"

"He's on his way to meet his sponsor," Toby surmised.

"Correct," she confirmed, "or he's working with Myerson."

"That might explain his meetings with the Imam, but what about the food poisoning business with the cyberspace nerds?" Toby reasoned.

"What now?" Claire pondered. "He's met you, so best bury your head in The Telegraph. I'm going for a walk."

Toby watched the Ice Queen stride through the carriage towards second class.

* * *

TINA WAS SURPRISED to see Brenda. She was busy attending to a patient but could see Brenda was agitated and seeking her attention. "I'll be with you in a couple of minutes Brenda go and wait in the Sanctuary, I'll be along ASAP."

That fecking Sanctuary could have paid for Brenda's trial and more besides, wait till I meet the fecking minister, she thought to herself.

She found Brenda siting in the Good Vibes room. "Can you lock the door Tina?" she asked with an urgency that surprised Tina.

"No problem. There, done." Tina pulled up a chair so her knees were touching Brenda's.

"What is it Brenda, is it about the trial business?"

"Sort of, I had a bit of shock this morning."

"What sort of shock Brenda?"

"I got a package put through my door this morning with this note." Brenda showed Tina the yellow post note.

"For your trial, hope it helps," Tina read it aloud and looked quizzically at Brenda who opened her hand bag. Tina peered inside.

"Jesus," she exclaimed.

"Maybe Tina, maybe it's a gift from the gods because I haven't got a clue who else it could be from, but wherever it's from, this is wrong! How the hell am I going to tell John? There's five grand there, he'll go mad with worry."

"Tina thought immediately about the hundred pounds Mo left, she thought about the SIM cards, his disappearance. She didn't really know how to respond, it would cost a lot more than that to finance the trial.

"I'll fetch us a nice cup of tea Brenda and we'll think this through."

* * *

BRENDA LIED TO her husband for the first time in thirty-five years of marriage. She told him she'd been called to the hospital to see Tina, the Sanctuary had been handed funds to help its patients and four thousand pounds had been put in their account. She never mentioned the thousand pounds cash she hid in her knicker drawer. John finished his pork chop and confirmed, "That's great news dear, I'd read about Macmillan giving out hardship payments but didn't want interfere love."

Brenda's guilt vanished slightly but she couldn't stop wondering who and where the money came from. They sat in their respective armchairs to watch Eastenders but Brenda's mind was elsewhere. She thought of her relatives. Her children, nieces and nephews would all help if she asked or they would approach her maybe with a cheque in a card, but wouldn't stuff the cash through her door. Her friends likewise.

Her thoughts turned to Tina, who'd suggested the ruse, and then to her fellow patients. Veronica had the money but they'd not really clicked, she was too common for Veronica. Hassan worked all the hours god gave him for his family, Brian spent all his spare cash on therapeutic weed. He was a nice man, but no, not him. The Professor was possibly the nastiest, most obnoxious man she'd ever met. Micky, a dark horse, bit of a rouge, doubtful. Oh and Mo, she'd never even had a conversation with him, so, no way.

21

THE CONFESSION

CLAIRE STRODE PURPOSELY through three carriages, Mo was easy to spot among the mainly Caucasian passengers. He had his back to her, there was a spare seat next to him, opposite him was a mother and young daughter.

She stopped and glanced at the empty aisle seat. The chef made a subtle gesture with his right hand inviting her to sit. He looked more dishevelled than ill she thought. He didn't smell too good, probably the effort of running for the train. She noticed the black rucksack above his head.

She spread her Telegraph on the table in front of her and took out a pen from her handbag before finding the crossword. She was enjoying this unexpected turn of events. This was what she joined up for, action in the field, but all her experience thus far in her meteoric rise through the ranks had been endless meetings and computer screens. *How do I start a conversation with an Afghani chef stroke terrorist?*

Toby sat alone back in first class with just his iPhone for company. He'd called Christine and brought her up to speed. She was to gather what info she could on the sponsor's movements. This was not what he'd been planning, yes he'd expected work related conversation but he hoped that during the four and a half hour journey he could melt some of his boss' ice. *Why was he even bothered, why did he obsess so much about her?* She wasn't called the Ice Queen for no good reason but the Myerson business had got to him. A skirt for fucks sake, and that brief glimpse of a stocking top was stuck in his head. He lost a night's sleep over that one thought. But here he was on his own whilst she played James Bond.

Sometimes God works in mysterious ways, she thought looking at the crossword clues.

"Shit," she said aloud. "Bloody hell, sorry about that." She spoke quietly to her neighbours so as not to offend the mother and young daughter opposite. "I'm stuck on the capital of Uzbekistan, I should know it, my best client's from there, I've got brain freeze."

"Tashkent," Mo replied.

"Thanks, you sure?" Claire engaged.

"One hundred per cent miss, I'm from that part of the world."

"Really, Uzbekistan?"

"No miss, next door, Afghanistan."

"Wow, I've never met an Afghani person before. I shouldn't have had to bother you, as I said, I have a client from there. I should have remembered he was from Tashkent." Claire was rather pleased with herself, the hardest part of starting a dialogue had come easily. Her first case had been as part of a team investigating a member of the ruling Uzbek family who lived in luxurious splendour in Chelsea but was suspected of having been radicalised.

She took her jacket off and placed it on her lap.

"What kind of work do you do miss?"

"Interior design. My name's Claire."

"I'm Mo."

They shook hands formally.

"Thank you once again Mo. You going to Edinburgh?"

She noticed he hesitated before answering. "No, Newcastle, I'm going for a job interview."

"Really, what kind of work do you do Mo?"

"I'm a chef."

"Wow, that's fantastic," she answered enthusiastically, whilst wondering if it could be a coincidence him being on the same train and that he actually could be genuine. *No, that's ridiculous,* she realised.

"And you Claire, where you heading?"

"Edinburgh, to see a potential client," she answered convincingly.

"You're travelling very light," Mo commented, looking at her small nondescript handbag.

"Oh, no I left my overnight bag back there," she nodded back at the luggage rack, wondering if he was onto her. She returned to her crossword before texting Toby: *Sitting next to chef! He's going to Newcastle. Let Christine know. Speak soon. P.S. I'm an interior designer.*

Poor Toby, the poor fool was obviously all worked up over yesterday's performance, he probably spent all night wanking. She smiled at the wicked thought, put her pen down and closed her eyes for a few minutes.

Mo glanced at her left hand. No rings, no nail varnish.

Claire was churning the options in her head, she opened her eyes and feigned a stretch.

"What kind of restaurant is it you're hoping to work in?" she asked.

"Asian fusion sort of thing."

"I didn't know they were so trendy up there."

"No idea, never been," he confirmed.

"Where have you been working up to now then?"

"I worked for a company that specialised in supplying healthy lunches for offices, conferences in London sort of thing. But I'm fed up with London clients, they drive me crazy."

"In what way?"

"Bloody online comments, petty criticism, I ended up wanting to kill some of them."

"I can imagine."

"And I've been unwell to be honest."

"Sorry to hear that Mo."

"I'm on the mend now thanks, thanks to the NHS."

"God bless the NHS," Claire agreed, before making her excuses on the pretext of going to the toilet.

She scurried back to Toby to collect her small case.

"So are we getting off in Newcastle then?" Toby asked.

"I think so, any news from Christine."

"Yes, the sponsor left the Shetlands on a flight to Edinburgh an hour ago."

"Oh, maybe she's going to drive to Newcastle. I thinks it's safe to say she's on her way to meet our chef."

"And how is our chef?"

"Quite a gent, I'd say, I'm going back to join him."

She returned with two coffees. "Here Mo, got you a coffee for helping me with 'Tashkent'."

"Thank you Claire, here let me put your case up." He leaned across her reaching for her smart silver carry on case.

"So some of your clients drove you mad then? I've got a few of them." She reopened the dialogue.

"Maybe it's my age, maybe my illness, but I've got less and less patience with small minded people worrying about small things. I've seen poverty like you couldn't conceive, I've seen war! It's not easy to react calmly when someone gets irate because their canapés are too effing dry."

"I can imagine Mo, blimey I don't know what I'd do in your position."

"I'll be honest Claire it's got to me so badly I've lost my last two jobs reacting badly to criticism."

"Oh dear Mo. I've got a chef friend that spits in client's dinners if they complain, I'm minded never to comment till after the cheese board." Claire laughed.

Mo smiled. "Oh I've done worse, much worse."

"Really Mo, like what?"

"You don't what to know believe me."

"You going to let me guess Mo?" she teased.

"You're too much of a lady to guess I'm sure."

Claire smiled and pretended to look at her paper.

Mo was disappointed she'd stopped the conversation, he didn't know what but there was something about her that he both liked and despised. She seemed interested but at the same time aloof. After a short silence he continued. "I'm hoping a change of scene will help calm me down, I'm certain the clientele up north will be less demanding, more down to Earth."

Claire nodded, she felt things were going well, he wanted to talk to her.

"Well Mo, my uncle Cyril, who was from Liverpool, used to say 'the further north you go, the colder the weather but the warmer the people'."

"I hope your uncle is right about the people at least, I do have concerns about being Asian, I don't think there's many about up there."

Claire wondered why he'd brought this up as she seriously doubted he was actually planning to stay in Newcastle.

"I'm sure you'll be fine, there's good and bad everywhere, mostly good. Have you got any friends up there, any contacts?"

She noticed he hesitated for a minute before answering. "Yes, I have an old friend up there who helped me come into this country."

"A good friend I'd say, is she a Geordie?"

"No she's Scottish, I haven't seen her for many many years."

"You must be excited to see her."

"Sort of, it's been a long time."

Claire didn't want to press him too hard, she needed to decide what to do. Did they get out at Newcastle or Edinburgh? She smiled at Mo and closed her eyes, feigning sleep.

* * *

MICKY TAPPED ON his daughter's front door, she took some time to let him and his partner Tracey in. "The baby's fast asleep. Come in, I'll put the kettle on," she whispered.

It wasn't an easy situation for Tracey, Mickey's baggage had put a strain on their relationship but she was no fool, she knew he was a man with both history and mystery when she met him. She hoped to tame him but accepted it would be a slow process. She wasn't sure what his daughter made of her, she wanted to be there for her but realised she'd have to tread carefully.

Micky went and sat next to the crib, he stared at his granddaughter in wonder for twenty minutes before joining the girls in the small living room.

"She ok dad?"

"She's just beautiful."

They indulged in small talk for a few minutes before Micky asked how Frankie was.

"How's his job going?"

He noticed her mood changed at the mention of her partner's name.

"Ok," she answered dismissively.

"Just ok," Micky pressed, but they heard a small yelp from the crib and the conversation ended abruptly.

After the baby was changed Micky held her in his arms for a few minutes whilst his daughter had a shower, he reluctantly handed the little bundle of joy over to Tracey for a cuddle.

His daughter took over, some twenty minutes later and they said their goodbyes.

Micky felt something wasn't right.

They made their way to the car park and were about to leave when a sporty silver Merc sped in and parked. Micky watched as Frankie emerged from the driver's seat with a bunch of flowers and a bag of nappies.

"Aww look Micky, Frankie's bought Shirl some flowers, how sweet." Tracey swooned, but Micky was staring at his swanky new motor, his anger rising.

"Cunt," he mumbled.

"What did you say Micky?"

"Fucking little cunt." This time he raised his voice. "Wait here Trace," he commanded and went to get out the motor.

I'm going to blow his fucking brains out if he doesn't hand me the car keys. How can I have been so naïve? He stopped in his tracks, his mind racing. *Fuck it, why did I put the gun in with Mo's deposit, I'll have to get it back.*

* * *

MO'S PHONE BUZZED, Claire pretended to be asleep whilst listening.

"Micky," Mo said. "No I'm in a train to Edin- Newcastle. Going to visit an old friend."

Claire could only make out indistinct chatter on the other end of the phone.

"No idea, maybe two or three days," Mo continued, "…got it with me mate."

She pretended to wake up just in time to see him look up at his bag. "Something up Micky?" Mo asked. "I thought it was a present," he responded to whatever his friend had said. "No problem, I'll meet you as soon as I return...Yep, it's not my thing anyway, I told you that...I'll call you as soon as I'm back." Mo ended the call, he smiled at Claire and rested his head against the window, within seconds he was snoring.

Claire text Toby: *I think he is getting off at Newcastle, keep a low profile. I'll message you.*

A moment later came his reply: *Ok, I've mustered some troops just in case, see you soon.*

Claire looked up at his bag sitting next to hers and then at the mother and daughter sitting opposite. She'd dreamt about this moment since she was approached at uni. This is what she signed up for, not attending endless meetings with wankers like Toby and Myerson.

The mother and daughter got off at York, leaving Claire alone with Mo. She moved around to the seat opposite.

He opened an eye. "Where are we?"

"York," she confirmed.

Mo drifted back to sleep.

She was recalling the call he'd received from his mate, he had something in his bag. She didn't want curiosity to come before professionalism. She waited twenty minutes or so before reaching up to get her case down, patting the side of his sports bag, feeling for anything unusual. She heard Mo cough, she nervously brought her case down and opened the zip to pull out a makeup bag. Mo woke up and saw Claire applying a subtle amount of lipstick.

"Would you watch my bag Claire while I visit the small room?"

"No problem Mo," she replied. Another slice of luck, but then again she'd made that luck by earning his trust.

She waited till he was out of sight before placing her case back in the rack and pulling down his bag, another look around and a deep breath before she opened it. A change of top and pants, interestingly a couple of Tesco pay as you go phones, a toiletry bag. She felt something hard and plastic on the bottom and pulled it out. She reckoned she had around two minutes to make a decision that would change the course of the operation. There was no time to confer, it was her decision alone. She stuffed the object into her handbag before putting his bag back up next to hers and then waited, and waited.

He must be doing a number two, she thought, *maybe it was his illness.* She didn't want to dwell on the details.

He had been gone an age, but she was still minding his bag so she was confident he would be back.

Suddenly there was an announcement that the train would shortly be stopping in Newcastle. She tried to call Toby but they were in a tunnel and she had no signal.

The train pulled into Newcastle station. "Shit," she said aloud.

A man who was sitting behind her shouted in a Scottish accent, "Is that your bag love?"

"No," she mumbled trying to stay calm.

"It's that Muslim fellas, where the fuck is he?"

"Calm down, it's fine, he's only gone to the loo."

"He's been gone ages, call the guard!" a woman yelled, as other passengers started to take notice.

The doors opened, there was no sign of Mo.

"There might be a bomb in it!" the woman screamed.

"Calm down, there's no bomb in it."

"How do you know?"

"Because I looked in it," Clare said firmly and truthfully.

There was pause before the women asked her why she looked in the bag.

"I'm an off duty policewoman, I didn't trust him." Claire half lied as the train pulled away. She thought she caught a glimpse of Toby lurking by a kiosk. *Shit, Toby,* she thought.

Just then Mo came bursting into the carriage shouting, "Shit, I've missed my stop!"

"We thought you'd left your bag you idiot," the Scottish women scolded him.

"We nearly called the bomb squad Mo. Where on earth have you been? What you going to do now?"

He sat down covered in sweat and water from the tap. "I bloody fell asleep on the loo Claire, it's my illness. Shit, I'll have to get a train back from Edinburgh, how long is it till we get there?"

"About an hour and a half," Claire informed him.

They both sensed the hostile atmosphere in the carriage. Claire stood up and beckoned Mo. "Come with me Mo, best move to a different carriage."

He took his bag and followed her up the aisle.

"Idiot," they heard behind them.

He followed her to the first class compartment she pointed to Toby's vacant seat. She sat opposite and held up a finger and mouthed, "One minute."

She saw three missed calls from poor old Toby, she called him back. "Hi."

"Where are you?"

"On route to Edinburgh."

"You have company?"

"Yes."

"You okay?"

"I'm fine, in first class, you ok?"

"I'm good, shall I get the next train? It's in forty minutes."

"Good idea."

"Christine is waiting for you with cavalry at the station, if needed."

"Great, be in touch."

Toby cursed as the rain started to sheet down, he was freezing his nuts off whilst a suspected terrorist was in his first class seat.

Mo realised how close he'd come to being arrested for causing a bomb scare. In hindsight the Newcastle story was stupid but he recalled Alice's warning, trust no one. Thank god he decided to entrust his friend with Micky's gun. If someone had looked in the bag, that could have been five years inside.

Claire decided it was time to make a move, she removed her hair band and let her impossibly blonde hair loose, shaking her head.

She stared at Mo, he noticed just how blue her eyes were.

"You're not an interior designer are you Claire?"

Mo got in first, briefly unsettling her but she was the Ice Queen, she quickly composed herself.

"No I'm not Mo, most interior designers are the bored wives of rich husbands." She smiled before returning to her icy stare. "And you are not on your way to an interview in Newcastle, are you Mo?"

He shook his head.

"You're on your way to meet Alice, your sponsor?"

Mo looked upset, she thought she detected a tear in his eye.

He nodded. "I am, if you're telling me Alice has done something wrong, I won't believe it."

"No Mo, I'm not at all worried about Alice, I've got my eye on you."

"You're police?"

"No Mo, it's more serious than that."

"The conference centre?"

"Not my main issue but there are one or two people I know, serious people, very upset about that."

"It was a batch of bad prawns, it was bad luck. I had no idea they were important people."

"Do you know who they were, the people who got sick?"

"No, but I know they were important clients, I lost my job, they got better."

"Ok Mo, tell me about the Imam."

Mo looked confused. "What Imam?"

"The Imam that visited you in hospital."

"Oh that nutter. He's dead you know, the poor nutter was killed in that mosque attack."

"Yes I know, why do you call him a nutter?"

"How do you know I met him?"

"Because he was on our watch list and because he met you, you are now on our watch list and I'm giving you a unique chance to come off it."

"You're MI5?"

"Something like that."

"Have you got the power to arrest me Claire, should I have a solicitor?"

She leaned forward and tied her hair back into a bun. "Mo, I have the power to do a lot more than arrest you. I must warn you there is a small army waiting at Edinburgh Station, I can hand you over to them or, if I'm happy with your answers between now and when we arrive, I will deliver you to Alice personally."

The chef stared at Clare considering his options. "I think I met one of your colleagues yesterday, he mentioned Scott, that is why I'm going to see Alice, I was shocked to hear his name after all these years."

"And that's why we're on our way to meet Alice as well, we planned to visit her at her home in the Shetlands."

"But why now, why bring Scott up now?"

"Because you are a puzzle to us Mo and your relationship with Scott is a big piece which we want to understand."

"So watch the documentary, I told your colleague, watch the documentary."

"I'd like to Mo but I'm trying to locate the elusive tape, we thought Alice might have it." She told him about the unedited tapes she saw and how they'd been recorded over.

"Here, problem solved, he opened his bag and rampaged through the contents.

"Fuck it's gone!" he yelled. He saw Claire holding it up. "You took it from my bag!"

"It's my job Mo, you offering it to me has been duly noted, thank you."

Mo was flushed with relief he didn't bring the gun.

"Your honesty deserves mine, Mo. I'm under a lot of pressure from the organisers of that conference, they want blood and I want to make sure they get the right blood. You called the Imam a nutter, why?"

"Aren't they all, bloody religious nutters."

"Why did he visit you?"

"You tell me, I never invited him, he just turned up because I was Muslim and was ill."

"I see, what did he say?"

"What didn't he say. he went on and on about how I had lost my way and I needed to find my religion again before I died."

"Does that make him a nutter?"

"No, but on his second visit he told me I had a unique opportunity to do my duty and he mentioned…" Mo hesitated. "He talked about jihad."

"What about jihad?"

"It was as if he was trying to get a reaction from me, testing me."

"What was your reply Mo?"

"I told him to fuck off and don't come back, then I heard he was killed by another nutter. I was sad but not too disappointed to be honest."

"Ok Mo, I have one last issue." Claire sat back and paused for a second. "What the fuck are you and your mates from the Good Vibes Club up to?"

"What mates?" he replied, feeling hot.

She leaned forward again. "Now listen Mo I believe you have been very honest with me thus far but when I say you're on the watch list I mean we know when you take a shit, we know when you hang around Golden Square. Now tell me about your plot to poison the Minister of Health and who's going to give you fifteen grand."

Mo was confused, he hadn't planned to poison the minister, though he'd like to give him a piece of his mind about Brenda's trial.

"You've lost me Claire, I won't say another word until I have a solicitor."

Claire sent a short text then gave Mo that stare again. "Don't fuck with me Mo, we've got you three musketeers on tape. We will be in Edinburgh in half an hour or so, think very carefully about your options."

Mo sat in silence eyeballing Claire, she returned the stare for several minutes until she got a message. She glanced at her phone and then out the window. She gestured with her eyes for him to do the same. A police helicopter was serenading the train.

"I'm in big trouble aren't I Claire?" he broke the silence.

"Depends on the next fifteen minutes Mo."

He thought about his uncle slapping him when he questioned God and then in his late teens beating him senseless for backing down in an argument with a woman. He looked at Claire. *She's played me, she's enjoyed playing with me, the fucking arrogant bitch.* If only he had that gun, he'd put her to sleep, he thought.

Claire looked at her watch. "I must be honest with you Mo, getting back to the small matter of your freedom. The minister will not be attending the hospital, he will be under the weather that day so no need to plot and plan now."

Mo took a deep breath before confessing. "I wasn't going to poison the minister Claire, it was someone else."

* * *

CHRISTINE SAW THE Ice Queen striding towards her with an air of triumph, followed by the chef, dishevelled and defeated.

"Christine." Claire greeted her with a formal handshake.

"Good journey boss?"

"Interesting."

"Follow me boss, there's a car waiting."

Mo shuffled behind the two women tired and confused. Christine introduced the driver, Tommy, who opened the back doors. Claire and Mo climbed in.

"Where to boss?"

"Drop Mo off at the cottage where Alice is waiting first, then take me to the hotel where I'll wait whilst you go and collect Toby from the station."

"Oh yes Toby, I hear he's bringing up the rear," Christine laughed.

The journey to the rented cottage just outside Livingstone was spent in silence. They pulled up outside the cottage, Christine handed Claire a tag, Claire placed it around Mo's ankle. They then got out and escorted Mo to the front door.

"Ok Mo, hope your reunion goes well, we will pick you up midday tomorrow, don't forget our deal," Claire said.

She shook his hand, he nodded, turned and knocked on the door.

22

THE DINNER PARTY

TINA NEEDED A drink. She cursed as she headed for the train home. Notwithstanding the lack of staff, she couldn't get the Brenda business out of head. She seriously needed company, and a second opinion.

She called Jed but he was starting two night shifts, he promised a big night out Saturday instead. She was about to phone her father but that would probably go badly so she made a snap decision and ended up sending a message to Freddie: *Bad day, need to bore somebody. Will be in World's End 6.30.*

She concealed as much of her uniform as possible with her black leather jacket and found a seat in a discreet alcove in the cavernous pub. She downed half of her pint in seconds and played with her phone whilst she waited. At seven she was well into her second pint, despite having started a strict diet recently. *This fecking job*, she thought.

She received a message from Freddie, she looked at it tentatively, expecting another rejection. *In pub, where art thou? x.* She quickly text back: *In pub, in the bowels!! x.*

A few minutes later Freddie emerged with a two pints of Guinness. "Happy New Year!" she bellowed, despite it being mid-April.

"And Happy New Year to you Tina."

They kissed and clinked glasses.

She told him the whole story starting with the hundred pounds Mo left her, up to Brenda's surprise.

"So your man Mo is an out of work chef?" he confirmed.

"Yep."

"You definitely sure it was him?"

"It figures, but there's something else I should tell you, I found a load of pay as you go SIM cards when he left. What's that about?"

"Sounds dodgy, what did you do with them?"

"I threw them away but it's played on my mind."

"Well the advice you gave Brenda seems to have worked, seeing as she phoned you to say her other half accepted her story. How much would the trial drugs cost out of interest?"

"A lot more than that," Tina sighed. "There is another possibility, he's a fellow patient, Micky, he's a professional gambler. I don't think he's the kind of man to give his money away but he's gone a bit soft since he became a grandfather."

"Maybe you should just ask them?"

"Maybe I should."

Freddie took a gulp of his drink. "And how's your love life?"

"Well that's another story…" Tina related the whole fireman episode.

"Simple test Tina," Freddie responded after hearing her predicament.

"Really Freddie?"

"Yep, next time you're in his bedroom tell him it's your secret fantasy to have sex with a man dressed only in his helmet, and axe of course!"

"Freddie you're a genius! I'm getting you another pint."

* * *

DENNIS RETURNED FROM his shopping run with a sense of dread. Yes he was still euphoric over the unexpected turn of events but the atmosphere at home was difficult to say the least. *How much crying could a woman do for god's sake?*

He opened the front door and carried the two heavy bags to the kitchen, where he was met with the first of two surprises. Sandra was up, dressed and cooking up a storm. "Sandra?"

"Hello Den. I'm cooking dinner, we have a guest."

He noticed she had made an effort with hair and makeup and had done an excellent job of concealing forty-eight hours of wailing and gnashing.

"Go into the dining room, someone wants to meet you."

The second surprise was much bigger.

"Hi Dennis."

Dennis stared at the dinner guest in disbelief, he noticed the dining table had been set out for three people. The surprise guest held out his hand, Sandra entered the room with a bottle of Prosecco.

"I know this is awkward but Sandra and I thought it best to have a clear the air meeting."

Dennis gave Raymond a reluctant hand shake.

"Sit, I'll get the starters," Sandra insisted.

The two men sat opposite each other at the four seater table. Dennis was slightly overwhelmed by Raymond's aftershave. *He stinks of the suburbs*, he thought.

"How's your health Dennis?"

Dennis didn't reply. He knew he looked like shit. He stared at Raymond's trendy hairstyle and well-groomed goatee beard, smart white shirt and tailored trousers. He could see his reflection in his wife's lover's shoes. *Hang on, ex-lover*, he corrected himself. He looked at the best cutlery she'd placed out. He assumed fish was the main course. Could he kill someone with a fish knife, he doubted it. If only she'd cooked steak.

He still hadn't uttered a word when Sandra returned with the small plates of avocado filled with prawns. *Fucking smothered in a pink 1970s sauce*, Dennis thought.

She placed the starters on the table. "I'll do the honours," Raymond said as he opened the fizz and poured.

Dennis noticed how steady his hand was considering the situation.

"So," Sandra stated with a mouth full of food, "we need to clear the air, none of us will benefit from the recent atmosphere."

"Agreed," Raymond mumbled.

Dennis looked at his starter and the glass of Prosecco. *This is like fucking 'Annabelle's party', this is a nightmare*, he thought. *Never mind steak knives, I'll go and get that new rake and impale the both of them*. He imagined doing his wife first, he would then apologise profusely to her lover, ex-lover, about the embarrassing choice of starter, before killing him.

"What's for the main course?" Dennis spoke for the first time, causing bewildered glances between the other two.

"Salmon en croute, why?" Sandra asked.

"Fish and fish," Dennis chided her.

She was about to snap at him but Raymond intervened. "We thought a frank civilised conversation would be helpful to all three of us Dennis."

"What veg have you done with the salmon?" Dennis asked his wife, ignoring Raymond

"New potatoes, asparagus spears and baby carrots," she confirmed.

"Good combination Sandra. Sorry Raymond, you were saying?" Dennis asked calmly.

"We need to be frank with each other Dennis."

Dennis took a mouthful of his starter. "A bit too 1970s for me, avocado's nice and ripe though, I must say. Anyway, Raymond, I thought you'd been a naughty boy?"

Raymond wasn't sure which misdemeanour Dennis was referring too. But he took a chance. "I put my hands up, I messed up, I've confessed everything to Sandra and apologised profusely," he took Sandra's hand, "and Sandra's forgiven me."

Dennis watched them smile at each other. *Where's Micky? Where's Mo?* he wondered. A bullet, poison, he didn't care which at this point. "What happens now then?" he enquired.

Sandra and Raymond looked at each other for reassurance for a few seconds, she took a large swig of her fizz, emptying her glass. "Raymond is moving in Den."

Dennis couldn't recall the last time she called him Den, suddenly he was Den again. "Moving in where?"

"Here Den."

Raymond refilled her glass.

"May I ask how that's going to work?" the Professor asked.

"We've talked this through Dennis, Sandra and me. I want to be completely upfront with you. I'm going to rent my house out and move in here. I'm going to sell the Porches and give you the proceeds as compensation for the inconvenience caused. I'm talking around fifty grand Dennis. Do with it what you want mate, nice deposit on a flat, five star holiday?"

"It would be very helpful for the time you've got left Den," Sandra added.

"And supposing I don't want to move out?"

"It's perfectly up to you Den."

"And supposing I don't want him moving in?"

"I'm sorry Den, we've made a decision, Raymond is moving in today. I best go and check on the main course."

There was an uncomfortable silence whilst Sandra cleaned the plates and disappeared to the kitchen before Raymond piped up, "I know this is difficult for you Dennis, it's rather embarrassing I know, but I'm sure we can make this work and I want you to know that when…when you've gone I'll take good care of her."

Dennis thought about Sandra standing at the end of the bed with her stockings on. "Have you got green fingers Raymond?"

"Pardon."

"Are you any good in the garden?"

"Not bad mate, I tinker, why?"

"Because after I'm gone I won't be worried about Sandra, but I'd like the garden maintained to my high standards."

Raymond was hoping Sandra would return and help him out. "Come on Dennis, you don't mean that mate."

"Oh yes I do, my sons won't be interested and Sandra won't be around to look after it."

"I'm sorry Dennis, what do you mean mate?"

The Professor looked Raymond in the eye. "Move in, sell your fucking fancy cars, it doesn't matter to me. Enjoy my wife, her fit body, her fucking prehistoric cooking while you can because she's going to be on a fucking slab long before me matey."

23

THE SLEEPOVER

TOBY WAS MIGHTILY relieved to find Christine waiting for him at the station. "That was not the best day I've ever had Chris, I can tell you."

"It's not over yet, the boss is waiting for us in the hotel, I don't think she's planning a night on the town." Christine bigged up their driver Terry, explaining he'd not only organised the helicopter and back up troops but, at the bosses request, sourced an electric tag and VHS video recorder within an hour. Toby wondered just what he'd missed on the epic journey.

Christine received a message from the Ice Queen and related the info to the others. "Blimey O'Reilly, the boss has suggested we freshen up and meet in the hotel restaurant in an hour. I can quote her, 'everyone must be thirsty and hungry'. Wow she does have a soul after all. You're welcome to join us as well Terry."

"That's very kind but I'm sorted thanks. Tell your boss if there's anything you need I'll be five minutes away."

Toby reflected on what a bloody frustrating day he'd had and now he was facing a working dinner for sure.

* * *

"What exactly have they asked you about Scott and why?" Alice asked Mo whilst pouring her second glass of wine.

Mo shrugged, "Well, my phone was stolen by the CIA who passed it to the British anti-terror unit at Paddington Green, where I was invited to pick it up. The guy there casually asks me how Scott is-"

"Is?" Alice interrupted.

"Exactly."

"Did you correct him Mo?"

"Sort of, but he panicked me, which is why I contacted you. Then I'm joined on the train by this bitch from MI5."

"And she wanted to know about Scott?"

"Yes, but only so she could know about me."

"Why you, have you done something wrong Mo?"

"Not yet, but everything started with some clients getting food poisoning at a conference I catered for, turns out these were very important clients." He went on to explain everything that had happened since, regarding the Imam and the conversation with the Ice Queen, though he left out the bit about the business with the Minister of Health.

"So you gave her the tape I sent you?"

"Yes, I'm hoping by the time she picks me up tomorrow she would have seen it and that will be the end of the matter."

"What did you mean by 'not yet' Mo?"

* * *

TOBY HAD SPENT an unnatural amount of time thinking about the possibilities of a night away with his boss, he hadn't factored in sharing a twin room with Christine. He liked her a lot as colleague and a person. She was a great drinking partner down the Red Lion. She could laugh at herself because she was one of the lads. She'd recently announced her engagement to her partner Charlotte, who was a civil servant in the foreign office. Toby had been earmarked to make a speech at their wedding, Christine said he could use all the big five syllable words he liked.

Toby was OCD when it came to tidiness and appearance, Christine was the polar opposite. She'd already annoyed him by emptying her stuff over her bed to change into an outfit he thought was more suitable for gardening.

They sat at the table their boss had booked, making sure they were a few minutes early. She, as expected, was dead on time. Neither recognised her as she entered the bar area of the restaurant. Toby and Christine exchanged surprised glances as they surveyed her outfit. A low cut light blue sleeveless top and the tight short black skirt she'd entertained Myerson in. She was chatting to the maître d' and pointing to their table.

"Look at those heels, she's wearing high heels," Christine observed.

"And a pearl necklace," Toby mumbled, trying to look unfazed.

"I would," Christine whispered.

"Would what?" he replied, averting his gaze from his boss.

"Give her one," Christine confirmed.

"Christine!" Toby chortled.

"Are you telling me Toby you wouldn't given half a chance?"

Their conversation was cut short as their boss headed to their discreet table. "I've just ordered some Prosecco, hope that's ok?" Claire announced.

"I'm more of a beer girl to be honest boss," Christine stated.

"No problem Chris. What about you Toby? Good to see you at last," she laughed.

"Prosecco is good for me Claire."

"Ok, let's order, I'm famished." She smiled at the maître d' who was over in a shot to get everything organised.

"OK, let's get work out the way." Claire gave edited highlights of her conversation with the chef. "Finally, I cut a deal with him."

"A deal?" Toby chipped in.

"Yes, I gave him permission to meet his sponsor, sort himself out, on the condition he wears a tag. Terry will keep an eye on things. In the meantime we watch the tape. We pick him up midday tomorrow and he gives us what we need to know on the train back to London. We decide by Watford what we do with him. That's it."

"Sounds like a plan boss." Christine was impressed.

"When do we watch the tape Claire?" Toby enquired.

"Breakfast, eight sharp in my room tomorrow, and a film show. That ok? It's been to long a day, enough of work, here comes our drinks."

Christine and Toby nodded agreement.

She definitely has boobs, Toby thought, looking at her tight silk top. The colour matched her eyes exactly.

* * *

DENNIS SAT WATCHING the TV whilst Raymond struggled with a large suitcase up the stairs.

Sandra brought him in a coffee. "What did you think of the salmon en croute Den?" she asked nonchalantly.

"Not bad," he lied. He thought the meal was a joke.

"I'll do you lamb chops tomorrow. Now I'm retired I'm enjoying cooking again. Raymond loves his lamb chops."

Dennis stared at the crap on TV not really concentrating on it.

"I think I'll turn in now, see you in the morning." She leaned down and kissed him on the cheek. "Everything will turn out ok Den, I'm sure. This way there are no more lies, no more deceit, everything out in the open."

He watched her leave the room and disappear up the stairs. He sent a text to Mo: *Where are you? Need to talk.*

He realised he was watching a reality show, he hated reality shows, *Fucking chavs, fucking suburban chavs*, he thought. He took to staring at the ceiling instead. His head was pounding, was it the stress or his tumour, possibly both.

He took his cup into the kitchen and looked at the carving knives in the wooden rack. He'd been down this road before. *Fuck it*, he thought, he'd just cut her throat and let loverboy do his worst. He was past caring, he'd be dead soon so he might as well enjoy his last days. Fuck the final trip to the Lake District he was planning after the Minister of Health had visited the Good Poison Club. He'd been there enough. The look on Raymond's face as he slaughtered his lover would beat Lake Coniston any day of the week.

Once again he found himself climbing the stairs with murder on his mind. He got to the bedroom, his bedroom. He didn't need to put his ear to the door, he could hear everything. First the loud continuous thumping of solid oak against concrete as the headboard smashed repetitively against the wall, then he heard his wife's primal screams as she climaxed.

He plunged the knife into the door and turned the handle before entering the bedroom.

The bedside light was on, illuminating Raymond's plump backside making one last heroic thrust as he collapsed onto Sandra who saw her husband opening a wardrobe door searching for his pyjamas.

"Dennis!" she screamed. "What are you doing for Christ's sake!"

Raymond rolled off and slid under the duvet.

Dennis calmly took off his clothes in front of them and put his maroon pyjamas on. "I'm just going to clean my teeth and then I'm going to sleep in my bed."

Dennis removed the knife from the door and went to the bathroom. He returned five minutes later to his bedroom, the bed was empty. He placed the knife in his bedside cupboard and climbed in. He lay staring at the two large designer cases in the corner of the room and sobbed like a baby.

* * *

CLAIRE ORDERED ANOTHER bottle of Prosecco, Christine was now indulging in the fizzy stuff. "I would have loved to see your face when you realised we were still on the train," Claire laughed at Toby's expense.

"What irked me was that the bloody chef was sitting in my first class seat," Toby protested.

The three engaged in trivial chit chat over desert.

After their dishes were taken away Christine winked at Toby and decided to shoot from the hip. "So boss, is there any special person in your life?"

Claire toyed with her drink. "No Chris, no one special, not enough time."

"Apart from Myerson of course," Toby chanced his arm.

Claire glared at Toby.

Shit, he thought, *just as she was loosening up for the first time he'd gone too far.*

She downed the whole glass before answering. "In his dreams."

Toby and Christine didn't know where to take the conversation next. Their boss refilled their glasses. "You probably wonder why I have that American shit in my pocket."

"It has been on my mind Claire."

"Well, I'm sorry guys, what happens in Vegas stays in Vegas. If I told you I'd have to kill you." She smiled. "What about you Toby? You must have a posse of Made in Chelsea types chasing you with those chiselled features and that Sloane Square accent."

Claire put Toby on the back foot. "Like you Claire there isn't enough time for fun, I catch up with an old girlfriend from uni now and again but, like Chrissy's partner, she's in the foreign office. She's stationed in Chile so there's quite a few miles between us." Toby confessed. "Must just pop to the loo, talk about me while I'm gone." Toby kicked his chair and staggered off feeling more than merry.

"He's a good hound is Toby but like most men I'm around he's such a pathetic wanker," Claire whispered, causing Christine to spit her drink out.

"That's so funny boss. Can I ask you a personal question?"

"As long as it doesn't involve any CIA station chiefs."

"Are you gay?"

Claire laughed and played with her hair. "Why do you ask?"

"Well tonight's the first night I've seen you let you let your hair down in two years of working with you, I was just wondering."

"Well, between you and me, I've had a dabble a couple of times. I'm not ruling it out but I do like a good shag now and again. For god's sake don't tell Toby, he'll literally combust!"

"You think he fancies you boss?"

"He doesn't so much fancy the person I am at work, you know, in my sexless suit, no makeup etc., he fancies what I could be if let my hair down. They all do Christine, Toby, Craig, Mittall, even Achtar, Myerson and I dare say, Sir Martin. The more unattainable I am the more they want me, it's all a ruse, a game, that's why I'm boss Christine. Here comes Toby, watch me blow his mind."

"What you going to say boss?"

"Trust me just play along, believe me you are about to see a man blow his gasket."

"You can stop talking about me now ladies," Toby chuckled.

"Don't flatter yourself Toby, we were just sorting the sleeping arrangements. Christine is going to sleep in my room, you can have your room to yourself." Claire put her hand on Christine's thigh.

Toby thought he might die there and then.

* * *

MO TOYED WITH his croissant, he looked at the two empty wine bottles that Alice had consumed sitting by the bin. "I'm sorry Alice."

"What for?"

"Causing you all this grief."

"It's not your fault Mo, life is just shit sometimes. But it's great to see you, I'm sure all will be fine."

Mo sipped his fresh orange juice wondering if Claire had seen the tape yet. "I lied to you Alice," he confessed.

"About what?"

"About the conference, the food poisoning."

"What about it? You said it was genuine."

"Yep, and that's what I told that MI5 bitch, but I was lying. I caused the food poisoning, I added something."

"Oh shit Mo, what was it?"

"Just a little cocktail my grandfather taught me to make, never going to kill anybody, just slow them down for a day or two."

"Did you know who you were poisoning Mo? Tell me the truth."

"No, I just wanted to fuck up the reputation of the centre after the petty online comments. Honestly I had no idea they were so important."

"You once told me your family's poison recipes were untraceable."

"They were back in the eighties but science has moved on since then, it's only a matter of time before someone in some lab somewhere finds a fly in the ointment!"

"Oh dear Mo, what are you going to do?"

"Claire, the MI5 woman, told me that the Americans were out to get me and that if I cooperated with her she'd sort everything out."

"A minute ago you were calling her a bitch Mo. What about disappearing for a while? I could help you."

"Again," Mo laughed, "you've done enough for me Alice. I owe you and Scott everything. There's nowhere to hide from Clare." He looked down at his tag.

"I'm sure we can sort that somehow Mo."

"Maybe Alice, but that Claire would soon track me down. I don't think she's the kind of person you can run away from."

They were interrupted by a knock on the door. "They're early, I thought you said they are collecting you at midday," Alice stated.

"Change of plan maybe," Mo suggested, as he went to peer through the closed curtain. He saw what looked like a courier van parked outside. "It's a delivery I think Alice."

Alice went and opened the door, a man stood smiling holding a small package. "Special delivery for Mohamed Zaheer madam, sign here please."

Alice was concerned by the courier's accent, it was forced, almost Hollywood.

"Hang on I'll get him to sign himself."

She caught a glimpse of the back door of the van opening, she saw a figure climbing out in a black balaclava. She turned anxiously into the house, slamming the front door shut behind her. "Run Mo! Run!" she yelled, pointing to the back door.

24

THE TAG

CLAIRE SAT UP and stretched. "Well, I must say I thoroughly enjoyed that."

Christine was curled up in the foetal position on the other side of the bed, she had the mother of all hangovers. She watched through blurry eyes as Claire jumped out of bed naked. *A bit to skinny for my taste but I definitely would*, she thought.

"Enjoyed what boss?" Christine queried as she watched her boss get dressed into a jogging bottoms and a tight running vest.

"The thought of Toby tossing and turning next door."

"A lot of tossing I should think boss."

"Ha yep, he'll probably be cross eyed this morning. I'm off for a run Chris, could you get everything organised for our working breakfast please?"

"Will do boss." She watched Claire check her watch and leave the room. *Wonder Woman*, she thought, reaching for the pain killers.

* * *

THE WARNING ALARM on their app went off simultaneously. It had been set to warn them if the chef and his tag strayed more than a hundred meters from the hired cottage. Claire was some fifteen minutes, fast jog, from the hotel. She stopped to see what caused her phone to vibrate against her upper arm. "Shit!" she said aloud and started to sprint towards the hotel.

Terry, their driver, was parked up at a café five minutes drive from the hotel, he left his cooked breakfast realising he'd be needed right away.

Toby banged on Christine's door. "Where's Clare?" he bellowed.

"She's gone for a jog. I know, I know, I got the alarm!"

"Have you called her? Where's Terry?" Toby was in panic mode, not helped by his massive hangover.

Christine received a text from Terry, he'd meet them outside in five minutes.

Claire sprinted along the rush hour streets, sheeting rain lashing her face. *What an idiot,* she thought, he'd know they'd be tracking him, they had a deal. *Which bit had he lied about? What hadn't he told her?*

Christine and Toby jumped in the back of Terry's car. "Where's the boss?" he asked.

"Jogging, she'd have got the warning. Look, here she comes now."

Christine nodded to a very wet begrudged Claire as she dodged between the traffic across the busy road. She jumped in the front passenger seat, Terry put on a siren and whizzed off down roads only a native would know. "What do you reckon boss?" Christine asked.

"Not sure, where is he now Toby?"

Toby was tracking the tag on his phone. "Seems to be moving through a wooded area."

"Want the helicopter up there boss?" Terry added.

"Not yet Terry, only if he takes the tag off."

"What about your deal?" Toby asked and immediately regretted it as Claire turned round and gave him the thousand yard stare.

"He's still tagged, he knows we will be following him, let's not rush to conclusions."

"Am I following your man or are we going to the cottage?" Terry enquired.

Claire hesitated, Christine made the decision for her. "I would suggest the cottage first boss, Alice isn't in any shape or age to do a runner, she's got a walking stick for Christ's sake."

Claire agreed and twenty minutes later they pulled up outside the cottage. "Christine you've met Alice, you come with me. Wait here lads."

Toby watched the Ice Queen stride purposefully towards the cottage, despite the situation he was transfixed by her posterior in her tight jogging bottoms. He wasn't so impressed with Christine's ill fitting jeans and builder's bum.

Claire's phone rang, she stopped in her tracks, it was Sir Martin. She put a restraining arm on Christine's and showed her the name on her phone.

"Fuck," Christine mouthed.

"Sir," Claire answered.

"Where are you Claire?"

"Edinburgh, sir."

"I know that Claire, where exactly?"

"At the sponsors hired cottage, there's a complication sir."

"I know Claire."

Claire looked at Christine perplexed.

"Listen carefully Claire, do exactly as I say."

"Ok sir."

"I've had a call from Myerson."

"Myerson?"

"Yes, Myerson, he claims they have absolute proof the cyber conference food was tampered with."

"The yanks are after the chef then sir?"

"Yes, they've just made a house call but he was most concerned you get there ASAP, he said there's a key under the doormat."

She pointed to the doormat and Christine looked under it finding the key, she gave a thumbs up. "Got it sir."

"Ok, you'll find the old lady tied up."

Claire gestured for Christine to open the door. "We are going in now sir, entering the living room."

"Good morning girls," Alice greeted them.

"Found her sir."

Christine started to untie Alice, Claire noticed they'd left one hand free and a bottle of water and cheese roll next to her.

"She's fine sir, shall we go after the chef sir?"

"No, Claire. Myerson's crew are armed and on his tail but I don't think they can track his tag, unless they get hold of your phones of course. I suggest you disable the app on your team's phones. Debrief the old lady and come back to me with an update."

"Will do sir."

"And Claire, no heroics. You know what those yanks are like we don't want any friendly fire."

Claire sprang into action, instructing the team to disable the tracking app. She invited Toby in whilst Christine made Alice a cup of tea. Alice told them about the delivery van, how she realised they were bogus and spoke Scottish with a Hollywood accent. She managed to warn Mo, who legged out the back door. "I went back to the front door and told the man Mohamed would be down in a minute he was just in the loo."

"Quick thinking Alice," Toby chipped in.

"I closed the door again but they must have got suspicious, they started banging on the door. I opened it and there were two armed men dressed head to foot in black, balaclavas, the lot, carrying machine guns. They ran past me and started searching the cottage. I didn't want to lose my deposit so I told the courier who seemed to be directing operations that Mo had skipped out the back. They were very apologetic about tying me up and made sure they were gentle with me. The leader said they were American and if I contact the embassy I will be compensated for any inconvenience caused. They also said you'd be along shortly so I wasn't too bothered. But what about poor Mo?"

"Is there anything he told you that might be helpful to us Alice?" Toby asked.

"No he told me all about his phone and then his conversation with you," she nodded at Claire, who went and kneeled in front of Alice and took her hands.

"Are you sure Alice?"

"I'm sure. You've seen the tape, the documentary?"

Claire looked around guiltily at Toby and then turned back to Alice. "We were about to all watch it but then all this happened. The Americans want to arrest Mo because they believe he poisoned some very important people, it's vital we find him before they do Alice."

There was a pause in the conversation, Claire checked her phone. She could see he was moving quite fast, probably in some kind of vehicle, hopefully a bus and not a van.

"He did," Alice suddenly announced.

"Did what?" Toby enquired.

"He told me he poisoned them, but he didn't want to kill them, only upset the reputation of the conference centre."

"I believe you Alice." Claire squeezed her hands reassuringly. "Ok, Christine you wait here with Alice, I'm going to arrange for you both to be picked up and taken back to the hotel. Toby and I will jump in with Terry and see if we can get one over on the yanks."

"He's on a bus to Edinburgh I reckon," Claire proclaimed, as they sat in the back of the car. "He knows the yanks are not going to be playing James Bond in the centre of town."

"I think I know the bus route boss," Terry interrupted. "I reckon I can intercept it in five minutes."

"Go for it," Claire ordered.

He put his foot down and made it in four minutes, they were right behind the bus.

"Shall we intercept at the next bus stop Claire?" Toby suggested.

"No, it's too open round here, he's going to the bus station I'm sure." She looked at her app. "Keep a discrete distance in case he jumps off before."

They slowed down at four more stops, they were relieved the bus was now in heavy traffic in the city centre. The last two stops seemed to take forever, Claire was tempted to phone Mo but knew the Americans could possibly be tracking it. *If he's clever he would have destroyed it*, she thought. The bus reached the terminus and they exited the vehicle. Terry waited at the front doors, Claire and Toby the rear.

They watched the half full bus empty with no sign of their chef.

Terry showed the driver his accreditation and boarded the bus, the other two stayed put. He searched every seat till he reached the rear seat. "Boss!" he shouted, Claire and Toby jumped on and joined him staring at a discarded tag under a seat.

"Shit, the yanks must have him," Toby said.

"Not necessarily," Claire stated. "He might have removed it himself, I reckon he might have shaken us all off."

"Is that a good thing boss?" Terry asked.

"Who knows," she shrugged, "you get your colleagues out there, Toby and me will join the others back at the hotel, we've got a film to watch."

* * *

OVER IN ISLINGTON, the Professor hardly slept a wink. His headache was worse and he was burning hot so he decided he'd make an emergency appointment at the doctors after breakfast. He fancied a cold shower, he clambered out of bed, his pyjamas wet through with sweat. He shuffled down the corridor towards the bathroom but stopped in his tracks as he heard singing and the sound of the shower.

Sandra emerged from the second bedroom naked. "Sorry Den, thought you would be up by now. Raymond won't be long, why don't you pop down and get some breakfast ready."

He made his way downstairs without complaint and made himself a cup of coffee. He had no appetite but thought he'd try a slice of toast. Raymond emerged a few minutes later wearing a white towelling bathrobe with his initials RY emblazoned on it in gold letters.

Dennis could see he worked out, he hadn't noticed how tall he was before, at least six two he guessed. "What's for breakfast Dennis? I'm starving."

Dennis sat at the breakfast bar eating his toast. "Fuck you," he mumbled with his mouth full.

Raymond walked over to him and, without warning, rabbit punched him in his kidney. In a mixture of pain and shock the Professor collapsed to the marble tiled floor. He coughed up some sick.

Raymond sat on the vacated bar stool towering over the prostrate figure. "Now listen to me Dennis, Sandra and I have tried to be civil with you. She's told me all about your misdemeanour, you're lucky she didn't throw you out years ago. Hopefully you'll be dead soon, until then either move out or show some respect. I shall be fucking your wife in your bed tonight and every night, except Thursdays. You will be sleeping in the second bedroom. And lastly, when we ask for breakfast you will fucking well sort it."

Dennis writhed on the floor not quite believing this new reality. He tried to nod but couldn't function for the agony he was in. Raymond then jumped off the stool and kicked him in his other side.

Dennis screamed.

Raymond got on all fours and put has face against the poor wretch. "I'm going upstairs to give you missus the kind of treatment you should be providing you pathetic little wanker. This little episode stays between us ok."

Raymond picked the Professor up and threw him over his shoulder, he couldn't believe how light he was. He opened the kitchen door and carried him down the garden to the Professor's beloved greenhouse. He placed him on the floor. "You stay here till we've gone for lunch, one peep out of you I'm going to give you another dig."

After a few minutes Dennis sat up and leaned against a plant pot. He lifted his shirt, his side was black. He fumbled for his phone and rang Mo but there was no answer. He phoned Micky.

"Professor, you're a bit early."

"You've got to help me," Dennis pleaded. "I'll pay you more, anything, you've got to help me!"

* * *

MICKY WAS IMPRESSED with the Professor's front door, 'proper Islington', no suburban porch and paved front garden here. He rang the bell and waited, then gave a hard knock, but no reply. He sighed impatiently before calling him. "Where are you mate?"

"Come round the back, I'm in the greenhouse, I can't get up."

Mystified he made his way down the side passage and through the garden. *Nice*, he thought, *very bohemian*. He opened the greenhouse door and there was Dennis lying on the floor holding his side, his face twisted with pain.

"Fucking hell mate what happened to you? Come on let's get you inside."

He helped him to his feet and led him gently to the back door, through the kitchen and into the living room, placing him in his armchair. "Shall I put the kettle on mate?"

"No, just a glass of water please."

Micky obliged and on returning to the living room saw Dennis inspecting his heavily bruised side. "Shit Professor, did you fall?"

"No, he punched me."

"Who punched you?"

"Raymond."

"Raymond?"

"Yes, Raymond, my wife's lover."

"I thought he was history mate."

"He's moved in."

"What do you mean he's moved in?"

Dennis told him about recent events concluding with the punch to his kidney and the parting kick.

"Fuck me mate, you poor bastard," Micky said.

"Where's Mo?" Dennis asked.

"Edinburgh, visiting an old friend, you're stuck with me mate."

"When can you kill them?"

"Hang on mate, I'm a granddad now, I've got a new perspective on life. I'm leaving this to Mo."

"When's he back?"

"Fuck knows."

"How much do you want, how much extra to kill them today?"

"Sorry mate, I've got other issues to worry about."

"The gun!" Dennis shouted. "Your gun, I will buy it off you now, how much?"

"I'd be only too pleased to sell it to you but Mo's got it with him."

"Why?" the Professor pleaded.

"I'm sorry mate, I'll let Mo know the situation as soon as he returns."

25

KENNY DALGLISH

THE PROFESSOR HAD struggled from his chair after Micky left and poured himself a glass of malt whiskey. He knew he wasn't supposed to drink alcohol whilst on the heavy duty medication he was prescribed, but he was way past caring.

He left the glass on top of the teak cocktail cabinet and took the bottle back to his chair. Just then Raymond's black Land Rover parked outside with its hazards on. Shortly after he heard the key in the front door as Raymond entered carrying two Waitrose bags, which he dropped off in the kitchen, before striding into the living room.

"Bit early for that Dennis," he chortled, pointing at the bottle on the table by the Professor's chair.

"Here's the plan, I've just popped back with some food shopping, whilst we're at lunch I'd appreciate it if you'd put the shopping away and organise a resident's parking permit for me, there's a good man."

Dennis didn't answer, the whiskey and drugs were taking affect.

Raymond came and sat on the arm of Dennis's chair. "Sorry about this morning Den, I hope we don't have to go down that route again. We want to make your last days as comfortable as possible." He placed his hand on the Professor's shoulder. "I want you to be assured that after you've passed, I will make sure I keep the garden maintained to your high standards Den."

"Thanks," the Professor croaked, thinking about his number one hobby.

"Unfortunately you haven't maintained your lovely wife with the same passion as the garden, but don't fret, I will more than keep her happy on that front." He gave Dennis a playful slap on the cheek and stood up to go.

"Except on Thursday's," Dennis coughed as he spoke, his side still hurting, his cheek was stinging from the slap.

"I'm sorry Den?" Raymond snarled.

Dennis cleared his throat. "You said last night that you'd be fucking my wife every night except Thursdays."

"You're correct Den, glad you were paying attention to the fine details. Thursday nights I spend with Grace."

"Grace?"

"Yes, Grace, Dennis, she was the cause of the little spat between me and Sandra, but we've sorted the arrangements amicably. You can do what you want on a Thursday night Den, you can even sleep with your missus if you're up to it, up to you mate. Anyway Sandra's waiting in my charabang so must run. Don't forget your chores Den."

* * *

CLAIRE AND CHRISTINE sat on the edge of the bed, Toby and Alice in chairs. They were munching on pizzas that Claire had ordered.

"We'll watch the tape once everyone's finished," she stated.

Christine demolished hers and a muffin well before the others. "You don't get hangovers then boss?"

"No Chris, it's the Viking blood, I'm hardcore."

Toby looked at his boss still in her jogging gear. The sports bra didn't do her any favours, he pondered.

"How did you sleep Toby?" she quipped, winking at Christine.

"Not too bad Clare, thank you," he lied.

"At least you had a room to yourself Toby, I had to put up with Chris snoring all night!"

Toby wasn't used to this kind of jovial chit chat, he struggled to understand how his boss kept so cool whilst the pressure was on.

She gave him the tape and it took a few minutes for him to set everything up.

"I'm glad one of us knows what they're doing," Christine announced.

Claire explained where they'd got up to with the unedited tapes.

"I'm sorry about recording over the other two tapes, I'm an alcoholic you know!" Alice confessed.

The others just smiled not knowing whether she was serious or not.

"The last part we saw was very disturbing Alice. Scott found his colleagues hanged, he was then picked up by one the Afghani policemen."

"In that case you might want to wizz the first five minutes on, it's the same introduction as you've seen and a brief description of the betrayal by the team leader Felix, culminating in the massacre you've already heard about."

Toby pressed the fast forward button, it reminded him of his youth, watching videos of Rugby Internationals with his father.

The room fell silent as Scott took up the story, his profile filling the TV screen.

"ACHMED DROVE IN silence for hours down endless tracks that were not on any map. I was in complete shock, I presumed he was keeping us out of harm's way. I dozed off for a couple of hours and when I awoke, the Jeep was stationary. I realised Achmed was out of the vehicle talking to some tribesman whom I presumed were his friends. I heard laughter in the darkness and was flushed with relief. It didn't last long though as the door opened and a rifle was thrust in my face.

"The last thing I saw before I was hooded and tied up was my captors handing over a finder's fee to Achmed. I was bundled into the boot of another vehicle and driven for several hours until I was dragged into a basement. This was to be my world for the next eight months." Some grainy footage of the basement is shown. "In my 'room' was a dirty blanket for me to sleep on and a bucket. I didn't see another human for three days until a huge man appeared and dragged me into an adjoining room that had a plastic table and two chairs.

"On the table was bread and water which I devoured. He gestured for me to walk around the room, presumably to get some exercise, he then beat me with a large wooden post and dragged me back to the cell. This ritual carried on for two weeks. Then, next to the bread and water was another drink of what looked like fruit juice. I was reluctant to try it but he picked up his post and waved it at me. I drank the 'juice' and he led me back to my room without a beating. This procedure was then was repeated for a further two weeks. After that it was just bread and water again, this mentally crushed me. No beatings, but I was banging on my door screaming for my juice. The day after, the juice was there. So was my video camera!"

"SORRY TOBY, COULD you press pause please?" Claire interrupted as she received a message from Terry.

"Terry's team have found what they believe is Mo's phone. It was disassembled and scattered behind a bus stop between Livingstone and the terminus."

"So he got on the bus?" Toby surmised.

"It's certainly looks that way," Claire agreed.

"Do you think we should get there and help search boss?" Christine suggested.

"What do you think Alice? You know Mo better than anyone," Claire asked.

"I think you should watch the rest of the film, I find it very upsetting, if it's alright with you I'll go and wait in the bar."

"Of course Alice, we'll join you when we are done, carry on Toby." She gestured for him to press play.

"*I SWALLOWED THE juice in a frenzy, my captor calmly pointed to the camera and then to me and started screaming 'CIA' at me. I said no ten times but he beat me unconscious. I woke up screaming for juice. They threw me back into my room and gave me filthy water. My bucket was overflowing. I decided to try and kill myself or provoke my captor to kill me.*

"*After a few days I was back sitting at the plastic table. On it was some kind of meat and lentils, bread, water, and believe it or not a bowl of marshmallows! I scoffed the lot down, he placed a glass of 'juice' on the table. I tried to grab it, but he kept moving it away, he pointed to the doorway and I noticed a small boy, barely a teenager, standing there holding my video camera. My captor ushered him in and spoke to him gently as the boy stood next to him, I guessed they were related.*

"'*You KGB?' the boy asked.*

"'*You speak English!' I screamed in excitement.*

"'*You KGB? You CIA?' he asked again. 'You Soviet? You American?'*

"'*No, no, I'm Scottish! I'm British!' I yelled. 'I'm not KGB, not CIA, I'm not a spy! I make films for television.'*

"*The boy looked confused but spoke to the captor who laughed and then spoke to the boy at length. I thought I heard the word Scotland in the conversation. 'That's right I'm Scottish, not Russian, not a yank,' I said again.*

"*My captor passed me the 'juice', which I knocked back like a shot. My captor took the empty beaker and gave it to the boy who ran off with it. I finished the marshmallows, several were stuck to my face. 'Scotland,' my captor said clearly and in a serious tone.*

"'*Yes, yes, I'm Scottish,' I answered.*

"*He leaned forward and said two words I will remember till my dying day. 'Kenny Dalglish!' he roared.*

"'*Yes, Kenny Dalglish! Scottish like me!' I replied.*

"*The boy returned with the beaker full of more 'juice'. I held the beaker up and toasted Kenny Dalglish. The boy laughed. 'My uncle love Kenny Dalglish, my uncle love Liverpool,' he said.*

"'*I love Celtic,' I replied. The uncle went quiet for a moment and then put his hand on my shoulder. '*

"'*Jimmy Johnstone!' he yelled and then sent the boy out again.*

"'*Bring more 'juice' boy!' I bellowed. The boy returned with a lad in his early twenties who was wearing a traditional hat, the captor whipped it off revealing a shock of ginger hair.*

"'*Jimmy Johnstone!' he roared. I was laughing and crying all at the same time.*

"*They led me back to my room. I was convinced they would see it's all a misunderstanding and I'd soon be on my way home to see Alice. For the next few days I only saw the boy, who spoke a tiny bit of English. I could now spend more time in the big room, he told me his uncle wanted me to teach him 'good' English. I figured the more I taught him, the more I could learn about my captors and win my release. His name was Mohamed and for the next seven months he was my best friend in the world.*

"*The food got better, the juice, which I soon realised obviously contained opium, was plentiful. After a couple of months Mohamed told me that they were trying to contact the British embassy to let them know I was alive and negotiate a ransom. I was their first hostage and they had no contacts or knowledge of how to go about this. I suggested they film me with my recorder. They were hesitant at first because they were still concerned I was a spy, but eventually Mohamed's uncle, who was clearly in charge, relented and they sat me at the table with Mohamed filming as I'd taught him.*"

At this point the video shows the actual footage. Scott, cheek bones almost skeletal, his eyes glazed, he's clearly drugged. He looks at the camera, coughs, then speaks. "*I am Scott Murdoch, I'm being held prisoner because I'm accused of being a spy.*" A few seconds later, a voice is heard and the film ends.

"*I tried to explain that I should say much more but Uncle gave me a severe beating and I was dragged back to my room. No 'juice' or Mohamed for a week. I was going out of my mind, having suicidal thoughts again. I dreamt and thought endlessly of my girlfriend Alice back in Scotland. I'd met her at Edinburgh University where we were both studying journalism. I decided I'd try and strangle the boy when he came with my food the next day, that would surely provoke the uncle enough to kill me. I was all prepared but when he opened my door I saw he was holding the beaker! I was back on the juice, he also told me they'd somehow sent the tape to the British embassy in Kabul. Not for the first time, Mohamed saved my life.*

"*The days turned to weeks, Mohamed spent more and more time with me. I taught him English, he taught his language, mainly useful swear words. He told me his father had been killed when he was six, in a dispute with a rival tribe. His mother died of an unknown illness two years later. His grandfather and uncle had looked after him but now he was thirteen he could be a soldier and would be married soon. I taught him about Scotland and our way of life. He was fascinated by cricket, a game I explained was played by the rich English. I asked him constantly about the tape and if there was any news but he claimed he didn't know such information.*

"*I'd been in the basement seven months, I'd only seen Uncle, Mohamed and the ginger 'Jimmy Johnstone' in the seven months I'd been a hostage. Then one day I was introduced to the Mohamed's grandfather who, along with Uncle, joined me for lunch. The old man had one tooth and seemed to permanently have a massive spliff wedged between his lips. Mohamed translated as Uncle explained that they'd got nowhere with the embassy but their 'intermediary' was in talks with the Russian's. I was also told at the end of the day grandfather, as the village elder, would have the final say. I explained that they shouldn't trust the Russians, as I'd already been betrayed by them and I felt they'd endanger themselves.*

"*None of them had ever met a Russian so I presumed the village must be very remote. The next day Mohamed explained that his grandfather liked me, which was very important as he was the village boss and, more worryingly, he'd killed many people. I asked why and he explained that every few years there'd be a flare up with rival tribes and villages. After his father was killed, his grandfather exacted revenge by killing everybody in the village responsible. He poisoned the food at a wedding feast, within a day everyone was dead! He explained his grandfather was an alchemist, the most legendary in the whole of Afghanistan, and that he was teaching Mohamed to be his successor."*

Claire and Toby exchanged glances, they both knew what each other were thinking.

"I was in a better place mentally now but the thought of the Russians being notified of my whereabouts kept me awake at night, even if I'd been on the 'juice', which I now knew was a potion concocted by the legendary alchemist. My fears were well founded, after exactly eight months to the day since my capture a Russian jet dropped a massive bomb on the village at six in the morning. I was sound asleep when the roof caved in. I think I was unconscious for a few minutes, when I came round my whole body was covered in masonry, I couldn't breathe, my eyes were filled with hot dust. I could hear muffled shouting, then I heard my name, 'Scott, Scott.' I felt Mohamed's hands clawing away the debris from around my head. I felt water being poured over my eyes and suddenly for the first time since I was put in the boot of that Jeep I could see the sky.

"It's was the most vivid blue I'd ever seen. I saw Mohamed kneeling next to me clearing more dust from my face. Then I saw a woman, I hadn't seen one of those for a long time! She was wearing a black hijab, I can still recall her eyes, as black as her veil."

There is footage taken by Scott of the smouldering remains of the village. *"Uncle and the rest of the villagers frantically tried to clear the mound of rubble that was once the Alchemist's home. I knew their mission had failed when I heard first the women wailing and then the cries of hardened warriors, led by Uncle. That day the villagers sought sanctuary in the few remaining shelters. Uncle and Ginger came and chained me to a metal trough, where the ponies came to drink. They had no one else to take their grief out on so they beat me senseless. I truly believe their intention was to kill me but as they aimed endless kicks at my head I heard Mohamed's voice screaming at them to stop.*

"I passed out and came to the next day, I was still chained to the trough, it was blisteringly hot, I could feel my head burning. Mohamed emerged with some water and rice but no juice. The entire village suddenly gathered near me, sitting on the ground. Uncle came and stood on a cart and addressed the crowd. His speech was interspersed with cries from the gathering of 'Allahu Akbar!' I asked Mohamed what was going on, 'We must honour the memory of my grandfather, we must spill the blood of our attackers, we are declaring war on the Russians.'

"I started to laugh. 'How do you propose to exact revenge on the mighty soviet army?' I pleaded.

"'With our bare hands if necessary. Ginger knows of a Russian garrison two hundred miles away, we are going to attack it' he replied.

"I grabbed hold of Mohamed and screamed at him. 'You will all be slaughtered! It will be suicide!' The villagers then turned towards me, Uncle stepped forward and unleashed his sword, a couple of men grabbed me and exposed my neck. I prayed to a god I never believed in and thought of Alice as I waited to be decapitated. I shouted at Mohamed as Uncle came towards me, his face contorted with rage. 'I know where there's a gun, a great big fucking gun,' I said, desperately trying to save myself.

"The crowd were screaming 'Allahu Akbar!' as Uncle took aim above me, shading me from the burning sun. 'A howitzer it could kill hundreds of Russians!' I screamed. Mohamed shouted at his uncle, the word howitzer was tossed back and forwards between them. Uncle dropped to one knee and held the blade to my neck.

"'Where howitzer?' he growled at me.

"'Near where you captured me, in the village the Russians napalmed. I can take you. You can kill many Russians,' I gasped.

"He spoke to Mohamed who translated. 'You take us to howitzer? If Russian blood spilt, you go free!' he replied eventually.

"'I laughed and cried all at once. 'Let's go!' I shouted. 'Juice please!'"

TOBY PAUSED THE tape. "Got to use the loo," he said, jumping up.

"I could do with a coffee break, my god this is heavy shit," Christine commented.

"Yes, good idea Christine. This is…quite a story," Claire replied.

26

OLD DUNDEE

CLAIRE DECIDED TO take advantage of the break to shower and change.

Toby and Christine sat on the edge of the bed sipping their coffee. Toby needed some light relief from the documentary.

"So, how was last night then Christine?" he asked.

"A massive disappointment to be honest Toby, despite me wearing my stripy jim jams, nothing happened."

"Nothing? I thought the Ice Queen was going to seduce you."

"I should be so lucky."

"So she really is, really is…"

"Straight?"

"Yes, straight."

"I'm not so sure Toby, I think the Red Lion theory that she is asexual might be true."

"That is very disappointing Christine, I was relying on you."

"What, to seduce the boss? Sorry to crush your dreams matey."

"Well Chris I must tell you, you let your country down."

Claire emerged from the ensuite in her familiar trouser suit, the glamour of last night a memory. "Ok Toby, let's get this done."

Toby pressed play.

"THAT AFTERNOON I was unchained and invited to what was basically a council of war. Mohamed did his best to translate. I tried to pinpoint the exact position of 'Old Dundee' on the only map they had. There was an argument about whether they'd be better selling me off to another tribe for either money or weapons, but I made a proposal that suited both Uncle and myself. I suggested they let me film the mission and make it the subject of my documentary. That way the outside world would see what was happening

in Afghanistan. I'd get my documentary made and if I made some money I could help them rebuild the village."

The warriors are visible for the first time in the video, a line up with their faces half covered with rough scarves and rags. Mohamed is obvious by his size at the end of the line. Footage of the crushed buildings are shown, followed by the convoy of men and horses leaving the village.

"So the epic journey began, it was to be a painfully slow journey into the unknown. Eighteen men including Mohamed, who was not yet fourteen, and a Scotsman, who'd never even had a fist fight. There were four ponies, the Jeep had been destroyed in the bombing. I learnt that Uncle's real name was Omar. His eyes seemed to be constantly on me, he insisted I was in front of him. We covered about fifty miles the first two days. The terrain was completely featureless and it made me realise just how remote their village was. The days were blisteringly hot, the nights freezing. On the third day we came to what at last could be called a road. Omar insisted we could only use it under the cover of darkness due to the various roadblocks, which were basically tax collection points manned by different tribes. Some were friendly, some not, fortunately Omar knew which was which.

"I'd counted only seven rifles among our group and just as dawn broke on the fourth day Omar, Ginger, and the next five most senior warriors left us in the overnight camp we'd made some two hundred yards from the road. I was dozing when I was woken by gunfire. I was paralysed with fear and considered making a run for it but Mohamed and his cousin grabbed me as they charged down a hill towards the battle. We got to within fifty yards of the road and I could make out five prostrate bodies lying there. As we got closer I could see the blood. Omar and Ginger were now standing over them. I grabbed the camera but was too late to film the two men put a bullet in the heads of two survivors."

The footage cuts to bodies lined up at the side of the road, next to a pile of tyres that was the temporary roadblock. The warriors look triumphant, making defiant gestures to the camera.

"Mohamed told me to stop filming before spitting in the eyes of the dead bodies. I quickly realised this was personal. These poor souls were from the same tribe that killed his father. The bad news was they used all their ammunition on the raid, the good news, after the raid they now had five Kalashnikovs and three handguns. I hadn't told them the howitzer only had two useable shells. With the newly acquired weaponry they might not need the services of 'Old Dundee'. I mentioned this to Mohamed but he said that with 'Old Dundee' and the machine guns they could slaughter the whole garrison. We marched another three days without incident. We'd covered around three quarters of the distance to where I thought the destroyed village should be. We struck camp by a stream where I spent a good hour bathing my blistered feet.

"I was making my way back with my chaperone when the first shots rang out. It was dusk, the light was rapidly fading, there was pandemonium as it became clear we were being ambushed. We made it back to the camp, the gunfire from both sides was relentless, it seemed to go on for hours but eventually subsided. We all lay motionless till first light, hoping they'd given up and moved on. Suddenly Omar was going crazy running

around the camp, checking on everyone. Ginger was missing. Omar told everyone to lay low whilst he went to investigate. We soon heard shouting."

The video cuts to a clip of Scott talking to his own camera, sitting in a ditch. "Omar has made contact with the attackers. They have Ginger, they say they will release him in exchange for the weapons and two surviving ponies we stole at the checkpoint. Seems a case of easy come, easy go."

Scott's voice continues to narrate. "So we continued our mission with Ginger but no weapons. My life was totally in the hands of 'Old Dundee'. After nine days marching we reached the ghost town. Nine months on I could still smell the napalm."

The camera pans around the demolished buildings and the warriors removing the debris covering the basement. Someone shines a light into the pit and reveals the rusty hunk of metal that is 'Old Dundee'. There's footage of them pulling the howitzer out of the pit and trying to clean it up.

"We took it in turns to drag the beast through the desert towards the objective. We were now deep in Mujahideen territory, our progress was painfully slow, eventually we reached a hill overlooking the Russian garrison. Nobody slept that night.

"We collectively waited for the sun to rise, which it did just a fraction after six. Omar nodded to me, I went to the back of 'Old Dundee' and loaded the first of our two shells. We'd already discussed the coordinates, I fiddled with the pretty basic guidance system whilst Omar spied the garrison through a pair of stolen binoculars. The plan was to drop the first shell in the parade ground that would hopefully wake up the camp and cause some chaos into which we'd fire the second shell. I closed my eyes and prayed. Omar raised his hand and then lowered it. I fired the shell into the valley and waited for the explosion. I lost sight of the shell but eventually heard a dull thud as it overshot the camp and landed disappointingly with a low thud, causing just a plume of dust to rise in the far distance."

27

MO

"WHERE IS GOD?' A fair and, I would have thought, quite astute question for a thirteen-year-old boy. I say 'boy' but Mohamed has seen and experienced more pain and hardship than most people would in an entire lifetime. I suppose to his peers he was very much a man, particularly to his uncle.

'Mohamed's reaction to his uncle's harsh slap was initially a boyish bewildered look of injustice, he sulked for a few seconds, then defiantly took the binoculars off his uncle and pressed them to his eyes, to stare at the valley below. His cheek burned red from the vicious slap but there was no trace of tears. 'What can you see?' I asked in English, trying to defuse the situation.

'Uncle Omar glared at me, his nephew answered, 'I see where 'shell' hit, bit too far. I see Russians in garrison, maybe seven, no nine, they not running, they not see 'shell'. They-'

'Uncle Omar cut him short as he snatched back the binoculars. After a couple of minutes he put them down and looked directly at me, I'd never seen eyes so dark and angry. He leaned over Mohamed and pulled me over him, turning me onto my back as he placed a knife against my Adam's apple. Calmly he told his nephew that he was to fire the second and last shell and, if he didn't kill at least one Russian, he would slit my throat.

'Time stood still as I strained to see Mohamed load the shell into the rusty old howitzer. I knew Uncle Omar never trusted me and I couldn't in all honesty blame him, for I had little trust myself in the old relic of a gun. In my heart of hearts I knew it would fail miserably but that wasn't the point. It was a double whammy, 'Old Dundee', as I'd christened this useless hunk of old metal, had kept me alive thus far and also it was highly unlikely that I'd be responsible for anyone's demise. I was completely helpless as I glimpsed Mohamed pick up the remaining shell and disappear to the rear of 'Old Dundee'. The rest of the Omar's tribe were silent, all I could hear was a slight metallic

scraping as the shell was loaded. The pressure of Omar's blade was choking me, I gasped for air, dry unforgiving air that even at dawn was burning hot.

"'Where is God?' I thought. It was a good question. I'd settle for a slap, but prayer seemed my last chance, as 'Old Dundee' could in no way be relied on to save me now. She'd bought me the extra weeks it had taken to push the sad old beast to this god forsaken hill top. I knew Mohamed would do his best for both his family and my good self. In the nine months his village had kept me captive I'd taught him English and he'd done his best to lessen the beatings. My life was in the hands of a 'man' barely in his teens and a thirty-nine-year-old artillery piece. It would take Mohamed, with the help of a couple of villagers, around five minutes to fire the last shell, a futile effort to take revenge for his grandfather's death by killing a Russian soldier. Or, if the mission fails, kill a spy, for that is what uncle Omar believed I was. So, I had just a few moments to reflect on my twenty-eight years on this planet. To think of mum and dad back home in my beloved Scottish highlands, friends, family, lovers, and of course my beautiful Alice.

"With one hand holding his dagger to my throat and the other holding the binoculars to his terrifying eyes, Omar prepared to give the signal to fire again. There was a chilling silence, which was suddenly interrupted by an almighty roar as a huge helicopter swept nearly fifty meters above our heads. I stretched every sinew to see the helicopter sweep into the valley below and then land in the middle of the garrison. At least a dozen commandos emerged from various accommodation blocks and started to climb in the rear ramp as it unfolded onto the dusty ground. Other soldiers rushed over with boxes of supplies and ammunition. It was clear we all thought the same, the pilot would have seen us and it wouldn't be long before we were under attack.

"Omar shouted the command to fire and the ground vibrated as 'Old Dundee' recoiled. Mohamed rushed forward and was beside me. At first no one could see where the shell landed before Ginger pointed out a commotion around the helicopter as a group of soldiers were gesturing to a plume of dust some ten meters from them. The helicopter blades started to rotate and the rear ramp slowly closed before it started to leave the ground. Some thirty-seconds elapsed and Omar dug his knee into my back and started screaming incoherently at me, the dagger pierced my skin. Mohamed jumped on his uncle's back pleading with him to spare me. 'Where is God? Not here', was my last thought as the helicopter was now ten feet off the ground, directly above the useless shell.

"Suddenly there was a boom, the shell exploded causing a piece of shrapnel to penetrate the helicopter, possibly hitting one of the boxes of ammunition. Omar and everyone dived to the ground as the helicopter become a giant fireball. I broke free as Omar lost his grip on me. I saw the crazy fireball hover out of control and spin around the garrison causing absolute carnage as various buildings and vehicles were set alight. Mohamed had grabbed my camera and filmed the aftermath, he was now hugging me. 'We did it! We did it, Scott!' he screamed. Then we started to run and run and run some more. We all knew it wouldn't be long before migs would be up in the air hunting us down.

"We got to a road, Omar and his men stopped to catch their breath. Omar handed me his canteen of water. We could hear a jet in the distance as he started to give everyone *instructions. Mohamed came and explained that everyone was to split into small groups and head back to the village in the hope they wouldn't be spotted. I was a free man. We embraced. 'Thank you Scott, thank you for blessing my grandfather. Now go!' Omar shouted in English. 'Go!'.*

"A mig circled above, I started to make my way along the road. I turned and saw Mo walking in the opposite direction as he started the journey back to his god forsaken village. 'I'll come back for you Mo!' I shouted, but my promise was drowned out by the Russian jet fighter as it fired at the road.

"Four days later, on my track towards Kabul, I collapsed exhausted for the night in a deserted half built building. I slept for some twelve hours before being woken by a Kalashnikov tapping my head. I looked up at five Russian soldiers, one of which spoke English. I explained I'd been a hostage for nine months but had escaped. They accepted my story and drove me to Kabul. I learnt on the journey that there'd been a Mujahideen assault on their comrades garrison. A troop carrying helicopter was hit, resulting in dozens of dead and injured. The Alchemist had been well and truly avenged.

"I got to the safety of the British embassy and was interviewed by someone I presumed was an intelligence officer. I told him all about Felix and how I was convinced he was working for the Russians. 'Felix Douglas?' he asked.

"'Yes, you know him?' I replied.

"'He was found in his hotel room two weeks ago with his brains all over the walls,' he confirmed.

"'Who did it?' I asked, wishing it was me.

"'Who knows,' the Embassy man shrugged. 'CIA, MOSSAD, KGB, MI6, Mujahideen, could be anybody. Are you bothered?' he replied.

"I realised I wasn't. I returned home to Scotland with my tapes. In my absence Alice had worked tirelessly to get the powers that be to secure my release. We moved in together, she was busy with her blossoming career with BBC Scotland, I was busy editing my documentary titled Mo."

28

THE AFTER SHOW

"JESUS," CHRISTINE SIGHED.

"Yes, that was intense," Toby added.

"I think we need to ask Alice what happened next," Claire suggested.

"Don't disagree boss but I'm up for doubling our efforts in finding Mo. Shouldn't we get out there?" Christine asked.

"I agree," Toby concurred. "If the yanks get him I reckon they'll put him on a plane out the country on his way to Guantanamo."

Christine nodded. "Toby's right boss."

Claire stood up, pausing for thought. "One moment, I'm going to make a call," she said coldly. The other two weren't sure if she meant a judgment call or a phone call. They soon discovered they were the same thing as she searched her contacts under M and put her phone on loud speaker.

"Claire, I've been expecting your call," Myerson answered.

If Toby and Christine didn't realise who it was already, they soon would. "Where's Mohamed, Mr Myerson?"

"Probably on his way to Poland by now Claire."

Toby was surprised the head of CIA Europe knew his boss' first name.

"I think you're bullshitting me, you've lost him haven't you?"

"You think what you want Clare. You have definitely lost your friend haven't you?"

"He is my friend and let me make the situation perfectly clear, I will do anything to help my friends Mr Myerson and I mean anything."

"Very admirable Claire but I doubt if you have any friends."

Toby and Christine exchanged glances as Claire paused.

"Have I touched a nerve Clare?"

"If Mohamed is not in my hotel by eight o'clock this evening you will regret it Mr Myerson."

"Ok Clare, let me spell out the situation, if I don't bring this mass poisoner to book, my idiot president will sack me. If I do, some stuck up English bitch will come out with some tittle tattle about an alleged conversation, her word against mine. Who are people going to believe?"

Clare looked at her colleagues and winked. "To be honest sir, the only person who will believe that the head of CIA Europe suggested to a junior member of the British Intelligence service that he'd like to bend her over his desk and fuck her up the arse just to put a smile on her miserable face would be your wife sir. I'll be in the hotel bar waiting for the arrival of a fit and well friend of mine. Thank you Mr Myerson."

There was stunned silence in the room, Claire sat down in an armchair. "You ok boss?" Christine asked.

"I need a drink, let's go and see Alice," Clare suggested casually.

There was a very uncomfortable silence in the lift, Toby's Etonian cheeks were once again burning red. They exited on the ground floor and before they reached the bar Clare stopped and looked coldly at Toby and Christine. "You do know what you just heard is grade A classified and one word down the Red Lion, or anywhere, I will make sure you're finished."

"Yes boss," they answered in unison.

"Can I at least boast about spending the night with you boss?" Christine tried to lighten the atmosphere.

"Of course Chris, don't spare the sordid details." Claire winked. "You ok Toby? You're looking hot and bothered," she teased, as they went to join Alice in the bar.

Alice was nowhere to be seen, they thought she might be in the toilet but after ten minutes there was no sign of her. Toby went to reception, he showed his accreditation with the intention of looking at the hotel CCTV but the receptionist handed him an envelope, written on it was 'CLAIRE PETERSON, ROOM 425'.

He returned to the bar and the trio adjourned to an alcove.

Claire opened the envelope and read the contents aloud. "Dear all. So you all now know that Mo is no terrorist. The only thing he is guilty of is of being a frustrated chef! The yanks must be mad to assume he was plotting anything sinister. They won't catch Mo, he is a man who defied famine, disease, the Russian army and the Taliban! Rest assured he is still a free man. As for Scott, he returned home to me. The documentary had limited success, mainly on the university circuit. I was busy with my career but things rapidly fell apart between us because of the cruel legacy of the Alchemist's 'juice' that was stuck in his veins. The only way he could cope with the hideous cravings was to seek sanctuary in the dark world of heroin addiction.

"He moved to London and then Glasgow. I didn't hear from him for five years. He made contact with me in 1991 claiming he was clean and heading back to make a follow up documentary about whatever happened to Mo, who never left Scott's mind. He asked me to use my influence, as I was now an executive producer with the Beeb, to act as a sponsor should he manage to persuade Mo to come back to the UK with him. I received a letter from Scott six months later informing me that he'd found Mo and was planning to bring him back with him, but Scott had been ill and was resting up in Kubal. Three months later I had a call from an immigration officer at Heathrow explaining he was with an Afghani citizen named Mohamed Zaheer. I took a taxi to Heathrow with the director general of the BBC. After five hours of interviews we were on the M4, Mo had leave to remain. He then told me Scott was found dead two weeks earlier in a Kabul hotel. He died of a heroin overdose the day after purchasing flights for himself and Mo. Sorry I didn't hang around. I needed to get home. Good luck. I'm entrusting sponsorship of Mo to you now Claire. He doesn't like you very much but I know you're a fair and resourceful women. Yours faithfully, Alice MacDonald." Claire finished reading and placed the letter back in the envelope.

"Quite a story," she said at last.

"Where do you reckon he is?" Christine asked.

"He'll head back to London I reckon," Toby surmised.

"Wherever he is we need to talk to him," Claire added.

"The Minister of Health business?" Toby guessed.

"He hinted there was a misunderstanding. Before I totally give him the benefit of the doubt, I need to hear his side of the story."

They were interrupted by three young men entering the bar, one of which approached them. "Hi you must be Claire Peterson, I'm Brian. Apparently we owe you an apology," he said. He spoke with a heavy New York accent.

Claire realised who they were immediately. "Yes you do, where's our man?" she replied.

"We lost him mam," he shrugged.

"Were you ever close?"

"He threw us with that bus business mam."

"So the three of you, armed with those big guns, were fucked over by an old lady and a chef," Claire said. She was in her element.

"Looks like it mam."

"I'm surprised that your boss didn't use special forces."

"We are special forces mam."

"Really?" In one word she reduced the three Americans to naughty school boys.

Toby and Christine marvelled at their boss as they saw their adversaries squirm in front of them.

"Is that it?"

"Is that what mam?"

"Your apology, is that it then?"

"Yes mam, we just wanted to apologise for the misunderstanding."

"There was no misunderstanding on our part, we had our man and now thanks to you, the USA's finest, we haven't. So whilst I accept you do not have our man, fuck your apology and fuck you."

The three Americans looked at each other awkwardly. "Understood mam," Brian reluctantly replied and off they slinked with tails between their legs.

"High five boss," Christine offered, Toby likewise.

29

THE DAY OFF

"SO WHAT DO you plan to do with your day off Dennis?" Raymond asked, as the Professor prepared breakfast.

"I'm going to hospital."

"I must say Den, you do look like shit."

"I feel like shit but that's not why I'm going to the hospital, it's the Good Poison Club."

"The what?" Raymond queried.

Dennis explained what the meetings were all about, suddenly realising that he was actually having a normal conversation with Raymond.

"Sounds a good idea Den, it must be therapeutic for you."

"It gets me out."

"I thought you'd want to take advantage of my absence and enjoy some quality time with your missus."

"I don't think she wants to spend quality time with me to be honest."

"You need to man up, stop whinging, have a shave and haircut mate. Smarten yourself up. You're her husband, you're not dead yet, get a grip." Raymond gave Dennis one of his playful slaps. "Got to get going, Grace will be waiting for me."

* * *

IT HAD BEEN quite a morning at HQ.

Toby had received a call from Claire explaining that she'd been involved in an accident whilst jogging early that morning and that she'd be in a bit late. Sir Martin had popped into the office to be debriefed about the Edinburgh trip. He was surprised she wasn't there but Toby gave him the edited highlights, careful to avoid any mention of his boss' difficult relationship with Myerson. Toby was just about to explain their outstanding concern about Mo and the Minister of Health when Clare hobbled into the office on crutches.

"What the hell happened to you Claire?" Sir Martin asked.

Toby noticed, alongside her right foot being heavily bandaged, she also had a nasty graze on her forehead. "Blimey Claire you've been in the wars," he remarked sympathetically.

"I tripped whilst on my early morning jog, my pride hurts more than anything else."

"Well, take it easy Claire, we've got a meeting with the joint intelligence committee tomorrow, eleven am prompt. See you then. Thanks for the update Toby."

Toby nodded as the big white chief left them to it.

"No news then Toby?" Claire queried.

"Nope, I winged it with Sir Martin, I'm going to listen in to today's Good Vibes Club, see if there's any hint of the Golden Square conversation."

"Good idea Toby, keep me updated."

"So what really happened to you Claire?" Toby asked looking at her wounds.

She hesitated for a few seconds. "Well I didn't trip."

"Go on."

"I was jogging on my usual route when a Land Rover swerved onto the pavement and came straight for me."

"You think it was deliberate?"

"I know it was."

"Who do you think it was?"

"The Americans, the Russians, the Israelis, the Arabs, I've upset virtually all of them in my short career." She shrugged.

"Do you want me to arrange some backup Claire? Whoever it was might have another go."

"Achtar is looking at any possible CCTV, in the meantime I can look after myself."

* * *

TINA CAUGHT A glimpse of Micky and Dennis sitting together in the canteen. *The Professor looks awful,* she thought. She made a mental note to look up when his next appointment was.

"Where the fuck is Mo and where the fuck is your gun?" Dennis exclaimed to Micky.

"Calm down mate. A few weeks ago you were a retired lecturer, now you've turned into a crazy psycho," Micky whispered in reply.

"Well, since you aren't prepared to do the business, I'm relying on Mo to help me."

"Believe me, I'm as desperate to see him as you. I need my gun back."

"So you will do it then?"

"Sorry Professor, I've got more pressing problems to take care of."

"You're coming out of retirement?"

"Not really, this isn't business, it's personal."

"Welcome to my world," Dennis mused.

* * *

TOBY SAT IN front of the screen, feet on the desk, munching on a hoisin duck wrap. He watched Tina setting out the chairs and felt a pang of guilt. He liked her, he wondered what she made of 'Rupert'.

Brenda was the first to arrive.

"Brenda, how are you?" Tina was genuinely pleased to see her.

"I'm good Tina."

"All quiet on the western front?"

"All quiet Tina, I came early because I'm concerned everyone's going to be on the minister's case next week on my behalf and I don't really want any fuss."

"I understand Brenda, I'd like to give him a piece of my mind, but maybe we should show a dignified silence."

"I'm not sure the others will see it that way Tina."

"I'm sure Dennis will have something to say," Tina laughed.

Brenda smiled and took a seat. "I think I know who gave me the gift Tina."

Tina had her own suspicions and was curious to see if Brenda thought the same, but Brenda's reveal was interrupted by the arrival of Veronica, Brian and Hassan. They were soon followed by Micky and Dennis.

"Hi everyone, looks like this is it. No Mo then?"

"Last spotted in Edinburgh!" Micky declared.

Toby discarded his lunch and turned the sound up, he recalled the conversation at Golden Square. 'I still want my fifteen grand,' this character had said.

What were they plotting? If it was the Minister of Health, they were going to be disappointed.

"I see Uber is in trouble thanks to our wonderful mayor." Dennis' comment got straight into Hassan's ribs.

"He doesn't stand a chance of stopping Uber, the only people against them are middle class racists like you."

"Racist!" the Professor shouted. "What do you mean racist?"

"Everyone knows most drivers are from ethnic minorities, if you had your way we'd all lose our jobs."

"It's got nothing to do with race you fool, it's about globalisation!" Dennis screamed.

"There, you heard it, the eminent Professor called me a fool. I'll tell you what's wrong with you, you've never lived in the real world. You went to infant school, then primary, then grammar school, then uni, then you ended up teaching. You've theorised all your life mate."

"How do you know I went to a grammar school?" Dennis retorted, wishing he hadn't because it was true.

"Ok boys, let's calm down, we need to discuss next weeks visit from the Minister of Health," Tina said. "Now let me just tell you that I've also been fantasising about humiliating the idiot but I'm now of the opinion of us showing some dignified silence, what you reckon?"

"Bollocks, this a one off opportunity to vent our anger about Brenda's trial," Micky intervened.

"Tina's right, we shouldn't stoop to his level," Brenda stated.

"Yeah, you're right Bren, but I'd like to turn my back on him."

"Not a bad idea Brian," Veronica concurred. "When he asks us why we've turned our backs we can explain about them not funding drug trials."

"Look at me," Dennis proclaimed standing up. "I'll be in a hospice before too long, Hassan is right, it's not about Uber. He's right about me. I've spent a fucking lifetime pontificating about how society should be run without actually doing anything practical to change it. This is my chance to leave my mark. I can do anything I like now, what can they do to me, I'm a dead man just about walking. What would you like me to do to that hideous parasite?"

The Professor's rant was interrupted by loud clapping from someone standing at the door dressed in a hoodie.

They all turned to look.

Watching the screen in his office, Toby couldn't see the source of the applause, he leaned forward to try to get a better look.

"Well hello stranger, pull up a chair." Tina beckoned the latecomer into the room.

Toby couldn't believe his eyes as Mo came into view. He looked behind him through the glass panels towards Claire's desk. She wasn't there. He grabbed his phone. "Claire, I've found him, our chef!" he said as she answered.

"Mo?"

"Yes Mo, he's just walked into the Good Vibes Club!"

"Oh, really? I'm on my way home, not feeling too good. Use your initiative, send me a recording."

"Will do Claire, take care, speak later."

"I think our Professor is the man to put the government man in his place," Mo stated to everyone's surprise.

"Thank you Mo. What do you think I should do?" Dennis asked.

"Offer him one of these," Mo opened a tupperware box containing what looked like chocolate brownies. "They contain a strong laxative, it won't change his policy but we will have the satisfaction of knowing he will be spending the night in the loo in great discomfort."

"Blimey Mo, what's in them?" Tina queried.

"My own recipe."

Toby was confused at this new development. Claire told Mo the minister wouldn't be attending, yet he is encouraging the others to take action? *Was this some kind of message?*

We need to question him about the fifteen grand business, he pondered. *What if the yanks get hold of him?*

He called Christine and updated her, suggesting she get a team to the hospital before they lose him again.

Dennis took the box of cakes and thanked the Professor. "What would happen if I gave him all eight cakes?" he asked, looking inside the perspex lid.

"That would be an assasination," Mo declared.

"Interesting," Dennis replied. "Is there a sell by date?"

Mo put has hand on the Professor's shoulder. "They are good for the next two weeks my friend," he winked and then turned to Micky. "Thank you for helping me out mate, here's what I owe you." He placed a twenty pound note in Micky's hand as he shook it and then made for the door. "Sorry it's been a flying visit but I've got myself a chef's job in sunnier climes. Thank you for everything Tina. Bye all." He was gone.

Toby jumped out of his seat. "Fuck it!" he shouted as he ran to Achtar's desk. "Get everything you can around the hospital, contact all ports and airports, our chef's on the run again."

* * *

TINA WAS GLAD things wound up without any more drama. As everyone was leaving she took Dennis aside and suggested he see his consultant as soon as possible.

She noticed Brenda approach Micky. "It was you, wasn't it Micky?" Brenda asked.

"What have I done Brenda?"

"The gift, it was from you."

"Sorry Brenda, what gift?"

"You don't have to be so coy, I presume you won it or something. I don't care, it's greatly appreciated. God bless you."

"I'm sorry Brenda it wasn't me, I'm presuming someone gave you some money."

"Yes, for my trial."

"I'm guessing it was five grand cash?" Micky suggested.

"Yes," Brenda confirmed.

"It wasn't me Bren, but I know who it was."

* * *

WHILST TOBY, CHRISTINE and their colleagues were running like headless chickens, Claire was reclined on her sofa nursing her wounds, sipping a glass of red whilst watching Made in Chelsea on catch up.

What a bunch of Tobys, she laughed to herself.

Her peace was disturbed by her phone buzzing on the coffee table. It was an unknown number, she hesitated before answering. "Hi," she said tentatively.

"Claire, it's Mo."

"Where are you Mo?"

"Lurking about Claire. I lied to you."

"About the minister?"

"Yes."

"Why do you want to poison the minister Mo?"

"Because he's denying us life saving drugs."

"It's not that simple Mo, you know that, besides I don't believe he's your target as I told you his visit would be cancelled."

"I wanted the group to believe the visit was going ahead. It's literally kept them going."

"Fifteen grand, what about the fifteen grand Mo? And what about the slow untraceable death? You're on tape. The Professor offered the money, fifteen grand to humiliate the Minister of Health."

"I exaggerated the effects to impress him."

"Why did he want to humiliate him?" Claire pressed.

"He's a Marxist and he's dying, he wants to be remembered as some kind of lefty martyr in the war against austerity." Mo had been cooking up this scenario since he got to Edinburgh. He was quite impressed with himself.

"One last question Mo."

"Go on."

"What's in the cakes?"

"Nothing Claire, they're placebos. Anyway, why you bothered? The minister's not going to eat one of my delicious brownies."

"No but the poor Professor's family might, we don't want another accidental poisoning do we."

Mo hesitated before answering. "No Claire, I suppose we don't. So are you going to look for me?"

"I've seen the documentary Mo, it's a powerful story. I'm sorry about Scott. You could be arrested for attempted murder of the cyber geeks or conspiracy to harm a Member of Parliament. I'm going to visit a friend of yours in the morning. Call me this time tomorrow, I'll let you know then."

"What friend?" Mo asked.

"Speak to you tomorrow Mo." She hung up, happy that she'd ended the conversation on the front foot.

30

THE NIGHT OFF

MICKY HAD SPENT the afternoon after leaving the Good Poison Club following Frankie. He watched his daughter's partner emerge from his local and cross the road to the bookies.

He did this three times in an hour.

Micky sat in his car seething, now and again he'd look at the note Mo gave him: *Anna 07786556345. Shetland pony.* He entered the number into his phone and tore up the note.

Frankie emerged from the pub laughing and joking with his mates. Micky thought about the Professor's rant about the suburbs. He thought about the five grand he gave the little shit and the flash motor he'd seen the other day. "Cunt," he said, then phoned the number. "Anna?"

"Yes."

"I'm Mo's friend, Micky, I believe he gave you something that belongs to me to look after."

"Yes."

"I'd like to pop round and collect it please."

"I'm working till late, you can come in the morning."

"Where do you live Anna?"

"Come to Acton station and call me. You must give me the code word when you call, I will give you the address details then."

"Ok," Micky confirmed. *Mo certainly covers his tracks*, he thought.

* * *

CLAIRE WOKE WITH a start, she must have dozed off for at least three hours, and grabbed her phone out of habit. The world could have ended on her watch whilst she was dreaming.

There was one message from Achtar: *Claire. Car was registered to the Russians.*

"Russians?" she said aloud. She tried to call Achtar but his phone went to voicemail. "Shit, Russians," she repeated, reading the message again, her mind was racing. She pressed another number.

"Christine."

"Boss," Christine replied.

"Have you spoken to Achtar?"

"Toby called me, fucking Russians."

"Mad isn't it Christine?"

"Very strange boss."

"Where are you?"

"Outside your apartment block boss, with Toby."

"What?" Claire exclaimed, "How do you know where I live?"

"Sir Martin sent us boss."

"Sir Martin?"

"He told us to keep an eye on you and get you to Whitehall safe and sound in the morning."

Claire considered the situation for a moment. "Do you want to come up Chris?"

"Not another night of passion boss?" she teased.

"Once you see my flat I'd have to kill you, so send Toby up. Give me ten minutes to put some clothes on."

"Right you are boss."

* * *

DENNIS OPENED HIS own front door feeling like an unwelcome stranger.

"Dennis, I'm in the kitchen!" Sandra shouted.

He reluctantly put his head round the door.

"I've done you dinner, it will be ready in twenty minutes, go and relax Den."

Dennis tried not to smile, he nodded and put the bag of Mo's cakes in the bread bin.

"They look nice Den," Sandra said, nodding towards the cakes.

"Yes, one of my fellow patients made them for everyone at the club, he's a chef."

"That's nice Den, I'll try one for pudding."

"Good idea," the Professor agreed.

He went upstairs to shower and change before joining his wife for dinner.

"A nice light starter Den, spears of asparagus."

"Nice," Dennis lied.

"Steak Diane for mains," she confirmed.

Sharp knife required, he pondered.

* * *

TOBY STUDIED HIMSELF in the lift mirror sweeping back his hair and dusting off some dandruff from the collar of his jacket. He felt bad wondering what Claire would be wearing rather than who had tried to kill her. He reached the fourth floor and found her apartment.

She was wearing an unflattering casual grey tracksuit, he was disappointed once again.

"Come in Toby, I'm flattered that you're looking out for me, take a seat." She gestured to the armchair.

Sky news was on the TV but muted. Portishead emitted from a set of speakers.

"Sir Martin is very concerned about your safety Claire?"

"I realise that. Fancy a beer, wine?"

"A beer would be good thanks."

He watched her disappear into the kitchen and took the chance to look around the apartment. It was modern, minimalist, lacking warmth. He wasn't surprised.

She returned with a bottle of a Mexican lager. "No lime I'm afraid."

"No worries Claire. So what do you think about this morning?"

"I don't think they were trying to kill me, I think it was a warning."

"A warning about what?"

Claire shrugged and took a sip of her red wine. "I've got a bit of history with the Uzbek business, but I doubt if it's that."

"I had two initial thoughts Claire," Toby offered.

"Go on."

"My first thought was Myerson."

"And mine," she concurred.

"Then I thought it might be something to do with the documentary."

"My thoughts entirely Toby."

"I've done a bit of digging Claire." Toby picked up his iPad and gestured to the vacant space on the sofa. "May I?"

Claire gave a positive double tap on the brown leather beside her. He sat next to her and keyed in his code before showing her a screenshot of a Russian newspaper.

"This is an article from 1980 describing the massacre of an entire platoon of conscripts in the village Scott saw napalmed by Russian migs. I've got the translation which describes the massacre by the 'Mujahideen', claiming the soldiers were ambushed, mutilated and then their bodies burned."

"A cover up," Claire surmised.

"Exactly, and it gets more interesting. In 1984 a delegation of the rouge platoon's relatives made representations to government officials but with no success. But with Gorbachev and Glasnost opening things up during the late eighties one or two articles emerged giving a different account." Toby showed Claire more screenshot photos of various newspaper cuttings and documents.

"This is very impressive Toby, you dug all this up in an afternoon?"

"No Claire, I started digging as we were watching the documentary."

"Why?"

"I had a bad feeling about it. Look, 1991, compensation was paid to the families after the government admitted the platoon hadn't been killed by the Mujahideen, they'd died in a friendly fire accident."

"Friendly fire," Claire said cynically.

"Exactly, that's not how Scott saw it and his documentary points to collusion with that guy Felix and the KGB stroke military intelligence. Alice was high up in the BBC but the documentary was only aired on Open University. Scott tried to sell it to all and sundry but nobody would touch it. Why?"

Claire looked at Toby. "I've misjudged you Toby. You're on the ball."

"Thanks Claire, but this is my job."

"Yes it is, thank you for your efforts and thank you for looking after me," she said, placing a hand on his arm.

"No problem Claire. So do you think the Russians were warning you not to bring up old wounds?"

"It's possible Toby." Claire refilled her glass and stretched. "I'm thinking Scott didn't die of a heroin overdose when he went back to get Mo."

"I'm thinking the same."

* * *

THE PROFESSOR CUT into his Steak Diane with the steak knife he'd requested. He looked at his wife with total disdain, he imagined plunging the knife into her heart there and then. Well, between courses. He could then wait until morning and do the same to loverboy when he returned from his night with lover number two.

"Are you ok Den?"

"It's fine, nice sauce," he replied dishonesty.

"No, I meant are you ok? Are you okay with Raymond living here?"

"Have I got a choice?"

"Not really Den but I'd like you to be comfortable with the situation."

"I'm happy with Thursdays."

"Don't be like that Den."

He couldn't resist it. "So are you comfortable with Raymond spending his Thursday's with a young lady?"

Sandra gave her husband the look. "You can't blame me Dennis after the uni business you put me through and we haven't had any kind of physical relationship for years have we?"

Dennis toyed with his steak. "Do you want me to leave?" he asked. "Pack my bags and move out?"

"Where to?" she responded.

"The coast, I sometimes think I'd like to spend my last days by the sea."

"You'd hate it Den, you're such a townie."

"It would be easier for you if I just disappeared."

"I know you're very ill Dennis, I'd like to agree some kind of cease fire between us. Do you think it's possible?"

Dennis paused for thought, he cogitated on seeing his wife being fucked by another man in his own bed. He was still bruised from Raymond's punch in his kidney.

"Are you going to try one of my friend's brownies?" he asked pleasantly.

"I'm full as a blister Den, maybe tomorrow. I've got a better idea, let's go to bed."

* * *

MICKY COULDN'T GET to sleep, he was chewed up thinking about Frankie. Tracey had been kept awake by his tossing and turning.

"You're stressed ain't you Micky?" she asked finally.

He turned his back on her and stared at wall.

"It's that Frankie ain't it?"

She knew him too well.

"It's that motor, you think he's flash, should have spent the money on the baby."

"I'd like to kill the little cunt," he seethed.

Tracey sat up and put the bedside light on. "Honestly Micky you're pathetic. Who are you to judge him? You've gambled, womanised and god knows what all your life, you ignored your daughter for most of her life now you're being holier than thou because she's with a fella who is just like her father."

"I gave him five grand Trace," he sulked.

"Why for fucks sake?" she chided him.

"For the baby."

"So why didn't you give it to Shirley?"

Micky didn't reply.

Tracey answered her own question, "Well we both know the answer to that, she'd think the same as me, where'd that dosh come from? Honestly Micky if someone gave you five grand when you were Frankie's age what would you have wasted it on? The horses, football, boxing. You would have lost it on some stupid bet, at least he has spent it on something he can get his money back from. For god's sake you men, you're pathetic!"

31

THE DAY AFTER THE NIGHT BEFORE

RAYMOND AND GRACE sat naked on the sofa, they both leaned forward in unison and snorted a line of cocaine that he'd distributed on the glass coffee table.

They reclined laughing and clawing each other.

"So how's the master plan coming along Raymondo?" Grace quipped.

"Well I reckon hubby will be under the soil within three months," he guessed.

"Three months!" Grace protested.

"Yes, which means I've got to put up with the woman's ridiculous cooking and drink all those fucking 1970s liqueurs." Raymond thought that Dennis would agree with him on this point. *Who still fucking drinks Dubonnet for Christ's sake.*

"Oh poor Raymondo, and all that sex you have put up with, you poor thing."

"Thanks for your sympathy Grace, it's all for a good cause remember, once he's popped his clogs and she's signed her house away to me, we can start making plans for that gaff in Spain."

* * *

SANDRA LOOKED AT her husband lying naked next to her on their matrimonial bed. He looked almost skeletal. She'd never seen anyone so pale. The only redeeming factor was the smile on his sleeping face, and she'd put it there.

She derived no pleasure from the act, in fact she was repulsed by it. But there was method in her madness, as he was about to find out.

He opened an eye, for a moment he was disorientated before recalling the night before.

"You're awake Den?"

"I think so, should I get up? Is Raymond due back?"

"There's no rush Den, you're still my husband, we are all adults."

He wasn't sure what she meant, he recalled Raymond challenging him to sleep with Sandra. "What happens now Sandra?"

"I enjoyed last night Den, let's make a date for next Thursday," she lied, running her hand over his beard.

"I might be arrested next Thursday," he mumbled.

"What?"

The Professor told her about the Minister of Health's visit and his intentions.

"Blimey Den! You're crazy!"

"That's the point, it's my chance to do something crazy."

"So what do you propose to do to him?"

"Stab him in the heart with this," he reached beside the bed and showed her the unwashed steak knife with which he'd eaten the Diane.

Sandra looked at her husband, slowly a smile lit up her face.

"Keep the knife Den but I've got a better use for it." She took hold of his manhood and stroked it back to attention. "I want you to kill someone for me Den."

SANDRA RETURNED TO the bedroom after showering. The Professor was still lying on the bed feeling completely drained. He watched her get dressed. *A repeat performance*, he thought, as she teased him pulling up her stockings.

"Raymond's got a thing about sexy underwear," she declared. "I'm going to the hairdressers, Raymond's taking me to the theatre tonight. I'll be back in a couple of hours but Raymond should be here soon. Enjoy your lie in Den."

Dennis dozed off for a good hour, he was woken by Raymond slamming the front door. He could hear a lot of door banging in the kitchen as Raymond searched for suitable breakfast food.

There was a sudden brief silence, then he heard Raymond bounding up the stairs. Dennis was nervous for some reason, he pressed the record option on his phone on the bedside chest.

Raymond entered the bedroom munching on one of Mo's brownies. "Well, well, the lord of the manor has been carrying out his duties." He spoke with his mouth full, he was holding the bag of cakes, it looked to be his second. "I'm bloody starving, I was thinking a fry up but these brownies are gorgeous."

"I think it was more of a duty for Sandra to be honest, I just laid back and thought of England," Dennis piped up.

"A sympathy fuck I would imagine," Raymond laughed.

"How was Grace?"

"Insatiable, I'm knackered. I hope you've sorted your missus cause I need the day to recover." Raymond sat on the edge of the bed. "It must be strange having sex thinking this could be the last time," he smirked.

Dennis glanced at the steak knife, Raymond started on his third cake. He noticed the knife. "So you decided to fuck your wife rather than kill her then?"

"That's not for Sandra," Dennis stated calmly.

"Oh, you want to stab me? Who could blame you, after all, I've taken over your home, bed, wife. You must really hate me."

"I do hate you but the knife's not for you or Sandra."

Raymond picked up the knife. "Really? Who's it for, yourself?" he asked sceptically. "Ouch!" He winced in pain holding his gut. "Don't know what that was. Had a takeaway curry last night, must have been a bit dodgy. So who's the knife for?"

"Grace," Dennis whispered.

"What did you say?"

"It's for Grace, Sandra wants me to kill Grace."

Raymond was sweating profusely, he grabbed Dennis by the throat but had to move one hand to his stomach as it spasmed. He was consumed with a mixture of pain and anger. His one hand was enough to choke the Professor's scrawny neck though. He sat astride Dennis looking down on the cancer ridden shell of a man. "You fucking stupid lying cunt!"

"It's true," Dennis croaked, gasping for air.

Raymond turned Dennis on his front pushing his face into the pillow. Raymond put his face next to Dennis'. "You want to fuck with me Dennis, you want to fuck with me?"

Dennis was suffocating but then Raymond eased the pressure and spoke into his exposed ear. "Listen to me Dennis, listen good. This is how it ends, in a second I'm going to fuck you, I've fucked your wife, now I'm going to fuck you."

He shoved his index finger into Dennis' anus, Dennis screamed and tried to turn over but didn't have the strength.

Raymond winced with pain and then vomited all over the Professor's back. "Fucking hell!" he bawled, then composed himself as the pain subsided. "Where was I? Oh yes, I'm going to fuck you Dennis, then I'm going to suffocate you. Your last few moments of life will be very distressing for you. Being buggered by your wife's lover. Being buggered by your wife's lover who will then suffocate you. When Sandra comes home I'll suggest we go to bed where we will discover poor Dennis dead as a dodo having succumbed to his cancer. Sandra and I will be surprised but delighted. I shall break open some fizz and fuck your wife next to your dead body. Then in the coming weeks I'm going to get your house signed over to me, after which Sandra is going to meet exactly the same end as you mate. Face down in a pillow being buggered senseless by Raymondo."

He vomited again, over Dennis' head but it didn't seem to deter him. Raymond put his hand in his pocket and pulled out a small packet of cocaine, which he sniffed up in one go.

"No one will miss her will they Den? She's got no friends. If your boys ever turn up I'll tell them she walked out on me and has disappeared. Then when the dust settles I will move Grace in. Believe me Den, Grace is one hell of a woman and a bloody good cook. I won't miss your wife's cooking and neither will you."

Raymond pushed Dennis's face into the pillow with one hand and opened his fly with the other. "So quite a finale eh Den?"

Dennis prepared to die, he felt a searing pain as Raymond entered him. He thought of a holiday he had on the Italian island of Ischia in an effort to blank out the dreadful scenario his torturer had painted.

"One last thing Den, I'm going to pave your fucking garden over," Raymond tormented him.

Tears started to run from Dennis' eyes as he began to lose consciousness. Suddenly he heard a stifled cry as Raymond relaxed his grip and slumped forward collapsing like a dead weight on top of him.

Dennis desperately tried to move but couldn't, Raymond's lifeless body was too heavy.

He could see the bag of Mo's brownies laying on the floor next to the empty cellophane packet that had contained Raymond's 'Charlie'. The Professor, a confirmed atheist all his life, managed a feint smile. *Maybe there is a God after all.*

THE PROFESSOR TRIED without success to get the dead weight off him. He was too frail, besides any movement and he felt Raymond's still erect penis inside him.

He managed to reach for his phone and remembered he'd pressed record. He was about to phone 999 but couldn't face the embarrassment. He phoned Micky instead.

"Professor," Micky answered, whilst he walked back to the station wondering whether the police had found Mo, the gun, or both.

"He's dead! He's dead!" Dennis yelled.

"Slow down mate, who's dead?"

"Raymond, my wife's lover, he's dead."

"How-what?"

"The ca-" He was about to say cakes, Mo's cakes, but remembered their deal.

"He's had a heart attack, he's dead."

Just then he heard a key in the door. "Shit, Sandra's home!" He hung up.

"Fuck me, what a morning," Micky exclaimed as he walked into the station.

"Raymond!" Sandra called out from the bottom of the stairs. "Someone's hit your wing mirror! I'll be up in a minute, where's Dennis?"

The Professor started to laugh. He hated Raymond's gas guzzling beast of a motor, it was far too wide for their Islington mews.

He could feel Raymond's manhood start to shrink as he heard Sandra climb the stairs. "I'll be one minute, I've got that new underwear on you told me to buy, I hope you didn't overdo it yesterday."

Dennis tried desperately to wriggle free but it was too late, Sandra opened the bedroom door. He heard her scream and then a thud as his wife fainted.

32

INAPPROPRIATE BEHAVIOUR

SIR MARTIN WAS waiting in the reception area at the Ministry of Defence.

Toby escorted Claire into the building, nodding to the familiar security guards.

"Good morning Claire, how are you feeling?"

"I'm fine Sir Martin."

"Toby, thanks so much for keeping an eye out."

"No problem Sir Martin, all quiet on the western front. Let me know if we are needed," Toby replied, and left to join Christine.

"Not a great morning to be meeting the minister Claire, the papers are full of rumours of scandalous behaviour in Westminster."

"So I heard on the news Sir Martin, the minister will be a bit sensitive about it."

"Why so Claire?"

"Because he left his first wife for a much younger researcher."

"So he did. Still, who casteth the first stone and all that."

Claire gave him her disapproving stare.

They were escorted to the minister's office. He emerged from behind his solid mahogany desk, a tall slim man in his mid-fifties with what Claire took to be a patronising manor.

"Sir Martin," the two old Etonians shook hands warmly.

"Robert, good to see you."

"You too Sir Martin and you must be Claire, Sir Martin's told me all about you. Reckons you'll be in his seat sooner or later."

Claire gave a slight dutiful smile and shook his hand. He directed them towards the corner of the office to a casual circular table surrounded by four chairs. An assistant poured coffee and left the room.

"So I will cut straight to the chase, the only thing on the agenda this morning should be the spate of vehicle attacks across the West and the fallout from the fall of Raqqa etcetera. But unfortunately we have, I feel, been side-lined by other time consuming, energy sapping, and in my opinion, trivial events."

Sir Martin and Claire exchanged quizzical glances.

"With respect minister, I wouldn't regard yesterday's incident with Claire a trivial matter," Sir Martin jumped in.

"I appreciate that Sir Martin, but the chain of events that have led to the despicable attack on Claire have come about simply because of political events on the other side of the pond."

"Minister?" The head of M15 pretended to be mystified.

"I'll be frank, Trump and his team have put enormous pressure on the CIA, who in turn have put pressure on us. This bloody fiasco with the cyber-crime conference has snowballed out of control. Now listen, we need to refocus, our priority must be the situation in Syria and Iraq. With ISIS on the back foot we can expect a lot of their serving fighters with British passports seeking to return to the UK. You know my views on this, one returning from the battlefield is one too many. I want to see them eliminated over there before they return and cause havoc on our streets. We are reliant on Russian boots on the ground and American drones to help us clear up this mess, so I need them onside.

"First, I want this Afghani chef arrested and charged ASAP. Second, this expensive charade at the hospital that seems to have created a plot rather than solved one, I want the co-conspirators arrested and charged. Lastly, Claire, I understand there's some friction between you and Wayne Myerson. Whatever it's about, it ends now. I'm about to have a meeting with him where I shall be giving him a hit list with over three hundred names on it. As I said we can't afford to be side-tracked."

They were interrupted by the minister's private secretary putting his head around the door. "Sir," he beckoned the minister.

"Is it urgent Miles?" the minister replied.

"Yes, sir."

"Excuse me I'll be back in a sec, help yourselves to more coffee."

Claire looked at her phone, Sir Martin noticed a slight smirk as she showed him the screenshot of breaking news that Christine had just sent her:

FIVE CABINET MINISTERS ACCUSED OF INAPPROPRIATE SEXUAL BEHAVIOUR ON POLITICAL BLOG.

A few minutes later the minister returned looking slightly ashen faced. "Where was I?" he asked.

"Something about being sidetracked," Claire reminded him.

***

MICKY CALLED ANNA, quoting the password 'Shetland pony' and was directed to a nearby pub where he shuffled uncomfortably outside, feeling like an alcoholic waiting for his first beer of the day.

He was still thinking about Tracey's lecture, he knew she was right, he'd have to move on and let it go. His plan was now to get his gun back and sell it to the Professor, he'd then open a long term account for his granddaughter.

His phone rang. "Anna," he answered.

"Ok, you see the alley opposite you? There's a service road running behind the shops, turn right, walk about fifty meters you'll see a metal staircase leading to a yellow door above a kebab shop."

"Ok." Micky crossed the road. "I'll just take my package and go," he confirmed as he walked down the alley.

"Ok, but your friend's here."

"Friend?"

"Yes, your friend."

Mo, Micky thought to himself, as he turned into the service road. The metal staircase came into view, he could see a Range Rover parked beside it. The driver got out and opened the passenger door for a young lady who climbed out and looked up at the yellow door.

"Old bill," he said aloud as he dodged into a car mechanic workshop. The young women was wearing a black trouser suit, she had impossibly blonde hair. Definitely police, he pondered, calling Anna as the policewomen started to climb the metal steps.

"Anna, it's Micky, I think the police are outside, one's going up the steps-" The call was interrupted by a banging on the door.

Micky turned on his heels and headed back to the station.

Anna swore as the TV blared and the kettle hissed, she was obviously in. She opened the door peeking through the gap as she left the chain on. "Can I help you?" she asked.

"Hi Anna, I'm Claire Peterson, you met my colleague Toby. I have some paperwork for you to sign so we can issue you a National Insurance Number as promised."

Anna reluctantly unhooked the chain and let Claire into her tiny studio flat. There was basically one room with a dingy bathroom off it. There was a tiny kitchenette in one corner and a hospital style curtain concealing a recess housing a bed.

Anna offered Claire a coffee, they sat at a small 1970s formica table. Claire put some documents and a pen down.

"You want me to sign something?" Anna offered.

"I've a few things I'd like to ask you first Anna, relating to Mohamed. Have you heard from him at all?"

"Who?"

"Oh I see, sorry. Mo, the chef," Claire confirmed.

"No, is he still in trouble?"

"I hope not but I need to find him urgently, there are other interested parties who aren't as friendly as me."

"But he's just a chef miss, that's all."

"I hope you're right Anna but you can't go round poisoning your clients even if they possibly deserve it."

"I know miss, but I think his illness and everything got on top of him."

"So you don't harbour any bad feelings about him, his inappropriate behaviour?"

"What inappropriate behaviour?"

"Toby played me the recording Anna, I'd call him adding extra tang to the salad dressing inappropriate behaviour."

Anna blushed and briefly glanced at the curtain. "He didn't force me, honest."

"I believe you Anna, I understand you were in no position to resist. I'm sure the atmosphere in restaurant kitchens is no different to the Houses of Parliament." Claire gave a wry smile.

"It was our little thing miss, our way of striking back at those fuckers who put our jobs at risk."

"So you were an equal partner in creating some extra tang, you didn't feel forced into it by chef? It was strictly for revenge and some bonus cash?"

Tears welled in the Moldovan's eyes. "I went through all this with your partner."

"I'm his boss," Claire quickly confirmed. "I think he was a bit embarrassed. You see Anna, you might not know this but Mo, chef, is a hero. I want to help him but I don't want to put my neck on the block for him if he's done anything to tarnish my opinion. Let me ask you a couple of questions then I'll be on my way."

Anna nodded.

"Is there any way he could flirt with radical Islam?"

"No chance miss, I'd stake my family's lives on it."

"Could the poisoning of the conference be anything other than revenge?"

"No, he'd have no way of knowing who the guests were."

"Ok, one last question, please be honest Anna it's very important. Did he at any time force you to carry out any acts of a sexual nature, against your will?"

Anna looked uncomfortable, she glanced round again at the curtain. Claire gestured towards the curtain with her pale blue eyes.

Anna nodded.

Claire stood up, strode over to the curtain and slid it open.

"Hi Claire." Mo sat on the bed holding Micky's gun.

"Mo, what are you doing?" She tried to remain calm.

"He's my guest!" Anna shouted. "Put the gun down it's not yours," she added.

"Whose gun is it Mo?" Claire chipped in.

"Go out Anna this is nothing to do with you!" Mo shouted.

She ran out, almost falling down the stairs. Christine and Craig jumped out the Range Rover and grabbed her. "He's got a gun, he's got a gun!" she screamed at them.

Craig reached into the glove compartment and pulled out his own weapon whilst Christine held onto Anna.

"It's the Professor's Claire, he pleaded with me to look after it for him."

"The Professor, a gun, why?"

"He's hell bent on killing the Minister of Health."

"Give me the gun Mo," she demanded, just as Craig banged on the door.

"You ok Claire?" he shouted.

"I'm ok Craig, just give us a couple of minutes!" she shouted back. "The gun Mo."

"You know I'm not a terrorist Claire."

"I know that Mo, but possession of an un-registered firearm will get you five years, so hand it over."

He pointed the gun directly at Claire. "I'm sorry Claire, I'm not going to prison. I don't want to hurt you or anybody else, I just want to cook and live my life."

"I understand Mo but the Americans want their pound of flesh and the Russians are after you as well, you'd be better off letting me arrest you."

"The Russians?"

"They don't want the documentary to be aired again, they gave me a warning the other day." She pointed to the graze on her forehead. "They won't warn you Mo, they will find you and kill you, probably poison you, which would be ironic."

They both heard sirens in the distance.

"Sorry Claire. You know me, I'm a survivor, I'll take my chances."

He held the gun to her side and led her to the kitchen area where he found some gaffer tape. He wrapped the entire roll around her hands behind her back. He then led her to the bathroom and helped her lay down in the bath. He put the last of the tape around her mouth, put the gun in the bath next to her and climbed onto the toilet seat to open the window.

"I'm sorry Claire, I won't trouble you again. I came back to try and help Brenda get her drug trial, we all want the same thing, maybe you could help. I'm going to keep running till I find a kitchen far away enough from you, the yanks, the fucking Russians. Take care."

She watched Mo disappear out of the bathroom window.

She wondered if she'd ever see him again.

33

THE SIEGE

TOBY AND MITTAL arrived half an hour after Anna had fled the flat.

They were quickly briefed on the situation. Marksman were in position, the area had been completely sealed off. A police helicopter hovered above and a news one flew nearby.

They were given a description of the flat and told special forces were on their way if needed.

Toby looked at Mittal and glanced towards the steps. Craig joined them and the three discussed the situation for a couple of moments. Toby then casually climbed the stairs and knocked on the door. "Claire! Mo! It's Toby, can I join you please?"

There was no response.

"Mo, it's very important we have a chat. I'm very concerned about Alice. We think she might be in great danger, we need your help."

Toby waited a couple of minutes, then spoke into his wire for Craig to send Christine up. A minute later Christine joined Toby. "You heard my comments re. Alice?" he whispered.

"Yes Toby, clever, he should have responded."

"I concur."

"What now?"

"Let's go for it Chris, on the count of three."

They both brought out their hand guns. Toby, in hushed tones, counted down, "One, two, three, go!"

They both shoulder barged the yellow door. It didn't budge.

Craig ran up the stairs with Mittal to join the scrum. The door gave way and Toby rushed in whilst the other three fell over each other, landing in an undignified heap.

Toby scoured the room, adrenaline pumping through his veins. He saw the room was empty, the curtain above the bed open. He rolled onto the floor and pointed the gun underneath. He jumped back up as Craig was moving towards the bathroom.

"Cover me!" Toby yelled as he tried to open the bathroom door. It was locked. He put his ear to the door and gestured for silence. He heard a knocking noise and a muffled yell. Toby nodded to the others who repeated the assault on the bathroom door, which caved in easily.

Toby rushed in screaming, "Drop the gun! Drop the gun!"

He stumbled towards the toilet then saw his boss tied up in the bath lying next to the discarded gun. Christine and Craig came in, Craig went to Claire and ripped the tape off her mouth and arms.

"I'm ok, I'm ok," Claire assured.

"Where is he?" Toby shouted, expecting Mo to be hiding in the flat.

"He's gone, he went out the window ages ago," she nodded at the bathroom window, "he's not armed, he left the gun with me."

Christine helped Claire get out the bath guiding her to the sofa in the main living space. Toby told Craig to inform the armed police to stand down and alert everyone the situation was under control.

"You ok Claire?" Christine asked as she gave her a glass of water.

"I'm absolutely fine, there's nothing here for us, let's go back to HQ. Craig drops us off and then get the gun to forensics."

"What about Anna?" Christine asked. "She warned us."

"Put her in a hotel till the cleaners have fixed up her flat."

Toby was concerned the Ice Queen was acting as if nothing had happened.

She brushed off some hair from her suit. "That's not the most savoury bath I've ever been in," she laughed. Claire thought about the last question she asked Anna. She didn't get an answer which was probably a good thing. *Men were so disappointing*, she pondered.

* * *

THE PROFESSOR WAS relieved Raymond's corpse was now no longer attached to him. He managed with great effort to wriggle free just as Sandra came to.

"Raymond!" she screamed and moved over to the bed. "Raymond what have you done?" she shouted, shaking him.

"He's dead. He tried to rape me, he had a heart attack, he tried to bugger me," Dennis said.

Sandra started to scream uncontrollably, Dennis attempted to calm her down. She saw the steak knife on the bedside chest and made a grab for it.

"You bastard!" she yelled at her husband and slashed at him with the knife. He slid off the bed as she screamed, "I'm going to kill you, you bastard!"

Suddenly the doorbell rang, Dennis scrambled up and ran to the stairs yelling, "Help me! Help me!"

Sandra slammed the door shut behind him and lunged at him as he legged it down the stairs. She lost her balance and fell down the stairs beside him, the knife fell from her hand to the bottom of the stairs.

Dennis opened the door, Micky stood dumbstruck at the scene before him.

"Micky help me, for god sake help me," Dennis pleaded, out of breath. "She tried to stab me, Raymond's dead, you've got to help me, where's your gun?"

"Ok, ok, calm down," Micky replied, stepping into the house and closing the front door. Sandra was semi-conscious at the bottom of the stairs. "Get some rope or something we can tie her up with," Micky demanded, "and put some fucking clothes on mate."

Micky dragged Sandra onto the sofa in the living room and closed the curtains. The Professor emerged from the garden shed with an assortment of string, cord and cable.

"Go and find something to gag her with," Micky ordered.

When Dennis returned with his dressing gown tie, his wife was trussed up like a turkey. "I've got to have a bath Micky, I'll leave you with her. There's wine, beer, help yourself."

After a few minutes Sandra came round, she tried to scream but realised she was bound and gagged. She was face down. She tried to kick her legs but Micky had tied them with cord. Her skirt hitched up with her wriggling, exposing the new sexy underwear she'd bought to please her recently departed lover.

"Wow, nice, I can see why Raymond went to all that trouble," Micky whispered in her ear. "What we going to do with you?"

He thought about the fifteen grand, he could buy his daughter and granddaughter a decent house up north. He couldn't see Frankie moving out of London, it would be a win-win situation.

He looked at his phone, there was a message from an unknown number: *Hi Micky, Sorry mate, the police have your property! I gave it a good clean and told them it was the Professor's. I left a magic potion in my left luggage locker, it will work in seconds. Please give my fifteen grand to Brenda. Good luck, pleasure to have known you. Mo.*

"WHAT ARE WE going to do with Raymond's body?" the Professor enquired as he emerged bathed and dressed.

"Well, there are three scenarios mate. First, you transfer the fifteen grand you owe Mo to me. Mo wants his money in cash to go directly to

Brenda for her trial. Then for another twenty grand I would get rid of Raymond's body, which is a bit risky for all of us. Second option is you dial 999 and tell the truth. The third is…" Micky went up to Dennis and whispered in his ear, "Mo left me a pot of his signature poison. In a minute I'm going to see my granddaughter, let me know which route you want to go. Now let's sort out the finances."

Dennis ushered Micky into the kitchen. "I don't owe you anything, you haven't done anything," Dennis said.

"Excuse me mate, what's that dead body upstairs then?"

"That wasn't the deal, and besides he had a heart attack."

Micky noticed the remaining brownies in the tupperware box. "What are they then?" Micky pointed at Mo's cakes.

"They didn't kill him, he had a fucking massive heart attack, probably brought on by his cocaine habit. They would have just given him the shits."

Micky grabbed a cake and offered it to Dennis.

"Fuck off Micky, I'm dying anyway!"

Micky turned and went back to the living room, he slipped off Sandra's gag and stuffed the cake in her mouth before retying the gag. "You've got twenty-four hours to sort out the dosh, don't fuck me about or I'll be back with Mo's signature dish."

It was half an hour since Micky left, Dennis had sat staring at his trussed up wife considering the options. He walked over to his 1970s turntable, picked out a record from his vinyl collection and turned the volume up to ten. Prog rock omitted from the speakers.

He lifted Sandra's legs and sat down next to her. "You hated this album Sandra and to be honest I wasn't too keen, but I loved the cover and the name. *Look at yourself.*" He showed her the cover which was simply a mirror.

She looked at her hazy reflection, she was sweating profusely.

"I'm not sure if those brownies killed Raymond. Of course the greedy bastard had three of them, probably all that sex and cocaine made him peckish. I'm going to show you something then I'm going to untie you and dial 999. I've had enough Sandra."

He put his face next to hers and held the album cover up. "Look at us, how did we come to this."

He picked up his phone and played the video recording which started when Raymond entered the bedroom and ended when he first entered Dennis.

He watched his wife sob uncontrollably, shaking her head.

"You probably think I deserved that for what I did all those years ago and you may be right but what with the cancer and now this I think I've suffered enough. I'd just like to spend the short time I've got left in the garden please."

He untied her and released the gag, if she did scream she would be drowned out by the heavy riffs of Uriah Heep.

She winced in pain. "Dennis I've just shit myself. I think that cake killed him, I think I'm dying."

Dennis dialled 999. He asked for both the ambulance and police.

34

THE RED LION

TOBY GOT THE first round in, he couldn't recall ever being so desperate for a pint. "What a fucking day," he announced to the tired and weary troops gathered in the Red Lion for Friday drinks.

"Tell me about it!" Christine hollered, she'd only just arrived.

"How's the boss?" Craig asked.

"She's back at her desk, I had to go and buy her a change of clothes," Christine replied.

"Agent Provocateur?" one of the minions jibed.

No-one else laughed. She was well and truly the boss now, respect had replaced tittle tattle.

"Strictly M&S, a functional tracksuit, if you must know," Christine confirmed.

They discussed the state of the Moldovan's bath and other incidental details relating to the 'siege'. They were on their third round when their collective jaws were on the floor in shock.

"Is someone going to get me a large gin and tonic?" The Ice Queen stood before them in a snug pale blue tracksuit. There was a pregnant pause whilst her team got over their shock.

"Bombay Sapphire ok Claire?" Toby mumbled.

"As long as it's large, I don't really care," she replied.

"You ok boss?" Craig enquired.

"I'm not sure what was worse, being held at gun point or the now ex Minister of Defence's aftershave," she quipped.

The crowd dutifully laughed.

"So this is the infamous Red Lion, I hope I'm not crashing your party?"

"Well, we'll obviously have to find someone else to bitch about boss," Christine laughed.

"So what do you think of Chris' fashion sense?" Claire gave a twirl, immediately putting everyone at ease.

"With respect boss, I would have done better," Mittal chipped in.

"Really Mittal? What would you have got me?"

"A nice sexy off the shoulder number," he replied seriously.

His boss gave him an icy stare, his colleagues thought he'd overstepped the mark. "Really Mittal, I've got a date tomorrow night, would you like to be my dresser?"

"Does that mean I'm fired?" Christine enquired.

"You're my chaperone Chris, and Craig, Sir Martin won't let me out alone until he meets his Russian counterpart on Monday."

"Where're we all going on this date boss?" he queried.

"Dinner, a concert and then who knows. Of course I'm going to have to kill you both afterwards."

"What happens in Vegas stays in Vegas!" Christine shouted above the Friday night din.

"Shouldn't we vet your date first Claire?" Toby joked, and pried, at the same time.

"No need Toby, you've already met him."

Claire gave him her glare and downed her drink in one. "Ok, what's everyone drinking?" she asked.

* * *

TOBY WAS NURSING the hangover from hell, the Ice Queen's surprise appearance had prolonged the Friday night session. He was due the day off but Sir Martin himself had messaged him asking him to look into the history of the gun Mo had discarded, claiming his fellow patient had asked him to look after it.

Toby was uncomfortable visiting the Professor in hospital, albeit a long way from Tina's.

He met the detectives who'd initially arrested him, Toby looked at the statement with disbelief. "The deceased died whilst sodomising the defendant?" he addressed the detectives.

"Apparently so sir."

"I've been fighting the war on terror too long, the world's gone mad," Toby continued.

"It has sir."

"Thank god my brief is to put together the history of the gun," he announced as he entered the Professor's room.

"Mr Coates, I'm Toby. I'd like to ask you some questions regarding the firearm that your friend claims he was looking after for you."

Dennis just wanted to rest, he'd answered enough questions. "I've told your colleagues everything I know."

"Sorry Mr Coates, I'm not a policeman, I'm from the intelligence services."

"The what?" Dennis sniped.

"The intelligence services, I'm only interested in the gun."

"You're MI5?"

"I'm not James Bond, but I do have the UK's security at heart." He looked down at his iPad at his list of questions. "Please describe the gun Mr Coates."

"What?"

"What make and model is the gun?"

"What?" Dennis repeated.

"The gun you supposedly gave your friend to look after, what kind of gun is it?" Toby was getting exasperated.

"A hand gun," Dennis shrugged.

Toby's head was hurting and this poor old fool wasn't helping. "Make and model Mr Coates?" he snapped.

"It's a hand gun, I haven't got a clue what the make is. I'm a retired lecturer for fuck's sake."

Toby held his aching head. "What car do you drive Mr Coates?" he asked.

"I haven't had a car for six years, no need, I live in town."

Toby recalled the Professor's dislike of the suburbs. "What car did you drive?"

"A Honda Jazz, it was blue. Why?"

"So you recall the make of car you had but not the gun. I don't believe it's yours Mr Coates."

Dennis knew he'd been found out, he just hoped he'd bought Mo enough time to get as far away from the shitstorm as possible. He wanted to come clean but wasn't about to betray Micky. "I'm sorry, you're right it's not mine, it's Mo's."

"Thank you. Why are you covering for him?"

"Because I was hoping he could help me kill the Minister of Health."

"Yes, I heard about this little plot. I must inform you as soon as you're better you will be arrested for conspiracy to commit murder, along with your fellow patient Micky Toms, and of course Mo, once we track him down. Any ideas where he might have gone?"

"Newcastle," Dennis proclaimed.

* * *

SANDRA CAME TO after a long, drug induced sleep. The stomach cramps had died down, as had her bowels. She focused on the tall slim brunette woman sitting beside her. "Who are you?" she enquired.

"I'm Detective Inspector Trish Collins, I'm afraid you're under arrest Mrs Coates."

"What the hell for?" Sandra mumbled weakly.

"Conspiracy to murder."

"Oh that, how's my husband?"

"Quite poorly Mrs Coates, what with his illness and the ordeal the poor fellas been through."

"I presume you've seen the video, is he under arrest too?"

"Yes, I've seen his phone footage and I'm afraid he's under arrest not just for conspiracy to murder but also for his part in a plot against the now ex Minister of Health."

Sandra laughed at the thought of her husband getting involved in such a thing.

"We've also taken Miss Grace Conti into custody."

"Good," Sandra stated.

* * *

MICKY LOOKED AT the mini statement in amazement, he had to apologise to a couple of people queuing at the hole in the wall as he stood staring at the balance in his account. *God bless the Professor,* he thought, the old blighter has been true to his word. He wondered what he'd do about Mo, no doubt the crafty chef had sorted everything out before he disappeared.

He drove to his daughter's, stopping to buy a massive cuddly bear on his way. She opened the door, he knew right away there was something wrong. "What is it love?" he asked, as she collapsed into his arms and sobbed.

"He's left me and the baby dad, Frankie's gone."

Micky felt a mixture of anger and relief. He thought about the car Frankie bought, then he thought about the support he could now give his daughter.

He took her inside and consoled her whilst rocking his granddaughter to sleep. "Don't worry little angel, Grandad's going to get you out of this place. I'm going to get you your own garden," he promised the little mite.

THEY'D BEEN SITTING watching TV for most of the afternoon. "Not more football," Tracey complained, as Micky went to put on another match.

"Yes dad, we want to watch Strictly," Micky's daughter protested.

Micky sat in his favourite chair, his granddaughter asleep in his arms. "Oi, you're a guest in my house love and I only have one rule. If West Ham are playing I get first pick, simple."

There was a knock at the door just as his team kicked off, Tracey went to answer it. "Good evening Mam, I'm DI Collins, is Micky Toms at home?"

Tracey saw two uniformed officers behind her and two police cars parked in the street. She reluctantly went to get Micky. "It's the old bill dear, what's up?"

"I think it's probably to do with the Professor." He passed the baby to his daughter and went to the front door.

"Micky Toms?"

"That's me."

"I'm DI Trish Collins and I'm arresting you for kidnap and conspiracy to murder."

Her colleagues cuffed him and led him to one of the cars.

35

ROCK CHICKS

CHRISTINE AND CRAIG arrived at Claire's apartment a few minutes early, ready for their chaperone duties.

"I wonder who the mystery date is?" Craig asked.

"Don't you start, I've had three texts from Toby today, it's doing his tiny mind in," Christine laughed.

"What you reckon, male or female?" he jibed.

"Honestly you men are ridiculous." She messaged her boss to say they were outside, a few minutes later Claire emerged.

"Wow," Craig commented.

"Hot stuff," Christine said.

Claire was wearing a black sleeveless Ramones t-shirt, a red leather mini skirt, fishnet stockings and red Dr Martens boots. She climbed into the back.

"Didn't know you were a rock chick boss."

"Only at weekends Chris."

"Where to boss?" Craig asked, eyeing her up in the rear view mirror.

"Brixton, meeting my date at Brixton village, then off to a gig at the Academy."

"Right you are boss, who's on? Anyone I'd have heard of?" he asked.

"The Pixies."

"I've heard of them, more of a Coldplay man though to be honest."

"Me too boss, last concert I went to was the Stereophonics," Christine said.

"Lame," Claire answered them both.

They drove in silence to Brixton, parking at the police station. "I'll see you later," Claire announced climbing out of the car.

"Ah ah boss, sorry we need to stick close," Craig said, shaking his head.

"That's right boss, besides I've promised to put Toby out of his misery ASAP," Christine added.

"Poor Toby," Claire sympathised.

They went to a small Thai cafe in the village, Claire's date emerged from the shadows wearing a black Pixies t-shirt and jeans. Craig recognised him before Christine. "Chris, Craig, this is Ricky, your paths have crossed before."

"How you doing?" The American shook their hands, he looked slightly sheepish.

"See you later," Claire said. "Concert should be over eleven-ish, Ricky will walk me back to the car. I'm sure I'm in safe hands."

Claire and Ricky disappeared into the restaurant leaving her colleagues gobsmacked on the sidewalk. "Toby will not like this one bit," Craig shook his head.

Christine laughed. "I wonder what Myerson would make of this liaison," she said.

"So here we are, thanks for accepting my invitation Claire." Ricky smiled.

"Well you're very brave Ricky but the Pixies tickets was an offer I couldn't refuse."

"Nothing to do with my good clean American looks then."

"I did admire your teeth and you've got a good barnet."

"Barnet?"

"Barnet fayre. Hair. It's cockney."

"My sister thinks my hair's very eighties Morrissey, whom she's in love with."

"Your sister has excellent taste."

"She loves the Pixies as well."

"So why did you take the chance of being humiliated by asking me out?" Claire gave him the glare.

"I was scared shitless to be honest Claire, you terrify me, and not just me…"

"Myerson?"

"Yes, you've certainly wound him up, which, to be honest, is a good thing."

"Really, why's that?"

"He's a bully, he hates you Brits and I'm of the mind that we have a special relationship."

"So he didn't encourage you to ask me out?"

"What?"

"It did cross my mind that your invitation was an attempt to either humiliate me or divert my attention in some way," Claire admitted.

Ricky took her hand. "But you accepted?"

"The Pixies are worth the risk," she smiled.

* * *

THE TEXT HAD put Toby off his microwave dinner. He'd asked Christine to let him know who the mystery date was, but he was drunk at the time.

"That fucking yank!" he exclaimed. *The Pixies? When did the Ice Queen start loving the Pixies?*

He tried to get tickets himself. He thought about jumping on the tube and finding a tout, but that may be construed as stalking.

It's a ruse, he decided, *Myerson was behind this.*

But Ricky, he would confess, was a bit of a charmer, in that crass American way.

Toby's day was done, he hoped. He lay in his bath reflecting on the long day. He realised the enemies of the state didn't generally take the weekend off so neither could he. He briefly reflected on the successful rounding up of Mo's motley crew. The 'domestic' drama had entertained him but the whereabouts of Mo and the gun business was exhausting him. Hopefully Monday would bring some news from the ballistics experts as to the weapon's history.

His thoughts turned to his boss. He didn't know if he was more jealous of her seeing the Pixies or her spending the evening with his American counterpart. He tried not to reflect on her conversation with Myerson, he'd had his own dark thoughts about the Ice Queen, but the head of CIA Europe had clearly abused his position.

He didn't understand why men got so worked up by her. Maybe it was she who had the power and knew exactly what she was doing.

Whatever.

He shook his head, trying to get himself out of his thoughts. He knew he spent too much time either fretting or fantasising about her.

* * *

CLAIRE WAITED FOR Ricky, who was jostling for position at the bar in the legendary Brixton Academy. She'd really enjoyed the authentic Thai cuisine in the village, after the week she'd had she needed a fun weekend.

She received a text: *Ricky!? Just be careful Claire, Toby.* She smiled to herself. Was he genuinely concerned for her welfare in a professional capacity or was he just jealous?

A woman walked past her clutching two pints, she did a double take, she knew her from somewhere. It was annoying her, she was fairly certain she'd seen her during the hundreds of hours of CCTV she watched on a daily basis.

Ricky found her and handed her a large glass of red.

"That girl over there in the black leather jacket, I know her from somewhere." She pointed her out to Ricky.

He placed his hand on the back her impossibly blonde head. "Where is your mind?" he asked, playing with the title of a Pixies classic.

Claire ran her index finger over his lips, sufficiently distracted from the woman she thought she recognised. "You really do have perfect Hollywood teeth Ricky."

* * *

"HI CHRIS," CLAIRE said, on the other end of the phone.

"Hi boss." Christine and Craig were relieved to get the call as they waited in the police station car park.

"The gig's over but Ricky's got us backstage passes, no need to hang around, I'm in safe hands."

"Sorry boss, you enjoy yourself but we've got our orders. We'll wait for you, we are on duty till eight am."

"Ok Chris, I'll let you know when we leave the venue," she replied and hung up.

Claire was very impressed that Ricky had got them to the backstage bar, where she'd already spotted quite a few celebs. Ricky disappeared to the toilet and she found herself standing by the young lady she'd seen in the bar earlier. They exchanged smiles.

"This is so exciting isn't it, I'm sure I know you from somewhere," she said to her neighbour.

"Really exciting. Are you a friend of the band?" the women replied.

"I wish, my friend knows someone who knows the promoter or something like that. What about you? You look so familiar, are you famous?" Claire probed.

"God no, I'm just a humble nurse, my boyfriend knows the head of security here, they're both firemen."

"Ha, we're both gatecrashers then. I'm Claire."

"I'm definitely a gatecrasher. I'm more of a metal head to be honest, but I loved the gig. Hi, I'm Tina." They shook hands. "And this is Jed," Tina introduced her man as he brought their drinks over.

"Hi Jed, I'm Claire, another gatecrasher."

"Nice one," he said, smiling. "Love the Ramones," he added, looking at her top.

"What hospital do you work at Tina?" Claire asked.

"Saint Peters. I'm a sister on the chemo ward."

Everything clicked as she realised where she'd seen Tina before. This was 'Toxic Tina' from the Good Poison Club. *What a coincidence,* she thought.

"That's where I might have seen you, I had a relative there," she lied.

"Unfortunately we have a lot of people pass through our doors, I hope your relative is ok. What do you do Claire? Apart from gate crashing."

"Sadly I'm a boring civil servant."

"Not the Ministry of Health?" Jed chipped in.

"No, even worse, international trade, all boring shit like Brexit."

Ricky joined them soon after and quickly engaged in small talk with Jed.

"You must love your job, it's a vocation," Claire said to Tina.

"I used to Claire but we are too stretched to give our patients the care they deserve. Austerity and all that. I might look elsewhere soon, I'm tired of all the politics involved."

"That's really sad Tina. Unfortunately politics rears its ugly head in every job. I know a few people in the health department, they are pulling their hair out, particularly now their boss has been caught with his hand in the cookie jar."

"Yeah, I heard about that. Funny thing is he was supposed to be paying us a visit next Thursday, I was really hoping to give him a piece of my mind. Some of my patients were planning to humiliate him, or worse."

"Really, that's funny, at least you and your colleagues won't have to worry about his straying hands," Claire laughed.

"No, we have enough of that with the consultants! You don't know someone in the health department called Rupert do you?"

"Rupert, I do know a Rupert, very posh." Claire just about recalled Toby's alias.

"Yes, the poshest man I've ever met, but quite cute in an old Etonian way."

"Yes, nice chap, heart's in the right place I suppose. Not as cute as your Jed though." She winked.

36

THE NAKED TRUTH

ANNA HAD COUNTED out the fifteen thousand pounds into two bundles. She'd placed half in a large brown envelope and printed 'Brenda' on it. She'd then travelled by bus and tube to Brenda's suburban semi and put it through the letter box.

She'd carried out Mo's wishes, she felt free, and a lot richer.

Brenda was at the hairdressers, her regular Saturday treat. John was in the kitchen enjoying tea, bacon butty and reading the *Racing Post* when he heard the letter box shudder. He had a rule never to spoil his weekends by opening the post, bills could wait till Monday. So if nature hadn't called he'd have not seen the large envelope on the doormat, but it did and curiosity got the better of him. The slight tear he made in the corner of the envelope revealed the cash enclosed.

He opened the packet and emptied the contents onto the kitchen table. He counted the contents four times. Seven thousand five hundred pounds in fifty pound notes. "Sweet Mary of Jesus, what in god's name has that woman been up to?" he exclaimed.

Brenda felt unsteady as she found her husband in the kitchen playing with a mountain of cash, sat on his paper. "I backed a rank outsider in the three thirty at Doncaster yesterday dear," he jibed.

"Where the hell?" she started, before he threw her the envelope with her name scrawled on it.

"Someone's just given you seven thousand pounds dear." He forgot about the five hundred pound 'finder's fee' he'd stuffed in his back pocket.

"Jesus Christ, this is getting out of control," Brenda muttered.

"What is? Who the hell is this from?" he raised his voice, a rare occurrence indeed.

"It's a long story dear."

"I've got all day," he relied sharply.

* * *

TOBY WAS WOKEN by his phone just after midnight, he was disorientated, he'd crashed out on the sofa whilst watching the day's rugby highlights.

He sluggishly picked up his phone and answered the call.

"Toby."

"What is it Mittal?" He knew it must be serious, it was gone midnight.

"Remember Terry in Edinburgh?" Mittal asked.

"Sure, top fella, he had our backs. Why?"

"Well, apparently he was one of Sir Martin's top guys back in the Hereford days. After the business with Claire and the Russians he sent Terry and a couple of his oppos to the Shetlands to keep an eye on our chef's sponsor."

"Alice, why?" Toby queried.

"First, he was concerned the Russians would turn up to put the freighters on her or worse. He also thought our chef might make his way there," Mittal replied.

"Um, interesting. And?"

"Terry's turned up and her house has been completely ransacked."

"Shit, is Alice ok?"

"There's no sign of her Toby, you'd better let the boss know ASAP."

"She's on a date."

"I know, with the yank. Do you trust him Toby?"

"I don't like him but that's not the point. Do I give Claire a call?"

"Good luck Toby, I'm done for the weekend," Mittal said, ignoring the question, and then hung up.

After a couple of minutes deliberation he phoned Christine and updated her. "What do you think Chris?"

"Leave it to me Toby," she replied.

"How's the date going?" he asked casually.

"Horribly well I'm afraid, the yank's blagged backstage passes- Got to go Toby, just got a message from the boss."

Christine ended the call and read the message. "The boss is out on the street, she's called an Uber," Christine said.

Next to her Craig shook his head. "No way, call her."

Christine nodded and called Claire, she picked up after two rings. "Boss, sorry to trouble you but our Russian friends are being a pain, I suggest you stick to orders and come and join us."

"Hang on Chris," Claire replied.

She heard her boss ask Ricky if he was worried about the Russians and then confirm that neither was she. "I'll text you the Uber details, you can follow ok?"

"Ok boss," Chris agreed reluctantly.

* * *

"IMPRESSIVE," CLAIRE SAID approvingly, as they pulled up outside a swanky Chelsea townhouse.

"I'm in the basement, don't get too excited," Ricky said.

She looked around, she could see the headlights of her colleagues vehicle double parked behind. "I'm sorry Ricky, nothing personal but I'm not comfortable with the situation. I have a reputation to live up to."

"What kind of reputation?" Ricky asked.

"Well let me quote a mutual friend, I'm a stuck up miserable English bitch with no friends. My colleagues call me the Ice Queen apparently," Claire explained.

"You're definitely English," Ricky chuckled.

Claire put her hand on his cheek. "I've really enjoyed tonight Ricky."

He looked at her light blue eyes, wide and inviting, but he couldn't put it off any longer. "I'm sorry Claire, but you really do need to come into my humble abode, someone wants to speak to you."

Claire tried to remain cool. She slowly got out the car, attempting to not show any disappointment, suddenly realising this whole situation may not be what she thought it was. "This isn't your home is it Ricky?"

"No, I live in Stockwell, the CIA don't pay that well." He nodded towards the basement door. "It's a safe house. Please take this." He handed her the key. "I'll wait with your friends. I am sorry Claire."

"I know Ricky, you were just obeying orders," she said honestly. "Listen I saw the Pixies, got a selfie with the drummer, I'm more than happy."

She walked over to the building, opened the basement door and switched on the light. She found herself in a very minimalist living space housing just two black canvas chairs and a small square black gloss table with a laptop on it. Wayne Myerson sat in one of the chairs, he gestured to the other. "Please Claire, take a seat."

She tried to conceal her surprise as she sat down, she'd thought it might be Mo she was meeting.

"I'm sorry about the subterfuge, I hope you had a good evening."

Claire said nothing, she just glared at him.

"I needed a one to one with you Claire, I didn't think you'd accept an invitation and of course I don't blame you. I'm being transferred to Pakistan, some say it's a promotion, I think it's a punishment."

"For what?" Claire spoke for the first time since entering the basement.

"A series of setbacks, losing the Imam, the cyber conference debacle and tomorrow's newspapers," he shrugged.

"Newspapers?"

"It seems that the current climate of whistleblowing for inappropriate behaviour is not just in Hollywood and Westminster."

"I haven't-"

"I know you're not involved Claire, though I wouldn't blame you. I've been under so much pressure but that doesn't excuse my behaviour. You won't be surprised by the allegations."

"Will your wife?" Claire chipped in.

"She's left me Claire, flew back to the States this morning."

Claire didn't reply, she just stared unblinking.

"Most people would show me a little sympathy, I suppose you're not one of them though Claire?"

"No, I'm not."

"You hate me that much?" he asked.

"I don't hate you. I don't like you."

"That's fair. You do like Sir Martin don't you?"

"I respect Sir Martin," she answered honestly.

"He respects you."

Claire gave a faint smile. "Why am I here Mr Myerson?"

The head of CIA Europe leaned forward. "This war on terror is going to last all my working life and possibly yours, we are and always will be on the same side. Sir Martin has high hopes for you, he reckons you'll be in his chair one day and it's important to me that my successor along the line has a good working relationship with our greatest ally."

Claire nodded in approval.

"I can't undo what I said, they were the words of a wound up misogynist and not a representative of the American government."

"They were the words of a bully," she sniped.

"I abused my position of power, that is bullying, you're right. I can't put right the wrong but I would like to part on, if not good personal terms, good professional terms. I know you weren't impressed with my special forces team up in Scotland-"

"They were no match for our chef," she reminded him icily.

"There's no force on earth that's a match for your chef," he confirmed. "Well, acting on intelligence, unusual I know, they followed a

Russian team to your friend Alice's house. The Russians ransacked the house and were in the process of kidnapping her when my boys intervened. We tipped off the Royal Navy who saw off a Ruski Sub, intended to be used to whisk the old lady off to god knows where."

"Shit, this tape has really stirred them up," Claire said.

"Yes, exactly, the Russians nose has been put out of joint by your chef and the back story in 1980s Afghanistan. We've got our collective knickers in a twist over the chef and the conference hall poisoning. My last meeting is on Monday with Sir Martin and our Russian counterpart. We are going to collaborate on a joint drone attack on the remaining ISIS leaders. The Russians particularly want to drop a bomb on this man." Myerson slid the laptop to Claire who looked at a photo and profile of a Chechen fighter. "This character decapitated three Russian journalists, one was the brother of a top dog in the Kremlin. We know where this guy is, the Russians don't. I'd like to give them the co-ordinates in exchange for them calling a halt to their activities regarding yourself, Alice, and of course your chef," Myserson concluded.

"And?" Claire shrugged.

"I'd like your agreement, you've seen the tape, you've heard the story. I've no doubt that poor soul Scott was murdered when he went back to Kabul but that was then and the fall of Raqqa is now, do you agree?"

"I do Mr Myerson, we need to refocus on our mutual enemy. We all need to look forward. So I presume you and, more importantly, your successor is going to forget about the cyber conference business."

Myerson smiled and held out his hand. "I can see why Sir Martin has such high hopes for you Claire."

They shook hands, he led her to the door. "One last thing Claire, tomorrow's story in the newspaper about me is fake news planted by the Russians. It doesn't matter because there are real misdemeanours on my part that could have just as easily surfaced. In the scheme of things it's not important but their meddling in western elections is very important and disturbing. They are hell bent on causing as much division and chaos as possible, it's what they do and they are very good at it. They know they can play games with the States, but they truly believe they can bring Europe to its knees, starting with the UK."

"You truly believe that?" Claire commented.

"It's started Claire, Brexit. Keep those blue eyes wide open. Now! More importantly, what do you think of my man Ricky?" he said smiling.

"Good hair, good teeth, great taste in music," she said.

"So this is where you really live?" Claire scolded Ricky, as Craig pulled up in a nondescript Stockwell side street.

"Yes, this really is my very humble abode I'm afraid." He thanked Craig and Christine for being "such wonderful chaperones" and stepped out onto the South London pavement.

Claire asked them to wait whilst she got out the car to join him.

"I'm sorry Claire," Ricky said finally.

"I know you were only obeying orders."

"I won't miss him Claire." He smiled.

"Neither will I but you know what they say, better the devil you know," she quipped.

"I owe you, we owe you. You've got my number if ever you need our help."

She thought he might ask her out for real but he kissed her on the cheek, then shook her hand. "At least we got to meet the Pixies! See you around," he said finally.

She watched him climb the stairs, then she retreated back to her car.

Christine thought she saw a tear on the Ice Queen's cheek. "You ok boss?" Christine asked.

"It's been a very strange date Chris, very strange."

"Probably because there was a man involved boss. Sorry Craig."

"Very true Chris, two men to be exact."

"Talking about men, I promised to keep Toby updated on your welfare, should I call him?"

"It's gone two in the morning, won't he be cuddling his teddy?" Craig intervened.

"Probably cuddling himself," Christine laughed. Suddenly her phone buzzed. "Talk of the devil," she whispered. "Hi Toby!"

"What's happening?"

"Quite a lot really, do you want to speak to the boss? She's right here." She handed Claire the phone.

"Sorry to interrupt your evening Claire."

"No problem Toby, heard about Alice?"

"Yes, she's safe and sound. Is Ricky still with you?"

"Why?" she replied curtly.

"Listen Claire just be careful, I wouldn't put it past him to put a listening device in your flat or worse."

"You don't trust him?"

Toby quickly surmised by her answer he wasn't with her. "I don't trust Myerson, Claire."

"Neither do I Toby. What you up to tomorrow?"

"Unless the war on terror intervenes, chilling."

"Fancy brunch in our Soho cafe? I'll bring you up to speed on my non date and other matters arising."

"Sounds good, not too early please Claire."

"See you there 11.30?"

"Ok. How were the Pixies by the way?"

"Brilliant, and would you believe I met a friend of yours there, I'll send you a photo of us with the drummer. See you in the morning."

Toby received the photo a few seconds later, he recognised the drummer but couldn't recall his name. He thought Claire looked good as a rock chick, then he focused on Tina. "What the fuck?" he said aloud. He didn't get much sleep that night.

37

SUNDAY BRUNCH

TOBY ARRIVED AT the Soho cafe his usual five minutes early, surprised to find Claire already there. He was also surprised to see her in her suit, he was hoping for something casual being a Sunday.

She was reading a printout of Toby's report into the Good Poison Club shenanigans.

"I want to finish this Toby. Here, have a look at the papers." She passed him The Times, which led on the latest cabinet resignations.

"Where you up to Claire?"

"The gun business, moving onto the protagonist's police statements."

Toby smiled, he was looking forward to her reaction to the Professor's story. He looked at the headlines briefly but was soon studying his iPad.

He spends his life looking at that thing, Claire thought.

Toby ordered a latte and studied the Ice Queen's face as she turned the pages. He punched in a proposed itinerary into his notes app just in case his mind wandered off topic, as it did often when he was in Claire's company. *PIXIES TINA BAIL MOH ALICE.*

"Ouch!" she exclaimed.

He knew instantly where she was up to.

"Christ, the poor Professor. This Raymond character must have gone to the same school as Myerson." She looked at Toby and winked. "Now I know why so many men are arseholes, they're obsessed with buggery."

Toby's cheeks turned crimson.

"I suppose buggery was a sport at your public school Toby?" she jested.

Toby looked at item four on his agenda and thought it would be the perfect time to bring up 'MOH', but she was too involved in the statements and reports to interrupt. He immersed himself in the sports section of The Times until she closed the file.

"I'm rather hoping you have the recording from the Professor's phone on your beloved iPad Toby?"

He didn't know why she made a point about his tablet but he was rather pleased she'd asked. "Yes, I'll find it for you Claire. It's not pleasant listening, it might put you off your brunch."

"Nothing will put me off my brunch Toby, not even sodomy, I'm famished."

She plugged in the earphones, Toby pressed play for her, sat back and studied her pale blue eyes, waiting for a change in her expression. He waited for the four minutes plus recording to end, she remained expressionless before taking out the earphones and sliding the iPad back to him.

"Wow, what a way to go," she stated. "Rape is no joking matter though Toby," she added as an afterthought, looking somewhere beyond Toby.

Toby let the moment pass and they eventually placed their food orders.

"So how were the Pixies?" he asked, meaning something else.

"They were fantastic, great venue."

"What about the encore?" he asked, trying to be clever.

"What, 'Monkey Gone to Heaven' or Myerson?" She said, knowing what he actually meant.

"Were you surprised Claire?"

"No, not at all, I knew as soon as Ricky contacted me there would be a catch," she lied. "I wouldn't have ever gone on an actual date with him," she lied again.

Toby felt good about her answers, which he knew was irrational. "And you coincidentally ran into Tina the nurse?"

"Yes, that was strange…she likes you, 'Rupert', I think she fancies you!" she teased him, and went on to relate the conversation with her. "I'm of the mind that she must come out all this completely untarnished by the sideshow around her," Claire concluded.

"I agree one hundred percent," Toby concurred.

"I'm going to make sure all charges of conspiracy re the Minister of Health are dropped immediately. We created the Good Poison Club simply to keep an eye on Mo, it's proven a complicated and expensive diversion, a good lawyer would crucify us for entrapment."

"Absolutely," Toby agreed again. "What about the Brenda business, the cash?"

"Once again we need to find a happy, or at least realistic, conclusion to this matter. Leave it to me."

"I'd be grateful if I could leave it to you Claire, I wouldn't want Tina to discover Rupert is a sham."

"No problem Toby. What's next?"

"The Minister of Health," Toby sighed.

"Which one?" Claire asked. "The one who's just resigned or his replacement?"

"The former Claire, yes he resigned but he's innocent, it's fake news."

"The Russians?"

"Spot on Claire."

"Myerson warned me, their fingers are everywhere."

"My eldest brother was at school with him, he wants to meet me. I'd like you to be there Claire."

"The school of buggery I presume Toby. If I can help I will, but if he's innocent, why did he resign?"

"He'll tell you himself, we are invited to his club this afternoon."

"Well I'm glad I'm dressed for clubbing," she jested.

Their food arrived and they discussed the Alice business and surmised to where Mo could be. "We should have both the ballistics report and the autopsy on loverboy tomorrow. I'll be very disappointed if either points to Mo, particularly the gun. I can understand his frustration at the client's negative petty complaints. Spunking on their salad was pretty gross but a gun would rekindle suspicions over more sinister motives," Claire concluded.

She lost Toby at 'spunking'. *What a fantastically descriptive word*, he pondered, *two great syllables*.

They headed to meet the ex-Minister of Health. Clare phoned detective inspector Trish Collins demanding that bail be granted to all the protagonists, with the exception of Grace, who was of no interest to her. She could rot in her cell.

The minister shook Claire's hand, he clearly knew Toby personally. They sat whilst tea and small crustless sandwiches were served. "I'll get to the point Claire, I've been stitched up. I've never even shaken hands with the woman in question."

"So why resign?" she asked coldly.

"Because whilst I'm completely innocent of this misdemeanour, I was concerned one or two other skeletons may rear their ugly head."

"Oh dear." Claire pretended to sound sympathetic, whilst thinking, *here we have another misogynistic public school wanker.* "So how can I help minister?" she asked, thinking that the man before her could be the same as the Minister of Defence who she'd met a few days earlier. *There must be a cloning factory somewhere that produces these politicians, probably Eton*, she thought.

"Well Miss Peterson, whilst the press have accepted my resignation, the Prime Minister, and, most importantly, my wife, hasn't. Toby tells me you're very resourceful, despite my unpopularity with some sections of the NHS I have big plans and hopes, unfinished business if you like."

What a load of bollocks, she thought. As did Toby.

"I will do my best minister but there is something I want from you in return."

"If I'm still at my desk Miss Peterson your wish will be my command, what can I do for you?"

* * *

TINA SLEPT LATE, she looked at her phone for the time, 10.30am. There were three messages. The first was from Claire with the selfie.

Next was Brenda: *Must see you! Another gift?!?*

Lastly was one from Freddie: *Sorry to bother you Tina, just to let you know my dad passed away last night after a short illness.*

Feck, she thought. She didn't even know he was ill. She would phone Freddie later.

She presumed Jed was cooking her breakfast with just his firefighter's helmet on. She was gasping for a mug of coffee.

Suddenly her phone rang, it was Jed. "Jed, where's my breakfast?"

"Sorry Tina I'm in West London, put the news on there's a tower block ablaze. I've reported for work, sorry love, got to go. I'll call you soon."

"Be careful!" she pleaded, but he'd hung up.

She went into the living room and put on the news, the fire was breaking on every news channel. She phoned work to see if she could help in any way. She was told the terrible news that there was very few injured but a huge amount of fatalities, they'd call her if she was needed.

She stood naked waiting for the kettle to boil, thinking. She knew it was wrong but she was going to have a good root about and find proof that Jed was indeed a firefighter.

She started by revisiting his sliding door wardrobes in the bedroom. A lot of black leather and black tops but no hint of his alleged profession. She looked around the room but there seemed to be no further storage options. She sat on the bed perplexed.

"The bed!" she shouted triumphantly. She ripped off the duvet to discover it was one of the those hollow divans that lifts up. She lifted the base excitedly but the moment didn't last long as she saw a collection of spare duvets, pillows and assorted bedding paraphernalia.

Tina retreated to the living room and forlornly looked through the low drawers and cupboards where Jed stored his CDs and vinyl. She stood hands on hips looking round the room, which was dominated by a black gloss fitted shelving unit. Her last option was the meter cupboard, she opened the door to rummage through hoovers, ironing board and cleaning products.

Finally giving up, she phoned her father and suggested they meet in his local for pint and a Sunday roast. She left a message for Freddie expressing her sympathy and asking if there was anything she could do.

An hour later, Tina and her father tucked into their Sunday roast.

"How's your fireman? No ring yet," he teased.

"Ha ha, funny you should mention it, he's lovely, don't get me wrong, but there's a fly in the ointment."

"There always is love."

"I still have no proof he's a firefighter. I was in his flat this morning, there's no sign of any uniforms or photos or anything."

"This is really worrying you isn't it? I'm sure he's bonafide love." He thought about his visit to the fire station but daren't say anything. "I think you should nip this the bud and confront him, not that I'm in any position to lecture you, but a relationship should be built on mutual trust."

Tina looked at him and shook her head.

* * *

SIR MARTIN WAS surprised to find Claire at her desk on late Sunday afternoon. "I suggest you go home and get some rest Claire, I need you by my side tomorrow, the meeting has been upgraded in the light of Myerson's transfer."

"Really sir?" She looked surprised but had already been tipped off that she'd be in the meeting.

"There's been a cyber attack on cabinet members closed email groups, Russians again. In the light of the recent resignations and the situation in Syria and Iraq it's been upgraded to a COBRA meeting in Whitehall."

"Really sir?" Claire tried to sound unfazed. "Do you know about the Minister of Health sir?" she asked.

"Yes Claire, fake news. I preferred things in the old days when we fought our battles with real weapons, I'm getting to old for all this nonsense."

"So Myerson won't be there sir?"

"No thank god, hence the upgrade, keep this under your hat but the Secretary of Defence is flying in tonight."

"Wow, no pressure then. So who's chairing the meeting sir?"

Sir Martin paused and gave a wry smile. "The PM," he whispered.

38

THE INNER CIRCLE

DI COLLINS GAVE Dennis the good news. He was bailed on condition he didn't make contact with his wife, Micky, or Mo. He was tagged and transferred to St Peters.

She informed him that she'd arranged for Micky to be bailed on condition he was tagged and did not make any contact with Dennis, Sandra, or Mo. Sandra was bailed on condition she was tagged and made no contact with her husband.

Dennis was transferred by ambulance to St Peters. In the Monday rush hour the journey seemed to take forever.

He was put in the side room that Mo had frequented. He felt awful and was unsure if the staff knew anything about him, realising the tag would cause some consternation. He stared at the ceiling wondering how he got to be in this situation. He wondered how Sandra was.

"Good grief Dennis, what the hell have you been up to?" Tina interrupted his thoughts.

"It's a long story," he grunted.

"Well, it will have to wait Dennis, I'm snowed under on Mondays."

He was relieved to be left alone.

* * *

MICKY COULDN'T SLEEP. His own bed was definitely more comfy than the cell but the tag was annoying him and he couldn't help thinking that if the Professor didn't confess, ballistic science would prove him guilty of possessing an illegal firearm.

Tracey wasn't speaking to him and he couldn't blame her. She'd gone to her sister's in Ramsgate. He hoped absence might make her heart grow fonder and defuse her anger.

He decided he'd get up and see his daughter and the baby first thing, just in case things went against him.

* * *

* * *

SANDRA STOOD STARING at the bedroom door, after a few minutes she opened it just enough to peep through at the unmade bed. She shuddered as she recalled the sight of her dead lover on top of her soon-to-be dead husband. She wasn't ready to relive the moment and slammed the door shut.

She made her way to the bathroom to run a bath. She stripped off and looked down at the tag on her left foot. She hadn't thought to ask if she could bathe with the tag on. She was about to go downstairs and google the answer but decided to take a chance, she needed to wash away the last few days.

She sunk into the soapy water and tried to get the image out of her mind, along with the memory of the stomach pains she'd felt after being forced to eat Mo's muffin. She closed her eyes, wishing this was just a bad dream rather than a living nightmare.

She decided she'd not leave the house until her husband had died. Her marriage was long dead anyway. She wouldn't miss his bad hair and teeth, his ridiculous politics. In fact there was nothing about him she'd miss.

She was already missing Raymond though, despite his last actions. She could forgive him for his Thursday rendezvous with Grace, but then there was the final betrayal...

Raymond had at least put a bit of colour in her drab, miserable, grey life, she thought.

* * *

TINA SAW BRENDA standing at the nurses station, she finished setting up a drip for the third of seven patients she was looking after and held up five fingers.

Brenda nodded and chatted to the staff that came and went. Olu, the cleaner, gave her a hug and during their conversation told her about the Professor's tag. Brenda was taken aback.

She looked at Tina working flat out and felt bad disturbing her but she and her husband felt it best they tell Tina about the money. She thought about the money she hid in the drawer, she'd earmarked it for her grandchildren but maybe Tina could do with it.

She decided she'd kill a bit of waiting time by popping in to see the Professor. Brenda put her head round the open door. She found him sitting up doing The Guardian crossword. The sheets covered the tag, which was a relief to them both.

"Hi Dennis, I heard you were here, how are you?"

"Dying," he grunted.

Brenda was taken aback, deciding on second thoughts she didn't want any of his usual negative attitude. She was just turning away when he shouted, "Did you get the money?"

Brenda froze, then replied, "What money?"

"The fifteen grand," Dennis snapped.

Brenda hesitated and then turned and entered his side room properly. "It was from you Dennis?" she asked.

"Indirectly yes, but directly it was from Mo."

"Mo?"

"Yes Mo, I think we all misjudged him," the Professor added.

"But...why Dennis? Why?"

"It's a long story but I owed Mo the money, he asked that it was given to you for your trial."

"So it's not stolen money then?"

"No, I gave him the money in return for his services."

"His catering services?" she questioned.

"Sort of," he laughed, which hurt his ribs.

She just twigged to the fact that he mentioned fifteen thousand. "I've received two payments Dennis, one for five thousand and a second for seven and a half?"

"Really?" he asked, sounding surprised. "I think there might be more to come, unless it's gone on commission," he wondered aloud.

"Where is Mo? Doesn't he need it?"

"Maybe Newcastle, maybe he's gone home, who knows."

She stared at him for a moment, still totally bewildered by recent events. She lifted the bedding to expose the tag. "What's this for Dennis? Has it anything to do with the money?"

"No Brenda, not really," he said wearily. "I suggest you go home, you don't want to know."

"But I do. I do. Why are you were wearing a tag Dennis?"

"Because I was planning to kill the Minister of Health," he stated matter of factly.

"Really?" she said disbelievingly and turned to leave.

"Fuck off back to the suburbs!" he shouted.

When Tina came to look for Brenda she was nowhere to be seen.

* * *

CRAIG AND CHRISTINE dropped Claire off outside the cabinet offices at 78 Whitehall. She'd not spoken a word on the journey, they guessed she was mentally preparing for an important meeting.

Claire winked at Christine as she got out the back seat and headed towards the security box at the entrance. As she waited for her accreditation to be checked, various men in suits were waived through. She felt like it was her first day a school as the head of security stared her down while she waited.

She returned the stare refusing to blink.

"Claire."

She heard Sir Martin's voice beside her but continued to glare at the guard.

"In we go Claire. It's ok, she's with me."

"Right you are sir," the guard sheepishly replied and averted his stare.

Sir Martin led her through several check points until they reached a nondescript room with a long table accommodating twenty-four chairs. There was a folder marked classified and a flag carefully positioned in front of each chair. Eight British, eight American and eight Russian.

Sir Martin explained that the meeting would take place in an hour and that each country had an office earmarked for briefing and debriefing, plus there were other empty offices available for rivals to negotiate in private.

"So who's in our team sir?" she asked.

"Come on Claire, I'll introduce you."

He led her down the hall to a door with a Union Jack rather crudely sellotaped to it. He knocked out of politeness while turning the handle. They were the last arrive. Sir Martin worked the room enthusiastically introducing the Claire to 'Team GB', as he called it. The Chief of Staff and the Commander of the airforce certainly had strong military handshakes. She was intrigued to meet the supposed head of MI6 and his rather handsome sidekick from the Middle East desk.

She harboured thoughts of working with the sister service sometime in the future. Her language skills plus her handling of recent events would make her an ideal candidate. She engaged them in some small talk before being led away politely by her boss.

"Prime Minister, I'd like to introduce you to my colleague Claire Peterson."

"Good to meet you Claire."

She thought the PM's handshake was firmer than the generals.

"Let's adjourn to somewhere quieter, I need five minutes of your valuable time Sir Martin."

They both followed the PM into a side room, her private secretary locking the door behind them. There was a small table with four casual chairs. "Please sit," the PM said and gestured to the chairs.

Claire had the feeling the country's political leader was pleased to have another female in the room. She thought she looked older in the flesh than on TV, but there again with all that was going on she probably got less sleep than her, if that were possible.

"Ok, so this morning's meeting is essentially to reinforce and update a previous agreement between the Americans, Russians and us, not to tread on each other's toes in, or to be more specific, over, Syria. There will be a lot of technical baloney about whose planes and whose drones go where. I will leave all that boring detail to the generals, but the main point is the final defeat of ISIS. However, as you aware, we have other issues blurring the lines, i.e. the Russians.

"The Secretary of State, who I'm told is on his way from Heathrow, is going to bring up the Russian's cyber attacks and blatant attempts to interfere with our democratic processes. I intend to put my pennies worth in as well. Particularly as their meddling has caused my cabinet to fall apart and this morning I've got over four hundred MP's panicking due to the internal email system apparently being hacked. I'm not looking forward to introducing my team this morning, watching their smirking faces because I have no Minister of Defence by my side, with respect to present company of course." She smiled at Sir Martin and Claire. "I understand you've spoken to the health minister?"

"Claire met him and has looked into the situation," Sir Martin confirmed.

The PM and her private secretary looked at Claire, for a brief second she wished Toby was in his seat with his cut glass accent and connections. "Yes Prime Minister, I can confirm he is the victim of a classic fake news story."

"You're one hundred percent sure Claire?" The PM looked her in the eye.

"I'm a hundred percent sure he is the victim of misinformation on this occasion," Claire confirmed.

"On this occasion," the PM replied with a wry smile.

Claire gave a knowing nod. Like her, the Prime Minister was also surrounded by old Etonian misogynistic wankers, she thought to herself.

"Thank you Claire. I need to reshuffle ASAP, I don't want lose a good man."

"Claire made an interesting suggestion Prime Minister," Sir Martin interrupted.

Did I? Claire pondered.

"If you want to send a clear message to the Russians that their mischief making will have no effect on the UK government, why not promote the minister to Minister of Defence."

The PM looked at her private secretary who gave a subtle nod in response. Claire looked at her boss and he winked.

"We discussed the same scenario this morning," the PM whispered. "And what's more I'm going to call him now and invite him to come to the meeting in his new role, that will make the introductions interesting."

"That will put our Russian friends on the back foot Prime Minister," Sir Martin added.

"One small problem," the private secretary spoke up. "We only have eight places at the meeting," she said looking slightly embarrassed.

"No problem, Claire would be bored out of her mind listening to all that drone business. You wouldn't mind keeping an eye on some of the hangers on would you Claire?"

"No, not at all," she agreed, secretly feeling a little disappointed.

* * *

TOBY SAT AT his desk talking cricket with Mittal when they saw the breaking news regarding the reshuffle. "Bloody hell, the PM spends half an hour with the Ice Queen and all hell breaks loose!" Toby laughed.

"She's won you a few brownie points mate," Mittal commented.

"The girls done well!" Toby chortled, knowing that between them they had got themselves a serious ally at the top table.

* * *

FOR A FEW moments Claire felt like a spare part as she surveyed the room full of support players. She poured herself an orange juice and picked up a digestive biscuit.

She was surprised by a youngish man in military uniform who asked her if there was vodka in her juice. She noticed 'NATO' insignia on his arm, alongside the Danish flag, and replied in fluent Danish that she never touched alcohol before midday.

"You're Danish?" he expressed his surprise, speaking in English.

"Half, and half Norwegian."

"But you work for the British government?" he enquired.

"I'm British, I was born here, my father was a diplomat. You're not invited to the ball either then?" she asked.

"No, my boss is in there as a guest of the UK, I'm here as a translator."

"Danish?"

"No no, I'm fluent in Russian. To be honest I'm no longer in the army, it's just easier to wear this uniform. I work in the trade department at the Dutch embassy here in London."

"You're a spy then?" she suggested.

"No, I really am in trade," he insisted.

"And a linguist?" she probed.

"I suppose so. I'm Yohan by the way."

"I'm Claire, nice to meet you. Can I borrow you for a minute Yohan?"

"Why not, I reckon we will be waiting around for quite a while."

She led him out of the office and down the corridor to a door with a hammer and sickle temporally stuck on it. "That's a first," Sir Martin had pointed out.

She knocked on the door a shaven headed man opened it a fraction. "Hi, I'm Clare Peterson, can I come in please?" she said sharply.

The man grunted a few words and pointed to the flag.

"You're not on the guest list," Yohan translated.

"Can you tell him I need to speak to whoever is in charge, I have important information for them."

"Wow Claire, you're not going to defect are you?"

"No thanks, just ask him. I'll treat you to lunch, but not in that uniform," she said.

"Deal Claire." He turned to the Russian and quoted Claire, there was a brief exchange before Yohan translated. "He's sorry but his boss is in the meeting, he's happy to pass on a message when the meeting's over."

"Ok, tell him that I'm the jogger one of his colleagues tried to run over last week. I'd like an apology." She stared the Russian in the eye and pointed to the fading bruise on her forehead.

Yohan hesitated but Claire turned her glare to him. "You sure about this? Sometimes these guys shoot the messenger," he stated.

"You want that lunch?" she replied.

He relayed the message, they then returned to the neutral office where they passed the time discussing Copenhagen. Eventually the meeting of the inner circle finished and the room was suddenly a hive of activity. "It reminds me of the staff room at midday," Claire mentioned to Johan.

"You were a teacher?"

"Yep, my first job after uni."

"I bet you were strict."

"Very," she confirmed. "I still am."

They were interrupted by Sir Martin who tapped Clare on the shoulder, "Someone wants to meet you Claire, follow me."

She winked at Yohan, thinking she was going to meet the Russians. Sir Martin led her to another office with the Union Jack on it and tapped on the door. A familiar face opened it. "Good morning Claire." The brand new Minister of Defence welcomed them in.

"I just wanted to thank you personally for your help in what I understand has been a difficult week for you," he said.

"No problem minister."

"I've got to hit the ground running, I've got to be at number ten shortly. Rest assured my second duty after signing off a few drone attacks on Raqqa will be to put in place my promise to you."

"Thank you and good luck sir." Claire shook his hand.

"No, thank you Claire, and thank you Sir Martin," he said sincerely.

They were returning to the neutral office with a sense of satisfaction when Yohan emerged with the shaven headed Russian. "Hi Claire someone from the Russian delegation wants to meet you," Yohan said.

Claire looked back as the new Minister of Defence left. "I've arranged an impromptu meeting with the Russians sir, is that ok?"

"No problem Claire, can I be of any assistance?"

"That's ok, NATO has my back. I'll join you shortly."

Yohan and Claire followed the Russian to yet another office. He knocked on the door, they waited a few seconds before it was opened by a familiar face. It took Claire a few seconds to recognise her. She tried to look casual and aloof but she was more than surprised.

"Hi Claire, good to you see you in one piece."

"Well, I have to be totally honest, I never saw this coming," Claire said.

39

THE RUSSIANS ARE COMING

MICKY FELT GOOD about himself for the first time in ages. He sat on the park bench rocking the pram gently backwards and forwards. His daughter really appreciated him giving her a much needed break, she'd also reacted positively to his suggestion that he help her find her own property, though he hadn't mentioned it might have to be up north.

He still harboured ill feeling towards Frankie but had put his plotting and planning on hold. His health seemed to be stable, he knew Tracey had the hump with him and of course he deserved it but he was hoping a few days away would bring her back onside.

The baby grizzled and a strong smell of poo filled the air, he laughed as he changed his first nappy.

* * *

TOBY AND EVERYONE back at HQ were busy digesting the breaking news of the reshuffle. Mittal and a few others were underwhelmed. Toby kept his own council, quietly feeling a great sense of satisfaction that he'd introduced Claire to the minister. Both their careers would surely benefit from their endeavours, as would the whole team.

It was clear 'Operation Chef' as they unofficially called the latest project was about to be wound up, he was confident they would be handed something juicy.

He thought about his boss meeting the PM and maybe even the Secretary of State. Whoever or whatever, he knew she would bow down to no-one. She'd earned his total respect during the challenging last few weeks.

* * *

CLAIRE READ THE accreditation on her lanyard. "Nice suit Anna," she stated cooly. She looked a lot smarter than the last time they met.

"Thanks Claire, I trust you've had yours dry cleaned, sorry but that bath is disgusting," Anna said smiling.

"It was totally disgusting, it was beyond dry cleaning. The British tax payer had to buy me a new suit."

They dismissed their minders and sat in two heavily upholstered armchairs facing each other. "So, you're not a kitchen assistant," Claire observed.

"Well, I was, but the pay was shit."

"So someone made you an offer you couldn't refuse?"

"Something like that Claire."

"I'm guessing this was just before the cyber conference?"

Anna nodded. "You've seen where I live Claire, seemed like a good way out."

"And were you on the motherland's payroll when you tossed our friend off Anna? I'm presuming your name is Anna?"

"Yes, and yes Claire. And I am Moldovan."

Claire gave that icy stare.

"I sucked him off as well Claire, I took my job seriously," she said, trying to shock the Ice Queen.

"Wow Anna, a double whammy, beer money and extra tang. I can't wait to tell my colleague Toby about this, he will spontaneously combust. I suppose this was one time when the fella encouraged spitting rather than-"

"Haha Claire you surprise me, I thought you'd be shocked?"

"Nothing shocks me Anna, that's why I'm the boss. So where is our friend now, I presume he's also on the payroll?"

"When they first approached him the deal was to poison the cyber experts in return for them forgetting he was responsible for the deaths of thirty-seven Russian commandos. Things got complicated by his illness and his new friends at the hospital. The gun wasn't his by the way, he was looking after it for one of his fellow patients."

"Really which one?" Claire interrupted.

"Micky. He was a hit man apparently," Anna confirmed.

"Interesting."

"Then of course things got out of hand with the tape business, the Russians don't want bad news from the past resurfacing. They have offered him a shit load of cash to poison a Chechnan."

"The one who decapitated the journalists?"

"I believe so."

"But isn't he in Syria? Hence the meeting today?" Claire asked. She was concerned.

"Possibly. Mo was offered safe passage to Turkey, they would arrange for him to get to where the terrorist was, which I believe has just been confirmed by the Americans."

"Oh shit," Claire exclaimed.

"Exactly Claire, that's why I'm here."

"I was wondering," Claire said.

"Well to be honest, I'm supposed to tell you that as long as the Scott thing is put to bed no-one's going to try and run you over or kidnap the Scottish lady."

"Who's Scott?" Claire smiled.

"Exactly Claire. But Mo, as you know, is a loose cannon, he's supposed to join the retreating ISIS fighters declaring his hatred of the Russians and then poison the Chechnan. The thing is, of course, Mo actually does hate the Russians more than ISIS, which worries me."

"And me," Claire concurred.

"But what really worries me Claire is that the Russians will drop a bomb on both of them."

"Kill two birds with one stone," Claire thought aloud.

"So apart from offering you a ceasefire I was hoping your people could get to Mo before he's taken across the border."

"I'm MI5, I only deal with domestic problems Anna, surely you could speak to one of your Russian friends?"

"I'm a 'disrupter' Claire, not a spy, I have very little influence."

"A 'disrupter'?"

"Yes Claire, I'm a 'disrupter', paid nobodies on zero hour contracts. We are all over Europe, paid to cause confusion."

"To what end Anna?"

"Fuck knows Claire," Anna shrugged. "It's all a power game to the powers that be. They want a return to the Cold War days, a carve up between them and the yanks. Putin hates you, and the French, particularly the Germans. He wants to be top dog. He plans to slowly break your will with endless cyber war, social media manipulation and encouraging immigration chaos. There's nothing you can do about it."

"Wow Anna, as if I'm not aware of all this. But for now let's see what we can do for to save Mo. I'll meet you in this cafe tomorrow, ten sharp." She handed her the card from the Soho cafe.

"And then what Claire?"

"And then you either work for me or I'll deport you."

* * *

NOT FOR THE first time Tina was diverted from her hectic schedule of patients. She was called to the nurses station where someone had come to see Dennis.

"Hello love, I'm Eric from Security First, I've come to remove the tag from one Dennis Coates." He showed Tina his accreditation and paperwork.

"He's asleep but I think the tag will just slip off, follow me Eric."

They entered the side room, the Professor was fast asleep. Tina lifted the bed covers to expose his pathetically thin ankle.

"I think you're right love, I can get that off easily, poor sod." He slipped it off in seconds. "The problem is love he has to sign these papers."

"Can I not sign them Eric?" Tina queried.

"Sorry love, has to be," he looked at the paperwork, "Mr Coates, love. I'll have to wait, it's his release conditions."

"I'll be honest Eric, he's not going anywhere soon except either up there or down there," Tina motioned with her head.

"I'll tell you what love, I'd like to get out of here as soon as poss so I can release his co-defendants today, you could put a pen in his hand and help him do a couple of squiggles, if you don't mind counter signing?"

Tina looked at the poor soul snoring raucously. "Ok as long as I'm not breaking the law."

He gave her the pen, which she gently placed in Dennis' right hand and moved it where the x's were.

"Thanks love, I'm hoping to get done so I can take my grandson swimming later."

"That's ok Eric. Strange job you have."

"You're right love, it's a part-time retirement job to be honest. I'm a locksmith by trade. I'm a legend in the East End, everyone knows me as Eric the locksmith."

He left Tina readjusting the bedding. She was relieved to see Dennis unshackled and she knew he would be pleased to have his dignity back. How on earth did he get into such a pickle, she wondered. She knew he could be a cantankerous old git but she was certain his illness was the cause of his recent excessive behaviour.

* * *

SANDRA WAS HALFWAY through a bottle of gin when Eric rang the doorbell. She hadn't seen the email from DI Collins so was surprised when he explained he had come to remove her tag. She led him to the living room and slumped onto the sofa, lifting her skirt to expose the tag.

He saw the gin, he'd smelt it when she answered the door. "Bombay Sapphire love, you've got expensive taste," Eric quipped.

"Only the best," she stated. "Would you like one?"

"Bit early love, if you were my last call I'd join you." He removed the tag and gave her the paperwork to sign. She started to read it but couldn't focus.

"The main condition of release is highlighted love, the rest is just gobbledygook." He pointed to the pink felt tip line.

"Read it to me please?" she asked.

"It basically says that you are not to make any contact with the following persons, Micky Walker, Grace Minotti, Dennis Coates."

"I see, you know Dennis is my husband?"

"I didn't know that love."

"Have you removed his tag, how's he doing?"

"I'm not meant to say but let's just say he's not looking too sparkling love."

Sandra poured another gin with a small amount of tonic. "Hopefully he will pop his clogs soon," she muttered.

"That's a bit strong love, I think you might have had one too many."

"What's your name?" she asked, holding his gnarly hand.

"Eric, love."

"Well Eric, that fucking waste of space you saw in hospital is responsible for the death of my lover, fuck him."

Blimey, Eric thought. *I'd better get out of here.*

"My Raymond was ten times the man Dennis was," she slurred.

"Sorry love I've got to get going, please sign at the two crosses."

"You have to help me Eric."

He guided her hand. *What a pair,* he thought.

"You sure you don't want to join me for drink Eric?" she winked.

"Another time," he replied and looked up the address of the next 'client'.

He found himself on familiar territory, a lot of his old pals had escaped to Romford from the East End.

Micky answered the door. Eric was standing there with a huge grin.

"Fuck me," Micky swore. "The legend himself. Eric the locksmith, I don't believe it, you're working for the man."

"Micky Toms, well, well, well, the man in black."

"Come in, I'll put the kettle on, and get this fucking tag off me sharpish."

They exchanged stories for the next half hour, it had been fifteen years since their paths had crossed.

"So what's with this job Eric, what happened with the locksmith business?"

"Got to a significant age, wanted to wind down, saw the ad in the Standard and here I am." He removed the tag and got the paperwork signed.

"How the fuck did you get caught up with these mad fuckers Micky?" he asked.

"Long story mate, got a touch of the big C, saw an opportunity, got messy."

They chewed the fat for a while longer before Micky had a thought. "Tell me Eric do you still do a bit of locksmith work?"

"Little bit for friends, why?"

"Do you deal with vehicles Eric?"

"Now n' again, is it kosher?"

"Not exactly Eric, not exactly…"

40

THE ICE AGE

CLAIRE GOT THE call at six thirty am, fifteen minutes before her alarm was due to go off.

"Claire," the caller said.

"Oh morning Sir Martin," she mumbled.

"Sorry I've woken you. I thought I'd tell you before it's on the news, the Russians are claiming they killed their Chechnan in a drone attack an hour ago. Putin has sent a private message of thanks to the White House, so everyone is happy."

Claire paused for thought.

"I'm sorry Claire, I know what you're thinking and I don't have an answer, I guess we never will."

Claire carried on with her usual routine, a 6k jog, shower, light breakfast. She thought about the train trip to Edinburgh, the excitement of actually being out in the field, taking the seat opposite Mo.

She took the tube to Leicester Square, when she emerged it was peeing down, she was soaked through by the time she got to the cafe. She found Anna outside looking at her phone map. She took her arm and led her into the cafe.

"Good to see you Anna." Claire was a little surprised the Moldovan had accepted her invitation.

"Any news Claire?"

"You haven't heard anything Anna?"

"No."

"Your Russians got their man this morning." Claire stared Anna out, looking for a trace of emotion. She got what she was looking for, a tear trickled down Anna's pale cheek.

"Any details Claire?" she asked, as she tried to compose herself.

"Sorry Anna, no details. I doubt there will be, do you?"

Anna shook her head.

They ordered coffee and sat in silence for a few moments before Claire stated matter of factly, " I'd like to offer you a job Anna."

"Does it pay well?"

"Better than kitchen work, even with the extras," she sniped.

"Do I have a choice Claire?"

"You can go home. Today."

"What is the job description?"

"Disrupting the disrupters," Claire teased.

"I can't go home Claire, there's nothing for me there."

"Family?"

"My parents are long divorced and totally fucked up. I had a brother who drank himself to death and a sister who is working in a hotel in Greece. When do I start and what do I do Claire?"

"'Operation Chef' is winding down this week. Toby will contact you in few days with any details you need to know, your history and language skills, particularly being fluent in Romanian and Russian, will be helpful. In the meantime carry on with what you are doing and if you hear from your Russian friends let us know."

"Now that Mo has-" Anna hesitated. "I don't think they have any use for me now."

Claire sipped her coffee. "Do you think Mo would have been keen to carry out the mission into Syria Anna?"

"No I don't Claire, he would know the stakes. Kill the Chechnan and possibly win his freedom would be a tempting offer but he'd know the risks, he certainly wouldn't trust the Russians."

"Would he contact you if he was still alive somewhere?"

"I doubt it, what about you?"

"I don't know. If he is alive, maybe, his curiosity about his fellow patients might be a pull, who knows."

"He had a lot of respect for his nurse."

"Tina?" Claire thought about her chance meeting with her.

"Yes, that's the one, he told me she was a very good person."

"He was right, I met her, she's very nice."

* * *

THE CONSULTANT HELD his daily meeting with his team, it was always a rushed soulless affair due to the pressure they were all under. He came to Dennis' notes last. He looked directly at Tina. "I'm afraid the latest scans have shown a rapid decline in his prognosis. You may want to speak to both him and his family about going to a hospice, we are talking a few weeks if he's lucky."

Tina thought this was going to be tricky but resolved to speak to the Professor after her break. A quick coffee and biscuit before the storm. She sat in her office reading an old OK magazine when her phone buzzed.

"Hello?" she whispered, not knowing the number.

"Hi Tina, it's Rupert."

She recognised the posh accent. "Good morning Rupert."

"Yes, good morning Tina, how's things?" Toby really was hating playing this game.

"Hectic, as usual. I presume you're calling re. Thursday's meeting. We presumed the Minister of Health wasn't coming, that was a turn up," she laughed.

"Well Tina, they say a week is a long time in politics and it is, but I've some interesting news for you. The new Minister of Health is making her first public appearance at your Good Vibes Group."

"Wow that's thrown me. I was planning to give the ex-minister a piece of my mind," Tina replied honestly.

"Well feel free to give the new minister a baptism of fire Tina, but I must warn you, she will have a ferocious minder with her as well as the press."

"Is that minder you Rupert?"

"Unfortunately I'm away on a course on Thursday. I'm sending a Rottweiler."

Tina thought about the press and her motley crew. "When you say press, I hope you don't mean TV Rupert. I won't have time to get my hair done!"

"Strictly between you and me Tina, I think the minister has good news she will want to share with all major TV news outlets."

"Oh feck!" Tina exclaimed. They ended the call. Tina took a sharp intake of breath before heading to see the Professor.

"I'm not asleep," Dennis grunted with his eyes closed, as Tina crept around his bed.

"Sorry Dennis just making sure you're still with us," she joked wickedly.

"Just," he replied.

"Good news about Thursday Dennis," she was delaying the bad news.

"Thursday? What day is it today?" he asked confused.

"Today's Tuesday Dennis, Thursday's the Good Poison Club and there's a special guest coming."

"I heard the Minister of Health resigned, I was planning to poison him you know."

"Yes Dennis, well I've just been told his replacement is making her first appearance here, there's going to be press, TV, the lot."

"Well, I'm going to have my say even if I have to crawl there."

"I'll make sure you're there Dennis but then I think we should be thinking about…about you moving to-" She hesitated.

"Moving me to the last chance saloon."

"Yes Dennis, that's a good way of putting it."

"If I'm not arrested on Thursday you can do what you want with me, I'm past caring."

"What about your family, do you want me to contact them?" Tina offered.

"Family, what family?" he snarled.

Tina thought his memory might be going rapidly. "Your wife Dennis and your sons."

"I'm not allowed to see my wife, don't you know why I was tagged?"

"I'm too busy for tittle tattle, I'm sure due to the circumstances arrangements could be made. What's the worst that could happen?"

"You've not met my wife," the Professor hissed.

* * *

MICKY HAD MET Eric in the last surviving boozer on their old East End manor. They reminisced about old friends, most of them rouges. Some had died, some spent time in prison. Micky told Eric about his health problems and efforts to support his daughter and baby.

"We've been offered a job you and me Micky?" Eric surprised him.

"A job, what kind of job?"

"Mrs Coates."

"What about her?" Micky didn't expect this.

"She asked me if I had green fingers when I removed her tag. I told her my fingers were multi skilled but yes I liked gardening and she asked if I'd be interested in maintaining her garden now her husband was incapable."

"Fucking hell Eric, believe me you don't want to get involved with her mate. She's dangerous."

"I guessed that when I saw your name on the bail conditions Micky."

"It's a long story Eric, you don't want to know. Anyhow you said she's got a job for me."

"She didn't elaborate but she wants to meet you, says it would be worth your while, she asked if I could arrange a meet."

Micky knew he shouldn't get involved but what the hell, he was curious. Besides, anything that swelled the deposit for his daughter's house should be considered. "I'll let you know a time and place Eric, but you be careful mate, this could end in tears, ask Mr Coates." Micky then remembered his reason for meeting his old friend. He told him he wanted to steal Frankie's car and demand his five grand back but the car had a state of the art coded ignition. "I don't want you getting into trouble on my account Eric, you don't want to jeopardise your cushy job mate."

"That's why I'm sending you to see my friend Vio, he'll sort you out with a Bucharest Box."

"What the fuck is a Bucharest Box?"

"Vio will explain everything, he's in his workshop till six."

Vio's explanation wasn't rocket science, Micky handed over the cash and left with two homemade key fob decoders. One to point at Frankie's fob, the other to receive the code and start the ignition, simple.

All he had to do was find Frankie.

* * *

TOBY RECEIVED THE call from DI Collins explaining the situation regarding Dennis Coates' deteriorating health and his request to receive a visit from his wife, despite the bail conditions. He couldn't see there being a problem given the circumstances, besides he had more pressing issues to contemplate. "I can't see a problem Trish, why not, what harm could it do."

"Apart from guns, kidnap, murder and sodomy?" the detective replied sarcastically.

He thought about the Good Poison Club, he was disappointed he wouldn't be able to chair Thursday's meeting with the minister but the recent unforeseeable events and his direct involvement in the firearm enquiries had compromised his further involvement. The Sanctuary was his idea, it seemed a good one at the time but events had taken a direction no one could have envisaged. He was relieved that 'Operation Chef' was nearing completion.

He was unsure about whether he'd be in Claire's team for much longer but the one big positive to come out of the Mo business was he now had a key ally in the new Minister of Defence.

A big job in the foreign office was his ultimate ambition, maybe an ambassador role. In the short term he looked forward to showing Anna the ropes, he found her kind of cute. Though Toby knew he still spent an unnatural amount of time obsessing about his boss, particularly her rant at Wayne Myerson.

* * *

SANDRA FELT A lot better for the bubble bath. She knew it wouldn't wash away her sins but it had got her off the sofa for the first time in days and although she'd brought a glass of red with her she was now focusing on moving forward and tying up the loose ends.

She was missing Raymond but was starting to question whether she truly loved him. Yes he made her feel like a sensuous woman again, made her feel needed, but maybe the part she truly enjoyed had been humiliating Dennis. She was disgusted by what Raymond did to him but there was a part of her that rejoiced in her husband's humiliation.

He'd be gone soon, she pondered.

She had permission to go and see him on Saturday before he was moved to the hospice. She was undecided on what she'd say to him. She'd loved him once, she saw him as a young, fiery, radical hippy when they first met. But he became boringly cynical. The boys never warmed to him, but there again, there was the possibility they weren't actually his boys...

Theirs was a strange marriage to be sure but she should have ended it after his misdemeanour at work. Since then their relationship had been a slow lingering death, literally.

She was pleased she'd found someone to sort the garden, he was a rough diamond but quite handsome, in a gangster-ish way. She'd be selling the house soon anyway and would move to a much smaller place in the suburbs. This would both open up some equity, which she'd use for travel and fine living, and also cause Dennis to turn in his grave.

She was smiling again and looking forward to the meeting with Micky.

Eric had called her to tell her Micky would meet her at 2pm on Friday in Golden Square Soho, by the giant high heeled shoe.

Now, he *really is a good looking man,* she thought, *another rogue.*

She felt a wave of pleasure thinking about when he tied her up. How he came to befriend her pathetic husband she didn't know but she was hopeful he'd be up for one more job.

41

FRIENDS AND FOES

TINA DIDN'T SLEEP well, she spent too much time mulling over what she'd like to say to the new minister and, more worryingly, what the others might come up with. She'd decided she'd arrive late, claiming there were too many patients and not enough staff, which would be the truth anyhow.

After showering, dressing and wolfing down peanut butter on toast, she checked her phone. There was a good luck message from Rupert.

What a nice guy, she thought.

There was also an email from the Chief Executive: *Hi Tina, Please come to my office at midday for pre Good Vibes meeting with the minister's team. Thanks, Sebastian.*

"Bollocks!" she shouted. That's all she needed, meetings about meetings, the fucking NHS, she could scream.

* * *

DENNIS RAVED AND ranted as the newly qualified nurse gave him his morning medication. "Leave me a fucking lone, I want Tina to inject me!" he screamed, as she prepared a shot of morphine.

His headache was literally killing him.

"You must calm down Dennis, Nurse Gallagher isn't here for another hour. This will kill the pain, if you're calm I'll find your vein easier."

He just about understood it would be a good idea to cooperate. She managed to successfully administer the drug before he vomited on her hand and arm. She went to get help, in the chaos the Professor picked up the discarded syringe driver and slipped it into his dressing gown pocket draped on the chair next to his bed. They returned, cleaned him up and gave him a drink of water before leaving him in peace.

He sat up looking at the news on TV but not concentrating.

If I can get close enough I could stab the stupid bitch in the neck. Dark thoughts swirled round his tortured mind.

* * *

SANDRA HAD VENTURED out to the shops for the first time since that dreadful day. She struggled home with two for life bags full of provisions, including two bottles of red, having taken advantage of a two for one offer. She went to climb up the concrete steps to her front door when she made eye contact with a woman sitting in the driver's seat of a red Mini Cooper. She appeared familiar, the woman quickly looked away.

Sandra unpacked her shopping, considered opening one of the bottles but thought it a bit too early. She put the kettle on instead and popped a couple of slices of bread in the toaster.

She thought about the woman in the Mini and went to open Dennis' man drawer. She rifled through the assortment of batteries and old phone chargers before she found Raymond's iPhone. It was as dead as a dodo. She tried two or three chargers before a battery sign finally flashed on the screen.

She buttered the toast and sat at the breakfast bar reading the Daily Mail. Dennis would go ballistic if he knew she'd brought the Mail into the house.

The phone pinged into life, she started to look through his photo album, stopping suddenly at a pretty smiling face. She knew she'd seen the face before. *Grace.*

She raced to the front door and into the street just as the red Mini disappeared up the road.

What the fuck was she up to?

* * *

TINA POPPED INTO see Dennis. She was pleased to see he was sitting up doing *The Guardian* crossword. "I'm coming to the meeting," he grunted without looking up.

"That's good Dennis," she lied. "Are you going to behave yourself?"

"Fuck no! I'm going to give that stupid woman a piece of my mind."

"Unlike you to be sexist Dennis, what has her sex got to do with anything?"

Tina touched a nerve.

"It's got everything to do with it," the Professor growled. "How can a woman be a fucking Tory? Heck, how can a woman who has the maternal instinct champion 'austerity'. It's disgraceful!"

"It's her first week in the job, give her a chance Dennis," Tina tried to reason.

"Why? She's part of the problem, she's out to destroy the NHS, she's part of the machine denying Brenda her drug trial. Fuck her."

This is going to be a long day, Tina thought to herself, making a note for a porter to get a wheelchair for Dennis.

Dennis had returned to his crossword, pausing briefly to check the syringe was still in his dressing gown pocket.

* * *

IT DIDN'T TAKE Micky long to track down Frankie, it was just a matter of narrowing down his choice of betting shops. He soon spotted the new father illegally parked in a disabled bay. His plan was to follow him to wherever he was living and then get the code with the Bucharest Box, but as Frankie was the only person in the shop, he decided to strike now whilst the iron was hot.

He reached into his backpack for the code catcher' gismo, crossed the road and stood out of sight just outside the betting shop.

He was obscured by an advert stating 'WEST HAM TO BEAT ARSENAL 2-1. 5 TO 1.' *Might have a punt on that,* he thought, considering the odds before pointing the gismo into the shop and pressing a small black knob. After a few seconds a green light flashed intermittently.

He walked casually to the car and pulled out the second box pressing the button again. This time a green light flashed on the receiving box. He excitedly slipped beside the driver's door and pressed the button, pointing it towards the ignition through the window. Within seconds the door unlocked.

He climbed in and then, nothing. He frantically pressed the button on both gizmos but nothing happened. He managed to lock the doors just as Frankie was returning to his car.

Frankie was too busy perusing his betting slip to notice Micky sitting in the driver's seat. He pointed the fob at the car but nothing happened, he put the slip in his pocket and tried again.

"What the fuck!" he blurted out, finally noticing Micky.

"Hi Frankie," Micky said as he opened the window. "You left it unlocked, not sure what I've done."

Frankie put his hand in and pressed something which unlocked the doors. "Fucking fob, can't beat the old keys," he said, as Micky reluctantly slid across to the passenger seat. "What the fuck you doing in my car Micky?"

"I've got a large share in it, I'd like a ride."

"Where to Micky?"

"Not far mate, Dagenham. I want to show you something."

He directed Frankie to his old manor, they otherwise sat in silence until he told him to pull up in a side street outside a row of 1940s maisonettes. One had a for sale sign outside.

"I grew up in this area, good memories, good people."

"So what we doing here Micky?"

"I think you're a cunt Frankie, but not as big a cunt as me. Believe me you don't want your daughter turning up in twenty years to remind you. I want to buy this house for our daughter's Frankie, get them out of that fucking hell hole they're living in. I'm trying to get the deposit together, I'd like some help."

Frankie looked around the car not sure how to react.

"Drive down to the end of the road I want to show you something else," Micky instructed.

Frankie followed his order, driving directly to a cemetery.

"My mum and dad are buried in there Frankie, so is Bobby 'The Pilchard' McVie."

"The Pilchard, I heard about him, bit of a face."

"Yes he was, a nasty fucker. Do you know why they called him The Pilchard, Frankie?"

"No."

"Because of his horrible fish eyes, right ugly bastard he was. He's buried somewhere in there Frankie. I put him there."

Frankie looked sheepishly at Micky.

"Hard men would slip out the back doors of East End boozers when he walked in, he was feared. I put a bullet in one of those big slimy fish eyes Frankie, got forty grand for it. It was the hottest day of the year, I pulled up on my motorbike at traffic lights off the A13. His window was down because of the heat. I can still see the surprise on his face. Nobody missed him, especially the old bill."

"I'd like to do my bit Micky, besides this car is fucking heavy on the fuel. Maybe you could speak to Shirley, let me see my daughter now and again?"

"Good lad. One last thing, you can chauffeur me to hospital. I'm going to take tea with the Minister of Health."

* * *

TINA GOT TO the chief executive's office ten minutes late due to lack of cover. She had decided to tell him she no longer wanted to run the Good Poison Club. She was surprised to see Sebastian Phelps standing outside his office door.

"Ah Tina, you're here."

He looked harassed. She wanted to tell him her intentions right away but he cut her short.

"Someone from the minister's team wants to see you Tina. I've given over my office so you can have some privacy, I'll see you at the Sanctuary. The press are already setting up, no pressure but I reckon you're going to be on the evening news!"

Tina wished she'd had a blow dry, she checked there were no stains on her uniform before entering the chief exec's office.

"Hi Tina, how you doing, remember me?"

Tina couldn't quite place the young lady in the black trouser suit, though she looked a little familiar. "Sorry, where do I know you from?" she queried, shaking her hand.

"This might help you." The familiar stranger handed Tina her phone. She looked at the photo of the Pixies drummer backstage at the Brixton Academy.

"Claire!" she suddenly remembered and gave her a hug. "Christ Claire you look so different." Tina couldn't equate this dour business woman with the rock chick she'd met before.

"Not the done thing to wear my Ramones t-shirt at work."

"What you doing here, in the big white chief's office?" Tina was confused.

"Please sit, I'll explain everything."

"Sebastian told me the minister's team want to see me, you're in her team?"

"Not exactly Tina, I've never met her."

"You told me you were a civil servant but I was too drunk to recall what department, was it health?"

"No, I told you I was in trade development, which was a fib," Claire reminded Tina. "I'm a civil servant for sure, it's a long story. I told you I knew you from somewhere when I first met you. Well, I ran into Rupert and told him I met you. We got talking and he mentioned the Minister of Health's visit to your hospital, he couldn't make it so I offered to look after the minister."

"But you mentioned you knew me from somewhere?" Tina queried.

"Yes that's right Tina, it's not a total coincidence Saint Peters was chosen to launch the Sanctuary. My department heard about the concept and suggested it be given to your hospital."

"Your department, which is?" Tina interrupted.

"The intelligence service," Claire confirmed matter of factly.

"Feck, sounds serious Claire."

"Well, I'm going to have kill you now Tina, obviously."

"So how the feck did you think you know me, I know I'm Irish but-"

"Mo," Claire interrupted coldly.

"Mo?"

"My department designated him a person of interest after he poisoned a conference for NATO's top cyber geeks. It was feared he might have further bad intentions, turns out he was just an angry chef seeking revenge for online criticism of his cooking." Claire thought it best not to elaborate on the Russian connection.

"So what have I got to do with all this?"

"Nothing, but we were concerned he might be radicalised whilst in hospital. I would probably have seen your photo amongst many others as we ruled out any members of hospital staff."

"Ruled them out of what?"

"A plot Tina."

"What kind of plot?"

"Sorry, I can't elaborate."

"Because he was Muslim, you thought he was a terrorist?"

"Not exactly, it's complicated. My conclusion is that Mo is far from a terrorist, he's a hero, but I want to be sure. When's the last time you heard from him Tina?"

"When he was discharged, why?"

"I was hoping he might have contacted you, we believe he is abroad. I'm sorry Tina there's a chance he may have been killed, I'm trying to find out for sure."

"Killed? How? Where?" Tina was visibly upset.

"Syria, he may have been killed there."

"No way, there's no fecking way Mo would have gone to Syria, no way. I remember him telling me he didn't want to see the visiting Imam anymore, he was quite firm about it."

"I know Tina, like I say it's complicated. I'm hoping he's ok, I thought he might contact you because he trusts you."

Tina looked down at the floor for a few seconds. "There was something strange Claire, when we were cleaning his side room I found loads of SIM cards, I thought it odd but was too busy to bother about it."

"What did you do with them?" Claire asked.

"I threw them down the rubbish shoot, but what I didn't throw away was this." Tina opened her handbag and handed Claire the note Mo left her.

Claire read it aloud, "Thanks for everything Tina, see you at the minister's visit."

"He left me one hundred pounds with it, I gave it to the ward manager for the xmas party fund. It was the most generous present a patient's ever left."

"How many SIM cards do you reckon Tina?"

"At least eight, why? I threw them away, I'm sorry."

"Don't worry, I'm not sure it's relevant, anyway let's agree if either of us hear from Mo we will let each other know. You never know Tina, he might turn up like he promised."

"Agreed. So what are you doing looking after the new Minister of Health Claire?"

"A favour to Rupert I suppose." *Half true*, she thought. "I hope none of your patients are planning to ruin her first official day."

"Funny you should say that, I think they all are, as am I," Tina confirmed truthfully.

"I'd give her a chance before you all attack," Claire smiled. "How's that handsome fireman of yours?" she said, lightening the mood.

"Still handsome, but not as handsome as your yanky boyfriend!"

"My ex yanky boyfriend I'm afraid."

"Oh, sorry Claire. He was far too chiselled for his own good though. Anyone else on the go?"

"Had lunch with a Danish chap the other day, I'm waiting for a call but not holding my breath."

"Actually Claire I could do with your skills. I'm not convinced Jed is a fireman."

She related the story to Claire over coffee.

"Well, I can't do anything naughty like look him up on our database but if I was to accidentally run into you both in a bar I could give you my professional opinion," Claire said with a wink.

* * *

TOBY HAD BEEN waiting in the Soho cafe for half hour, there was no sign of Anna. He studied his beloved iPad, watching the live feed from the Sanctuary. The press and TV networks were just setting up. He spotted Christine standing amongst them.

He received a message: *Sorry Toby, I won't be joining you, please tell Claire I hope to be in touch soon X Anna.*

"Shit," he said quietly. He had been looking forward to reacquainting with Anna but he was to be disappointed. He forwarded the message to the Claire and ordered another coffee.

There were a couple of very loud guys on the next table, he guessed they were Bulgarian or Hungarian by their accents. One of them turned to him and asked him if he wanted to buy a 'swanky' watch. He declined but the guy was in his face, repeating, "Swanky watch, very good watch."

In the split second his attention was diverted the accomplice grabbed Toby's iPad and made for the door, quickly joined by his friend.

Toby jumped up stunned and legged it out into the busy Soho streets, shouting and screaming. He saw them disappearing into Piccadilly underground station.

He was just about to give chase when he recalled previous incidents. *Tracker*, he thought, reaching for his phone.

He called Achtar and told him the bad news, the techy sprang into action.

He called Toby back in minutes. "Craig's coming to pick you up, the second they hit a wifi spot you can track the iPad to a square inch. Is there anything sensitive open on it Toby?"

"Yes, fucking sensitive!" he bellowed.

"Ok, once it's in a wifi zone I will capture everything, unless of course the Russians have it, then you're fucked!"

Toby thought they looked like opportunist thieves, he prayed he was right.

42

THE ASSASSINATION

CLAIRE WAS SURPRISED by how young the new Minister of Health looked.

"So you're looking after me today Claire? My predecessor has told me all about you," the minister said when they met.

"I don't think you need looking after minister, I'm not sure they are the liveliest bunch," Claire replied.

"But they are probably a very angry, frustrated bunch Claire, I'm pleased you're here."

"Thank you minister. Shall we move towards the battlefield?" Claire suggested.

"They walked through the hospital grounds to the Sanctuary, where Phelps introduced the minister to the staff, ending up with Tina. Tina led them into the Good Vibes room, where she was stunned by the TV cameras and flash photography. The room was packed, she saw some familiar faces sat in a semi-circle of chairs - Veronica, Micky, Brian, Brenda, Hassan, alongside a couple of new faces. Both Tina and Claire were secretly hoping Mo might have shown up.

Brenda studied the cheque and rehearsed the scathing speech she and her husband had mutually worked on.

Micky wished he still had the gun.

Sebastian Phelps stepped forward and tested the microphone before introducing himself and then the Minister of Health. There was a roar of digital sound and light as she smiled and replaced the chief exec on the temporary podium. Claire stood beside her and gave her icy glare in expectation that she kept her side of bargain, or, to be more accurate, the new Minister of Defence's bargain.

"Good afternoon everyone, they say a week is a long time in politics, well it's fair to say I'm living proof that's it's true. This time last week I was visiting my father in his local hospital. It's ironic that he is at the beginning of a long difficult journey, one that I know all of you sitting in front of me have been on, and I'm sure everyone in this room," she nodded to the TV camera crews, "has had similar experiences with loved ones. You all probably feel the same bittersweet emotions as me, absolute admiration for the empathy and professionalism of the staff but frustration and anger that they are run off their feet."

"Because they're underpaid and understaffed!" Brian shouted, to a chorus of agreement from his fellow patients.

"Yes, I know, and let me promise you all this, I'm not interested in party politics I'm interested in well-staffed wards and well served patients. I'll come to the point, past ministers of all colours have looked at the big picture and ignored the small details and it's those small details that matter to you and my dad. So here are the details that matter to you. First, I will speak to nursing staff about their exact requirements, not Mr Phelps or his minions, I will be talking to Tina and her colleagues. I haven't got a magic wand but I'd rather have two extra Tina's on the ward and one less pen pusher."

"Fine talk minister, what about Brenda's drug trial?" Hassan stood up and patted Brenda on the shoulder, she was still waiting for her opportunity.

"My dad has also been denied a drug trial, it's personal and all I can say is that as long as the consultants agree it's viable on medical grounds everyone who has paid national insurance will not be refused. Now there is no magic money tree and this is why I'm here kicking off my revolution at the Sanctuary. It was my government's intention to roll out this amazing facility nationwide. I've put a halt to that idea. I will fund this one to the end of the year, it will then have to be funded by charitable contributions. The budget earmarked for the rolling out of the Sanctuary project will go directly to a trial fund."

The minister was interrupted by the metallic sound of a badly oiled wheelchair being pushed into the room.

"The legendary Professor," Claire correctly assumed.

"When…when will I get on my trial, how long will I have to wait minister?" Brenda pleaded.

"A week may be a long time in politics Brenda but a day with cancer is longer. If your consultant believes you should be on it, as far as I'm concerned you can start tomorrow."

"Excuse me minister." A tall, silver haired man in a white doctor's coat standing at the back raised his hand. "My name's Mike Shepherd, I'm Brenda's consultant and I'd like Brenda to start ASAP."

"How quickly can you obtain the drug in question Mr Shepherd?"

"Realistically Monday, if I order it now."

"Well get to it," she ordered.

Tina couldn't quite believe what she was hearing.

Claire had given up listening, she only had eyes on the Professor, who had been pushed to the space at the end of the semi-circle of chairs. She noticed he was sweating profusely and muttering to himself.

He started to turn the left hand wheel whilst clasping his dressing gown pocket with his other hand. The porter was transfixed on the minister and didn't notice his charge sliding away towards the front.

Dennis' head was throbbing with unbearable pain, he hadn't heard a word of what was said. "Fucking Tory parasite bitch," he croaked inaudibly. "I'm going to kill the fucker."

He clasped the syringe tight and tried to steer the wheelchair with the other hand. As he got towards striking distance, Claire saw the anger in his eyes and slipped behind Dennis. She discreetly pushed the chair past the minister and out the door, where she saw a watching nurse. "I don't think this chap is feeling too good, I think you should get him back to bed."

Dennis was led back to his room cursing.

The Good Poison Club's collective anger had been extinguished by the minister's promises. She asked Sebastian Phelps if she could commandeer his office to talk to Tina and her staff about their requirements.

Brenda crossed out 'Cancer Research' and wrote 'St Peters Sanctuary' on the cheque she'd planned to use to pay for her trial. She thanked the minister and handed her the cheque in front of the press.

"Our first contribution," the minister said, as she waved it to the cameras.

Micky gave Brenda a hug. "Mo would be proud of you Brenda."

"I know, what a shame he's not here, do you know how he is Micky?"

Micky shrugged indicating he didn't.

Claire came up and took Micky's arm, leading him to the TV room. "Sorry to trouble you I'd like a word," she said, as she gave him the stare.

"Sure, who are you?"

She flashed her lanyard. "I'm here to make sure nobody carried out their plans to decapitate, poison or shoot the minister."

Micky felt an immediate sense of guilt. "I'm sorry, not with you love," he said, feigning ignorance.

"I've seen the ballistics report, you're all over the weapon. I know Mo was covering for you. I suggest very strongly you behave yourself."

"Hang on love, if that was my gun how come I was bailed?"

"Not in the public interest, what with all the illness, but I just want you to be aware that I know you probably killed at least two people with that gun, so behave and don't call me love again." Claire opened a jacket to reveal a holster housing a hand gun.

"Fuck me!" Micky exclaimed.

"No thank you. Just remember you're out of your league now, we will be keeping an eye on you."

"Who is we?" he asked.

"Us," she hissed and left him to his thoughts.

The minister held her meetings and was whisked away, leaving a sense of optimism behind her.

Tina saw Claire in the car park about to climb into Christine's car. "Claire, thank you so much," Tina said, before she embraced her.

"What did I do?" Claire shrugged.

"I think you did more than you're letting on."

"Almost a perfect day," Claire said.

"Almost," Tina concurred. They both considered Mo's absence.

"Don't forget our accidental date." Claire winked. "Your Jed is definitely handsome, I'll let you know if he's definitely a firefighter as well!"

43

THE LAST WILL AND TESTAMENT

CLAIRE COULDN'T RECALL ever enjoying sending a message as much as the one she sent to Toby first thing that morning: *Toby, my office ASAP (After your emergency dental treatment).*

Toby couldn't recall ever receiving such a humiliating invitation.

Claire was at her desk at eight sharp, ready to officially wrap up 'Operation Chef'. Toby having his beloved iPad stolen and the madness that ensued after, perfectly summed up the random chaotic nature of the last few months. She rattled off a few emails including one to Sir Martin covering the salient points from the highly successful day with the new Minister of Health. She didn't mention the Toby fiasco, she was hoping there was no need.

Toby arrived just before ten, he nodded to Claire, who was on the phone to her mother arranging a weekend at a Cotswolds spa hotel. She stared at Toby's wounds as he sat opposite, studying his blackened eye and split lip. She finished the call in Danish before addressing her colleague, "So, not your finest day?"

"No Claire, but it seems you covered yourself in glory."

"Well, your old Etonian chum kept his side of the bargain."

"I hear the Good Poison Club is continuing and the drug trials have been financed. Sister Gallagher must be pleased," Toby stated.

"Sister Gallagher?"

"Tina," Toby confirmed.

"For the moment yes she is, but a politician's promise…well, we shall see. Anyway Toby, enough of me, what the fuck happened to you?"

"Where do I start?"

"With being stood up," Claire smirked.

"Yes, I'm afraid Anna didn't show, you've seen the message she sent?"

"Yes, I did."

"So did you draw any conclusions Claire?"

"I suspect she's gone home, who knows, it doesn't matter now."

"So you don't think she's taking up your offer?" Toby tested his boss, which he knew was a mistake.

"Like I said Toby, it doesn't matter. So your beloved iPad was stolen?"

"Yes," he confirmed sheepishly.

"And?"

"Just Romanian gypsies out thieving, Achtar killed all the info anyway."

"But you tracked it anyway?"

"Yes."

"Why?"

"Male pride I suppose. I know I was stupid…"

"Yes, you were. What happened?"

"Craig, Christine and I cruised around South London following the signal. They visited three different phone shops where they were either trying to unblock it or sell it. They kept just ahead of us until we tracked it to a tower block in Streatham. Chris and Craig told me to leave it to the police but I was totally pissed off and decided to confront the fuckers on my own."

"Resulting in your injuries, a black eye and two teeth knocked out."

"You should see the other fellas." Toby gave a painful smile.

"I've heard about them, that's the main reason we are having this meeting." Claire had never looked more serious.

"I pinpointed the flat and knocked on the door, one of the thieves answered it and I held up my ID told them I didn't want any trouble, just hand over the iPad and I'd be gone. He tried to slam the door but my size twelve stopped it, just as he caught me with a right hook." Toby pointed to his black eye. "I retaliated and knocked him clean out, I stepped over him into the dirtiest doss house I've ever seen and was confronted by at least five blokes. Next thing I was on the floor and getting a good kicking."

"So you reached for your firearm?" his boss interrupted.

"I had to Claire, they would have killed me. I reached for my weapon and managed to roll away from the baying mob. I pointed it at them and they stood back in shock. I grabbed one of them and…and…"

"And, Toby?"

"And I held it to his head and told him to pass over the iPad or I'd blow his brains out."

"Very professional, not," Claire interceded.

"I know Claire, things got out of control. The other guys scarpered, literally ran out the flat, the guy I was threatening bit my hand, so I just snapped. I pistol whipped him, knocked him unconscious."

"You pistol whipped him?"

"Yes, and then retrieved my iPad, which was on a coffee table with a load of what I presume were stolen phones."

"So you took your beloved iPad and left the guy unconscious?"

"Yes Claire."

"And where is your beloved iPad now?"

"Achtar is bringing it back to full working order."

"And you're assuming these Romanians won't involve the police?"

"I'm hoping Claire."

"You do know this could cost you your job?" Claire snapped.

"Sorry Claire, I don't know what I was thinking." Toby sulked.

She stared at him for a few seconds. "That fucking iPad Toby, you need to get yourself a girlfriend."

Toby didn't know if she was taking the piss. "I'm trying Claire but you know how difficult relationships are in this business." He knew his answer would touch a nerve.

"Ok Toby, what happens in Vegas. Let's just hope Sir Martin doesn't hear about this."

Toby felt humiliated but relieved, he thought about asking Claire if she'd like to join the team in the Red Lion for Friday drinks but didn't want to encourage further humiliation.

* * *

MICKY LOOKED AT his watch, Sandra would be on her way to meet him by the shoe in Golden Square. The Professor, Grace, what was Sandra thinking? Dennis would be dead within weeks, she knew that, so it had to be Grace. If he charged forty grand to kill a low life gangster, an innocent, albeit conniving, woman must be worth a lot more than that. He could set up his family for life.

He stood in front of the mirror, sharply dressed in his customary black. He examined and pulled out a grey hair that dyeing had missed.

If she wanted him to kill Grace he'd have to find a new method now that he no longer possessed his weapon of choice. He mulled over the options, stabbing her would be too messy, pushing her under a train too risky due to CCTV. He thought about Mo's poison, but how would he administer it? Then he thought about the young lady who gave him a warning, she was more than vague as to who she was but she was carrying a gun and seemed on top of her game. He had a feeling she wasn't the kind of person to mess with. She said 'us' were watching him. Whoever 'us' was Micky didn't think it was worth upsetting them.

He took another look at the ex-hitman in the mirror, phoned his daughter and volunteered to take the baby for a walk, which she happily accepted. He decided to change into something a bit brighter, his granddaughter deserved something more colourful.

* * *

GRACE TWIRLED WHAT she presumed were the keys to Sandra's front door between her fingers. She'd discovered them in the small overnight case Raymond kept his 'Thursday' night clothes in.

Whilst her rival was on red wine and vodka, she was on white wine and whiskey, plus a small supply of cocaine that Raymond had hidden away.

Both women were consumed with grief and anger but Grace reckoned that although Sandra had lost her lover and was about to lose her husband, she'd at least come out of this mess with a house, and in Grace's twisted mind this was an injustice she couldn't let stand!

* * *

TINA JOINED JED at their normal alcove in Camden's cavernous World's End pub. He asked for her autograph when they met up, having seen her on the regional news that day.

She told him about her momentous day culminating in the highly successful private meeting with the Minister of Health. She omitted any mention of Claire though.

They started to finalise details for their imminent trip to Donington Park for the Monsters of Rock festival. Whether he was a fireman or not, she was going to the festival come what may. Three days camping and heavy metal music with Mr Perfect, or almost perfect, was a no brainer.

* * *

CLAIRE SAT ON a bar stool, surrounded by excitable Friday night revellers, studying her minion's report on her phone. She looked out of place in her work suit, it wasn't the kind of pub that attracted an early doors after work crowd. The woman sitting next to her had half her hair dyed blue, the other half was jet black and close cropped. She reckoned she was the only person in there without a tattoo.

A familiar figure squeezed in beside her clutching a twenty pound note trying to get the barmaid's attention. He smiled at Claire, she smiled back whilst staring at him intently, no doubt making him feel uncomfortable.

"Jed!" She tried to sound surprised.

"Hi...where do I know you from?" He was mystified.

"I'm Claire, we met at the Pixies gig."

"Claire! God I didn't recognise you."

"I've come straight from the office, I'm afraid I'm only a plastic rock chick, unlike Tina who's totally cool."

"She's here! Are you meeting errr…"

"Ricky," she reminded him.

"Yeah, Ricky, the American fella," he remembered.

"We're not an item anymore, I'm waiting for a friend."

"Oh, okay. Well, we are just through there if you want to join us Claire."

"I'll come and say hi to Tina in a minute," she offered, as Jed turned to leave.

Claire returned to Christine and Craig's report, which came as a mixture of relief and disappointment. *Fucking men,* she thought to herself as she watched the object of the report disappear to join his girlfriend.

Jed told Tina about running into Claire, Tina tried to look surprised. "I didn't recognise her Tina, she looks like an accountant, nothing like she did at Brixton."

"You couldn't take your eyes off her tight little backside that night could you, admit it," she teased him.

"Rubbish, I prefer a bit of meat on the bone," he squeezed Tina's ample thigh, "she's far too skinny for me." They returned to the topic of Donington. A few minutes later Claire found them, she was on her own holding a gin and tonic.

Tina stood up and gave her a hug. "Jed told me you were here, blimey I wouldn't have recognised you."

Claire smiled and gave a twirl.

"Are you with Ricky?"

"Nope, he's history I'm afraid. I'm supposed to meet a colleague but she's delayed at work."

"Please join us." Jed gestured for her to take a seat.

"Did I see you on the news yesterday Tina?"

"My fifteen minutes of fame was more like fifteen-seconds!"

They all made small talk before Claire turned to Jed, "How's the firefighting?" she probed.

"Like nursing, overworked and underpaid," he replied.

"Except of course you're all moonlighting," she retorted, putting him on the back foot. "What do you get up to on your four days off then Jed?" Claire asked, she was enjoying this.

"This and that. So remind me what you do Claire?" He tried to change the subject.

"I'm a civil servant," she answered.

"Not Inland Revenue I hope." He sounded serious.

"Trade and industry," she said, her normal catch all answer.

Jed visibly relaxed.

"Well that's what I tell everyone," she teased him.

After half an hour Jed announced he had to get to work. "I'll leave you girls to it, see you tomorrow." He kissed Tina and shook Claire's hand. Her parting glare made him feel uncomfortable.

Tina went to get more drinks, Claire put some make up on and undid a couple of buttons. She untied her hair and shook her head in an effort look more grungy. She needed a couple of drinks, she was unsure how to break the news to Tina as she returned to the table.

"So what do you think Claire?"

"He's gorgeous," she replied.

"I know that but do you think he's a fireman?" Tina asked.

"Oh, I know he's a fireman," Claire confirmed.

"Really Claire? How on earth can you tell from your brief conversation with him?"

"I know he's a fireman because I had him checked out."

"Checked out, how do you mean checked out?" Tina was surprised.

"Yes, I had him checked out Tina. Are you ok with that?"

"I've no problem with it but you said you couldn't do anything naughty."

"Right, but I decided he was a person of interest," Claire confirmed.

"A person of interest Claire, in what way could Jed be a person of interest?"

Claire took a swig of her drink and pondered how much she should divulge to her new friend. "Like I told you at St Peters, we were interested in Mo, but in the complicated enquiry that followed there were one or two incidents that sidelined us."

"Like the Professor getting into trouble?" Tina guessed.

"Exactly Tina, we became aware of possible problems with the minister's visit and things got very messy with the resignations. There seemed to be a lot of different people interested in the visit and not in a positive way. I was put under a lot of pressure and when you, probably innocently, mentioned your suspicion that Jed wasn't exactly who he said he was, I got curious. Probably paranoid but I checked him out just in case."

"And he's definitely a fireman?" Tina interrupted.

"He's a fireman for sure. The problem is Tina, he's also a man."

"I'm sorry?" Tina was taken aback.

Claire hesitated. "I'm sorry Tina, he is a fireman but his name's not Jed."

"What! What do you mean?"

"Why did you suspect him of not being a fireman Tina?"

"My dad."

"Your dad?"

"He sowed the seeds, didn't reckon a fireman would look like Jed, but then for some reason he changed his mind. But that's my dad, most of his views are fuelled by alcohol."

"But you were suspicious despite your dad?"

"No uniform in his flat, I even tempted him to wear nothing but his helmet and I still haven't seen it!"

"That I'd like to see, but he'd keep most of his gear in his locker at the fire station."

"Yes I know Claire but they'd surely be something at home."

"Probably, but the fact is there's something about him that isn't genuine in your mind, despite me insisting he's a fireman."

"So what's his name then? Maybe Jed is his nickname."

"Maybe, but what do you know about him? You met him online, he's good looking, got a nice pad, loves heavy metal. That might be all you want, but has he introduced you to his family or any friends?"

"No, he hasn't Claire, you're right. I've had some doubts and the fireman thing is probably the most trivial of them."

"His name is Robert Eames and he has a wife and two children in Reading. I'm sorry Tina, as I said, he's a man."

IT TOOK SEVEN minutes to get from the World's End to Jed's, aka Robert Elms', flat. It took Tina those seven minutes to tell Claire about the pact she had with Freddie. She opened the front door and punched in the alarm code.

"This is it." Tina turned the lights on and gave Claire the tour.

"All very minimalist," Claire observed.

They entered the bedroom, Tina slid open the wardrobe doors exposing the scant collection of clothes. Tina suddenly understood why.

Claire stood hands on hips looking at the headboard that dominated the room from floor to ceiling. "That's a very deep headboard," she remarked, tapping on the front.

"To be honest with you Claire, I'd not considered its dimensions whilst in the throes of passion."

"I get that. Follow me Tina." She led her friend to the living room where she stood staring at the black gloss bookcase.

"What?" Tina queried.

"I'm doing the math Tina. The bookcase is very shallow, whereas the headboard on the other side is deep and hollow. She went over to the bookcase and studied it closely. She removed a couple of paperbacks and pressed a small spigot on the back causing the bookcase to open out like two huge doors.

"Feck…," Tina stood open mouthed as a secret cupboard was exposed. "You're fecking good Claire," she whispered, as they stared at the fireman uniforms hanging in the secret cupboard.

"It's what I do," Claire quipped, as she found a passport in a small hideaway section. She tossed it to Tina, who looked inside. Apart from confirming his real name there was a photo inside of who she presumed were his wife and kids in Reading. She placed it on the glass coffee table.

"Well, at least he's a fireman," Tina sighed. "It was fun while it lasted."

They left the flat in such a state that Jed/Robert would be in no doubt about their discovery. Tina wondered how long it would take him to discover the Monsters of Rock festival tickets were gone. She would text Freddie in the morning with an invite.

* * *

GRACE FELT HER heart beat a little faster as she turned the key in the Chubb lock and pushed Sandra's front door open. She'd parked her red Mini several streets away and in the process of approaching the house she saw Sandra leave and disappear towards the station.

The calendar in the kitchen confirmed that she'd be gone a while. *14.00 DENNIS HOSPITAL.* She guessed her rival wouldn't be back till the evening, plenty of time to explore and play.

Raymond had driven her past the house a couple of times previously. Now she could see the interior she could justify their efforts. Poor Raymond, he would have been like the lord of the manor in this well-established property. The kitchen would need a complete makeover but interior design was her thing.

She studied the rack of kitchen knives but decided the one in her backpack was sharper. The living room and dining room were exactly as Raymond had described them. She looked at the dining table, where he'd had to endure Sandra's dreadful 1980s cooking. She smiled as she recollected him describing how he initiated sex with her over the table for no other reason than to avoid eating the prehistoric dessert of oranges cooked in Cointreau. He made sure the Waterford glass bowl took a tumble during the act.

She made her way upstairs, finishing her tour in the master bedroom. She looked in Raymond's wardrobe, his clothes were still immaculately hung and folded. She removed his favourite linen suit, the one he wore when he took her to see Michael Bublé at the 02 arena one glorious Thursday night. She lay it out on the bed, along with a pair of his highly polished shoes and lay next it, plotting and planning.

The doorbell interrupted Grace's rehearsal. She'd decided she'd hide in the wardrobe and watch Sandra discover her creative work with Raymond's clothes neatly laid out on the bed. As she froze in surprise, Grace would creep behind her, place her left hand on Sandra's forehead and slit her throat with her right. She'd practiced this manoeuvre several times before the doorbell startled her. She clasped her knife tightly and crawled to the bay window, peeping down. The doorbell rang again. Maybe it was a delivery?

She waited a few minutes before crawling to the landing. There didn't appear to be anyone still there, maybe it *was* a delivery. Suddenly she heard the roar of a lawn mower in the back garden. She peered out the back bedroom window, sure enough Eric was carrying out his new duties. She was relieved the gardener didn't have a key and would hopefully be long gone before Sandra returned.

* * *

SANDRA TOOK BEING stood up by Micky philosophically, it was probably meant to be. She'd get over Grace, she'd move on. Eric, her new gardener, looked game, she'd also found a dating site online where she could find someone for more cultured pursuits. Once Dennis had passed she would consider her options. Sell the house, travel, the world would be her oyster. Her grief for her lover was beginning to dissipate already.

She wasn't looking forward to her meeting with her husband today, but at least it would be her last.

Dennis wasn't sure how long he'd been asleep. He was laying on top of his bed in pyjamas and a dressing gown that he'd put on to go to the toilet, the effort of which he thought would kill him. He smelt Sandra's perfume before he saw her, she sat on the bed beside him.

His vision, like everything else, was deteriorating rapidly. He thumbed for his glasses on the bedside locker. He saw Sandra was wearing a new red coat. "Very stylish," he croaked.

Sandra was shocked at the sight of him. The palliative care nurse had warned her that they didn't reckon he'd survive the journey to the hospice. She knew this would be her last ever conversation with him.

"Thank you, I splashed the cash up west yesterday, bought myself a few new outfits." She slipped off the coat to reveal a black dress that left little to the imagination. "Hospitals are always so hot," she complained.

Dennis managed a sip of water. "You look like you're going out on the town Sandra."

"Well Dennis, I won't beat about the bush, I've got a chap coming to sort the garden this afternoon. I want to make a good impression." She winked.

"You don't waste much time," he grunted.

"Raymond reminded me I am a sexy woman Dennis, I'm not going to let him down now he's gone. I've got everything organised."

"Does he know what he's doing?" he asked.

"I hope so, he's a bit older than I'd like but he's the rough and ready type."

"No Sandra, is he any good at gardening?"

"Fuck the garden Dennis, I'm more interested in him giving me a good seeing to." She adjusted her dress hem revealing a stocking top. "I've gone online as well Dennis, a dating site for those looking for someone a bit more cultured. I'll read you my portfolio: Sophisticated, mature, single, woman seeks well-groomed gent for theatre, opera and fun. I've got a date for next Thursday, do you think this dress is a bit short for the opera?"

Dennis was expecting this final humiliation, he deserved it, humiliation had been his constant companion since he first met her. "Do the boys know I'm dying Sandra?"

"No Dennis and quite frankly I don't think they'd be bothered. The nurse doesn't think you'll make the journey to the hospice." She looked at her husband, a shell of man, not that he was ever a proper man. She thought of him laying defenceless on their bed with her lover on top of him. "The quicker you die Dennis the better all round. I'm going to sell the house and move to the suburbs and travel and fuck and travel some more."

Dennis recalled his speech to the Good Poison Club. "Fuck the suburbs!" he cried. His throat was dry, he tried to tell her he'd instructed his lawyer that all his assets were to go to the communist party, but he was struggling to speak. *Fuck it*, he thought, *she's not going to fuck anybody else ever.*

He beckoned her to put her ear close to his mouth and reached for the syringe driver. He'd dreamt about this moment, watching her eyes dilate as he injects the vein in her neck with air. 'Give my regards to Raymond,' he planned to be the last words she'd ever hear.

As Sandra came near, he grasped at the pockets of his dressing gown but couldn't find the weapon, which unbeknown to him had fallen out on the toilet floor and was found by a cleaner. He was frantic, Sandra could see the mixture of hate and disappointment in his eyes.

He passed an hour after his wife had left for home.

* * *

TINA AND HER father worked their way through the shepherd's pie she'd cooked for them. "My signature dish," she boasted.

"It's your only dish," he jibed.

"Feck off dad!"

"I hope your fireman likes it."

"My ex fireman dad."

"Oh, oh dear, sorry Tina."

"You were right though dad."

"Right about what?"

"He was definitely a fireman."

"Well, I have a feeling for these things love."

It's a shame he didn't have a feeling he was a cunt, Tina thought to herself.

"What about your festival? You were looking forward to that."

"Freddie's coming." She was both surprised and pleased her father had remembered something she'd told him.

"That's good Tina, so I should still get my wedding suit dry cleaned," he joked.

* * *

"WOW, YOU REALLY know what you're doing Eric, I'm impressed!" Sandra genuinely was impressed. "I'll put the kettle on!" she shouted, as she opened the back door.

As she prepared tea and biscuits she noticed she'd missed a call from the hospital. She listened to the message, "I'm sorry Mrs Coates, this is palliative care nurse Angela at St Peters, your husband passed away a few minutes ago."

Sandra deleted the message.

She poured the tea and returned to the back door. "Tea's ready Eric!" she shouted.

Eric gave a thumbs up and headed to the shed to put away the assortment of Dennis' equipment. He assumed Sandra had been to some posh lunch, she was certainly dressed to kill. He made his way into the kitchen where he noticed Sandra's stylish red coat on the marble tiled floor. He washed his hands at the sink and guessed they were taking tea in the living room where he'd removed her tag.

As he walked into the hallway he saw her high heels abandoned at the foot of the stairs. He then noticed the black dress half way up the stairs. He recalled Micky's warning but...*fuck it,* he thought, he'd prefer cash but if this was her method of payment then so be it.

He hesitated for a second but saw her knickers and bra hanging on the banister at the top of the stars. Just as he started to climb the stars he heard a high pitched scream and muffled cries.

He ran up and headed towards the sound of a desperate struggle. The bedroom door was open, he stood frozen to the spot as he saw the two women wrestling in the bed.

He just about recognised Sandra, naked apart from stockings, but her face was covered in blood. The brunette, dressed in a pink tracksuit, was slashing Sandra with a long kitchen knife.

"What the fuck?!" he yelled, before Grace broke free and lunged at him like a wild banshee.

He held up his hand as she tried to stab him. He felt a searing pain as the knife sliced off the tips of his index and forefinger. He fell backwards and tried to grab the knife but only sustained more injuries to his hands and forearms.

The woman brought the knife down in a frenzied attack, he felt the blade imbed itself in his shoulder blade, he grabbed her throat with both hands in a final, desperate attempt to save himself.

He managed to turn her over so he was now on top. She was trying to retrieve the knife so she could finish him off but his massive hands were too strong, he squeezed until she released her grip. That was when he heard the most dreadful gargling noise from the bed.

Sandra tried to stand as blood was squirting from her neck.

A minute later he dialled 999 and requested an ambulance and two body bags.

44

THE RETURNERS
(Four Months Later)

"ANNA! ANNA!" THE maître d' called her over to his podium.

"What now?" she sighed.

"Table seven Anna, they're fucking returners, Mr and Mrs Franks. They're fucking returners!"

"Returners, what are returners?" she enquired.

"They return to this resort time after time, the Franks come twice a year. I fucking hate them. Go on, take their order, you'll see."

Anna waltzed over to the Franks. "Hi, I'm Anna, are you ready to order sir, madam?"

"Good evening Anna, where are you from?" Colin Franks asked.

"Moldova," she replied, wondering why he asked.

"Where's that?" his wife chuckled.

"Russia, stupid," he berated his wife.

"What's the weather like in Moldova?" she continued.

"Changeable," Anna offered, wishing she could set fire to them.

"We normally order with Carlo, we're regulars," Colin Franks claimed with pride.

"No problem sir I shall inform the maître d' you're here."

She returned to Carlo. "Your fucking returners are asking for you."

"See, you hate them already." He winked and reluctantly sidled over to take their order.

The sun was setting over the Med, it was busiest sitting of the day. Anna hated the job but loved the climate. Yes, the all inclusive attracted a certain type of clientele but at least she got to serve those with orange wristbands. Five star wankers, Carlo called them, but they were better than the scum with blue wristbands who frequented the pizzeria.

Carlo came back and continued his rant about returners. The Franks were typical, they actually believed the staff liked them. There was a hierarchy amongst them, the Franks were coming up to their twentieth visit, they were 'premier league returners' Carlo explained. Tomorrow, Pablo, the general manager, would reward them with a free week at a gala dinner. He would have to appear grateful and enthusiastic. Carlo revealed that rumour had it Pablo had enjoyed the occasional fling with Mrs Franks.

Anna could see they were an incongruous couple. He looked nerdy, whilst Heather Franks dressed to impress and liked to show off her manufactured boobs. He spent his days going on trips so he could indulge in his passion for photography. She spent all day sunbathing by the pool, disappearing for a siesta, not always in her own room.

Anna went to clear the Franks' table after their starters, they'd been joined by another couple.

"How were the starters?" she enquired.

"Delicious as usual, Anna," Colin Franks replied.

The mere fact he both remembered, and mentioned, her name annoyed her.

"Joe, Suzy, this is Anna from Latvia," he introduced her. She didn't bother to correct his mistake. "This is our friends first visit here, we're showing them the ropes," he stated with pride.

What a complete asshole, she thought, as she cleared the table, leaving Carlo to take their order for the main course. She watched the poor bloke grinning as the returners patronised and humiliated him.

He took his order into the kitchen, where he noticed Pablo looking stressed.

"The fucking Franks are here!" Pablo exclaimed.

"I know, I've just taken their order."

"That's all I need, fucking returners, this week of all weeks, we've got a bloody inspection from head office Thursday and Friday." He didn't tell his staff that the powers that be were considering an offer from a bigger hotel chain and redundancies were inevitable. He cowered in the kitchen, sweating profusely until the Franks order was ready.

Anna and Carlo collected two plates each. "Four rib eye steaks," the general manager observed.

"Three medium and one well done for you know who," Carlo confirmed.

"What a cunt," Pablo hissed, spotting the small cocktail stick emphasising the well done steak. "What a fucking Philistine," he added, before spitting on the sizzling meat and winking at Anna.

He expected a protest but she didn't even blink. *I've seen a lot worse,* she thought, smiling to herself.

* * *

"WOW TINA, YOU look great!" Claire greeted her new friend in a rustic hipster bar in Shoreditch. Tina was wearing a black velvet mini dress with a studded choker and thigh high boots.

"You're working today?" Tina guessed, as Claire was in her usual attire.

"Unfortunately we're snowed under, six day weeks, sometimes seven at the moment. So how was the festival?"

"Fantastic Claire, but things got out of hand."

"Really, in what way?"

"This is what happens when it's your birthday and you overindulge," she place her left hand on the table.

"My god, the pact, you're actually engaged!"

"Bonkers isn't it, Freddie got down on one knee during the Iron Maiden headline set."

"Wow congratulations, that's the second bit of good news I've had recently."

"Really, what's new in your world? Any love interest?" Tina enquired. "I thought you might have hit it off with Rupert, he's quite dishy in a public schoolboy kind of way."

"Far too posh for me Tina, he's got himself some Sloane ranger off that dreadful tv thingy, Made in Chelsea. Remember Ricky?"

"The yank?"

"Exactly, we've been out a few times. Our jobs are both equally complicated so it seems to be more a case of absence making the heart grow fonder, particularly as he's based in Helsinki right now."

"Well, I hope it works out for you. I take it you can't tell me what you're up to work wise?"

"Sorry Tina, I would seriously have to kill you." Claire laughed. "How's the Good Poison Club going?"

"It's not Claire, seems to have died a death. We got the extra staff the health minister promised but it's always a fecking vicious circle. It meant we got a load more patients, so I'm too busy to take care of the group. Fucking politicians, either lying or shagging."

Claire smiled and diplomatically nodded. "And Brenda?"

"Brenda's great, she's on the trial, she feeling good and off to Florida with all her lovely family shortly. So at least something positive came out of all the craziness."

"I've got some more interesting news," Claire stated, as she pulled a postcard out of her handbag and placed it in front of Tina.

Tina studied the beach scene on the front before turning it over and reading the message aloud, "Hi Claire, sorry I didn't take up your job I got better offer, weather wise, from an old friend of ours! Wish you were here, Anna".

Tina smiled and pulled out an envelope and passed it to her friend. It was two tickets for a week at an all inclusive resort in the Canary Islands.

"Nice," Claire said impressed.

"They arrived the other day, quite a surprise, no explanation, just the tickets." Tina shrugged.

"You going to use them?"

"I've booked the flights already, we're going in a couple of weeks. Fancy joining us? Maybe Ricky would be up for it?"

"Too busy I'm afraid, but be sure to say hi to Anna for me and our old friend of course."

"I certainly will."

"One thing Tina."

"What's that?"

"Don't under any circumstances complain about the food!"

* * *

PABLO AND CARLO stood in the centre of the pool bar. Ten tables had been laid out around them. Beyond the tables staff and bathers curiously gathered to see what was going on. Pablo tapped the microphone, he looked around at the expectant returners, he imagined he had a machine gun and could spray the room with deadly fire. He cleared his throat and smiled instead.

"Welcome everybody, it's a privilege to welcome you all here for our gala lunch to thank the exclusive club of visitors who have returned here ten times or more!" He paused for a ripple of applause. "To reward you all for your incredible loyalty we have placed gold wrist bands on your tables, which means free house wine with every meal, including breakfast!"

More applause and laughter.

"We are honoured to have two couples who are approaching their twentieth visit. Would the Franks from England and the Vollers from Germany please stand up?"

Carlo went over and presented the ladies with bouquets. Heather Franks' cleavage pressed against him as they hugged.

"To reward these two wonderful couples we would like to offer them a free twentieth week in our platinum suite."

The Franks squealed like wild banshees, Heather jumped up and down clapping her hands with excitement, her boobs almost popping out of her top.

As Anna and the rest of the team started to bring out the food, Pablo departed to his office, his smile replaced by a pained smirk.

Where's a tsunami when you need it, he thought.

"I'd liked to introduce you to our new chef," Carlo announced to the Franks, as Anna poured their free wine. "This is Colin and Heather Franks, chef."

"Delighted to meet you chef, our steaks were perfection last night, weren't they dear?" All eyes fixed on Heather Franks as she gave a doe eyed smile, the men's eyes fixed on her breasts.

"Very good, although mine was a little underdone, a little too bloody for my taste."

The new chef exchanged glances with Anna and gave his apologies to the returners.

Micky lay on his sun bed, supping his beer, watching his daughter playing with his granddaughter in the pool. Tracey snored gently on the adjacent sun bed as she topped up her tan. His phone pinged with a message, he took off his sunglasses and smiled at the 'What's up' from Eric. It was a selfie showing that he was out of hospital at last. He was giving a thumbs up with his right hand, two fingers missing.

"How are you my friend?"

He looked up as he was suddenly cast in shadow.

"I'd be better if you'd take that fucking chef's hat off mate." He stood up and embraced his old friend. "We're all good mate," he pointed to his family splashing about in the pool. "How you doing? Thanks for the holiday, we're loving it."

Micky gestured to the empty sun bed beside him, Tracey was oblivious, laying on her front.

"I'm good mate. And it's a pleasure, I'm pleased to see you."

"Well it's been an interesting time to say the least," Micky confirmed and then continued with the edited highlights of the past few months.

Mo listened intently, he was particularly pleased to hear about Brenda, and Micky buying his daughter a nice house. "The poor Professor," he said shaking his head.

"Yes, quite a palaver." He paused for a moment, looking out over the pool. "Anyway, what you been up to Mo? How'd you end up here?"

"A long story my friend," he shrugged, "I'll catch up with you later, I've got to get back to the fucking returners."

"The what?" Micky asked quizzically.

Mo gestured towards the Franks who were now joined by their friends, showing off the gold wrist bands, gulping down free house wine.

After leaving Mickey he found Anna alone in the kitchen.

"How're the fucking returners?" she asked. "Ready for their desserts chef?"

Mo reflected on the put down the revolting Heather Franks had given him. "I killed thirty-seven Russian commandos when I was thirteen Anna. I've taken on and beaten the CIA, KGB and MI5. Am I supposed to take this shit from some fucking returner from the fucking suburbs!" he ranted, momentarily remembering the Professor's disdain for the suburbs.

Anna had a good idea where this was heading, she would be surprised if the Franks would ever be returning for their platinum visit. She smiled as chef stood over the returner's creme brûlée and unzipped his trousers.

ALSO BY SIMON LYONS

How to Kidnap a String Quartet

Buy now on Amazon!

ABOUT THE AUTHOR

Having left his North London 'sink' comprehensive at the age of fifteen with few qualifications, Simon travelled extensively before settling down to family life and 'blagging' a living. A ferocious gig and festival goer, he always felt he had a story to tell and How to Kidnap a String Quartet, his debut novel, is an expression of his varied experiences of life and wild and whacky imagination. The follow up The Good Poison Club is an exciting thriller set in a London NHS hospital.

www.simonlyonsauthor.com
Facebook: simonlyonsauthor
Twitter: @simonlyonsbooks

Made in the USA
Columbia, SC
10 August 2018